SITA'S CURSE

Sreemoyee Piu Kundu is an ex Lifestyle Editor and former PR head, and now a full time novelist based in Delhi. Her next two releases are *You've Got the Wrong Girl* (Hachette) and *Cut!*. Sreemoyee is planning her fifth novel, a political tragedy, *Rahula*.

Dedicated to my parents, Mrs Sushmita Kundu Rao
and N. Krishna Rao

SITA'S CURSE

the language of desire

SREEMOYEE PIU KUNDU

First published in 2014 by Hachette India
(Registered name: Hachette Book Publishing India Pvt. Ltd)
An Hachette UK company
www.hachetteindia.com

1

ISBN 978-93-5009-780-9

Hachette Book Publishing India Pvt. Ltd
4th/5th Floors, Corporate Centre,
Sector 44, Gurgaon 122003, India

Typeset in Garamond Premier Pro 11/14
by Saanavi Graphics, Noida

Printed and bound in India by
Manipal Technologies Ltd, Manipal

Prologue
'Ram, Ram!'

It was light outside. The streetlights blurred in the sun. Someone had forgotten to switch them off as usual. Chhotu's school bus had departed a while ago, leaving a blanket of darkened soot. Tiny particles of auto-emitted dust crept in from a discoloured window that overlooked a cramped by-lane flanked by an open drain. Like yesterday and the day before, and all the days before that, the early morning stench was steadily on the rise.

There was no other sound.

Madhubala, the neighbour's parrot, slept soundly in her cheap wrought-iron cage, its edges as worn out as her voice – supposed once to have been saccharine-coated. Asha Tai, the old, raspy-voiced flower-seller whose neck veins turned bluish-green as she pleaded in her peculiarly nasal tone, with dishevelled housewives in their crumpled early morning saris, to purchase her flowers for their morning prayers, had also fallen silent.

Maybe all her flowers had wilted.

Tiny flies buzzed in and out of the surrounding stillness.

Not a single cloud shaded the sky.

Her arms flung over her head, Meera sprawled out on her hard wooden bed, twitching on her bare back as a faded green, mirror-work cushion callously chafed her inner thighs. Biting her lower lip, she *clamped her eyes tighter, filtering out the persistent light; knowing it was raining, somewhere, still.*

A slight breeze rose and fell, warm in parts.

Meera moved restlessly as the first power cut of the day kicked in and the ceiling fan ground sluggishly to a halt. A faint line of moisture trickled down the centre of her fulsome breasts, pausing for just a few seconds above her navel, before plummeting downward. And then another...

With a deep sigh, she began to loosen the tight folds of her sari. She'd forgotten to unfasten the safety-pin tucked into its pleats last night. The skin around it felt sore, suffocated from the dull heat. The pleats fell sideways in a slow motion of sorts. The smooth skin of her midriff tingled slightly as a stab of damp breeze blew on the moist spot.

'Ram Ram, Ram Ram,' Madhubala, the parrot cackled all of a sudden, dispelling the quiet.

Meera turned languidly on her side, causing her anklets to make a soft clamour... shuddering at the sensation they always caused.

The fan had come to a complete halt.

Propping herself up on one elbow, Meera shifted her heavy, loosely plaited hair to the side, off the nape of her mildly perspiring neck and pulled the confining fabric of her tight blouse off her shoulders to expose her breasts. She always took off her bra at night. A sharp sunbeam shimmered over her arched frame at that moment – like an old longing, reignited. With her left index finger, Meera dreamily began to caress her nipples, one by one. Her head lolled backward. With every passing second, this morning was growing more intimate, feeling grown-up all of a sudden. Or maybe it was the way she always felt at the beginning of things. She fell back among the pillows once again. Oh, to let go... to not look back; making that one last bid, before everything was washed asunder... like a boat leaving the tranquil shores on a stormy night.

Meera kicked off the block-printed chaddar – a gift from Mrs Deshmukh downstairs – her breath suddenly roughish; a collision of callous cravings. Drawing up her knees, she clumsily positioned the cushion under her hips. As her fingers gathered momentum on her breasts, she pressed the cushion tighter between her thighs, moaning softly as its rough edges abraded her insides. Turning her defences to liquid dust; her nipples ripe.

Like Asha Tai inspecting a garland before she quoted a price, Meera dreamily opened her eyes and studied her hand before she sucked gently on her right thumb, stroking herself below her navel with her left... at the same time. A part of her was already floating by then... lithe... like the paper boats Chhotu drifted in the drain below. From time to time, she dragged the cushion upwards; rubbing herself against it... faster, more frantically... her lips throbbing in the slow heat trapped between these four walls. Somewhere in Mumbai, the rains were coming down hard. Meera could smell the saltiness of them up close; her eyes rolled back slowly, like a blind man smiling serenely at a fading sun; reaching out from a place inside. Lifting up her petticoat she peeled away the layers, her sari cascading off the crumpled bedsheet like a riverine tributary – dark, dense, desolate.

Moving her right thumb in copious circles, Meera plunged in and out of her deeper hideaways, her hips thrusting, her cheeks flushed with the wanton abandon of an adolescent awakening... as if she'd just turned seventeen or something and was spinning round and round on a brightly lit merry-go-round; a merry-go-round in a village fair... one decorated with bright, yellow lights and garish, purple streamers... the one that made her feel as if she was flying.

Flying without wings... flying without the fear of falling... flying, just flying.

✤

'Meera Ben!' a familiar voice cried out. 'Open the door, or should we call for Dr Batliwala again?' The voice grew more insistent.

Outside, it was still.

'Meera, what are you doing? And why the hell is the bedroom door bolted? Do you know what time it is, huh? The breakfast paranthas have to be made... and what about Ba's pooja thali? Goddammit woman,' a harsher voice thundered, urgently banging on the door.

Meera hung her head over the edge of the bed. It was some minutes past nine, she sluggishly calculated, her eyelids opening and closing. Soon, her husband Mohan would depart for work – clutching a cloth folder and a small leather bag, his car key-chain dangling from his front trouser pocket.

Meera ignored his rants as she shivered lusciously, shoving in her entire right hand, drenched in dampness... rewarded by the rites of passage... at the ease with which it was transferred to her. She was soaring. It was the most alone she'd ever felt and yet she needed nothing else... not even her own fingers after a while... as she swayed at the furthermost edge of her dreams, in a place more intimate than the G spot – the playground of pleasure. Folding her legs like Goddess Lakshmi seated on a half open lotus, she clenched one corner of the chaddar with her teeth – to hold on when the descent finally began... when it would...

'I'm kicking this door right now!' someone screamed hoarsely as soon as Meera had pulled the sheet over her face, her limbs lost to lust. Turning weightless.

The banging was turning louder.

But Meera was past caring. Her body in raptures, her lips quivering as the cushion dropped from between her legs. Carelessly – sans a centre of gravity.

'Mar gayi manhoos,' the tirade outside resumed.

Meera finally opened her eyes. The hazy sunlight greeting her guilt-free gaze, almost alien to begin with. For the first few minutes, she remained motionless... naked, sprawled, spent... not moving, her petticoat ridden up to her waist.

'Ram Ram, Ram Ram,' Madhubala screeched again.

Meera smiled, slowly wiping her eyes...

Everything was a blur. The way her tongue tasted, the iciness of the mattress, the cracks in the ceiling above... the moth-eaten calendar that *now confronted her... most of the dates discoloured. One of her glass bangles had shattered leaving a fine line of blood along her right wrist.*

What if it was true? Meera asked herself, taking a deep breath, running her fingers along the thin sliver. What if she'd died a long time ago? What if she'd never been alive? What if she'd breathed her last in Ward 3, Bed 22? Or even before that? Back home in Sinor? What if everything was a lie? she mused as her attention drifted outside – to the throbbing tumultuousness of another pre-monsoon day.

What if Yosuf had been right? What if he'd been right all along? What if there was really another world... beyond this one? Beyond all this? This bed – this body – this rain – this road – this longing – this light – this speed – this stench – this desire – this debauchery – this morning – last night – the afternoon before – the months in between – the year to which it all belonged... before...

Part One

One

My Name is Meera

A woman grows up in many ways, in many stages. But each stage is painful; the woman inevitably at the receiving end of the lessons, like she called it upon herself, in the first place. The first time is inevitably the hardest. The day she realizes her body has changed; becoming her greatest enemy, in a sense. From being the friend she trusted – the only friend, at times. Betraying all her deep dark secrets, even the ones she buried herself, using her own hands sometimes... in the dark, when no one else was watching. The doors steadfastly bolted.

Turning into a swan. Trapped in a fairytale.

The beginning of which was to be decided by someone else.

❦

My name is Meera. I was born after three miscarriages, along with Kartik, my twin brother, delivered a minute-and-a-half before me, at the back of an airless, cramped cowshed, surrounded by pregnant mammals imparting desperate howls and other mothers-to-be whispering sullen secrets, their sweaty faces contorted, their belly-buttons exposed.

'*Jaanu chu,* they almost forgot about you. In fact, it's only when Ma wouldn't stop kicking her legs and hands about and mumbling incoherently under her breath, that the hunch-backed dai with a huge black mole on her left cheek, painfully yanked her knees apart once more, literally shoving in her entire hand this time, as Ma wailed, writhing in pain... Ma was hauled up and made to squat for a good hour or so. You know *na*, the way women pee, crouching awkwardly, their ankles twisted, their hips protruding?'

Far away, a long-distance passenger train whistled by. We must've been about twelve. Kartik and I used to have identically lean bodies back then, but now mine was beginning to fill out. '*Haan, haan*, you remember everything, don't you? You know what I think, Kartik?' I squealed, pushing his chest hard. 'I think you just made this *whole* story up... all the things you described to me... just to annoy me...'

Kartik laughed roguishly, clicking his tongue, before laying his head on my chest to whisper, 'I think it's a *great* story, Meeru. In fact, I would do anything to be born like that – forgotten, resisting, fighting. It's what makes you so strong, silly. Stronger than me, your big brother,' he sounded tender all of a sudden, caressing my forehead lightly.

Kartik was my twin, my alter ego and my best friend, an extension of me, really. We were inseparable in every way, even eating from the same stainless steel plate every night, sleeping on the same cot, sitting next to each other on the same wooden bench in school, on Ma's lap, on Bapuji's cycle... everywhere. We would always lean into each other – as though we were not two individuals, but a single person. We shared every thought, dissected every reaction, being able to feel each other's minutest pain; intuitively deciphering what the other was thinking.

'Okay, so you tell me which game you want to play? You decide, okay? Happy?' I bit my lower lip hard, trying to gently push him away as on the road beside us a bridal palanquin made its way, the coloured glass lanterns glimmering softly as it approached, briefly lighting up the forlorn face of the newly-married girl inside.

'Let's play touch-touch,' Kartik whispered suddenly, in a hoarse voice, bringing his mouth near mine.

But I was beginning to dislike our old game. I grimaced as he guided my hands inside his half pants. 'No, please Kartik... I told you I don't like it anymore... especially this thing of yours, it's like a snake... it feels yucky... and, and it smells weird too... like cow-dung,' I winced, making a gagging noise.

Kartik immediately stood up and trounced off. He was miffed with me, I could tell. He didn't speak to me for the rest of the day either, his fingers avoiding mine even when we ate our meal from the same thali that night. His face clamped tight in a sulk.

'What's the matter with you both today? You never fight...' It was Ma who finally dissipated the stubborn silence between us, while picking up the dishes after dinner that night as we sat around the hearth of our crowded kitchen.

We lived in Sinor, a small dusty town in the heart of the bustling district of Vadodhara. It was my father's biggest regret that we had never seen the city... that we hadn't been born there. Being strangers in some way to the lights, the noise, the tall tales that travelled back and forth almost daily, bringing us within inches of the world that lay outside our boundary wall; our banal, every-day existence. The one that had provided Bapuji the ability to fund two square meals a day, as also maintain four cows, twelve hens, and a pukka one-storeyed house.

'Ma, is it true,' I took a deep breath, 'that since Kartik was born first no one bothered about me? Did I have to fight and scream just so you would notice me and let me out?'

Ma looked up with an amused smile. 'Nonsense, Kartik and you are the same soul, Meera. It's just that God created you in separate bodies so that you could be born to me... to make the birthing process easier, you understand? It's why you both look so similar – same hands, same big brown eyes, same hair...' she paused, her lips still grease-lined from the last helping of *aam kheer* that Ma always saved for herself, to savour at the end of her meal.

It was Bapuji's favourite too. He invariably asked for a second helping as Ma spliced thick slivers of fresh mango, before squeezing the porous pulp into a flat-bottomed vessel filled to the brim with boiling, thickened milk, the colour rapidly changing – from dense to desirous.

'Then how come Kartik has a snake lodged between his legs, Ma?' I blurted, stepping onto Bapuji's dirty plate in my agitation, the leftover curry splattering onto the sides of my legs.

'Chhee, Meera!' Ma scolded. 'Who taught you all this nonsense, huh? From where have you picked up all this filth? Is this any way to speak? You know your father could walk in any moment...' she reprimanded, pulling me by my plait, her nostrils flaring.

'No one... no one, Ma... I, I am sorry, I mean...' I stuttered nervously.

'What's wrong? Why are you shrieking? What has Meera done now?' Bapuji interrupted rushing inside. 'What's the matter? Speak up, dickri, what have you gone and done this time?' he barked, walking closer to me, scratching his chest.

Instantly Kartik was by my side. 'It's nothing, Bapuji... there was a small accident. Meera knocked over your plate... I was deliberately teasing her... that is all really...'

I rose up with a start, standing with my back pressed to the wall, warm tears rolling down my cheeks.

Kartik always took the blame for any trouble I got into; he could never stay mad at me, no matter what I did. Even when it wasn't his fault... at all... His love was rare. Never asking for more than its share.

❦

'Why does he keep on staring at you like that? All the other girls talk about it after class... as if his eyes are pulled open or something. Idiot!' Kartik remarked sourly, as we walked back from my dance class one day, taking a shortcut through the open fields again. He had always been possessive about me, but these days he was getting increasingly suspicious.

'And what if he does? I don't care about such silly things anyway. Besides, why on earth are you always in on what the other girls in *my* dance class discuss?' I sniggered, pushing him back roughly. I found Vardaan Bhai's attention quite flattering, actually. But I knew the slightest mention of my feelings would only make Kartik more jealous.

Kartik grabbed my hand. 'Listen; let's get this clear. I come to drop and fetch you as instructed by Bapuji. Besides, that Vardaan guy *is* weird... and well, have you even seen yourself in the mirror? You're getting so fat, bulging everywhere...' he stopped, as I turned around to face him. My eyes ablaze.

'Vardaan Bhai happens to be my dance Masterji... that's all,' I cut him short, defensively folding my arms across my chest. 'And just what do you mean by calling me fat? I haven't put on any weight at all. Besides, look who's talking? Have you heard your own voice of late? Like a frog calling out to its mate... And *your* face? Filled with ugly boils. It's not like you've become any better looking in the past couple of years...' I smirked callously, tossing my plait over my shoulders. Then, instantly contrite, knowing I'd hurt Kartik, I ran back, gently cupping his face. 'Okay, okay sorry, na... you said fat first... you know I didn't really mean a thing... you are the *most* handsome boy in all of Gujarat!' I hugged him tight.

'I didn't mean fat, I meant *these*, okay,' Kartik cut me short, his slender fingers suddenly underneath my rainbow-coloured dupatta. 'When I said you are putting on weight, I meant like Ma... soon you will have to wear those strange things with thin straps that she purchases from Yashoda Fui, every time she visits us from Mumbai, hiding them under her arms...'

'Are you saying I'm ugly?' I questioned huskily; Kartik's touch singeing my skin.

'Are you saying our Ma is ugly? Don't put words in my mouth, Meeru!' he said gruffly, abruptly letting me go.

But I couldn't stop. 'Hey, what is this?' I whispered, teasingly tracing the faint line of hair sprouting over his upper lip.

'Bapuji says I have to grow a moustache... he claims it's a sign of a man...' Kartik answered tersely, swerving to his left, trying to avoid my intense gaze.

My stomach had been hurting since morning, now it churned once again.

'Ouch,' I grimaced, pressing my hands down over the rim of my ghagra, slowly stretching my legs.

'What's the matter? Where is it hurting, Meeru? Here?' Kartik lifted up my kameez, immediately concerned as I tightly clenched my stomach muscles. My tummy was slightly bloated. For a while we remained like that, Kartik's hands resting protectively over my stomach, rubbing the area around my navel tenderly.

'I'm sorry I said you were fat, okay? Just that, sometimes I think you are going away from me. Do you feel it as well? The way things seem to be happening too fast around us nowadays, everything spinning out of control in some way? One moment we are so close, just like we always were, and at other times I seem to hardly know you...' he sighed, lifting up my face.

'You should stop thinking about me all day! I know that's what all your silly friends do anyway, lurking behind me in class. Some of your friends even smoke, you know? I hate all of them. They are bad for you,' I retorted instead.

Kartik stared at me raptly for a few seconds. 'I feel the same way about Masterji... whenever he eyes you... looking you up and down as if you are a new bride, he's bad for you, Meeru, very bad,' Kartik's eyes were dark and brooding.

My face flushed at the memory of Vardaan Bhai's gaze.

Kartik's words echoed in my mind as I vividly recalled watching Masterji myself – the way he straightened my posture, his firm hands expertly pressing the small of my back. And when he danced, the supple grace of his muscular thighs and buttocks, and how he always scratched his chest when I walked in, as if distracted by me, slanting his mouth. Our eyes avoiding each other's for a while, before searching one another out again, as I crouched to fasten my ghungroos, raising each leg in turn, expertly balancing myself, my unruly tresses billowing in the musky evening air.

'Are you ready, Meera?' Masterji would clear his throat to ask, lending me a hand, touching my shoulders lightly, before walking away again, leaving me breathless.

I never answered Masterji, except occasionally smiling shyly at him. It was like our little secret.

The first that wasn't Kartik's and mine.

Two

Besharam

Shame and sin are like two sides of the same coin. Thinly divided. A paradox, really, as I was to discover the year I turned thirteen. Standing between both these worlds, with nothing. It was the most alone I had ever felt. Estranged from my childhood; distanced from Kartik, suddenly governed by the whims and fancies of a changing body and the tromiscuous passion of new-found emotions.

Ma constantly gave me instructions on what I should or should not do – lessons in propriety, as she constantly referred to them.

She had devised a 'proper' way for everything – the way I should carry myself. Or drape my dupatta over my head, carefully camouflaging my cleavage. Or even talk to Bapuji in front of others – lowering my glance, muting my voice. All the things good girls *should* do, those like me, who belonged to respectable families with a fair amount of wealth; born with certain privileges, such as the education my parents spent on, always emphasizing how it would help make me more eligible in the marriage market.

'Your Bapuji's dream is that you marry in the city. He doesn't want you to spend the rest of your life with these useless small-town blokes, who have no work other than to just sit and drink all day or spend time chasing girls. "Our Meera is different. So beautiful, so pure, she's meant for another life," your father tells me night and day,' Ma chided, while clumsily stuffing my breasts into a stiff contraption that made it difficult for me to breathe – it was conical-shaped with adjustable straps, starched white, the same colour as my panties. Cutting into parts of me; trapping me; taming me in some way.

Of late, Ma's eyes scrutinized my every move; her ire unbearable on occasion, especially if I happened to return late after dance class or even spent an extra minute in our makeshift toilet. 'What takes you so long these days?' she always wanted to know, studying me up and down as I dabbed myself between my legs. 'What is it? What is it dickri?' she'd sometimes yell, yanking the thin cotton towel I used to wipe myself, to inspect its damp edges as if she were searching for something.

'Why are you always so uptight these days, Ma?' I once mustered the courage to ask her as she sat on her haunches, oiling my hair, her fingers untangling the knots cruelly, the warm liquid stinging my scalp.

Kartik stood in a corner watching us both.

Suddenly Ma snapped at him: 'You! What are you standing there gawking for? Didn't Bapuji leave instructions that you need to go help Manohar Kaka unload the goods from the truck that came in last night from Surat? Do you know how upset you will make your father by this insolence? Have you no idea just how hard the poor man toils all day just so that his children can have a better life than he was handed down?' she spewed, tugging hurtfully at my hair.

I gasped, coughing for breath.

Kartik was unfazed. 'Bapuji says I have to drop Meera to her dance class; besides, there seems to be a storm approaching. How can I just leave her alone? It is a long walk...'

Ma picked up a stick and waved it at him. 'Do as I say, Kartik, you understand? Your sister can manage on her own. As if this is the first time she is going there. Besides, will you always be around to escort her to and fro, from just about everywhere? Meera is no longer a child... soon she will get married... Learn to live without her... focus instead on getting trained under Manohar Kaka... What will you do when Meera's palki leaves this courtyard? Will you follow her all the way to her in-laws' house?'

'Ma, please let Kartik drop me on the cycle, it's a tiring walk and my stomach is hurting. Manohar Kaka's house is on the way too. I will walk back home with the other girls, please,' I interrupted, settling my ghagra, pulling the dupatta modestly over my front, trying to look as proper as Ma wanted me to.

Kartik was silent as he took me on his cycle through the deserted fields, his arms innocuously pressing into the sides of my breasts, as I sat on the cycle rod in front of him.

'Are you angry with me for what Ma said earlier? Do you think it's my fault she's always so edgy of late?' I grabbed his arm, pressing it against my chest.

'You are wearing that thing again, aren't you?' he cut me short, drawing his hand away.

'As if I have a choice! Ma is literally breathing down my neck,' I shook my head a couple of times.

'You want me to open it for you, Meeru? Just to breathe?' Kartik broke into a smile all of a sudden, slowing down his cycle.

'I do... but you suppose it's okay? What if the other girls poke fun of me in class?' I asked nervously.

Kartik snorted: 'None of the other girls wear all this, you know. Maybe they can't afford it... or maybe they don't have a Yashoda Fui supplying them these luxuries from the city. Anyway, take off this thing before someone comes along. I will hide it for you in my bag, okay? Don't worry so much; I will reach home before you and put it back in the cupboard. You can quickly change into it before Ma notices...'

'Okay, turn around then, quick... stop wasting time talking,' I pushed Kartik away brusquely.

'Not so fast, silly girl,' he chortled, untying my choli strings one by one, his touch feeling very different from Ma's; the tips of his fingers sending small shocks down my back, the warmth of his breath brushing the nape of my neck.

A drop of rain landed on my lips just then.

'You better hurry...' Kartik murmured, pulling me closer, his chest grazing my bare back before he turned me around.

I swallowed; his breath lingered on the side of my ears, caressing the edges of my earlobes like a scented summer breeze, the smell of his sweat forging a surreal intimacy.

'Are you done tying my choli back? Have you finished...?'

By the time Kartik was done, it had started raining with greater intensity.

'You're all wet,' he muttered under his breath.

❧

Dance Masterji – Vardaan Bhai – was a distant relative from Bapuji's side. He had been summoned to choreograph the annual play for the Dussehra day celebrations in our school three years ago. Back then I had been tall for my age, my head sticking awkwardly above the others'. He had noticed me at once as our eyes awkwardly collided.

'We are honoured to have a classical dancer of such repute agree to choose one among you from this class today, to play the central part. It is a matter of great pride indeed,' Jignesh Sir, our headmaster, who stood rubbing shoulders with him, had announced.

Vardaan Bhai had sized me up frankly. 'Of the eight girls and twenty boys I have seen performing earlier on this afternoon, I think she will make the best fit. Her hips... the way she folds her fingers, in fact even her natural posture is ideal for traditional Indian dance, which you all know, demands a certain amount of innate grace and poise,' he paused expectantly, as I ducked my head, embarrassed and utterly mortified by the way he openly discussed my figure.

'Go on, Meera, say your name,' Jignesh Sir had shouted as the whole class broke out into peals of laughter.

'Meera Rajda, Sir...' I had whispered, preferring to stare straight ahead.

Vardaan Bhai walked up to me and had cupped my cheeks lightly, 'Someday you will make a fine Sita, the coveted heroine of the Dusshera play that marks the culmination of the Navratras in Sinor... People will come to see you, from far and wide... to look into your eyes... to burn in your fire... I will train you personally. I will train you free of cost. After school... every Wednesday and Friday. My dance classes await your presence,' he had added in a hushed tone before I could react.

Since that fateful day I had essayed the role of Sita three years running.

My heart racing when I saw him. Even today.

✤

The dance class was eventually cancelled that evening as the downpour kept everyone away. As it turned out, I was the only one who made it. Just Masterji and I, staring at each other, as thick drops of rain pelted the compound facing us, accumulating shallow pools of water.

'The weather is becoming thoroughly unpredictable nowadays, no wonder not a soul has turned up,' it was Masterji who spoke first, as I waited near the window, my arms drenched as I clasped the iron grilles lightly, catching drops of water in my hand. He sounded a bit agitated.

But I was in a playful mood. 'Isn't Sinor the loveliest place when it rains?' I turned around to question, taking my time, dabbing my damp wrists with the corners of my orange bandhni dupatta.

Masterji nodded his head, his eyes following the movement of my fingers, his chest heaving. 'It's not just the most beautiful place in the world, it also has some of the most beautiful dancers... and you...'

'And I...?' I repeated softly, removing a few stray strands of hair that had entered my mouth, experiencing a sudden sense of power in that moment.

Masterji stayed silent for the next few seconds. He hadn't shaved; his dimples concealed by a dense crop of facial hair... partially grey. He was breathing roughly. He looked away.

'Have you ever wanted to get drenched, Masterji?' I deliberately licked a drop of rain on my lower lip.

Masterji walked towards me taking slow, measured steps. 'And what if... if I were to drown in the waters, huh?' he spoke thickly under his breath, his hands suddenly on my shoulders.

On an impulse, I placed my right palm over his lips, darkened from smoking bidis. 'I'd save you... always...' I answered throatily.

For a while we stood in silence, Masterji trying to get a hold on himself, staring desperately towards the dimly-lit entrance from time to time, his earlobes reddening. 'Looks like the rain has slowed a bit, let me drop you home. Your parents must be worried sick,' he cleared his throat.

I smiled, twirling around, before teasingly splashing some rainwater on his chest, as one of the doors to the classroom suddenly flung wide open; a violent gust of wind rushing inside.

'Goddammit!' he swore, pulling his wet cotton kurta over his head, tufts of coarse, black armpit hair confronting my glance, adding to the darkness that engulfed us both. It was torture not to stare. I tried glancing down at my toes, a little scared by my own daring. 'Uh... Kartik will be late tonight... I told him it would be a long rehearsal...' I spoke breathlessly after a few seconds, lying easily, some of my kohl having bled, my throat almost parched, the ghungroos on my feet echoing the clamour of my feelings.

Another harsh breeze and the door swung open once again. Masterji's neatly combed locks were now completely dishevelled. He shivered slightly. Quickly lighting a bidi and inhaling a few puffs, he forced his eyes shut. The tobacco fumes made me cough and I immediately moved away, my back pressed awkwardly to the windowsill. Another dusty draft and my dupatta slid off me. I thought of the brassiere Kartik had taken off earlier as I tried concealing my clearly outlined breasts with both my hands, crossing my arms clumsily across my chest.

Without a word Masterji gently removed them, his touch at once tender and tumultuous. The tiny follicles of hair on his thick wrist brushed against mine causing a peculiar tingling sensation just below my navel. I gasped, the feeling strangely intimate; a delicious shiver that I usually felt when I urinated.

It was pitch dark outside. The smell of doused earth was overpowering.

'Meera,' was all he could manage, before slipping his fingers inside my choli and tracing my nipples with his long nails, his eyelids drooping with desire. I grimaced when he suddenly pushed me down on the cold, damp floor, my tresses billowing in his face, my plait coming undone. From the corner of my eyes I watched him expertly undo the choli strings...

'Oh Meera...' he repeated, cupping my breasts in his hands, as I vexed my ankles, moaning desperately as he bent down to suckle on them, swirling his tongue around each curve desperately. Beads of sweat crowding his otherwise placid face.

He was biting down now. The pain exquisite... novel. And yet, as Masterji climbed over me, drinking hungrily, freely, pinning me down with his bare hands, all I could think about was what Kartik had told me a year or so ago. The truth about men and women... and their bodies...

'Meera... you are so young, so ripe... so...' he grunted, as we embraced for the first time... my heart racing against his. 'At least look at me...' he muttered hoarsely, tugging feverishly at the thin silver waistband I wore.

'Why?' I shuddered, wantonly licking my lips, the blood rushing to my head as I slithered seductively underneath him.

'At least then I will feel this is not all my fault...' the rest of his words melted, as he folded my knees all of a sudden, one hand stroking my navel in a circular motion, twisting my nipples roughly with the other.

My body was aflame. I secured my arms around his neck, rubbing myself against his dhoti front, writhing in pleasure, as Masterji's movements grew more frenzied, his eyes bloodshot.

'You are so lush... so, so young... and... yet...' he whispered lifting my legs over his shoulders, as if this were a complicated dance composition. But then he stopped. 'Oh God no, what is this?' Masterji cried, horrified with himself, forcing me to look up in his direction, my body caught in the midst of a convulsion, his dhoti pleats loose under my hips... my ghagra too partially undone.

It took me a while me to focus back on Masterji's face, details that had seemed irrelevant till a few seconds ago. He was trying to say something else as well, as I tugged at his wrists in vain... my nipples still erect, pointing at his face.

I don't know what happened next.

'You should've told me, Meera... you should have told me you were perioding... Chhee... how could you do this to me? Just how?' he said agitatedly, hurriedly buttoning his crumpled kurta, looking visibly disappointed.

Outside it was flooded.

Inside, I bled.

Feeling let down by a man I had been greatly attracted to since the time I was a young girl; and had wanted desperately since I had turned into a woman.

It was the first lesson I ever learnt about sex anyway. As I walked home with my head hung low, covered in the same crushed dupatta that Masterji had used to wipe his fingers. Rubbing between them

– fiercely, frantically, fastidiously. I knew nothing would remain the same.

Our attraction silenced. Forever. A forced shame.

❦

I had never felt more betrayed by own body. And yet, in a strange way it was my body that proved to be my greatest ally – my first menses saving me from the guilt of what had really transpired between Masterji and me. The attack on my virginity concealed somehow by the dull stains of my period.

Maybe the rains have a way of blurring things...

When I got back Ma pretended as though she had been prepared all along, promptly undressing me, never once asking me why my clothes were dishevelled or why I still hadn't removed my ghungroos, even refraining from the most obvious question – how I had managed to make my way back alone in the heavy showers.

'Don't speak about it to anyone, child. Not till I take you to the temple first thing tomorrow morning. I should be the one to break the news to your Bapuji... make sure you don't breathe a word... not even to Kartik. Remember one thing, Meera, from now, every month, on more or less the same date, you will bleed for three to four or even seven whole days, experiencing a strange soreness. You might even feel a sharp pain in your lower abdomen. Learn to deal with it. Tears will have no effect. You must behave as normally as possible, cleaning yourself regularly, changing these cloth pads that I am going to now teach you to make. Insert them between your thighs, and suck in your stomach when the cramps come...' Ma's face was grim as she pointed at the soft mound of flesh between my legs, tiny tufts of hair camouflaging the entrance.

The moment Kartik entered, he instinctively knew something had happened. 'What's the matter with you?' he asked, shaking me violently, as always sensing my discomfort and pain.

'Just leave me alone,' I snapped, crouching in a distant corner of our bed.

Kartik clicked his tongue. 'Now that's not fair... I get to deal with your mood swings, while you get to have fun with Masterji... huh?' his words stank with sarcasm.

I sat up, clutching my stomach, the cotton slipping out of place, displaced by the sudden movement. 'Don't you ever speak to me like that... nothing happened between Vardaan Bhai and me, okay?' I screamed bitterly as Kartik leapt over to my side.

'What are you hiding from me, Meeru? I know everything...' he gritted his teeth menacingly, pressing his hands down on my chest.

I burst into tears at once, taken aback at Kartik's sudden transformation.

'This... this is what happened,' I shouted back in self-defence, hitching up my ghagra as drops of blood steadily trickled down the back of my legs.

Kartik wiped the blood gently with his fingers.

Ma walked in just then, looking aghast.

'What's going on here?' she hollered. Then before I could react, she said, 'Meera, you are a girl and Kartik, your brother, is a boy. Don't you understand the difference, you two? You must never touch one another like that. It is dirty; it is a disease, it must never occur again,' her thin fingers dug into my collarbones as she ordered Kartik out.

'But Ma, I, I can't sleep without him... and, and I hate the dark, I have never slept in this room by myself,' I went on undeterred, the tears not stopping.

'You will get used to it. Besides it's time, Meera... like I said you have entered a new life... one that Kartik has no place or right to be in anymore. Just like you made it back tonight, despite the rains, you must make this journey on your own,' she said, settling my ghagra, not batting an eye.

I clamped my eyes shut, nursing a familiar fatigue. Not knowing when Ma left. Or when the night gave way to day.

Kartik was gone the next morning. He must be in school by now, I calculated, running my hands over my breasts. They felt unusually heavy and plump. Ma was shouting instructions to Bapuji. Something about bringing home some groceries he had forgotten the previous evening, thanks to the rains. The sun was shining furiously as though nothing had happened.

Maybe nothing had.

I took a deep breath, before moving over to Kartik's side of the bed. Missing him in a way only a woman can miss a man. Without knowing why.

Three

Binal

'So tell me about yourself, I've been doing most of the talking. Tell me your dirtiest, deepest secret, now that we are finally alone...' she said, giggling and rolling over on my bed, her eyes the colour of molten jaggery. A rich girl from Baroda, an only child, Binal was related to Yashoda Fui in some complicated manner and was spending the summer in Sinor with us, in the room once shared by Kartik and myself. She had arrived the day before yesterday with a fancy white suitcase, overflowing with clothes of all colours and cuts... and a pair of heeled slippers that made a sharp, clicking sound. Everywhere.

Bapuji had told me to take special care of her. 'I've promised to look after her well, see to it that she has company always... she is very different from you,' he had said as we had waited for Binal at the station.

'Hey, Meera, can I ask you a question? I've been dying to since we got back from the tour of the river...' Bimal looked at me sideways as she tied her hair in a high ponytail. She was so open and frank; so unselfconscious in the way she conducted herself. I could see that Bapuji did not know what to make of her.

I nodded absent-mindedly, my attention riveted on her western style skirt. The way it had ridden up as she sat in bed. Exposing her plump, fair legs. Beads of dampness collecting near the entrance of her thighs when she clamped them together.

I felt a dull ache that refused to go away. Reminiscent of the afternoon that Kartik had been sent away. To work in Manohar Kaka's flourishing cloth business, somewhere in Surat.

'What's the matter, you look sad?' Bimal lowered her voice, stroking my hand, before resting our locked hands in the warmth of her lap.

It was the first time I was sharing this bed, my space, with anyone after Kartik's departure. I swallowed uncomfortably, glancing at the small bedside table on which Kartik's photograph stood... its edges frayed; tiny scratches across his face.

'You must earn your keep... I cannot keep wasting money paying for your failures, every single year...' I closed my eyes as Bapuji's booming voice rang afresh in my ears. Our school results had just been announced and Kartik had failed most his subjects again.

'I don't want to go away; Give me another chance...' he had begged.

'Son, we've never said no to you for anything, but you must remember that soon we have to cough up a sizeable amount for Meera's marriage. Try and understand your Bapuji's limitations, please. Besides, who knows what may happen if you can actually impress Manohar Kaka with your hard work and loyalty...' Ma had tried placating Kartik as he continued to stare expectantly at Bapuji's inscrutable face.

It was then that I had intruded, dashing out of the kitchen to confront my father, my eyes full of tears, my hands stiff from kneading dough for the night's dinner. *'Bapuji, I am not interested in marriage, please don't send Kartik away...'*

Ma tried saying something. *'No, Ma, you won't come between us anymore. Kartik will stay in this house... here...'* I must have yelled, the hot wind hissing through my hair.

Bapuji swivelled all of a sudden. *'Don't you dare answer back...'* he thundered, his eyes flaming, his right hand raised as if to strike me.

It was at this point that Kartik had lunged forward, grabbing my father's hand and pushing me back roughly. *'This is my problem, Meeru, and let's face it, Surat is way better than this shit-hole,' he had scoffed, staring coldly at Bapuji's face.*

'Hey, what's the matter? Are you crying or something?' Binal gently lifted up my chin. Forcing me to look at her.

'I'm sorry, I was just thinking of my brother. Actually, when Bapuji told me we were going to have a surprise visitor, I thought for a minute it might be Kartik. That he was back. It's just that he was the only friend I had... for a really long time. In school too, the other girls came and went, Kartik was my only constant, my soul-mate, and, and now with him gone...' I paused pensively, as Binal picked up the photograph from the table.

'This is him, right? Cute *chhe*,' she mused, caressing the frame, before facing me to add: 'You look so similar.'

'We have the same mouth and eyes... we are twins... Kartik must have grown a lot taller now, though... this snap was just after our tenth exam...' I sighed placing my head on the pillow next to Binal's head.

Kartik had left Sinor the day after his ugly showdown with Bapuji. He had not come home since. He was working hard with Manohar Kaka, Bapuji had reported matter-of-factly to us one afternoon, reading from Kaka's letter, sent some eight months after his departure.

'*Matha matthi bhoot kardhe*, at least he's thinking straight now,' Ma had commented, as she scrubbed the utensils, her back hunched.

Kartik never wrote. Not even to me. Not ever. Not a single detail about his new life away from our home.

'You have a boyfriend?' Binal questioned, playing with a strand of my hair, dispelling the rest of my thoughts.

I shrugged. 'Depends on what your definition of a boyfriend is... you big city folks have names for everything. It's easier I suppose... putting each relationship in a particular container and conveniently fixing a label...'

Binal drew my hands in hers. 'Well, all I know is that boyfriends make a girl happy... very happy... and know something... you are sad, very sad, Meera. In fact, it's the first thing I noticed about you.' Binal was so understanding, so unjudgemental. I slipped my fingers back inside hers as the fractured sunlight played hide and seek on our backs.

'I know we are very different. You the daughter of a rich trader... someone with a privileged city breeding... and, and I... this, this is my life... there is little here to be excited about really... especially during these lengthy summer vacations,' I paused to take a deep breath. 'But I don't know why I feel I can talk to you... it's the first time, really...'

Binal closed her eyes for a few seconds. Then placing her head on my chest, she confessed in a husky voice: 'I'm getting married soon. I hear it's all been fixed... it's why my father actually insisted I come here... you know, to see how women serve their husbands... theirs being a traditional family set up... Jamnagar based...'

I laughed aloud for the first time. Stroking her silken hair, I asked playfully, 'So what have you learnt, vali dickri?'

Binal had the most mischievous eyes. They sparkled all of a sudden. 'It's pretty simple, you listen to what a man says, nod your head demurely a couple of times... and, and then,' she stopped inadvertently, reaching out to caress my collarbones instead, our lips nearly touching.

'And then?' I shivered, my head falling backwards, thoughts of Kartik ebbing and flowing.

Binal paused for a couple of seconds. Carelessly undoing the buttons on her shirt, she murmured, 'You... you let them have their way with you...' Wordlessly, she guided my right hand inside her shirt. 'That's all it takes to turn on someone... anyone...' she whispered, her eyes closing as my fingers touched her firm, velvety breasts.

I shivered, Masterji's face flashing before my eyes in that instant. The way I had walked up to him... wanting so badly to be held... the first time I had been alone with him. His fingers climbing up my waist. The soft shudders. The incessant rains. His angry last glance. Had he been repulsed because I was bleeding? Before my time? Thoughts crowded my mind. Had I not played hard to get that evening? Hard enough?

Propelled forward by my own bodily hunger... the aching need to be loved... had my brazenness hurt his manhood? Was it why he had rejected me so easily after that solitary encounter? Not uttering a single sentence in the whole year that he taught me... bypassing me deliberately in the evenings, till he finally disappeared all of a sudden, to be replaced within a month or two by a fastidious elderly lady called Kanta Ben.

By then the heat from Binal's body was melting against mine. She had undone my shirt too, her breasts grazing my nipples, creating a familiar shudder... my hands turned clammy with wanton cravings.

'I, I don't understand what you mean, exactly,' I fumbled to find the right expression, as Binal impulsively planted a kiss on my forehead, her arms steadying my shoulders at the same time, settling my unruly tresses that flopped haphazardly over my eyelids. I was due to menstruate any day; my breasts were engorged, my earlobes tingling at her deliciously inappropriate touch.

Wordlessly, Binal ran her left thumb along my waistband, as we sat facing each other, the afternoon sun drenching our backs. Her skirt that had climbed up promiscuously. I could see her panties from under her legs. I evaded my stare, stopping at her mid-riff, at her cleavage peeking out from between a starched off-white shirt, the one with the oval buttons and a slim brown belt that bunched up her tiny breasts.

She had a mole just in the middle.

'Meera, you're so good looking; boys will die to just get one look from you. But, you are just too guarded... it's like you are petrified of the power your own body possesses, the things it can make you feel... I mean just look at your breasts... do you have the faintest idea how many women could also go crazy simply staring at *them*... as, as I am this minute,' she looked slyly in my direction, perhaps hoping to gauge my reaction.

A thin line of moisture trickled down my navel, as I felt my cheeks flush, tongue-tied at Binal's outspokenness. The way she became me. In that minute. 'So what do you suppose I *should* do then? Do you have a remedy, a cure?' I laughed awkwardly as she leaned forward, cupping my cheeks, both of us trying to make light of the moment.

Binal drew me closer, her lower lip opening and closing like her eyelids. Hers were the most thick dark brown eyelashes, I noticed, as she planted her lips on mine.

I tried saying something, hoping to get away; a part of me worried about Ma walking in on us just then, or perhaps my own feelings; thoughts that didn't seem to go away. The way I almost hopelessly succumbed to Binal's accidental touch, responding to her tongue as it insistently parted mine, slipping inside insidiously. Her lips creating a hollow sound as they closed over mine, as she squeezed the top of my breasts simultaneously.

My hips rocked in tandem with her buttocks, as we huddled closer on the bed, my panty clinging damply to my sex, the bed shaking like a sinking ship tossed on a tempestuous midnight ocean.

A train passed just then, its deafening whistle making Binal all the more desperate, as she swerved sideways, biting the side of my neck, pulling down my bra straps, moaning suggestively all the while.

I stared at her without words, in a state of sweet arousal. Feeling a heady mixture of shock and surprise, as we lay with our ankles entwined. And then I pulled her up by her ponytail, brusquely throwing her down on the mattress, kissing her with a copious carnal fervour, before I squatted over her stomach, yanking her skirt up to drink in the sight of her bare stomach.

Binal had a slight tummy bulge; she groaned, her body like putty as I wrapped my thighs tightly around hers. The sweat on her skin was akin to drops of summer rain. Smooth as silk.

'Meera...' she moaned, lifting up her hips, her pupils dilated.

Gently I slipped my left hand inside her shirt, sinking my teeth over her right nipple, watching as she manoeuvred mesmerically under me, imparting muffled groaning sounds, Kartik's picture dropping off the table with an inadvertent swing of her limbs.

I saw it fall from the corner of my eye when Binal parted both my legs with her knees, rubbing herself against my saltiness, swallowing some of my hair too, I think, her pale pink lipstick smudged, like the ochre clouds outside.

I held her tight; inhaling the muskiness of her sex, the sweet smell of her afterbreath.

My thoughts veered back to Kartik.

'When will you be back?'

I remembered his face. As we had waited for the overnight bus to arrive, a dust storm brewing up close, the trees around us mostly dead. Kartik hadn't shaved.

'Maybe it's time for you to make new friends, Meeru...' he had muttered, running his fingers through my hair, before I lurched forward, falling into Kartik's arms, clasping his chest. The way Binal grabbed me desperately now.

'That's different... we are more than friends you know...' I had mumbled, sobbing as the bus pulled up beside us..

Kartik had kissed me lightly just above my upper lip. Then turning around to pick up his misshapen tin suitcase, he whispered under his breath, 'Now you know why I have to leave!'

'What's the matter?' Binal raised her voice, caressing my eyelids, her breathing uneven.

I swallowed with some difficulty.

'Nothing...' I gritted my teeth, bending down to pick up Kartik's picture that lay on its back, forgotten... our arms sliding off one another's, as I climbed off her... the sheets a mass of moistness.

Binal wrapped my dupatta around herself, suddenly vulnerable, half naked, lowering her glance. 'I know you're not going to tell anyone about all this... just as you are not going to tell anyone your other secrets. It's just that you are so sensual, Meera. I just wanted to see how it felt to touch you once... we, we *are* friends, right?' she broke into a nervous smile, trying to settle her skirt, her hands still somewhat unsteady, her face partly frozen by my sudden withdrawal.

I pushed myself on my elbows. Straightening the mattress, I answered, 'What if we just stayed this way...'

Looking Binal in the eye.

The rest of Binal's three-week visit passed uneventfully. We never touched each other again or talked about what had transpired, treating our fleeting attraction as a necessary digression, perhaps a dress rehearsal at best, never holding the other fully accountable for the sequence of events, knowing somewhere that our lives would be altered irrevocably as soon as we parted. Hers, before mine, as had been previously decreed.

'I'll miss you,' she confessed the day she was leaving, wiping her eyes, her fingers slipping out of mine, as surreptitiously as they had slipped in that day.

'Looks like you have mastered the art of a true blue village belle. What happened to the girl from the big, bad city? Don't tell me I was the bad influence,' I joked, tugging at her ponytail

Binal looked up for a few seconds, then, not knowing what more to say, she disappeared inside the night train.

'Hey Meera,' she stuck out her head, adding hastily as the train chugged out of our deserted station:'We are more than friends you know...'

❦

My last year in school was quite gruelling. I struggled to concentrate, my thoughts always with my missing brother. Most of the girls in my class had already been married off, and the boys who remained whispered amongst themselves the second I entered class. I knew they were discussing me from the lewd, sidelong glances they cast in my direction – always waiting for a chance to peer at my cleavage, before dissecting the rest of my appearance.

With Bapuji determined to 'settle' my marriage at any cost before the year culminated, our courtyard was infested with so-called well-wishers, almost every single evening. There they sat, a bunch of village elders, munching on theplas and talking of this groom and that, armed with photographs and convoluted janam kundlis – aligning alliances and astrological positions.

I was even made to meet a few of my prospective suitors. My head always demurely covered, strategically draped in the ornate silk sari last worn by Ma on her marriage – with an intricate gold pin tucked into its centre, even as I complained about the choli being too tight or the fact that my temples were incessantly throbbing.

'Pain and pleasure mean the same things for us. Besides, get used to managing yourself in a sari, Meera. And how many times have I told you to ensure your pallu is neatly arranged over your breasts? Dickri, once you are married... your body too must adjust to the changes. Learn to walk slowly... and look down while speaking to a man, okay? You don't want to raise any untoward suspicions.' Ma mouthed instructions, sounding like a seasoned war general, unmoved by my plight.

I did as I was told. Feeling nothing. Staring benignly at my latest suitor. All the while holding imaginary conversations with Kartik. Thinking of his eyes over mine.

'I don't understand why you can't be happy anymore? I mean aren't you satisfied with any of the rishtas?' Kartik asked. He looked hauntingly handsome, clad in a thin silk kurta. His beautiful, curly hair glimmering in the setting sun.

'Kartik...' I interrupted, as we sat with our legs dangling over the bank on a makeshift, wooden platform that creaked ominously every now and then.

Kartik caught my left hand. Then pressing it to his mouth, he said, 'I only came for you, Meeru... I had to see you once before you were betrothed. Bapuji rang up Manohar Kaka... asking him for a loan to arrange your marriage... he said Meera is going away soon... sounding excited for the first time... I had to come back...'

I placed my head on his shoulders.

'I'm sorry I was angry with you, Kartik... not hugging you either when I first saw you walk in through the gates. Somehow, there is so much I have to tell you... these last few years... each day has been so...' I choked.

Kartik listened impassively.

'So, it's you going away this time, then?' he spoke after a while, his eyes searching my face.

'I miss you so much... promise me you won't leave Sinor now until things are finalized, I don't care how long this marriage natak takes,' I exhaled, lifting my face up for a few seconds.

'Meeru, your life is about to change. Most girls are so elated at the prospect of getting married...' he teased before falling strangely silent; saying nothing for a while as we studied the ripples in the waters below us. 'Everyone has to get married at some point... it's only natural,' Kartik cuddled me tenderly.

'Nonsense,' I scoffed, trying to get up, adding as I settled my dupatta: 'I am sick of everyone telling me things about myself that they seem to feel and I don't know already. I have my own dreams too you know. Besides, as opposed to what you may be speculating right this moment, I haven't said yes or no to even the last proposal, okay? Have you ever thought, Kartik, what if I was the one rejected... I mean...'

Kartik seized me by my hips, before bringing them closer to his. 'Meera, don't you understand, I... can't let you love anyone else... it's... it's not so simple... for me...' he looked strangely tortured.

I took a deep breath.

'Anyway, it doesn't matter really... I must leave now or I will get very late,' I pursed my lips.

Kartik picked up a stray pebble. Studying its shape, he said in a hushed voice, 'Ma tells me you were chosen to play Sita in the Dusshera play again this year... you have been practising night and day she claims, after dinner too... daily. I think you will make the perfect Sita... someday...'

'And... and after the play ends?' I breathed, as he stood up to dust the back of his kurta.

'We'll come down to this river. Just you and me, Kartik and...' he murmured, pulling up my chin.

'Meeru... your Meeru...' I whispered, falling into his sturdy arms, closing my eyes.

'You'll always be there, right? Watching me, even if it is from a distance... I'll always find you by the river, right?' I swallowed hard, pressing myself into his chest.

Kartik stiffened. His ribs poking me under my breasts... I ran both my hands to steady his back... the sun slipping into the horizon just then. The sky soaked in saffron.

'Why can't you be happy anymore either?' I rued.

'I know all about the Masterji incident...' he said all of a sudden, inaudibly almost, at first. 'Everything...' he spoke again, before burying his face into my hair.

I shuddered, pulling away at once, covering my eyes. My heart nearly skipping a beat.

Kartik gently removed my hands one by one.

'It's the real reason I went away. You've always wondered, haven't you?' he inhaled with difficulty, wiping my cheeks with his palms...

I searched for words.

'I, I was always afraid Bapuji would find out... or Ma... it's what I told myself when I spotted you... with that Vardaan Bhai... on the night of the rains... all the while hoping it was someone else... hating myself for it... all this time... needing to punish myself... in some way... for...' Kartik cupped my shoulders.

I shook my head vigorously.

'You've hated me... all this while you've hated me, haven't you?' I screamed hoarsely, tears flooding my face.

Kartik hung his head low.

'Or maybe... maybe...' he hesitated, drawing me into him.

A streak of silver lightning flashed across the evening sky.

I saw it reflect in his eyes.

Four

Agniparikhsha

I still remember the very last time I was dressed as Sita. It was the month of October. Kartik had been gone for a long while.

My eyes were kohl-lined. There were fresh jasmines tucked into my plait, a line of hairpins piercing my skull, causing a dull ache especially near the temples. A fake diamond tiara sat on the centre of my forehead, its weight enough to make me feel faint. Ma's dull gold lehenga clung to my bare legs, adorned with intricate patterns. My arms weighed with glass bangles of every kind... in every colour. Even purple... next to the red, second from the front, to the lime green and the off white... pearl necklaces crowding my cleavage.

I ran out of the make-shift green room the moment the performance culminated and raced down to the river, my anklets roughly colliding.

'*Agniiiiiparikhshaaaaaaaa,*' I screamed, feeling a chill run down my spine.

The river was freezing this time of the night. But it's where I always came to. Feeling a sudden sense of safety, remembering the game Kartik and I had once invented.

Each year, after the Dusshera play, when everyone flocked to witness a gigantic cut-out of Ravana being installed at the nearby chowk, Kartik would cycle down furiously with me on the carrier of his cycle, tearing off our elaborate costumes as we dove headlong into the aquamarine waters, jumping off a makeshift wooden diving board.

Trying to hold our breaths underwater for as long as we could.

It was fun seeing who chickened out first.

'And, what if I'd died? Drowned I mean? What if you hadn't caught me in the nick of time? Again?' I'd invariably complain, holding on to his chest desperately, tears gushing out of my swollen eyes, once we'd surfaced.

'Dying and drowning are not the same thing,' Kartik would shout back, his thighs holding my bare back in a pincer-like grip.

Before he let go and we drifted apart... slowly...

'I'd love to drown someday, melting into this river... swimming upstream with all the multi-coloured fishes... locating secret passages, maybe even rediscovering the sack stashed with a hundred gold coins Ma told us about during her bedtime tales, somewhere at the bed of this mighty river. Imagine a world where you'd never have to wake up, Meeru? Where everything is blue... no black, no white... not even a speck of grey...' he'd whispered, manoeuvring the raging currents expertly.

It was difficult to keep up.

'Kartik,' I sobbed now, my voice breaking, flapping my arms frantically as I jumped into the deep. 'You said I could come... you, you said I would always find you here... you said there is a river in all of us... Kartik...' I broke down completely, my sentences dissolving into the dusk.

It had been exactly a year since Kartik had died. They had found his body bloated out of shape, lying on his back by these very banks. His face had been calm, as beautiful and serene as I always remembered him.

❦

'Put your arms around me and hold tight. Hello, can't you hear me?' a young man with the fiercest black eyes hollered, grabbing my hips unexpectedly, emerging as if out of nowhere in the deep.

My make-up had melted... my lips tasted like rubber.

'It's fine... relax... you can breathe now, you are going to be okay,' he spluttered as water filled his mouth, trying to haul me up from the river. He pulled me back towards the shore, his strong arms crushing my breasts.

'What were you trying to do? Don't you know how to swim?' he panted, his powerful arms separating the ripples as the water became shallower near the shoreline.

I couldn't see his face. My kohl must've bled. My eyes burned.

'You could've died, the current is at its highest this time of the night, you have no business being here by yourself,' he spoke in an imposing baritone, managing to finally swim to the mud bank, stretching out his right arm, holding me in his left.

'I came here to look for something, something I lost... something important,' I cut him short tersely, shivering violently, watching him look away as he assessed the difficulty of the job ahead... the distant lights of the chowk reflected on his hard wet back, glistening dreamlike, together with specks of silver sand.

'That's ridiculous, anyway now listen to me carefully. I will climb out and then haul you up. These currents can't be trusted, you could slip again, so hold my hand properly, okay?' he instructed, clearing his throat a couple of times.

'I can't,' I said, my lips trembling.

'Just do it...' he commanded, the water beginning to collect near his toes, droplets of moisture coalescing on a bed of coarse sand.

'I, I can manage, you carry on, I'm sorry for the...' I stuttered, bowing my head, tongue-tied, shuddering as his fingers slipped out of mine in less than a second.

There was no moon.

'Nonsense. I'm not going to stand here and watch you kill yourself, stop sounding childish,' he said authoritatively, almost sounding like Bapuji, his lips tightly pursed together.

'I can't,' I whimpered, shaking my head vigorously this time.

He was no boy; his arms were powerful, virile. He must have been in his late twenties. He wasn't wearing a shirt. His chest was hairy, like Bapuji's. I could see the outline of his organ. One part of me was embarrassed at my own diffidence, the other craved to reach out... somehow.

'Step out of the waters at once, just do as I say,' his eyes glared angrily in the darkness.

'I... actually... I'm not...' I tried saying something coherent.

'I know you are naked,' he snapped.

I stepped out, faltering only a few seconds longer, before climbing out of the river, concealing my breasts, using both hands, my gait awkward, my legs crossed clumsily... scared to slip again.

For a few seconds, we stood clinging like that, the stranger and I, in a sort of suspended silence. My insides had turned icy; my long hair was soaking wet. My face was drained of colour.

A sharp shiver passed between my thighs as I clenched them together.

A night train passed in the distance just then, its piercing lights illuminating the shadowy branches shrouding us. I heard the man's sharp intake of breath.

'You can look if... if you want to, it's all right,' I finally spoke, dropping my arms to my side. It was difficult to see much, except a faint silhouette of his broad shoulders. The man turned his face away obstinately. 'Please can you stay, stay a while? Please...' I pleaded, running my hands down his stomach... the dense crop of hair coarse against my fingers.

'I am...' he was trying to reply when I suddenly pressed myself into him.

Now I could feel him fully. His breathing was uneven. I watched him grow as I raised myself on my toes, lolling my head backwards each time he squeezed my buttocks and tugged at my breasts urgently with his other hand. 'You're the girl who played Sita, right, two years ago too? I was there in the audience. I watched you... you were so...'

he muttered gruffly under his breath, deftly aligning my hips with his, his lips closing over mine.

Without a word, I stripped off his cotton underpants, taken aback at the redness of his organ, at how tender it looked, even in this light, oozing a sticky secretion, its tip inflamed. He parted his thighs at once, slipping his left thumb inside my vagina, stroking me with his index finger insistently. I convulsed, grabbing his back, my lips opening and closing as he repeated the same movement... this time probing deeper. My insides smarted. His own gaze drunken with a fierce potency as our limbs entwined. He pushed my thighs forcefully apart, using only the back of his knee, guiding my hands onto his hardness.

I pulled him over my breasts, wanting desperately to be taken.

We were both hungry, his tongue insatiable – as were my own fingers, picking up speed, before slipping back into a sedated, dizzying spell.

Another train passed, its deafening siren practically tearing us apart.

'Don't stop...' he commanded the moment I happened to slow down, biting my left earlobe gently, as if it were a signal, sending another delicious thrill through my privates. His manhood completely filled my palm.

I let him inside. Letting out a sharp cry, watching his pelvic muscles expand and flex with ease, as he swung back and forth like a dervish. His soaked trousers now lay bunched near my toes, his jaw hardened, his eyeballs rolled back as if he were having a fit or something. 'Faster, c'mon...' he gritted his teeth painfully, sucking on my shoulders, instructing me as he pulled my hair back, 'Touch me. Now...'

I did as I was told to, pulling him in deeper, our bodies buoyant... almost rendered weightless after a point.

We were breathing coarsely, our mouths locked. He'd moan whenever his bulge slipped out, rubbing it frantically over my belly button as I arched my back to make more space, my tangled tresses wrapped around my breasts, forging haphazard patterns.

'I'm so close...' was the last thing he muttered, as I caressed his nipples, his body shuddering, minutes before he jerked forward unexpectedly, spreading a warm mass of whiteness slowly down my stomach.

I clamped my eyes shut.

'*Meera*,' someone screeched irately from a distance.

The man glanced up distractedly for a moment. 'Ahhhh, Meera... Meera...' he mumbled, intoxicated, before pushing himself down with more vigour, grinding his buttocks, his cheeks flushed; his gaze as turbulent as the mysterious depths of the river. We kissed like long lost lovers.

And then he was gone.

I was to never see him again either.

A man who did not even know my full name... nor I his, for that matter. Like an unfinished love letter... or that one last glance over your shoulder. The one that you never take... scared of things you will never know nor understand.

By the time the month had ended, Bapuji announced that he had fixed my alliance to a boy from the city. 'Graduate, business background, roots in Ahmedabad, oldest son, own shop selling dress materials... even imported ones, somewhere in Mumbai,' I heard him inform Ma as I listened from behind their door one night.

'But Bapuji, I want to pursue dance, at least, if I can't go to college,' was my first reaction when the news was officially broken to me a day or two later.

'Stop sounding childish now, Meera. Don't trouble your Bapuji any further. This is the best marriage offer you can get, the whole of Sinor agrees on just how lucky we've been... considering this family's fate,' Ma grimly covered her mouth, about to break down, muttering as she slowly wiped her eyes, 'Haven't we all suffered enough? Have you forgotten your brother? The way he died? Besides, look around, Meera, you are probably the last surviving unmarried girl here... it is also a question of our reputation. And haven't you ever done something just to keep the people you love happy, huh? Marriage, it's called marriage, dickri...'

I stared at Ma as she scoured my face, searching for answers.

'What's his name?' I asked resignedly at last, a knot lodged at the base of my throat.

The mention of Kartik had numbed me. As it had Bapuji who hung his head low for the rest of the conversation, preferring to concentrate instead on the row of cow-dung cakes plastered on the boundary walls upfront.

'Mohan, his name is Mohan Patel,' Bapuji finally replied, getting up to wash his hands, two dry chapattis lying untouched on his plate, the curry half-eaten.

I didn't cry at my wedding; nor did my parents as we stood huddled around a fragrant fire, minutes before the commencement of the Mangal Pheras, its bluish-green flames jumping to a great height, every time the priest from our village temple poured a dollop of ghee into its centre. Maybe after Kartik, there were no more tears left.

I stood unmoved as my husband-to-be lifted my heavy ghunghat, staring back in silence once our eyes had finally settled on one another.

'Mohan, his name is Mohan Patel,' I recalled the expression in Bapuji's eyes, as my newly wed husband tilted my head sideways to place the mangalsutra around my neck.

Feeling strangely naked all over again... naked in a man's eyes... a man I had never met before – like the stranger from the river.

Five

'Shukha Karela'

Our whole lives are spent negotiating terms with our sex. Just as our womb decides our destiny in a way. The way we choose to live; what is right and wrong; which man touches us; which one defiles us. The tears that never seem to stop flowing. The first night. The first cut. The children we bear. Or cannot. The scowls. The silences. The sentences. The sum of our sex.

It's simple, really. And yet, it takes a lifetime to figure.

Maybe, that's the thing about fate. A woman's fate; my fate, which perhaps began the day I became Mrs Meera Patel – two tiny initials tattooed onto my left arm – my husband's name, as per our family tradition. Minutes later, Mohan was whisked off to a separate room by a boisterous group of cousins and family friends, into a private space clearly demarcated for the 'gents' of the household.

'Meera and Mohan... what a celestial union,' gushed Yashoda Fui, gloating in the newfound pride of having 'fixed' this marriage, constantly showing off the gold chain that Mohan's family had gifted her as a token of their appreciation... a sign, apparently, of their large-heartedness and wealth.

'You have no idea how lucky your daughter has got. Imagine owning a house in Mumbai! Imagine being in the same city as Amitabh Bachchan,' she smirked, pinching my cheeks as I closed my eyes.

The tip of the tattooing needle stung... like my insides. A million thoughts ran through my head as I searched for my husband in the crowd that thronged our home, wanting to hear his voice once, so bad; the reassuring sound of my name on his tongue.

From a distance I sensed someone's stare. I lifted my veil furtively, desperate for human contact. Bansi, Mohan's younger brother stood at a distance watching me. He was much taller than Mohan and fairer too; a thick crop of hair almost camouflaging his eyes. His well-toned arms were placed on his hips. A boyish smile spread across his face.

I looked down, tongue-tied, wondering if Bansi was Kartik's age. My eyes riveted by the sight of his deep-set dimples, which bore an uncanny resemblance to my lost brother's. Even his Adam's apple, which protruded slightly in the middle of his slender neck, reminded me of him... as if he, Kartik, was trying to say something to me. My heart felt suddenly weighed down with a lingering leftover sadness.

'Dickri,' Bapuji touched the top of my head as I stared in silence at my swollen arm, still smarting from the pain of the first few symbols being inscribed by a gypsy woman from a tribe that dwelled on the outskirts of our town. 'There is something we have to talk about...'

I nodded demurely. My neck muscles throbbed with the weight of the heavy gold set that rested on my bosom. It was the only one Bapuji had managed not to sell over the years. Saving it for Kartik's wife, Ma used to tease me, as I would turn red with envy.

I shifted sideways; making space on the jhula that had been temporarily erected in our courtyard, its ornate wooden beams carefully draped with freshly plucked blooms. The air scented – laden with the bitter-sweetness of ceremonial customs that seemed to continue unabated. My stomach churned. I was thirsty.

Some women in ghunghats and rich gharchola saris hummed songs in our native dialect, shaking their heads in time to the lyrics. The compound wall was lined with tiny oil diyas – prepared painstakingly by Ma herself.

'Damadji says there is a problem...' Bapuji whispered, leaning closer, parting my gold jhumkas that nearly touched the nape of my neck. Looking older all of a sudden... the lines around his eyes deep-set. His cheeks somewhat shrunken. The exhaustion of the past month-and-a-half had clearly taken a toll on him.

'More? Is it about more dahej?' I paused, breathless.

Bapuji wrapped his arms around mine protectively. Then staring benignly for a while at my face, he replied, 'Actually it was me... I was the one who told Mohan's mother that Mumbai seems so very far away. What if I never meet my daughter again? I was only making a joke though... but, but decent people that they are, they decided... on, on their own, that you can stay home for a few more weeks... here... in Sinor with us. And, and imagine they are so polite, Damadji even claimed it was due to some renovation work in their own house... just, just to make me feel better, I suppose...'

'Oh,' I looked up, distressed, tears rolling down my eyes, my waist-band piercing my skin. 'Mohan...?' I mused, whispering into the impenetrable darkness. The moon had disappeared completely behind the clouds by then. 'Where is he?' I asked aloud.

The women around me burst out laughing.

'Wait... wait... not so soon, dearest... you have to wait for your patidev... treat it like a tapasya... after all, isn't the fruit of waiting supposed to be sweet? The more you wait for one another the better... sometimes it can take a lifetime... a lifetime of waiting...' the gypsy woman hissed. Her entire torso was tattooed. Names. Numbers. Places. People. Husbands. Harems. Children. Concubines...

I swallowed hard.

❦

It was past midnight that Mohan and I were finally alone. Ma banged the door shut, turning the key from outside. The cacophony of female voices slowly died down. The diyas were now mostly doused. The room was shrouded in semi-darkness. The lone electric lamp flickered weakly because of the voltage fluctuation – common in these parts.

That Mohan wasn't very tall was the first thing I noticed about him, as I stealthily made my way towards a rather high wooden bed covered in rose petals, mostly wilted. He was barefoot, a pair of beige mojris lying on their backs, covered in a trail of scattered dust. He had small feet... at least smaller than Kartik's, I duly noted.

Mohan had removed his turban. He looked intriguingly handsome and austere in the fractured light. A thin moustache outlined his upper lip. He had a cleft in the centre of his chin. He was wheatish complexioned, of average build, constantly settling his hair, which was neatly combed to one side, his kurta clung to his arms... I tried guessing if he was hairy; if his chest would have a mat of hair.

I cleared my throat a couple of times, hoping to perhaps catch his attention... my ghunghat shifting out of place just then. The sides of my face were damp with sweat.

I stopped in my tracks to observe his next move as Mohan stared down at his lap, and smoothed the creases on his off-white silk kurta. I stood with my ankles crossed, the pain of the inscription a persistent ache, like the drone of the crickets outside. It was eerily ominous. I found myself drawn to the way Mohan's hands and mouth moved at almost the same time, drawing me into a secret place. But his pajama front was guarded zealously by a thick jasmine garland. Some of the petals had collected near his feet.

'Umm... should I heat a glass of milk for you?' I spoke up after a great deal of consternation, studying him constantly from the corner of my eyes; the veil that covered most of my face bothering the edges of my mouth.

Mohan pretended he hadn't heard.

Wordlessly, I moved back a couple of inches, my bridal lehenga clinging to my inner thighs, making it difficult to manoeuvre any faster.

'Bapuji... my, my father... said you wished that I stay back here...' I tried forcing conversation again, biting my lips in quiet desperation.

Mohan looked up this time, distractedly scratching his right knee.

I held out the glass at once. Unsure what to do next. For a while no one spoke. Then Mohan unfolded his legs, before spreading out on his side of the bed, placing the pillow horizontally under his arm.

'Should I press your legs for a while...?' I questioned, anxious about making any further advances.

Mohan pushed a pillow under his head impatiently, without looking at me. 'Just put the glass by the bedside table, and, and turn off that lamp... it's beginning to hurt my eyes,' he answered pithily, wiping his moustache.

Mohan had a slightly nasal voice. It made me curious, though I lowered my eyes instantly, sucking in my stomach, careful not to breathe too loudly even.

'It's always better when it's darker,' Mohan added curtly after a while, staring me in the eyes for the first time, fanning his face furiously... his eyebrows creased.

He was right.

He fell asleep in a few seconds. Snoring lightly.

Slowly, I turned on my side.

The milk stood untouched.

❦

Every woman lies in her marriage. Sometimes lies are like children... you need them to sustain a marriage, or just to survive... a bad day, a bad week, a bad year – sometimes more. It is difficult to tell after a while or analyze why they came about... what they had finally cost or what had brought them on in the first place. An ugly spat in the midst of an overcrowded marketplace, a stranger's dark eyes that never left you, even while you undressed, facing the mirror alone? Could it be that orgasm you never really had, the one you only read about in imported women's magazines that were confined to the back of your cupboard?

Or was it just that one forgotten *shaadi ka saalgira*, the first, perhaps? The first in a long line of leftovers... things you know you can never quite bring back?

Sometimes, all it takes is a lie to hold a man and woman together.

To make them close the door at night and turn the key, concealing all their secrets.

And so I lied.

'Did Damadji mention when he's coming back to fetch you? It's almost been a month since your wedding...' Yashoda Fui pryed, making no attempt to conceal her curiosity.

I covered my eyes. The afternoon sun felt unusually harsh all of a sudden as it slipped between my fingers. I parted them, and studied the elaborate henna patterns on my palm that had almost faded by now.

'I can go to him whenever I wish to, after all Mohan is my husband,' I said, rising up from the bed with an angry start.

It was the same bed on which Mohan and I had slept after our nuptials... for the seven days he had deigned to stay back in Sinor. Not touching each other once. Seldom conversing, even. We were surrounded by family on most occasions – Bansi especially – who always hovered around me, making silly jokes, trying to get me to lighten up; following me around even in the kitchen, squatting beside Ma, as she blew into the earthen chulha that we used to make phulkas. He teased me by drawing flattering comparisons between me and the reigning film heroines of the day, before going on to describe them in great detail... as if he knew all the leading-ladies of Mumbai!

It angered Mohan, I think. He never participated in the banter. Even asking Bansi to leave our room on one occasion, when he discovered us alone – Bansi's fingers running along my left arm, tracing the tattoo. Calling me 'dickri,' like Ma. His eager eyes alight.

But all that was a month ago, and there had been no correspondence since.

'My, my... that's some confidence, Meera... looks like you have trapped your man on the very first night itself,' Fui cackled, breaking my reverie, baring her tobacco-stained molars.

'So how was it, the first time, huh? The Patels are desperate for an heir... that's how I convinced your mother-in-law to give her older son's hand in marriage to a woman more than half his age... that too someone from a small town... you better prove me right, ' she resumed probing in her usual sing-song way, tugging at my plait, as if to prove a point.

I pushed her hands back this time, slowly walking on to the entrance.

Her voice followed me. 'You know your friend, Binal? I hear she's with child. My Badi Bahu's younger brother wrote from Jamnagar saying her in-laws are supposedly over the moon... gave her a diamond ring it seems... no mean feat considering how tight-fisted that family has always been,' she smirked.

I was almost at the door by then. 'Didn't you always say your Badi Bahu is a snake? Or something?' I snapped, not looking back once.

'What!' Yashoda Fui shrieked, horrified at my cheek.

I shrugged my shoulders.

❦

Binal had not attended my wedding.

'If your husband says yes to the milk immediately and laps it all up, it's a sureshot way of knowing that he will always be your love slave. Even in bed,' Binal had remarked, looking serious, as she sucked on a chuski. 'Let's go get one more of these, mmm,' she had moaned a few seconds later, stretching herself out on the bed in my room, one of her breasts nearly popping out of her blouse.

'Gosh you've really grown!' I had exclaimed, pointing towards Binal's crumpled, silk choli, my fingers accidentally brushing her nipple.

'Well, Purushottam can't have enough of these you know, he's like a newborn, really,' she smacked her lips salaciously.

'Didn't his own mother feed him enough?' I had tittered wrapping my arms around Binal, brushing off a strand of hair from her right eye. Before falling silent.

'Okay... now you are thinking what if even your to-be var raja wants to feed off your breasts? That's what's playing on your mind, right? Go on Meera, we can talk about anything,' Binal had restarted the conversation, licking the chuski juice from her fingers.

'I'm never getting married,' I had interrupted carelessly. 'Tell me about Jamnagar... your life there; what do you do all day? There must lots to keep you occupied...' I questioned instead.

Binal had sat up by then. 'If he doesn't drink the milk from your hands, when you walk in, just, just wait till he notices you. It can take very long, Meera... the soles of your feet may tire; your shoulders throb with the weight of your veil. But, don't sit until you're asked to, okay? Eventually, your husband... he will look up... in the end,' she had sighed wistfully, her voice sounding suddenly older.

'Like you'd know any of that,' I had said sarcastically, pinching Binal's arms, quickly adding, 'Purushottam, I remember you writing to me, the month after you had landed in Jamnagar had ripped off your choli, sucking desperately on these, the minute you both were alone. His, his... you know what... you had even compared it to a brinjal, saying how it was, "purple, plump... pleasure oozing out of every pore!" ... you dirty big city girl!'

'And, you believed every single word?' Binal quizzed wryly, settling her expensive ghagra.

'Naturally... I'd been waiting expectantly for days. As if you didn't know that?' I paused, pushing up Binal's chin.

'Meera, promise me,' she had whispered going serious all of a sudden, her breath caressing the corners of my lips, 'you won't tell anyone...'

'Tell them what?' I had pulled her into my arms roughly.

'There is someone else,' she spoke into my right ear, her tongue grazing my earlobe.

'What? Who someone else?'

Binal buried her head into mine, her breasts taut, as I slowly ran my hands over her back, trying to fight her fullness.

'Purushottam, he's a very good man... but, the thing is... he's... I mean, I...' she faltered.

For some reason I kissed Binal's left cheek just then.

'It's just that his organ is minuscule, Meera... smaller than a little boy's. In fact when Purushottam enters me, I feel nothing, you know... I, I was too embarrassed to write all of this to you earlier. I, I just didn't know how to say it,' her lips trembled, as she reached out for my arms again.

We sat in complete silence, the chatter of crickets the only sound, until I burst out laughing.

'What's so funny, huh?' Binal seemed angry.

'I'm... I'm sorry... but I couldn't stop imagining the brinjal you had described in so much detail...' I somehow managed to confess.

Binal still looked confused. 'What else could I have said, Meera? How else could I...' she paused pensively, her kohl bleeding.

I laughed aloud again, saying, 'Anything... you could have just said it was a karela or something...'

Binal had closed her eyes by then. Her arms still wrapped lightly around my neck. Our navels pressed into another. 'Shukha karela,' she had whispered sadly, sounding strangely distant.

Six

Jai Sri Krishna

Ma and Bapuji insisted I dressed as a new bride even though I was still with them in Sinor six months later. Muttering disapprovingly the minute they saw me prepare to leave the premises without a ghunghat. Always reminding me about how they wanted my arms to be weighed down with colourful glass bangles, my ornate jhumkas in place, my hair pulled back in a tight plait, the parting in my hair streaked a sharp red. Stressing on the word, 'suhagan' perennially.

'What if Damadji happened to walk in? Or, or say someone from their side... there are always common relatives. What will they say? You are now a married woman, dickri, not some footloose young thing... marriage changes everything. Learn to stay home... to act your age,' Ma scowled, as I slipped on my anklets.

I had just turned nineteen.

I took a deep breath, running my fingers over my mangalsutra, pausing for a few seconds at the entrance to my cleavage. My heart racing to a halt, like the afternoon Mohan had left Sinor. Our eyes. Mine. Lowering as soon as he bent down to touch my parents' feet... vaguely distant. Or maybe it was all in my mind, I told myself later that night. We were still strangers in every way. Confined to age-old customs and the suffocation induced by small talk. Inhabiting different sides of the same bed. Our lives entwined... and yet completely segregated.

My dearest Binal,

How's the little one? I'm sure he's kicking hard by now? I heard the good news. Being horribly cross with you for the whole of last month for not telling me so yourself. Is that why you even skipped my wedding?

Anyway, am sure you've come up with a name for the baby by now. Something tells me you're going to give birth to a boy...

Or were you also angry that I didn't inform you when my marriage was fixed? Actually speaking there was really nothing to write. Everything happening so very fast. As if it was all fate to begin with. Mohan... Mumbai... me.

Of course I'm not there yet. The last nine months feel so strange... so empty in a way... at least at first. You know like there's so much you want to know about your husband... the things he likes. Or not. The city he lives in... the one he always dreams of. Bapuji insists though that it's only a matter of time before Mohan and I will be united... perhaps it's for the best I tell myself.

I make it a point to write to Mohan too... almost every second day. He keeps very busy. Do you ever think big cities swallow our lives in some way? Mohan is also fighting hard to resurrect their family business. His paternal uncle is a very vile person I am told, having cheated his own younger brother, Mohan's father, of a lot of money. My poor father-in-law expired, a couple of years ago.

I so wish I could just drag you to the bed this very minute... our secret hide-out... and pour my heart out to you about my first night... everything after as well... each intimate detail that I'm dying to share with someone. Anyone...

Gosh, why are you so far away? Why is everyone so far away?

Do write back soonest.

Yours,

M.

P.S. Oh, and I am yet to have a taste of my 'brinjal.' You were dying to ask me that, right? You dirty big city girl...'

I lay in bed reading my last letter to Binal for the longest time, my eyes moistening. My mind crowded with a million niggling questions. Had she already delivered? Was it a boy? Was Binal adjusted now? With Puroshottam? The way she knew she could never be?

Jai Sri Krishna,

There has been some more delay in the house repair. My uncle seems to be continually poisoning our loyal customers,' spreading false rumours about the quality of our merchandise. Competition is fierce these days. Mumbai people always want better... it's really tough to survive.

This month again there was hardly enough to fix the roof that has been leaking continuously since the last monsoons. Before our wedding.

Ba is away on a trip with some of her Guru behens; I had to take a loan to send her off, thankfully managing the amount on time. Talks are on about my younger brother Bansi getting engaged soon. Hopefully, the house should also be complete by then. The walls will need some repair too, a fresh coat of paint perhaps...

It's past nine. I've just completed my dinner. The chappatis were slightly burnt tonight, so I made do with just the eggplant subzi... that also had less salt.

Bansi chose to go to the pilgrimage with Ba this year, saying he hates sitting at the shop all day. It angers me, the way Bansi always manages to get away. But then Ba insisted she needed him to travel back with her, claiming the break would also do him good, especially before he settles down himself. Always taking his side, since we were boys.

Anyway now that Bansi is gone at least I have the house all to myself.

I will return to reading the papers. Convey my pranam to your parents.

Mohan.

My heart sank as I neatly folded the letter. Most of the words had blurred from being read and re-read. Constantly. The letter had arrived the afternoon of Kartik's death anniversary, about a fortnight ago. Bapuji had ripped it open earlier, his face a dead giveaway about the contents. I had stood watching him whisper to Ma, from a safe distance, adjusting my ghunghat over my head. Instantly.

There was a storm brewing.

I closed my eyes, storing the letter within my bosom, turning over listlessly to stretch out on my stomach, craving Mohan physically for the first time in the last eleven months almost that we had spent away from each other. I stared out at the trees outside my window, the curtains billowing in the balmy midnight breeze. The barren branches bent together like the women in our town, huddling together to gossip, as they had the first time I had made a public appearance, sans Mohan, exactly a month after our nuptials. I was being paraded at a ceremonial puja that was supposed to have been attended by the groom and his extended family, before everyone proceeded for an elaborate feast cooked by the new bride; partaken on brand new silver thalis.

It wasn't the first time I had walked into a room full of strangers. And yet I could still recall that afternoon, feeling just the way I did now. Suddenly unsure about everything – despite Yashoda Fui filling me with tall tales of how the Patels were one of the richest business families, supposedly having struck gold after migrating to Mumbai... building up a veritable empire from nothing.

As I lay on my bed that night, I looked down at my feet; slowly parting my toes as one of the slim silver toe-rings slipped off... trying desperately to imagine what Mohan might be doing right at this very moment. Wondering if, like me, he too felt trapped. *Voiceless.* Reaching over to my bedside table I picked up Kartik's photograph and pressed it to my lips as my thoughts veered back to him.

'Isn't he the most handsome man... you think he can speak Gujarati also?' I had whispered, staring open-mouthed at a poster of Amitabh Bachchan through a cramped train window, as we passed by a neighbouring station at dawn.

'*Silly Meeru... stop fantasizing about Amitabh, as if you can ever touch him... back,*' I heard his laughter pierce the dark.

We were on our way back from a cousin's wedding. Our first overnight outing, sleeping next to each other on the top bunk. Kartik bursting into spurts of laughter, seeing me stretch out my arms, desperate to touch him, somehow... smacking my lips, imagining just how it would feel to be held in his long brawny arms. Bachchan wore a khaki police uniform, his trademark intense expression intact, his brows creased.

'*You will never get him... at least not in the way you want Meeru, not, not ever...*' Kartik had declared dismissively, as the station slipped away.

❧

Was Mohan as unattainable as Amitabh Bachchan, I couldn't help but wonder, as I imagined my husband lying alone on a large, four-poster bed, a newspaper clasped tightly within his palms, his chest bare, his face strangely handsome, his eyelashes thick, the cleft on his chin a perfect circle.

I could have dreamed of this image all night, because then he grabs my waist all of a sudden, sensing my presence, before planting my mouth over his hardness, dropping his ankle-length pajamas onto the mosaic floor...

For a while I remain like that, inert, passively letting Mohan unbraid my hair, my tresses covering him waist downwards, forging a surreal darkness that makes it easier to surrender my initial coyness... sucking on the head of his swollenness... Mohan surveys me from the corner of his eyes constantly, thrusting his hips back and forth in languid slow motion, his hands gripping my shoulders as my choli glides off my shoulders. His mouth parting the second I cup his buttocks, slipping my index finger inside, our moans multiplying.

I gulp him down greedily, my tongue on fire, licking the underside of his member each time he eases back. Our bodies melting and merging, before Mohan drags me onto his lap, parting my thighs, forcing me to arch my back, his balls slapping at the entrance of my wetness, his nails digging into me insistently.

It was hard to keep my eyes open after a point.

Mohan perspires profusely, the area behind his ears as hot as his afterbreath. Like a woman possessed, I push my left breast inside his mouth, convulsing when his teeth nibble my areola, biting insistently.

With every pore in my body, I want Mohan... more than once, in more ways than one, stroking his balls desperately, my legs parting in anticipation. Something he instinctively senses, thrusting his full grown shaft into my moistness, slamming faster, all the while calling my name, as if it is a divine chant.

The bed is creaking ominously, the sheets a warm wet patch of juices. Outside, the wind howls. Perhaps it is still July – the month of the floods in Mumbai.

Like the rains coming down furiously, tiny droplets of moisture trickle down the corridor between my uncovered breasts, as Mohan suckles on them, insatiable as a child. His eyes illumined every now and then, by a sharp sliver of silver lightning.

'I'm close...' I whisper as Mohan pulls me down by my tresses, tilting me backwards, jerking in and out with an almost super-human like strength.

I swivel my hips. First clockwise... and then the reverse... launching myself expertly over his over-ripened organ, feeling him stiffen whenever he eases out of me. Finally lifting me upwards – our movements frantic, fearless and feisty.

What if time was running out? I asked myself, allowing Mohan the rites of passage he has been seeking all along, as he bounces back and forth... faster... and faster... clutching the sides of my buttocks, his heels digging into their centre.

'You are mine!' I choke, picking up speed, having waited so long for this one night. My insides turn molten. 'Mohan, stay... please...' I think I scream hoarsely.

Slowly repeating his name. This time in a quieter voice... many times in the darkness... parting my lips...

My ghagra lay wilted beside me. A gust of salty wind shattering the slow heat, extinguished the lone oil diya that had burnt until now in a faraway corner, casting a faint light on a picture of Mohan and me, our faces frozen by the flashbulbs, minutes before the *mangal pheras* had commenced.

In their moist shadows, I sensed Mohan's face once again, as unmoved as it had been when our glances first intersected.

I clamped down my thighs over my right hand. Inhaling a delicious soreness that spread all over my fingers.

A strange peace...

Somewhere on the cusp between dreams and desires.

Seven

After Dark

At the beginning of next summer, another letter arrived. Neatly enclosed in a flat, brown envelope.

> 'Jai Sri Krishna,
> *Bansi is getting married at the end of next month. Everything is arranged. The girl is a graduate in Mathematics. I shall come to pick you up myself, before their wedding, on the first Saturday of next month. Our train to Ahmedabad leaves early the very next morning. Bansi's in-laws also belong to the same native place. I have decided to spend the night at your parents'. Please do inform them and give them my pranam.*
> *Mohan.*
>
> *P.S. Do not carry your elaborate ghagras; as it is, I will have a lot of luggage, mainly items for Bansi's bride. Besides, in Mumbai you're likely to find them most inconvenient to move around in and also do the housework. Ba has agreed to let you wear saris at home; it's very muggy here.*

I bit the corner of Mohan's letter, lying stretched out on my bed, the setting sun filtering down my insides. Something told me I should have been over the moon at the prospect of seeing my husband, except I wasn't. Too many nagging thoughts troubled me.

Did my husband never miss me? Was he happier staying alone, leading the life of a bachelor in many ways? Didn't he ever want to know what the colour of the sky was, right now, for instance... dusk descending, seeing it through my eyes, only? A familiar ache arose, piercing the surrounding stillness, as I craved to confide in Kartik, like old times, my head placed on his chest, his fingers slowly parting my hair, our toes touching occasionally. Telling him about how jealous I felt at the news of Bansi's impending marriage. When I should have been happy... for all of them. Or just how I secretly wished Bansi had been the man I was betrothed to. The way he always watched me. The way I wanted someone to... ever since...

I couldn't sleep much that night. Thinking about Mohan's letter again and again, especially the last paragraph, listlessly pushing my ghagra above my knees, shuddering at the familiar sensation.

What if Mohan also touched himself in the darkness? I finally said it out loud, placing my hands over my breasts.

What if he was just like me? I repeated in the half-light, a tear blurring the corner of my eye, as the rest of my fears tumbled out one by one... like a pile of old letters stacked at the back of an antique cupboard.

What if it was enough?

❦

Mohan's train arrived on time. He sported a stubble; his cleft barely visible. Walking in behind Bapuji, who struggled with his unwieldy suitcase. We ate in silence after he had bathed.

Mohan was running a slight temperature. He slept like a child, crouched in the foetal position; his knees folded under him, his head inches below my mouth. I ran my fingers gently through his hair, afraid to wake him. It was just after sunrise. I almost felt like it was the first time Mohan had been this close...

It had been over a year since I had slept next to him.

Every now and then I'd check his fever, placing my hand lightly over his forehead, watching him stir, saliva collecting near the corners of his mouth. Hoping somewhere he would grab my hand, take notice... acknowledge my presence.

Mohan had a habit of murmuring in his sleep, something I had noticed on our *suhaag raat* even. He did it now as I lightly placed my ear just below his chest, desperate not to miss out on a single whisper, treating even his sighs like missing clues in a complicated jigsaw puzzle.

Gazing in silence as he slowly parted his lips, not knowing when I drifted off to sleep myself, perhaps imagining being held in Mohan's arms, my own glued to my side, like a wispy cloud floating in a dark midnight sky.

All of a sudden, Mohan swivelled sideways; his wrists accidentally brushing my back, bringing me instantly awake. I had forgotten to change out of my new patola silk; sweat trickling down my stomach, the heavy pleats rustling loudly as I cautiously extricated my ankles, raising my hips first.

Soon Ma would be awake.

'Did you sleep at all?' Mohan asked, clearing his throat, suppressing a yawn, his eyes bleary.

I turned to face him, my voice caught in a trap. We tried falling back to sleep again.

Mohan sat up after a few minutes, glancing in my direction as I lay on my back, my arms thrown over my face, trying to keep out the faint morning light. From the gaps between my fingers, I stared at the bristles on his moustache.

'I'd better go bathe, what time is it?' he muttered awkwardly, fiddling with his kurta buttons, his voice husky as his eyes travelled down the length of my bosom.

A slight breeze billowed. The sheet shifting out of place...

'You can rest if you want to, I was getting up, the water needs to be heated for your bath,' I softly interrupted, my pallu falling over to reveal my cleavage.

Mohan seemed unfazed.

'Would you like some tea?' I added, propping myself up on my elbow.

'No, I don't like tea very much, gives me bad acidity,' he cut me short.

'Oh, I'm sorry, so what would you prefer in the mornings from now? Shall I heat some milk with kesar?' I volunteered eagerly, rearranging the folds near my navel, uncomfortable in the heavy fabric.

'Warm water, with a dash of honey and a thin slice of lime... it's a habit I formed in Mumbai... it helps fight flab as well,' Mohan answered deliberately, eyeing me.

'Do you... do you think I am fat? Is that what you are trying to imply?' I finally blurted, mustering a bit of bravado.

Mohan's eyes were clamped tightly shut. From the look of it, he seemed to be mouthing a prayer or maybe he just hadn't heard. So, I cleared my throat. He didn't respond.

'Fine then, I'll arrange for your hot water,' I spoke quickly.

I was almost out of the door, when Mohan called out. 'Meera, listen, wait,' he said from the edge of the bed.

I turned, taking longer than usual.

'Umm... the thing is...' Mohan fumbled for the right words as I walked back, tying my hair into a loose bun, some stray strands lingering near the nape of my neck.

I wasn't wearing a brassiere.

For a while, we stood facing one other wordlessly. With my left hand, I tried securing the sari pleats inside my waist, suddenly having grown conscious of my own contours, particularly since Mohan's earlier comment.

Before I could finish, my pallu had descended to the ground. Without saying anything, Mohan lifted it up, his fingers roughly brushing my belly button, pressing down lightly.

I sucked in my stomach at once, before gently slipping my palm inside his, forging a tight fist, as our eyes eventually settled on each other, in our first private dialogue... ever.

Mohan undid my sari clumsily, balancing himself on the corner of the mattress, smoothing his hands down my hips before lifting up my petticoat, using his right hand. Planting wet kisses all the way down as he dragged it to my knees... his saliva moistening the coarse line of my pubic hair.

I nearly came undone as Mohan slid three and then four fingers in, pressing me into himself, removing my panty next, his right thumb rotating in furious circles at the entrance to my sex.

'Did... did you miss me... like this... in Mumbai?' I tried giving words to everything I felt.

Mohan didn't answer.

From the corner of my eyes, I finally caught a glimpse of his manhood.

Why wasn't he hard yet? Thoughts formed and drowned.

'Open, open this nara, it seems to be stuck,' I moaned after a few seconds, fumbling with his pajama strings, still standing, stroking his shaft feverishly from the outside.

Mohan did as he was told, his organ falling into my hands, its head pulsating, a thick tuft of hair at its base, moistened in places. I pushed the foreskin back, hoping to get a firm grip; anxious it would slip out of my palm any minute.

Mohan tore at my blouse, his eyes narrowed, his nails sharp... his fingers slithering in and out of my sex... making a hissing noise.

'Turn over,' he ordered in a stony voice all of a sudden, jumping off the bed, his jaw set.

Before I could respond or make sense of what was to follow, Mohan promptly turned me over, using the force of his arms, his knees planted at the back of mine, as I crouched uneasily, my head lolling over one side of the bed.

As I writhed under the weight of his limbs, he positioned himself over my buttocks, rubbing his member over and over. Emitting small shrieks.

I winced. Had it diminished further?

But, but hadn't we only just started? I questioned myself, before Mohan pushed me forward forcefully, my hands groping the crumpled sheet corners, as he hoisted himself into me from the rear, thrusting in and out fastidiously.

I bit my lips, a line of warm tears rolling down both my cheeks.

'Shall we umm... try something else?' I was about to say, when Mohan tightened his grip on my plait, swinging back with greater vigour, perhaps hoping to lodge his entire length in me this time.

'Damn it Meera, you're so tight,' he'd mutter every now and then, dragging me up with him when I lost my balance.

'This hurts, I can't, I just can't go on, maybe... please we should,' I tried making sense of the whole experience, my shoulders stooped with exhaustion. And the weight of my expectations...

Mohan's organ was completely wilted by then.

'What did you say?' I heard him snarl, as I tried visualizing Binal's face at that moment – the sadness in her eyes the time she had dissected Purushottam's first sexual performance, the resultant disappointment – and the way I had secretly pitied her fate.

'I want to feel your juices on me, now...' Mohan dictated, kicking me hard, dispelling the rest of my thoughts, having managed to regain his ripeness somewhat.

I choked, his pelvic thrusts intensifying in tandem with his left thumb now rotating up and down my asshole, stretching my skin.

'Just do as I say okay, I'm close,' he grunted authoritatively, as I tried glancing back. Once.

Mohan's face was contorted. His hands massaged his shaft frantically, as he pushed it back and forth over my lower back... his breathing roguish.

It was then that I think I gave up the fight, bending on all fours like an animal, with whatever little strength I had left, Mohan gripping my breasts, wrapping his legs around mine, climbing over my back... squatting over my hips.

'Want more, huh?' he spoke like a man possessed.

I closed my eyes. Wanting nothing, frankly, except to shut out the real world. This experience. Us.

❦

Mohan's ancestral home in Ahmedabad had been sold before the family had relocated to Mumbai. For Bansi's wedding, we had rented a sprawling hall with tinted windows and large pedestal fans. Vrinda, his to-be-wife, hailed from a rich family of cloth traders. She was the only child. A match made in heaven, as Ba, my mother-in-law pompously declared the minute we met in person. Bansi looked away. Our eyes lingering on each other only for a few seconds, as I turned around to inspect Vrinda's photograph.

It had been shot in all probability in a rented studio, under harsh lighting. She had an unusually wide forehead with eyes that squinted strangely and thick lips... a limp curl was stuck down on the left side of her face. She was quite plump, her paunch visible under an ill-fitted silk choli that made her breasts look lumpy and shapeless. A beauty spot just over her mouth was her only saving grace.

'Isn't she a beauty... from such a big family... so rich...' Ba rattled on.

I searched the shadows. Not saying anything.

There was something about Vrinda that I did not trust.

❦

For the main marriage function I was made to don a flaming orange gharchola sari, gifted by Ba. It should have been a part of my wedding trousseau, a part of the dowry my father paid for, she told me sarcastically several times, harping on the expensive fabric and how progressive she was – allowing the eldest bahu in the family to give up the traditional lehenga, and paying for it besides!

'Remember to always keep your navel covered, though. Sometimes a sari can be the beginning of sin,' she warned, watching me as I wore my blouse, fumbling with the hooks.

I tried to smile, suddenly missing the simple cotton ghagra cholis Ma stitched for me with her own hands, her eyesight weakened by years of sewing mirrors and embroidered borders on to my lehengas. I decided to keep my arms unadorned and barren – without bangles.

'Has someone *died*? Is this any way a new bride should dress? What will our relatives say after seeing you, huh? And, could you at least try looking happier, Badi Bahu, it's not as if your husband is torturing you in bed or something... just look at your face, not even a hint of sindoor,' she taunted as I made my way out of the kitchen, my head demurely lowered, a heavy steel tray clasped in my hands, afraid that I might drop the silver glasses filled to the brim with sugary sweet sherbet.

I didn't see much of Mohan in those days. 'There's always so much work during a wedding... you fix one thing, and just when you think you've got it right, it breaks down again...' I heard him complain to Bansi one afternoon, while hoisting a string of fairy lights at the entrance, perched uncomfortably on a crooked stool.

There was always someone hovering around us, keeping us at arm's length, stifling out conversation – or so I convinced myself, as we continued to exist like strangers, moving out of each other's way whenever our paths intersected.

'Badi Bahu, are you dead? Who's going to fry all this? How can you leave the kitchen unmanned? Hasn't your mother taught you even this?' a shrill voice rang out from afar.

I glanced backwards, hoping to catch a glimpse of Mohan once more; his large eyes flickering as bright as a little boy's as he instructed someone to switch on the lights.

'Don't they look grand, Bansi?' Mohan proclaimed proudly.

'But... but it's not even dark yet, Bhaiyya,' I heard Bansi respond.

'That's the fun of these lights, Chhote... they are like my lover. They do as I say. Always obeying my orders, even appearing to glow in broad daylight... maybe I should have married them instead,' Mohan laughed lewdly.

Tiny jasmine buds crafted in pink glass... I gazed in their direction for a while.

'You tell the truth, Bhabhi. Can you actually see them shine? Tell Bhaiyya also because he always thinks he's right...' Bansi made a face, pointing in my direction as I pulled my ghunghat lower, feeling a hot flush surge through my insides.

'Say something. You're not dumb, are you?' I heard the words and sensed Mohan's impatient stare.

He faced me directly, his eyes scouring my face.

'Hmm,' I bit my lower lip as I turned around slowly to look at them. 'I just wish someone had saved their luminescence for the night. What if their power gradually diminishes by the time it actually gets dark? The way lovers sometimes have a change of heart... their moods fluctuating... giving away their souls to someone else...'

Eight

Antaryami

I didn't go to Mumbai even *after* Bansi's wedding. Vrinda did.

Instead, I accompanied Ba as we set off on a gruelling pilgrimage on foot, travelling for more than a month, for a proposed darshan with their family Guruji, in his sea-facing ashram, somewhere on the west coast of Gujarat. Supposedly, there were some complications in my natal chart; sins carried forward from my previous birth that I urgently needed to purge, undergoing an austere praschyatam – a rigorous cleansing ritual in this janam before it was too late – Ba went on and on, repeating the words like a mantra almost, routinely rehearsed.

But I wasn't interested. 'What's Mumbai like this time of the year?' I questioned Mohan, rubbing his left arm gently, as he packed his belongings.

'You're not going there yet, no?' he cut me short; giving a dry laugh, picking up his neatly ironed trousers.

'I know... I know it's just you going to Mumbai from Ahmedabad. And I've heard so much about the place already in this past year. In fact even Vrinda was talking about it last night while we ate dinner. She's been there before, she claims, as a child, even having visited an actual cinema hall to watch a Bachchan picture.' I slumped down on the bed.

Mohan seemed distracted as he struggled to close the suitcase lid. 'Lend me a hand...' he matter-of-factly ordered.

'Will you write to me? More often?' I probed, staring back into his eyes, our fingers touching.

'You won't have a fixed postal address where you're going,' Mohan muttered absent-mindedly, moving away from me.

'Oh yes, silly of me to forget,' I replied, adding softly: 'I will pray that we have a son soon. I'm observing a fast too, every Tuesday as you know. Ba insists it's good for us. I hope to give you the news by the time I arrive in Mumbai... soon.'

A tear rolled out of my eye.

'Take care of her, understand? I hope you've made a proper note of the timings of Ba's medicines...' Mohan retorted, pushing up my chin.

'You look after yourself too. I've asked Vrinda to take special care of your diet and to ensure that every morning you are served hot water with a slice of lime and one tablespoon of honey, just the way you like it... and... and that your night chapattis are the way you like them... soft, not scalded,' I raced to finish, clasping Mohan's waist, my lips parting in eager anticipation.

Without saying a word, he cursorily touched his left hand to my face, his fingers briefly brushing my lips. By the time I looked up, Mohan was gone.

I did nothing for a while, except lie back on the bed, inhaling Mohan's scent, burying my face into the crumpled bedclothes, feeling strangely soothed by the familiar scent of my husband.

It was the kind of intimacy no one had really told me of in the past – not even Binal or Ma or any other family members for that matter – despite having taken turns advising me on the nuptial chores of a newlywed, meticulously outlining the dos and don'ts, before our *suhaag raat*. They always emphasized on words like obedience and duty and loyalty, instead of the other way around. Preparing a girl for marriage; but telling her nothing about love. Making too much of a woman's strength; too little of her weaknesses.

Amarkant Maharaj wasn't as old as I'd expected, not having seen his photograph in the past, relying only on Ba's exaggerated versions each time I had tried etching a mental portrait of the man, when we'd halt for the night in a modest dharmshala or at a cheap motel – arriving exhausted – blisters burning our soles, our lips chapped by the lack of moisture in the air, our backs aching from the exertion of the walk as we abandoned one town after the other.

'Was Guru Amarkant ever married?' I questioned Ba once. We had just finished offering prayers at a local temple atop a steep hillock, saffron flags billowing in the August air.

'Guruji doesn't really like talking about his life before he retreated to the Himalayas, from where he's known to have descended after seven long years. All they say is his matted hair was so long it brushed the ground... and his face looked like he had stared death in the eye and returned triumphant. He's no ordinary mortal, Badi Bahu, he can read your mind... even when you say nothing at all,' she chewed on her paan thoughtfully, dark juices staining the corners of her mouth.

'*Antaryami*...' I whispered unbelievingly, lying awake on the thin mattress, my hands groping my breasts. Could Guruji see me like this, I wondered. Listlessly undoing the first two hooks of my blouse, pleasuring myself to feel a sense of inner calm I so desperately needed?

Lying on the mattress beside me, Ba snored heavily.

'*Antaryami*,' I moaned, the word feeling as intimate as the special spot underneath my navel, flaming to my own touch. I shuddered as the coarse cotton sheet slid off my body, as I pulled up my knees. Securing the sheet over me I worked silently, careful not to wake Ba at any cost... desperate to dream of Mohan, his face, the shape of his hands. Closing my eyes I imagined him making feverish love to me, grunting with pleasure as he thrust in and out... his hardness... his heat... all over again... Slowly, I raised my hips and inserted two fingers in from behind, squirming as I massaged harder on my sex, writhing back and forth, rubbing myself desperately, craving a familiar convulsion, that slow release, that sudden death. My mind glazed as I flicked faster and faster with my right thumb, my breasts heaving, my lips parting each time I eased off. Before drawing out my hand... just seconds after the shivering had stopped, the heat still burning in my privates... I quickly adjusted my petticoat, before opening my eyes to stare at my fingers.

They were soaked in blood. My period was proof that I was still without child. My heart sank at once, the way I had felt when Mohan had released himself all over my stomach. Like a promise after it's been broken.

☙

'This is the *exact* reason I'm taking you to meet Guruji. He'll set everything right, making your insides strong enough to bear my grandson. God knows, we need an heir at the earliest. Had I known you had trouble conceiving, I would have rethought this alliance. Just look at your hips – seems your folks haven't fed you adequately, just not wide enough. Listen, Badi Bahu, having a pretty face isn't enough, you need strong inners. A woman's body must be hardened to take what comes, be it pleasure or pain...' Ba lectured on, sounding bitter as I lathered my hair, squatting in an open bath beside her, my petticoat tied over my breasts. Flies buzzed all around us. Like their incessant drone, her words continued to irritate my ears even as I stood in a dimly lit corner, waiting for Amarkant Maharaj to arrive from his evening satsang.

It was a week or so after my menstrual cycle, my body was still ripe... ready for another cycle of consummation.

'Maharaj pranaam, this is my Badi Bahu, whom I had written to you about, Mohan's wife. Bless her, Guruji, purify her womb with your sacred hands so that she can give us a strong, healthy son...' Ba said, rocking her body as she bowed before him.

I kept my eyes firmly fixed on the floor.

'Is she observing the fast I had asked you to make her follow on Tuesdays? And what about the Ashwagandha herb I had instructed you to grind and make her drink in a glass of lukewarm milk, from the second day to the last of her womb breaking?' I heard the man enquire in an imposing baritone. His voice sounded familiar. I could have sworn I had heard the voice before. My lower lip quivered slightly.

Ba nodded fervently, letting go of my arm at once.

'It's all your will, Maharaj. If you so desire, my Badi Bahu will conceive without any complications... who doesn't know of your miraculous powers. Oh Holy One, I beg you to shower her with your kindness,' she went on, lowering her head devotedly.

'What is her name?' Guruji thundered, his wooden sandals scraping the ground.

'Meera... I had her janam kundli sent to you as soon as the alliance was fixed,' Ba reminded him.

For a while no one spoke, then I heard the kutir door creaking to a close. Ba had departed. It was only Guruji and I.

'Look at me, Meera,' he commanded.

The sound of his voice sent a sharp shiver down my spine.

'Step forward and look into my eyes. I'm not going to hurt you, I promise...' I heard the words up-close as a pair of brawny hands tugged at my wrists, pushing my ghunghat off my head.

As if in a hypnotic trance, I looked up at his looming silhouette.

'You have been thinking about me, haven't you?' Guruji scoured my face, stepping forward from the surrounding shadows, a sense of assuredness soaking his last words.

He had a handsome, bearded face. I confronted his intense, dark rimmed eyes, which brimmed over with the turbulence of the river back home.

My throat was completely parched.

'Do you think I will harm such an attractive woman as you?' he continued unperturbed, securing his muscular arms around my shoulders and drawing me to him.

'It's... I mean it's not so simple... you are a holy man... revered by one and all...' I don't know why I suddenly blurted.

Guruji held up my chin, his steel grey eyes penetrating my defences. 'Do you not recognize me, Meera? Why, then, do I feel as if we've already communicated, as if I already know all your secrets?' he spoke in a hushed voice, stroking my forehead tenderly, his eyes on my lips.

I wiped the sides of my face nervously before deliberately disengaging myself and slowly walking towards a pitcher of water perched on top of a high wooden stool. 'I have no secrets, Maharaj. Mohan, my husband... he lives in Mumbai. I, I've never been there, unlike... unlike Vrinda, my sister-in-law... Mohan doesn't like me too much I think...'

Unknown to me, Guruji was right by my side with his elbow nearly touching mine. 'There is something I must tell you, Meera,' he murmured.

I drank the first sip, my eyes still fixated on the intricate patterns inscribed on his forearm. I was mesmerized by Guruji's mouth – the pattern of his lips.

'Meera, you are an extraordinarily beautiful woman, and you will have an extraordinary life,' he said, slowly lifting a strand of hair near my left earlobe. 'But you see, this life can't begin, until you allow it to... Nothing starts in this universe, sans our approval. Except... birth and death...'

'And, and marriage?' I interrupted out of turn again; some of the water dribbling down my throat, journeying down my cleavage.

Guruji wiped the water away, his fingers lingering on my breast. Then he closed his eyes as if he were retreating back into pious prayer and added: 'It depends on what your definition of marriage is. There are many kinds in this world, Meera, just as there exist myriad definitions of happiness. The union of a man and a woman is never really uni-dimensional, especially not when it is a woman with heightened sexual senses like yourself.' I gasped as he continued, 'You have the power to control the thoughts of men... someone with a rare power... an invincibility...'

One of the diyas went out just then.

'Then... then why does it still hurt so much, Maharaj?' I cried hoarsely, dropping my hands to my side, my eyes filling with tears.

Guruji sat me down, explaining in a steady voice: 'Because you are seeking pleasure for yourself... searching for it greedily, since the day you were born, making it the central focus of your whole human existence, when, when it was never meant to be that way. No, Meera, no...'

I felt the heat rise to my head.

'The day you can let go of this body, discard it as an outer skin... as you will someday, as we all have to, you will finally realize how nothing can ever cause you any pain or disappointment, except beyond the immediate present. No man, no marriage, no physical limitation... these are all just a figment of our own minds, Meera... the meaning of maya... all you have to do is lift this wispy, thin veil... and, and...' his voice stalled as he pushed aside my ghunghat and stared intensely into my eyes.

'Then... how is it that I am not pregnant?'

Guruji remained seated. 'Meera, you must not feign ignorance... pretending not to know what is the answer to that question yourself...' he halted abruptly, as I covered my face with both my hands. I felt humiliated. My insides smarted with sheer indignation at his comments, the underlining arrogance... the manner in which he made so little of my life, my husband.

Guruji parted my tresses after a few seconds of silence and lightly stroked my back: 'Maybe you were not ready. The attraction to your spouse was not the primary response your body had... you reacted to Mohan's advances more out of your own isolation... maybe you are lonely in some way, Meera, as we all get at times... craving for human touch... however short-lived... perhaps you are a prisoner of the past... of memories and people who live in your head and your heart...'

I took a deep breath, and pleaded, 'So tell me what I should do? Teach me everything there is to learn.'

Guruji's eyes were closed.

'I will do whatever is asked of me... anything. I, I promised Ba...' I continued impatiently.

'Are you hungry, Meera?' Guruji cut me short, placing my hands inside his.

'And... and what if I said yes?' I replied slowly, feeling my heart skip a beat.

Guruji let out a thunderous laugh. 'Be careful what you wish for, woman. The Gods are known to have a weakness for beautiful girls... and you are no less than an apsara. What if this wish of yours is granted? You may have no way of going back then...' his words fell short as his eyes glowed like a predator's.

'What if I don't want to?' I responded, my back pressed to the cold mud wall by then.

Guruji moved closer to me, his saffron lungi dragging on the ground. He was bare-chested. His dark brown nipples were perfectly rounded. His sculpted chest covered in a dense crop of hair. Outlining my collarbone with his fingertips, he murmured, 'When was your last cycle, Meera?'

My head lolled backward, my senses succumbing easily to the play of his fingers.

'I, I actually just finished,' I licked my lower lip.

'Pull down your sari lower... I want to feel your womb,' he resumed matter-of-factly, lowering his face, his breath temperate, his hand pushing itself down my navel.

My head spun.

'Stay still, Meera... relax... now part your legs,' Guruji continued, fanning his palm out on my sex, undressing the rest of my thoughts.

'How long will this take?' I shivered, as I felt my insides moisten.

Guruji was on his knees now. With his right hand he expertly loosened my petticoat strings. 'As long as you wish for it to go on, Meera... the body has a mind of its own, it must be allowed its own explorations.'

I wondered if he ever shaved as the bristles of his long unruly beard tickled my breasts, as he went on to undo my sari next, pulling it out of the unloosened petticoat... from the sides, his left thumb deftly pressing on my nerve endings, his tongue over my sex sending small currents... slight shocks from which it seemed impossible to recover. The knot forming at the pit of my stomach hardened further. Was this happening for real? I asked myself, as Guruji expertly parted my thighs and began licking me slowly. I looked up, my face flushed, an inadvertent moan escaping my mouth as I took in the sight of the one piece of unstitched cloth strategically revealing Guruji's loins, every time his loincloth shifted out of place. The gigantic Rudraksh necklace dangling from his long neck, crushed into my bosom.

'What if this is viewed as a grave sin?' I finally managed to form a full sentence, stiffening slightly as he squeezed my buttocks, kneading them up and down, deftly grabbing my back at the same time, digging deeply into the centre of my spine.

Guruji stood up. He was staggeringly tall.

'Is that what you think?' he paused, looking down at me, the muscles on his chest tautening, stirring a host of decadent desires.

'What will you call this then Guru Amarkant?' I shuddered, tasting his name, the way the words felt on my tongue, as our glances directly connected.

A greasy red tilak blazed at the exact centre of his forehead, slightly smudged on both sides. My shoulders drooped, as he suckled me, as if in response to my question, pressing his front down at the same time, the tip of his thick organ probing my wetness.

The sheer weight of his mouth moved me up a few inches as Guruji's moist lips closed over my left breast, wrenching off my blouse, his tongue tracing tiny semi-circles in the space between my breasts.

'You haven't answered me,' I panted, pushing his mouth away weakly, my nipples reddened by his teeth.

'You really want me to stop?' Guruji uttered hoarsely, throwing my arms over my head. And lowering himself over my sex again, rubbed the swollen tip of his manhood furiously as it protruded into my panty, his flimsy loincloth slipping away... like my thoughts... my fears...

'Yes... I, I mean no...' I whimpered, hoping to curb his right thumb from plunging deeper, peeling away the artificial walls that had separated us until then.

'Meera, the mind will come up with a reason, it always does... in the end,' Guruji pursed his lips persuasively, scratching my stomach with his nails.

It was torture not to cave in. A part of me was desperate to stroke his shaft, to feel him grow, to surrender at long last, melting on his manhood. There was something exquisitely carnal about the risks involved, about exploring all the pent-up pleasures he had ignited.

'Are, are you through with your examination?' I questioned inaudibly, jerking back, just in time to fight my own climax.

'Aah,' Guruji groaned, his left hand slithering out, drenched in my juices.

He then took a deep breath to inhale my bitter sweetness, licking some of it from between his fingers. 'You were so close, Meera,' he muttered, running the same hand over my parted lips. 'Do you know what this nectar feels like on your own tongue? So sweet... so salty...' his words made me jump out of my own skin. The raw scent of my soreness became one with the dense midnight air, like a raging forest fire that scorched everything in its path.

'Touch me now, Meera... you want to do it, I know...' Guruji urged persuasively, nibbling at my earlobes, deciphering my mind at once.

This time I didn't resist.

The room was pitch dark by then. All I could see were the rim of his eyes as Guruji stood motionless facing me; his organ erect.

'I've been waiting for you for so long,' he growled as I massaged his muscular thighs feverishly.

Bringing my face closer, I said, 'I believe you... we've met before, as you mentioned... in the beginning... in another life... somewhere...'

It was I who made the next move. Thrusting Guruji's manhood inside my mouth. The sheer thrill of watching him come undone as I ran my tongue along its girth made me equally ravenous. Watching him beg for more, made me feel no less than a Goddess myself! I licked harder at the tip, swallowing him deeper, till he pervaded my tonsils, pressing furiously underneath as well. The power I seemed to demonstrate over a man thousands worshipped was especially exhilarating.

'Oh Meeraaaaa...' Guruji howled deliriously every time I stopped to take in some air, sounding like a woman in labour, his face twisted. 'Where did you learn to make a man feel like this?' he gritted his teeth, twisting my nipples with his rough hands. The ecstasy of his touch emboldening me as our ankles dug into the cold, uneven ground.

'Antaryami,' I salaciously retorted, balancing myself on my haunches, his hardness positioned between my breasts, his juices staining my lips.

'Antaryami...' Guruji repeated in ecstasy, lunging forward, gyrating his hips, his manhood slapping against my face. I clamped my eyes shut, savouring the aftertaste – the pleasure both perverse and potent. The way I had felt sucking on ripened mangoes, stolen from Manohar Kaka's garden at dusk. After the July rains had come and gone.

❧

Ba and I spent the next month and a half recuperating in Guruji's ashram, which overlooked a tumultuous ocean, its turquoise waters drawing me in, especially after the vivid afternoon sun had set. On most evenings, while Ba rested, I'd make some excuse to just walk alone along its shadowy shores, my feet sinking into the moist sand.

It felt so good to be alone again.

Sometimes, I'd sit for hours, just like that, by myself, staring in silence at the line of boats adrift, their oarsmen sometimes missing, waiting as the stars slowly surfaced.

Amarkant Maharaj had left suddenly on a solitary and silent maun vrat to an undisclosed location, his senior disciples at the math had informed us the morning after I had left his kutir, running down a narrow, cobbled pathway, before the first light of dawn, the dryness in the air stinging my senses.

'We will meet again... remember my words, Meera... let go now... sadness is another form of impermanence... nothing ends...' Guruji had whispered into my ears, standing at the entrance, bare-chested, when I left.

There had been no one around then. It was still dark.

The water tasting ice cold at first, some of it pushing insistently inside my petticoat, like Guruji's hands had once, my hips swaying rhythmically to the symphony of the waves.

'You are an extraordinary woman, Meera,' I thought I heard someone whisper my name as soon as I'd opened my mouth; feeling the rains descend.

The tides were rough. But I wasn't frightened of drowning any longer, flinging my arms wide open to embrace the waters. 'Whenever you are scared... say this to yourself... nothing lasts, be it pleasure or pain. Our body is just a medium, Meera, the marg is something else... mine, yours, ours. Unlike the atma... the soul that is ananta... limitless, never perishing. *Na hanyate hanyamane sarire*... I am not this body, but a spirit soul... it's why we are all equals... each a bird of flight. Fly now Meera... fly away... let go of this empty vessel... this body, this trap, this Maya,' I replayed Guruji's parting words to me, spoken as I was fixing my blouse back on.

'Kartik...?' I murmured out of breath, falling backwards, my feet completely rudderless. As if he were omnipresent. I felt someone run his lips through my darkened tresses.

Nine

Saali Mumbai

Our train to Mumbai was sixteen hours late. There was a Rail Roko agitation up ahead, some of the co-passengers grimly reported. I hadn't slept a wink. Nor had I touched my food.

'At least have the prasad, Badi Bahu, do you know how rare it is to procure this in the first place? Guruji says it will work wonders for your health, and oh, I almost forgot, Maharaj sent word just before we left his ashram that you can now forgo the fast you'd been observing since your marriage. The last Tuesday of Shravan is to be the last day of fasting,' Ba paused, handing me a stainless steel glass, its sides twisted out of shape.

Wordlessly, I drank up the last drop of the murky concoction, careful not to spill any of it on my starched kota sari.

'Remember that Kalsarpadosha dominating your birth chart, casting its evil eye on your unborn foetus? Well, Guruji insists that that too has been successfully arrested, at the end of his Maha Mritunjay Yagna. The might of the holy havan destroying every impure particle... leaving nothing except a trail of smouldering ashes.'

'What is this?' I interrupted listlessly, my throat starting to itch.

'Ashes from the same havan. Guruji had it specially hand-delivered for you, bahu. You must smear a bit on yourself, before taking a bath every morning. It will act as your Suraksha Kawaj,' Ba said.

I weighed the packet lightly in my palms as some of the ashes dropped into my lap.

'Careful now, you must treat this as a new lease of life,' Ba mumbled, before lifting up her blanket and covering herself

I stared ahead. It was pitch dark outside.

❧

Mohan was waiting at the station, Vrinda by his side, their shoulders occasionally touching each other's as they peered into each incoming train. Bansi was missing. It was my first time in Mumbai. It was the first thing I noticed.

Vrinda looked different from when I had last seen her, as she leaned onto Mohan's left arm, whispering into his ear. She wore flat chappals and a maroon silk sari. Looking shorter than before... somewhat paler too.

I tried lip reading what she might be saying, gazing at them both from a distance, missing Bansi's broad welcoming smile acutely as the train entered the station, minutes before it reached a complete halt. Vrinda at once moved away, to stand a few feet in front of Mohan and covered her head demurely.

Mohan had put on weight. He lowered his glance as well, clumsily adjusting his glasses. 'Bansi is at the shop, Ba. He couldn't get away, though he really wanted to be here. If only our uncle wasn't plotting to throw us out of business all the time. He has gone to the extent of telling some of our loyal customers how he will leave no stone unturned, until the Patels are completely destroyed. It didn't seem prudent to leave the shop unmanned... I mean, you just can't trust anyone these days,' Mohan remarked, glancing back every few seconds, as we sat huddled in the rear seat of a suffocatingly small Fiat taxi, half an hour or so later. I was in the middle, carrying a huge striped cloth bag on my lap, the sinful smell of Sukhdi's flitting around us, reminding me of Ma's hands.

'*Kem cho, dickra*? Why are you looking so pulled down?' Ba chided, changing the topic, caressing Mohan's shoulder from the back-seat.

'No way, Ba. Vrinda Ben has been managing the house more than proficiently; in fact I have put on five kilos. She's a fabulous cook too, we are being thoroughly spoilt!' Mohan reported animatedly, his eyes gleaming.

Sitting on my right, Vrinda giggled, biting her lips, blushing. 'Now that Meera Bhabhi is here, you'll not need any more looking after by me. Besides, these days, I'm up to no good honestly, I get tired so much, so easily,' she said, sticking out her tongue, as Mohan's head darted backwards instantly, gazing intently in her direction, bypassing mine.

I cringed, grabbing the bag closer, feeling a sudden stab of competitiveness; Mohan's closeness to Vrinda multiplying the distance between us in some way.

'Ba, actually, the thing is, Bansi wanted to break the news to you... first, I mean he should be the one telling you... but...' he paused, scratching his sideburns. 'I'm certain you would have guessed by now... the thing is... Vrinda Ben is expecting. This is her second month. I have organized a havan at the end of the week for the child's well-being... hope that is fine with you, Ba?'

I sat through the rest of the journey in silence.

❦

'This is it – home!' Mohan announced, as I staggered out of the taxi an hour later, my feet swollen, clutching the cloth bag tighter, not knowing where to go next.

Ba had walked on ahead with Vrinda, their hands entwined, chatting about the imminent arrival.

'Come on, I don't have all day... have to get back to the shop and relieve Bansi... he must be cursing me by now,' Mohan shouted impatiently, positioned halfway along a deserted by lane, his eyes narrowed, the veins on his arms clearly visible as he lugged the suitcases.

'This is it? Home?' I repeated wearily, vexing my ankles. My head spun. I looked around at my new address in Mumbai for the first time.

'Yes... there... the last building at the end of this lane... can't you see the colony gates? There, the only house in the whole chawl with a window... up ahead, on your extreme left... you get a window all to yourself, Meera. Now come on, will you,' he added agitatedly, pointing upwards, quickening his own feet.

It was still early. The rest of the street was pretty much deserted, the surrounding facades strangely barren, the paint fading. We entered through a discoloured wrought iron gate that creaked when it was pushed open. After passing by several blocks of the same size and shape, we finally arrived at a narrow doorway. A sour aftertaste permeated the air. Flies buzzed everywhere. Ba and Vrinda had already gone up the stairs.

I straggled behind hoping to catch a few moments alone with Mohan.

'Meera,' Mohan was about to say something, when I grabbed his hand all of a sudden, pressing it against my cheek, leaning forward as our bodies coalesced.

'Say my name... say it... the way you...' I moaned desperately, running my tongue over his cleft.

Mohan shuddered, pulling me roughly into a shaded area. We stood motionless there for a while, before he lightly cupped my face, his thumb slowly circling the corners of my mouth.

I closed my eyes, slumping into his chest, feeling the warmth of his breath over my eyelids. His trouser front was beginning to protrude provocatively. I pressed myself against his hips, stroking his manhood faster, pushing apart his legs with mine.

The drone of flies was still audible, somewhere.

'I thought you would have forgotten you had a wife, by now... since you are so well looked after... and...' I moaned in a husky voice, steadying his back.

Mohan was sweating profusely, his brow creased, his ears turning red. 'Can you not wait a single minute for all this? Is this the right place?' he said suddenly, breaking away, throwing off my hands to push the main door open.

'Mohan,' I raised my voice hoping to hold him back, my insides moistened.

A black cat jumped out of the shadows just then, snarling at the unwanted intrusion, baring its fangs ferociously. I squealed as it charged in my direction, the cloth bag falling on the ground. Guruji's pouch slipped out from its folds leaving a trail of ash scattered all over the dimly lit entrance.

'Saali Mumbai!' Mohan swore agitatedly, kicking the cat as it fled down the corridor, yelping in agony.

Stopping to glare at me from a distance.

Like it were an *apshagun*.

Ten

Vrinda

My homecoming coincided with the havan. It was a hectic time for the household as I soon learnt. The house felt as unfamiliar as the city, closing in on me, choking my arteries as I shuttled uneasily between two tiny bedrooms on both sides of a nondescript hall. Not knowing where I fitted in.

The kitchen was equally cramped. The air around us was thick with the smell of rich, Indian spices and wet clothes that hung from a twisted clothesline. Clothes that Bansi had hauled out and dried as soon as I had finished washing them – squatting in a windowless bathroom, my temples still throbbing from the long train journey.

'Our lives here revolve around water. Be sure to fill all the buckets tomorrow and finish all your washing related jobs by ten in the morning. The Municipality water only comes around again about five-ish. Also, Ba likes to bathe first, before anyone... she has a piles problem...' Vrinda said the minute I began unpacking.

'Arre, leave her alone... it's Bhabhi's first night in Mumbai with us. Let her rest a while. I will wash up tonight, not to worry, Mrs Patel,' Bansi interrupted, popping his head into the living room.

I tried to smile.

'Bhabhi, mind if I push your suitcases to one side? Actually I need to pull out the dining table...' he stopped as I stared intently, adding, 'That's the second thing. We Mumbaikars learn to live in limited spaces. So, what you think is a hall may double as a kitchen later... or a place to eat. Like this...'

I laughed at the simplicity of his telling. Bansi rushing to my side to help, while I hastily folded the rest of my clothes; storing them on the back of a faded plastic chair.

'Thank you, I hope to learn soon...' I whispered, taking some of my blouses out of his hands.

A panty fell out of the heap.

I blushed.

'Here...' Bansi handed it back to me casually, our fingers brushing one another's.

I turned my face away.

'Don't worry... it's just day one... I am here if you need anything,' he winked playfully, dashing off to assist Vrinda in the kitchen.

I stood up, settling my sari. Where would we sleep? I wanted to ask.

From the corner of my eyes, I thought I saw Bansi plant a kiss on Vrinda's neck – her face flushed, as she wrapped her arms around him impulsively.

I envied her all the more in that moment. Not her beauty or the lack of it, now that the news of her pregnancy was finally beginning to sink in.

'Clear this mess you have created, Meera... couldn't you have waited till dinner to unpack, huh? Everyone seems to be in a hurry in this house... in this city...' I heard Mohan crib.

❧

Bansi was right. Everything in Mumbai was a fight to survive. It's what I felt the few times I stepped out of our flat; my head spinning with the cacophony of cabs and buses; the omnipresent stench of dead fish.

Everywhere I looked, there were hordes of people, crawling around like ants. Every nook and corner was infested... as if anyone who had ever shifted base in India had moved here, to Mumbai. Adding to the mayhem.

On my fifth night at home, Mohan and I lay side by side in the living room, our ankles entwined, on a hard mattress, the bed sheet having fallen short by a couple of inches, revealing its frayed edges.

It would take me a while to get accustomed to the smallness of the house, I reminded myself. Ba had occupied the larger bedroom; Vrinda and Bansi the other one that was supposed to have been originally reserved for me.

From where I lay I could see Vrinda's navel as she massaged Bansi's head, dripping warm oil down the side of his face. She was starting to show a little. It was an hour or two after Mohan and Bansi had pushed the folding dining table back into the kitchen, as soon as we had finished dinner.

The house looked different. It was the night before the havan. The rest of the furniture was carefully rearranged on one side, the floor mopped with cow's milk, the curtains hand washed; a few pieces of silver that Ba stored in her safe carefully polished, the marigolds fresh, stored overnight in large stainless steel buckets, placed just outside our kitchen, doused in Gangajal.

My stomach churned. I was fasting along with Ba. Drops of sweat trickled slowly down my bosom.

Mohan had his back to me. 'I wish it was me instead of her...' I blurted, lowering my voice at once, dabbing my face with my pallu. Seeing him unmoved, I continued, touching his shoulder lightly, shifting closer by a few inches, 'It's like I'm in second place. Vrinda coming to this city, this house first, before me... and, and hers will also be the Patel family's firstborn. As if that isn't enough, she's even occupied our bedroom... the window that you said was mine... on my first day here. What it would be like to stare out at the moon from that window now?'

'So go and stand there at daytime,' Mohan muttered, sounding irked.

'That's different... as if you don't know the moon only comes out at night?' I cut him short, sounding bitter.

Mohan snorted, facing me, our hips aligned. 'What? Did you just say "moon"? You think people in Mumbai actually pay for a window to gaze at the moon?' he retorted sarcastically, propping himself on his right elbow, staring vaguely into my eyes.

I lay back; worried this may escalate into an argument... scared of waking Ba. And what if Vrinda was eavesdropping, I asked myself, studying the hall shrouded in a suspicious silence. No creaking of the bed or stifled shudders, like yesterday or the nights before. No nagging coughs or clandestine murmurs either. Not even the sound of hurried footsteps, followed by the harsh glare of a bulb, followed by the rhythmic churning of water in the overhead cistern.

'You didn't answer my question,' Mohan resumed, nudging me with his right toe.

'I don't know, maybe I haven't lived long enough in this city,' I answered listlessly, moving away, my buttocks grazing against one of the dining table chairs placed upside down on another.

There were only four of them.

'You're just plain homesick, admit it, Meera,' he concluded curtly, yawning after a few seconds, his eyes bloodshot.

'Jai Sri Krishna,' I whispered closing my eyes, thinking of Guruji.

'What, so now you are angry? Angry with me, with Vrinda, or angry with that damn window... or possibly at the whole of Mumbai?' Mohan snarled, suddenly sitting upright.

'I don't know. Maybe you are correct; perhaps I am just trying to adjust. Everything feels so different, you know. Maybe I was expecting more, more than *this* at least... to be lying here, on the floor, relegated to a mosquito infested corner with my husband. After all this time that we've spent apart, our bodies feeling so distant. I don't know what it is, Mohan, but I never thought I'd be so lonely here... in my own home... the one I had been dreaming of on all those nights...

when I had nothing really... except myself and my imagination,' I exhaled, tears beginning to form.

'Stop all this crying business. You're going to wake everyone up. Things take time to fall into place, Meera. Besides, who knew Vrinda Ben would get pregnant this fast...' Mohan stopped abruptly, glaring accusingly at me.

'I'm sorry I couldn't conceive... I mean, first. But, we can always try again, right? I've been doing everything Ba has asked of me. I am certain my chances of conceiving are very high at this moment,' I interrupted, panting slightly.

'Try where?' Mohan snapped, a fierce scowl descending on his face.

I tugged at his waist.

'I don't know... it's just, just been so long since I felt your touch... your hands... I was hoping we would have a place of our own... a room... something...' my voice choked.

Mohan yawned again. 'Well, since we don't, better we go on pretending we're still living apart, I guess... you in Sinor and me alone, in this house. It's the only thing to do Meera, at least till Vrinda Ben departs for her parents' place, which I am assuming she will, once the lady doctor grants her permission to travel by train, before her delivery. As in... till we get the bedroom back,' he tried reasoning, clearing his throat awkwardly.

'But, what if, there's no full moon, then? Tonight *is* my first full moon in Mumbai...' I shuddered, staring at the main door, bolted securely.

'Well, may as well make up that part as well,' Mohan murmured all of a sudden, dragging himself closer, before planting his head down on my chest.

I moaned, raising my buttocks to make more space.

'Shiish Meera, be quiet... I mean, all I am saying is... umm... I mean why don't you touch yourself tonight, please? For me? For my sake...' he urged suddenly, pressing into my wetness.

I cringed, my sari slipping away.

'Where are you running away now? See... it's really easy... all you have to do is to imagine you are alone in the darkness, stroking yourself. C'mon, stop acting so uptight... and do it for me once, okay? I want to see you pleasure yourself... It's been so long since I climaxed. Please, Meera, can't I watch tonight?' Mohan pleaded, his legs steadily hitching up my petticoat.

'But, but I don't understand any of this. I mean, why can't we just make love, here or, or sneak inside the bathroom, over there? I doubt Ba or Vrinda are likely to get up... it's all so quiet. And, and that's Bansi... snoring too. C'mon Mohan, let's... the toilet is the safest place right now, here, here take my hand,' I tried making sense, clumsily grabbing his chest.

'Stop your childishness, Meera. Don't you understand that it's only a matter of time before we are together in private? Can you not wait a bit? What's gotten into you ever since you came here? You seem so reckless all of a sudden... so damn needy all the time,' Mohan scorned, shoving my hands off him.

A few of my glass bangles cracked, making a slight clatter. 'How can I do it?' I spoke after a while, removing the rest of them, one by one.

Mohan's back faced me by then; he had removed his kurta a few minutes earlier, and was wearing only his vest. 'Nothing to it,' he stirred, taking his time to turn back, adding in a raspy undertone, 'Just think of all the things you want me to do... the places you want me to touch you... and, and...'

'Can you at least switch off the bathroom light?' was the last thing I recall saying as Mohan's hands plunged lower, yanking my knees apart to remove my panty.

I could sense his organ was still deflated.

'Meera...' he groaned, rubbing his own chest, the sound of his voice different.

The power went out just then. Making us look the same.

Strangely equal.

I don't know which of us drifted off first; or when the power returned. In any case, it was me who woke up with a slight shudder as the sound of suppressed voices wafted in from a distance.

Mohan's eyes were clamped shut; his pajama was partially undone, his organ drooping sideways. I scanned my surroundings anxiously, wondering if it was just Ba, in the throes of a bad dream or something, craning my neck to sneak a peek underneath her door.

Her lights were still out.

I lay still for the next few minutes, turning slowly to face Mohan when the voices returned. But then I sprung upright as they wafted closer, narrowing my eyes, even as my body tensed with fear. Could a thief have possibly entered, climbing the thick water pipe outside our kitchen? There was so much silver lying about. Thoughts raced through my head as the bathroom door creaked loudly.

Mohan had insisted on keeping the light on.

Was someone inside? I felt my throat go dry.

Just then someone moaned.

Was the intruder in the kitchen? Hiding behind the row of utensils and buckets that had been carefully assembled prior to tomorrow's function?

A part of me was desperate to wake up Mohan, but something in me resisted. Instead I rose as stealthily as I could, bringing myself a few feet away from the edge of the mattress, careful to keep my head lowered all the while.

'*Shiiiish*,' I heard a muffled voice, as if something had just dropped out of someone's hands, the shuffle of footsteps making Mohan whimper too, before he stretched out on his back, covering his face fully with the printed cotton sheet that we had draped ourselves in.

With great difficulty, I now held my breath, crouching near the other pair of chairs... the clink of glass bangles whetting my suspicions all over again. But, but my wrists were bare... I shivered slightly.

There were shadows everywhere making it hard to see anything clearly – till I finally located a slim crack on the side of the bathroom door. Through it, I saw Vrinda squatting on the toilet seat, her sari bunched around her ankles, her hips swaying wantonly.

I leaned closer. And gasped at the sight of Bansi's buttocks, the faint outline of his balls slapping up and down, a rough tuft of hair peeking out from beneath his folded thighs.

I knew I should have looked away... except I couldn't.

Bansi was much taller than Mohan and more muscular. He could do a hundred push-ups at one go, I recalled him bragging once. His head was nestled between Vrinda's thighs; his tongue was darting in and out of her sex, as he drank in her soreness, crouching acrobatically near her ankles.

Behind me Mohan murmured inaudibly.

I held my breath, not wanting to make the slightest sound. My eyes riveted anxiously on Bansi as he scooped Vrinda in his arms, the way Kartik did when I was young, minutes after I had got off the giant wheel, my head spinning deliciously – as it was at this very moment. I watched as Vrinda wrapped her legs around Bansi's thick waist, her newly bulging belly button rubbing against his swollenness as she quickened her thrusts, her breasts slapping against his stubble.

What if he accidentally dropped her? I thought.

Bansi suckled on her plump breasts, one by one, as Vrinda clawed deep into his arched back, using her long nails. Would she climax before him? A sharp shiver shot through my insides. I bit my lips, sweating profusely

When I managed to regain focus, Vrinda had mounted Bansi, who squatted expertly on his haunches. I reached out for the mattress, not wanting to lose my own balance, unable to control myself from staring at Bansi as he plunged upwards, lodging his full length inside Vrinda, the tips of her enlarged nipples glinting in the dark.

My heart fluttered at the sheer size of Bansi's manhood, the shape it had then taken, its head fully ripened, as it plunged into Vrinda one more time, jerking with pleasure, stroking her furiously all the while, their tongues passionately interlocked.

'*Shiiiish*,' another murmur rose and fell, as I glanced over my shoulders impatiently, pushing my left hand inside my petticoat, rewarded with dampness.

'Oh... Oh... Bansi...' I was about to moan myself. Only I couldn't. As another pair of eyes stared back. Equally lust-ridden.

Mohan was behind me, his breath as rushed as mine. His eyes glazed with guilt... and greed.

❦

I was halfway down the stairs the next morning when our glances first met. I was on my way to assist Ba's oldest sister who had travelled all the way from Indore.

There were no clouds in the sky; the sun unforgiving.

I covered my face with the corners of my pallu.

'I... I wasn't expecting you to be here, I thought you were still away,' I finally managed a full sentence, my back pressed against the wall. The filigreed silver key ring that I had been carrying around since the day I moved into Mumbai shone from my midriff.

Guruji touched the top of my head in blessing; his gaze sanguine, and then continued to climb the stairs. I said urgently: 'I've been thinking of you a lot... I, I mean... after what happened... wanting to make sense of things... everything...' I spoke fast, my thoughts colliding.

Guruji turned around and smiled and was about to say something when Ba appeared carrying a plate of fruit for him.

'Will you be here long? I, I mean... Mohan doesn't know anything... you know the way things turned out...' I whispered desperately. Before I finished speaking, Guruji was gone, disappearing into the crowd of worshippers who had descended on the house. 'Vrinda... Vrinda...' I heard him chant, saying the mantras in her name. My eyes swam with tears throughout the ceremony. I felt betrayed. A line of chappals and shoes lined the narrow entrance to our home, hordes of people streamed in and out of our airless living room, the sacred echo of kirtans filtering outside, followed by complicated Sanskrit shlokas. The scent of desi ghee was overpowering.

'Vrinda?' a guest questioned, staring at my face searchingly, touching my shoulders, as I stood watching Guruji pour a spoonful of ghee into a saffron flame from a distance.

I glanced up, distracted. Smiling through my tears, I said, 'No... I am not her. The havan has begun. Vrinda is inside with Amarkant Maharaj and the rest of the family. I am Meera... the Badi Bahu.'

'Guruji is *actually* here? Did you all know he was coming to Mumbai? I would have come sooner in that case. Anything to just touch him once... be touched by him... somehow!' the lady cried urgently, rushing to meet him.

Her words stung.

Eleven

Shani's Mahadasha

Exactly seven months later, Chhotu was born. There were some complications at the time of his birth, the doctors at JJ Hospital informed us, advising a C-Section – to ensure the safety of mother and child. Ba howled and Bansi paced furiously up and down the dimly-lit corridor, worry lines appearing on his otherwise cheerful face.

I waited outside, unsure of the part I was supposed to play. Bansi brought me a bottle of water before he left for the shop again. From a distance, I watched as Vrinda gently grasped Mohan's left arm, and his eyes suddenly turned tender. 'You'll be just fine,' he reassured her.

'Something just doesn't feel right. What if the child gets stuck inside? I heard the nurses say that I will be made unconscious. What if I never wake up?' she whimpered, reaching out once again for Mohan's kurta.

'Ba has already had the baby's birth chart drawn up. It's going to be a boy, Guruji himself predicted... someone who will grow up to be a real prince, just you wait and watch now. There is some major planetary movement; the cursed period is about to commence, Shani's Mahadasha or something. That is why there are all these sudden developments, Vrinda Ben. There is a satsang being organized in Thane to ward off this evil... Ba will go there to pray for him with Meera for you and the child...' Mohan paused, then moving closer, he added, 'I will be here, though...'

He stopped speaking when he saw me enter through the half open door.

'Vrinda,' I said, taking her hands gently out of Mohan's into mine. 'There is no need to fret this way. It's bad for the baby. Learn to trust your fate in these matters. Also, think about it – the surgery will free you of the excruciating birth pains a woman usually has to endure, the endless wait... the agonizing contractions known to rip your insides out. My grandmother was a dai. I accompanied her sometimes, when the cases were complicated and she needed an extra set of hands. I, I have seen it all...'

Before I had finished, Vrinda had moved away, clasping her stomach protectively, her facial muscles tense.

'Don't take Meera's words to heart, Vrinda Ben. She is thoroughly inexperienced in these matters,' Mohan stepped in, glaring irately in my direction, his nails digging into the sides of my waist.

'I didn't mean it in that sense. I was only repeating what I heard my grandmother say... that when a woman gives birth, the pain is supposed to be earth shattering. She'd often call it a woman's rebirth, a second life... a new lease of...' I raced to finish, embarrassed at being admonished by Mohan.

'You are lucky, Badi Bhabhi, you know. Unlike us, it seems you have just one birth to complete everything – wash away your sins, find all the happiness you need... everything in this one janam. At least, we get a second life as you claim, no matter how painful it all may seem at present. But for someone like you, it may just be this one, solitary lifetime, right? Imagine the agony in that? No less of a suffering there...' Vrinda grimaced, gritting her teeth, as she was wheeled out.

Her words hovering like a curse.

❧

'Shani's Mahadasha or something like that,' Mohan's voice played in my ears eerily as Ba and I travelled to Thane, changing trains twice.

'It's all Guruji's maya. Imagine, his satsang coinciding with the same day the doctor orders Chhoti Bahu's operation. As if Maharaj is assuring his disciples that he watches over each of us... playing a part in each of our stories, our lives...' Ba said, covering her head as we jostled through a swelling crowd on our way to the satsang.

A booming voice blared all the while from a couple of overhead speakers.

'I can't see him, is Guruji still not up on stage? The chants have commenced...' I muttered distractedly to myself as soon as we had located a place to be seated in the crowd, in the midst of a sprawling open field covered with a saffron shamiana; dull, gold marigolds adorning its sides.

Ba was led away to the front, to sit on a plastic chair, in an area reserved for the old and infirm. Her eyes were already closed, her mouth moving in prayer.

A hefty lady seated beside me, leaned in closer and asked, 'First time here? Thane satsang? The one always held before the commencement of Navratras...'

I placed my hands over my eyes, before craning my neck again. 'I just moved to Mumbai...' I distractedly replied.

The lady fanned herself with a newspaper. 'I know... I saw it from your eyes... even I felt like this... travelling all the way from Charni Road... in this heat... just to... you know...'

I turned to face her.

'Have you ever been alone in his presence?' I spoke fast, my blouse clinging to me, soaking wet.

The lady inched closer. Lowering her voice, she answered, 'I've been in Mumbai for the past five years. Our whole family believes in Guruji, worshipping him like God almost. His photograph is kept in the Puja room, brought down and cleaned daily with Gangajal, as per mother-in-law's strict instructions. I am not from here also... ours was a love marriage. We eloped... I'm a Muslim... don't tell anyone though... I was forced to convert, my husband also insisted on it to make peace. Every year since we moved in with my in-laws I am brought here... like a ritual or something. Yet, somehow I have not seen this man even once. Every year my mother-in-law assures me that we will be blessed with a private darshan... but, but...'

There was some movement on the podium upfront, swarming with Guruji's primary shishyas, their footsteps frenzied all of a sudden.

'Looks like your wish is being fulfilled this time – see they are clearing the stage,' I cleared my throat.

'That is usual. It happens after the havan... actually you came late. This function has been on since twelve in the afternoon...' she retorted matter-of-factly, pulling out a printed handkerchief from her bosom.

The announcements had started by then, someone in the row behind me tapped my shoulder a couple of times asking me to stop conversing.

'I have a question...' I yelled, raising my left hand, after the next two hours had passed, my ears smouldering in the stifling heat.

Everyone turned around to look at me.

I stood up.

'All this we just heard about Ram and Sita, now...' I paused for a few seconds, hoping to locate Ba, 'all this... the havan that was just completed, aimed at reinstating the virtues of Ram Rajya... the purity of Sita Maiyya... this detailed lecture we heard... that, that you say is being transmitted from Guruji's mouth directly into our ears... I, I wanted to ask one simple question...'

'Please come to the point...'

'What if Sita hadn't been kidnapped... what if Lord Ram and she went on to lead a simple life... maybe in a city like ours, dwelling in a modest colony, like most of us do. Would the Ramayana still be this relevant, all the things you just described... would it stand for anything, anything at all? What if Sita Maiyya was just as happy – as before, the way she must've been at her swayamvar, when their paths first crossed? Hers and Ram's – a woman and the man she was about to be betrothed to... would the Navratras be relevant, to this day? All the strict rules you have laid down... things we are supposed to eat and...' I stopped as the mike hissed hoarsely.

'Next question please...' a saffron clad man standing on the side of stage cut me short.

On the way back, I was separated from Ba. The return train spilling over with people, some faces strangely familiar this time.

'I liked your question,' someone murmured on my right. It was the same woman from the satsang. I flopped down beside her. Settling my hair into a loose bun, I said, 'Thanks. In a way, I suppose it's good they didn't bother answering it... just that I've never really related to Sita Maiyya somehow... she's always spelt bad luck for me...'

The lady said, 'I lost my child during Dusshera too... I had a fall... I was fasting... I must have passed out...'

We were nearing our station, so I probed impatiently, 'Why were you fasting... especially at a time when you were pregnant... I recall you said fasting earlier on too...'

'It was Ramzan... the month of penance. It always coincided with Dusshera somehow. Back then too...'

I don't know why my eyes suddenly moistened. Pressing my left hand gently over hers, I said, 'Forgive me, Ben... I had no intention of raking up the past... I know how painful it can be...'

She slipped her fingers into mine. Staring at the railway tracks blankly, she continued, 'I had asked the same question the year it happened. I was shattered when the doctors informed me I may never conceive again. My in-laws blamed it on my religion, screaming at my shauhar, saying it was his fault he never enforced his wishes on me or checked personally whether I had discarded my prayer mat... I was seething inside... especially when they went on and on about Sita, feeling the way you do probably, or, or did before...'

I stared back into her eyes.

'What was the answer you got?' I paused to take a deep breath, our shoulders touching.

'You won't believe what he said... the same fellow on stage today...' she pursed her lips, tilting her head sideways, her hennaed hair slapping my face.

'What?' I quizzed, getting restless.

'Nothing sells like a woman's suffering... everything begins, it seems, from a woman's tears... as if the Ramayana is a film or something... as if it is all a woman's life is really worth. It's why I come here every year, hoping to meet Amarkant Maharaj in person... ask him to his face... point blank, if he has really loved a woman himself? Ever?' her thin lips quivered as she clumsily shoved the black thread back in a taweez attached to its centre.

Every now and then, my thoughts travelled back to Guruji, especially over the next few days, as Ba and I spent most of our nights alone.

Mohan insisted on taking turns in staying at the hospital, till Vrinda was discharged, swapping places with Bansi, while he guarded the shop. The house had suddenly fallen silent, Bansi mostly preferring to eat his meals outside.

Ba and I slept on the same cot, as she babbled on endlessly, narrating the same story almost every night – of how her deceased husband's own brother – Mohan's paternal uncle, and once an equal business partner had fallen out bitterly, in the days following Ba's father-in-law's demise in Ahmedabad.

'If only the old man had been a little prudent and prepared a proper will distributing his assets equally amongst his two sons,' she complained, rubbing her eyes.

One night Ba was away too, attending an overnight jagran.

I was on my own, for the first time. The vacant corners of the house stared back at me. Mohan was expected home any moment, to bathe and have his dinner, before heading onwards to the shop.

I rushed to lay the table, nearly tripping over a tattered floor mat, some of the water spilling out from my hands.

'Vrinda Ben will be discharged by 10 a.m. tomorrow; Ba insists we organize a puja at home, once the baby crosses this threshold,' Mohan remarked, dipping a piece of chapatti into his urad dal.

I waited for him to try the Bateta Sukhi Bhaji, a dry potato curry I had tried out for the first time. It used to be Kartik's favourite.

'You know, it feels so strange being alone in this house, with you. Just us I mean,' I confessed, serving him another chapatti spread with an extra layer of ghee, my arms brushing his bare back.

Mohan had just bathed, his body felt cool to my touch, small droplets of moisture clinging to his armpits, the hair underneath neatly pressed.

Wordlessly, he finished the rest of the meal.

'Is the sabzi not to your liking tonight? I thought you might want to try something a different? Ba being away... also,' I paused, opening out my bun, feeling my hair flop over my chest, before descending in slow ripples over my stomach.

Mohan glanced upwards absent-mindedly, then before I could say anything more, he said, 'It's good we are alone actually; there is something I've been meaning to tell you all this while.'

I wiped my cleavage with my pallu, my cheeks flushed.

'You had absolutely no right to say all you did to Vrinda Ben in the hospital that day. She was most upset after you left. As it is, the operation was a bolt from the blue... the sudden expenditure... the time she will now require to recover... the fact that she couldn't return to Ahmedabad, to her parents' house. I just pray she hasn't said anything to Ba. The last thing I want at this point is her complaining about your bluntness... the way you tend to say the dumbest things... tactlessly... always.'

I rose awkwardly, the chair scraping the floor. Trying to suppress my rising anger at Mohan; at the way he always took Vrinda's side in everything. Even on a night such as this.

'Stop thinking you're too smart, Meera. I mean, do you actually feel people are stupid enough not to see just why you're jealous of Vrinda Ben? Saying mean things at a time when she needs extra care, just because you yourself aren't able to bear a child? A woman like you should just keep her mouth shut!'

The bhaji remained untouched. I swallowed hard.

'What are you still standing there, gawking at me for?'

I bit my lips, looking down. It was the second day of my cycle. My stomach throbbed.

'C'mon, Meera, I know you are dying to make a point...' Mohan taunted, grabbing my elbow all of a sudden, twisting it painfully. 'I'm sure you have another theory on this. Something your grandmother told you, perhaps? No? Maybe something you studied in Saraswati Maha Vidyalaya... huh?'

I was walking towards the kitchen, when he suddenly gripped my shoulders.

'Let's not start,' I passively remarked, backing away.

'Why? Not in the mood tonight? No moon in the Mumbai sky is it?' he smirked, his fingers digging into my spine, getting a grip on my open tresses.

'It's just that I've not been feeling too good; I'd like to rest early. Tomorrow will be a busy day again, with Vrinda returning home... I am sure you understand that...'

Mohan swung me around. 'What were you going to say to me? I know when something is playing on your mind, Meera... *hum tamara pati chum,* not some part-time lover you've had a romp with...' he retorted harshly, his jaws hardening.

'I don't want to fight, there is no point...' I cut him short.

But Mohan was relentless, holding me down by my hips this time as I tried warding him off. I'd barely eaten all day; my head starting to spin out of control.

'Say it...' Mohan growled, his stubble scraping my cheeks.

My legs felt wobbly, the discharge at its heaviest.

'You... do you think babies... I mean... do you *actually* think kids come out of *nowhere*? You think Vrinda Ben just blinked her eyes and received the blessing of motherhood? Why do you think we are the ones not getting pregnant? Is it all just my fault?' I bit my lower lip hard, trying to stop myself from crying.

Mohan breathed strangely, an acidic aftertaste emanating from his mouth. He had been drinking.

'You can't simply have a child by watching your wife stroke herself, or by asking her to rub her breasts, or even by pushing a ripe banana into her sex... doing nothing but touching yourself all the while. Please, please Mohan, try and take a look at yourself first. It's been ages since you even touched me properly, let alone us actually having intercourse. I am not a village idiot, Mohan. I am your wife... not some mistress or tramp...' I completely ran out of breath, tears finally streaming out.

'Excuse me, come again,' Mohan yelped as soon as I'd stepped aside. 'I said come again, Meera!' he thundered.

I turned to face him, shuddering with sobs.

'That's *your* job Mr Mohan Patel... come again,' I mimicked him deliberately.

'Are you calling me a *namard*? What do you mean by everything you just said, Meera... how dare you talk back to your husband this way? That too in my house, eating *my* dal chawal?' he screeched, his eyes drunken with rage.

'Mohan you are not in a state to talk... and, you're hurting me now, let go,' I cringed, desperate to wriggle out of his grasp.

'Really? But, I thought you liked the pain. C'mon, Meera, it's what you've been missing all this time, haven't you? Admit it! Isn't that the real reason you creep up to me every night... you are dying for it... even shamelessly coming out of the kitchen, without your ghunghat, falling all over Bansi... packing his tiffin so lovingly... your pallu conveniently slipping off...'

'Mohan, I was upset too... maybe even jealous of the way you always fight Vrinda's case, picking up a fight with me over nothing...' I tried reasoning, covering my breasts defensively, trying to pick myself up from the floor.

'Oh ho... I forgot... this is about Vrinda and Bansi right, and their happy sex life? See, we are even occupying their bedroom tonight. You must be over the moon!' he barked, yanking off his belt all of a sudden.

My cramps were coming in shorter waves now, hitting hard against my womb. 'Please, I don't feel well, can't you drop it for once?' I managed to speak up.

'Shut up!' Mohan screeched, wrapping his belt around my mouth and pushing me flat on the bed.

It was hard to breathe. The stench of cheap country liquor and faux leather coupled with the staleness of Mohan's sweat rendering me utterly nauseous as he dragged off my petticoat and pulled out the thick pile of cotton I had carefully inserted between my legs.

'C'mon, you whore, suck! What are you staring at me for again?' he ordered agitatedly, as I let out a hoarse howl, my head tilting dangerously from the edge of the bed.

Before I knew it, Mohan had shoved his entire right hand inside my sex. 'Go on... pretend it's my organ... swallow it like you want to, Meera, like you have been dying to,' he panted breathlessly, forcing my left leg over his shoulder while massaging his organ furiously with his own left hand, rolling the foreskin up and down, as it drooped, lifeless.

I looked away, biting into the cold metal instead, the edges of my mouth completely braised, pools of sweat running down my thighs.

'Faster... go faster... I want you to climax on this. Do as I say, Meera... I am bloody sick of your petty arguments... and your demands... trying to always be one up...' he slobbered, squatting uncomfortably on his haunches, his zipper undone, looking like a man possessed.

I bled furiously. The sheets were soiled; my lips cut. Before Mohan leaned closer, throwing my legs over my head, he inserted the buckle in through my rear, his eyes rolling backwards.

'I know you like it in here, I know everything about you, Meera, all your secrets... I am your husband, never forget that... you understand...' he wheezed hatefully, kneading the cheeks of my buttocks, forcing my hands over his deflated member.

I don't know when Mohan stopped or where. Or how much blood I lost that night.

Feeling nothing after a point, except a sense of humiliation and betrayal. A slow hurt.

Coming in short waves. Coming back...

Twelve

Chhotu

Chhotu's arrival transformed our dreary, everyday existence; our lives were touched as if by a magical fairy wand the day Ba carried him home from the hospital, cradling him in her arms, softly humming a lullaby as she walked carefully up the stairs. The worry lines around her eyes had disappeared, as if for just those moments.

We all fussed over Chhotu in much the same way – where his bed should be placed, whether it was too hot during the day, how many times his nappy should be changed, who was to boil the water for sanitizing his bottles. The sound of his gurgles was infectious; the barren corners of our home slowly began to be crowded with his belongings, someone or the other was always tripping on his umpteen toys and rattles.

It was hard to tell when the year had ended. Elaborate plans for Chhotu's first birthday were eagerly discussed, almost every night, mostly over dinner. Mohan was always the first one to suggest a celebration for the little boy, his eyes lighting up each time he placed Chhotu on his shoulder, closing his own eyes, gently rocking back and forth. Telling Bansi to either mind the shop or retire early with Vrinda.

Vrinda hadn't been keeping too well ever since her complicated C-section. She had been coughing bitterly of late. One night I had watched Bansi massaging warm mustard oil over her breasts. I caught Mohan staring at them stealthily too, one time, after I had made my way back from the toilet. I pretended to lie still in the darkness. Turning away. Knowing there was little I could do.

Perhaps it was to fill the spaces between us, that Mohan and I voluntarily started taking turns to tend to Chhotu, battling sleep on several occasions, our own arms aching, our feet dragging by the time we had tucked the infant into bed.

Talks were rife of a bigger store opening right after Chhotu's first birthday. The new store, double the size of the previous one, was supposedly bang opposite Praful Bhai's, in the same lane. Bansi was overseeing most of the last minute work, being stationed at the new shop on most nights, while Mohan stayed home, tending to Chhotu – laughing in a happy, carefree way, bathing the little one with his own hands, inventing the silliest of games to grab his attention.

I'd join in sometimes. Chhotu tried to stand up on his own, his cherubic arms holding on to ours, as we clicked our tongues to encourage him. Mohan even looked in my direction. We tried smiling...

It was time to finally settle scores, Ba declared victoriously, before departing on yet another pilgrimage – to thank the Gods for their sudden benevolence, a change of heart, as she often commented, to pray for the good fortune Chhotu's birth had supposedly ushered in.

'I should be back soon, but if Guruji returns from his retreat, I will have no choice but to stay on. Anything to receive his blessings...' she muttered as Mohan and I touched her feet.

Vrinda watched us from afar, her breasts uncovered, the bed a haphazard pile of Chhotu's clothes and soiled cotton swabs, the smell of milk oozing ubiquitously.

With Ba away the house was split down the middle this time. Mohan and I occupying Ba's room, lying on separate sides, a thick bolster between us, dividing us in some sense.

Till the week after Chhotu's first birthday.

Ba had sent a message telling us she had decided to extend her stay. Vrinda's pulmonary infection had worsened, the doctors at JJ

Hospital advising her not to breastfeed the baby for the next month or so.

Mohan immediately carried Chhotu into our bedroom, reassuring Vrinda that it was what I had wanted.

'Meera says it's the best thing to do under the circumstances. Besides, I am a light sleeper myself. Don't you worry; of course we will keep our door open... just in case. Only a mother knows what is best for her own child,' I heard him reassure Vrinda, as I pulled the bed sheet awkwardly over my ankles. Wondering, would Mohan do the same if it was me, in her place?

I couldn't sleep at all that night... or the next for that matter, waking up with a shudder at the slightest provocation.

Even when it was nothing; even when there was no one.

'I think he's more used to this room. It is breezier too. It's just for a short while, though, till your health improves; anything for Chhotu's comfort, really. Hope this arrangement is fine by you?' Mohan questioned Vrinda awkwardly the morning after we had finally decided to swap rooms, complying with Chhotu's irregular sleep patterns.

Children are a habit, as I was to learn over the following weeks, finding myself getting hopelessly accustomed to the helpless, tiny creature sandwiched between Mohan and me.

I couldn't take my eyes off him, as I stood by the window alone, rocking Chhotu to sleep again, singing a song I remembered from my childhood. It was a song Kartik and I would often sing to each other at night, trying to put ourselves to sleep.

I held the wrought iron rails, staring out. Chhotu's soft hands fidgeting with the hooks on my blouse. 'Someday I'll take you to Sinor, my darling, and teach you how to swim, okay? And then we'll have chuski, just us, lying under the lazy afternoon sun, sharing all our secrets... walking back bare feet... chasing butterflies at dusk,' I whispered affectionately, rubbing his cheeks.

Chhotu purred at once, like he understood everything I was saying, gazing back with his large black eyes, melting a piece of my heart instantly.

Mohan and I didn't speak much, and fought even less. Our conversations mostly revolved around the new store... the old shop being put on sale... Chhotu's admission when the time came... or other mundane domestic issues. Mohan usually left home the minute Bansi returned from his nightshift, sometimes even without touching his breakfast – hurriedly stealing a glance at Chhotu just before he left, mouthing last- minute instructions to Bansi...

There wasn't much for me to say either, to be honest. And yet, something that night made me reach out to Mohan.

Maybe it was all Chhotu's doing, his oval face dream-like as he wrapped his pudgy hand around my left thumb. It was a full moon night too.

The first in a room that was supposed to have been once ours, the first moonlit night by my window, I instinctively calculated.

'What have you done with the kid?' Mohan quizzed irately, frantically rubbing his eyes, tufts of chest hair peeking out from between the pores in his transparent vest, when I woke him.

'Don't worry. I've tucked Chhotu to sleep; there he is, right over there. I doubt he will wake up before morning now. I changed him too, just in case,' I murmured, pointing to my side of the bed.

There was an awkward silence.

'I've been thinking, you know. The thing is, we haven't really had much time in the last few months, everyone is so preoccupied. So, I thought maybe tonight we could start, I mean... start over...' I gulped hesitantly, studying the shape of his ears.

'Why? Is it your happy birthday today?' he jeered, about to turn on his back, when I reached out and grabbed his shoulder.

'Are you not happy, Mohan? With me? With our marriage? With everything?' I raised my voice a couple of notches, pushing my hands down over his chest, hoping to win him over.

The bedroom door was ajar as usual, a night lamp glowing faintly in Vrinda's room.

'Meera, I'm in no mood for an analysis of our marital condition at this unearthly hour.' Mohan said, yawning in my face.

'I know. I realize that. But, but maybe, this is a good time to start, Mohan... fix things between us... mend whatever was broken, at least start over... try...' I resumed patiently, curling my toes.

'Why don't you just be frank with me? In the mood for sex, aren't you?' Mohan interrupted callously. 'I know what's on your mind. I can see it in your eyes... every time you bring up all this complicated stuff, trying hard to act mature. It's written all over your face... no wonder even all the men in the colony can't stop crowding under the stairs every time you walk down. You just want it all the time, don't you? I can see your desperation in your eyes, Meera!'

I glanced sideways. 'Maybe we should just get back to bed,' I said moving away from Mohan, patting Chhotu's forehead instead, settling the sheets carefully over his little chest.

'Just look at yourself once... when it comes to having sex, you couldn't care about anything or anyone... any time of the day, or night really... even now, with this infant lying between us... on the same bed!' Mohan snapped, his eyes scouring my face.

I lay back, preferring to remain silent; the midnight showers unabated... the only constant in this strange city.

⚓

'Why don't we go out somewhere in the evening today? You wanted to see a bit of Mumbai, right?' the sound of Mohan's voice made me jump out of my skin.

I had just bathed. Slowly, I turned around. My arms were damp, my sari clinging to my hips, drops of water collecting near my forehead. I hadn't combed my hair yet.

It was just after six sometime, the morning after.

I pretended not to have heard, folding Chhotu's washed clothes from yesterday, my fingers slippery.

'You forgot to drink this again, I had added some extra honey; no wonder you were coughing again in your sleep,' I remarked mechanically, removing a tall steel glass from the bedside table.

Mohan drank up the concoction in silence, using his left hand as always. I folded the sheets passively, deliberately avoiding eye contact. Wanting to punish Mohan for a change.

'What say we go for a film? You haven't ever been to an actual theatre in Mumbai since you moved here... and it's been a while since that too... gosh how time flies...' he attempted small talk, grabbing my hands all of a sudden, before pushing his face into my stomach.

I stood frozen.

'Should I take your *maun vrath* as a yes?' he spoke urgently, staring at me expectantly, rubbing the area around my navel.

I kept my head lowered, even as my heart fluttered.

'C'mon Meera, what do you want me to do? Want me to beg? Fall at your feet? Treat you like a Maharani?' Mohan continued dramatically, beginning to lose patience.

'And what happens to the shop? Isn't it your turn to keep watch tonight? Something about supplies being transferred in the new store, right? You've been repeating the same thing all week to Vrinda. Besides, Bansi and she should spend some time, just by themselves, now that Chhotu is well adjusted with us...' I cut him short dismissively, flopping down on the bed.

Mohan dragged me onto his lap, his hands disappearing beneath my pallu almost instantly, his slender fingers tugging at my nipples, massaging the area around them.

'And what happens to us?' he grunted, pressing his lips clumsily over the corners of my mouth.

I pushed him away roughly.

'Wait... listen... please... don't get up this way. Don't leave in a huff again...' he pleaded, groping my back, his overgrown nails clawing my skin.

A tear was beginning to form. I pushed it back at once. Knowing they meant nothing.

'You mentioned once that you loved Rajesh Khanna, right? You wrote to me. See; see... how I remember everything about you, huh? How about we go watch *Aradhana*? It's playing in town. Rajesh Khanna is in a double role in that picture,' he coaxed warmly, tugging at my arms, like Chhotu did ever so often.

A sign to denote he was hungry. A sign I knew well.

'Double role?' I quizzed listlessly, wiping my top lip, Mohan's moustache having thickened in the last few weeks.

The sun was just coming up. Mohan burst out laughing.

'Good lord! My small town belle – double role meaning one actor essaying two parts, in the same film. For instance, father and son, or two brothers separated at birth, perhaps lost in a village fair or something, one a saint, the other a sinner. Like Dr Jekyll and Mr Hyde...' he explained patiently, his midnight stubble grazing the nape of my neck.

'Dr Jekyll and Mr Hyde?' I paused feeling Mohan steady his grip over my waist, untying some of my pleats hastily.

'Yes, you know how it's said that in every man there actually exists two sides – one pure, the other evil? It's a famous novel, a classic. Let me see if I can get my hands on a Gujarati translation of the same... you will find it most intriguing,' he continued eagerly, securing his arms around me this time.

I sat expressionlessly, wondering if the same also applied to all men in general, including Mohan, as he went on furnishing facts about the book, his eyes glowing in the fuzzy early morning light. I found his sudden boyish candour hard to relate to.

Most of the stories I had grown up listening to or learning about in Sinor were based on good and evil, the characters clearly delineated; the battle-lines always etched decisively; the ending pre-empted in some way with good forever triumphing.

There were seldom any exceptions. Except the tales Kartik wove... as we swam together, our bodies slithering under each other's like multi-coloured fish.

'Listen carefully, Meera, meet me in front of Churchgate station, by 6 in the evening. I'll tell you how to go about it; trains as you know by now are easily available here... taking you almost anywhere, at anytime too. It's pretty simple... you just need to get the hang of things,' Mohan dispelled my thoughts.

'Hmm,' I nodded passively, squatting uncomfortably on his lap. The very image of Kartik's lips on mine drawing me in... the way he pretended to be resuscitating me, our limbs entangled, as I grappled with him, before rolling over on the wet mud.

Mohan sat still for a while, his chest thumping hard, before he reached out for me, slanting my chin upwards, his fingers delicately outlining the contours of my face.

'Don't, Vrinda Ben is awake... why take a chance?' I spoke coldly.

Mohan clamped his eyes shut, shaking his head a couple of times as if he were terribly disappointed by the turn of events.

Serves him right, I thought.

'You have the most exquisite hands, Meera. Have I ever told you that before? They can make a man so weak. You know, whenever I'd think of you... in the time we spent away from each other, it's the first thing that came to my mind... always... these fingers... do you know just how difficult it is for a man like me to match up to such a gorgeous wife? To keep up all the time... to all your desires, your dreams... fantasies that I fear I may not ever fulfil?' he spoke in a raspy undertone, placing my right hand over his mouth, parting my fingers to lightly suck on them, one by one.

'I should go, get breakfast organized,' I muttered, holding my breath. A part of me longed to kiss Mohan back with the same ferocity; the subtle scent of honey and lime on his afterbreath resulting in a dull intoxication as he tugged at my earlobes with his teeth.

'Bansi will be back; he's bound to be famished. God knows if he has even managed dinner...' I added, squirming in my place, feeling Mohan's organ slowly stir, its width widening as it nudged at my buttocks from inside his clothes.

'No, no, stay right here, Meera. Bansi won't be home before nine at least... trust me. And who matters more to you, huh? Bansi returning home hungry, or me? You're always giving him more attention...' he scowled, his head touching my chest.

I lightly caressed the cleft on his chin.

'You should stop leaving things unfinished always. It's a bad habit, it's what irks me at times too... things take time between a couple, Meera... especially these sort of things,' he breathed heavily, running his lips through my damp tresses, my blouse carelessly slipping off my shoulders. Mohan was quick to take advantage, as he arched his back to hold my hips down firmly, making sure I had no choice but to squat on his shaft.

'And stop fighting with me all the time, woman,' he groaned angst-ridden, as our tongues finally met, his swirling in and out of my mouth, increasingly demanding in its overtures.

I let him, taking my time to touch him... back. In the way he wanted. In the way I calculated.

'Oh Meera... Meera...' Mohan protested feebly, each time I shoved his face away, lowering mine to bite under his left nipple, guiding my fingers into his chest hair. Covering his face in my tangled tresses.

'Meeraaa... Meeraaa, your hands... oh...' he whimpered, thrusting his hips forward, unable to contain himself anymore as I stroked furiously over his pajama front, cupping his balls expertly from below, causing Mohan to convulse every now and then.

'I can't wait for this evening... I, I...' he stuttered, sweating profusely, before I shoved my thumb into his open mouth, rotating it to the rhythm of our bodies.

Mohan licked on it tenderly till I kissed him back ferociously, gripping his biceps to breathe him in.

'I'm, I will wet this bed any minute,' he howled, fluttering his eyelids and urgently sliding my hands over his hardness.

I held it there, not moving.

'Ahhhhhhh, oh, oh Meeraaaa... Meera... go slow... slower... please,' he now begged, pushing his organ out, its tip melting, clamping his own eyes shut.

Without the slightest movement, I slithered off him, thrusting my sex against his as I withdrew, Mohan's buttocks poised in mid air. Then, staring at him from a distance, I deliberately fastened my blouse, the sight of his twisted frame a new high. Enough to make me go over the edge...

'Oh... Chhotu is up,' I yelped the minute Mohan had pushed his foreskin back, fluttering my arms exasperatedly.

My words took Mohan completely by surprise as he sprung up with a start, his organ upright, pools of saliva dribbling down his chin.

'I, I didn't even know when you had walked away from me...' he rued, uncomfortably placing his palms over his crotch.

'We both completely forgot about him, I guess. I happened to look up and there Chhotu was, staring with his eyes wide open. I hope Vrinda hasn't seen us too, in this state?' I gasped, exhaling stiffly, before bending forward to scoop Chhotu into my arms.

Mohan looked down red-faced.

'See you at six then. By the way, my favourite hero is not Rajesh Khanna, Mohan. It's Amitabh Bachchan. It's what I would've written to you as well I suppose,' I smiled as he gauchely fiddled with his pajama strings.

'In any case, that was a long time ago. I should go now. I hope you don't suffer a change of heart though, this evening, changing colours or something... my Rajesh Khanna?' I giggled raunchily, placing my lips on Mohan's balmy forehead, squeezing the tip of his organ hard, before walking away.

With his head nestled in my breasts, Chhotu let out tiny air bubbles.

'Amitabh... you mean that Amitabh Bachchan, huh? Bachchan, right?' Mohan continued to fumble, sucking in his stomach.

I didn't bother glancing back. Revelling in a heightened sense of pride. The feeling a woman gets watching herself get away... the sense of winning in that one moment. Knowing somewhere it may not last... and yet not caring.

I think it mattered more than actual sex with Mohan that morning.

❧

'Are you in a hurry? Your voice seems different,' Guruji whispered, breathing heavily into the telephone.

I checked myself out in one of the window panes, one of the curtains billowing out of place just then. My ochre gharchola clung to my curves, a thin, gold waistband glinting precariously every time I moved my waist. My hair was still damp from my bath, my eyes kohl-lined, a tiny diamond nose pin facing the diminishing sunlight.

'Yes, I must leave immediately, I will miss the train otherwise, there are timings for each one here... once you miss a train... it is a really long wait... I was on my way out in fact,' I hurriedly answered, adjusting my pallu, slanting it sideways, the way a Gujarati woman is supposed to. The way I was taught to.

'What are you wearing?' he questioned slowly, undressing my thoughts.

I giggled, my hands clammy. 'I thought you could tell even such things... I mean, you've said that to me before, how you always know what is to happen... before it actually does,' I mused, inspecting the empty living room.

Vrinda and Chhotu were probably asleep. There was a minute or two of silence.

'I am told you haven't still... you know what I mean, right? How are things at home? I have been thinking of you, Meera,' he declared momentously, as a strong gust of wind blew inside.

'Mohan... Mohan is not a bad man... he is just someone I don't know too well, perhaps. Maybe the same applies to me too... intimacy needs practice, I feel. After all, in every man there exists a good and an evil side, contradictions that possibly make us all human, like it is the movies... Mohan calls it "double role"...' I cut him short.

Guruji let out a wry laugh.

'Promise to be careful now... times are bad everywhere and you are a beautiful creature, Meera... I should have taken off your nazar... if only I could have travelled to Mumbai more often... just so that we...' he groaned, his words pressed into each other.

I shuddered. 'Don't, not now, not tonight,' I don't know why I then blurted, banging the receiver down in a huff, as my heart raced.

Vrinda frowned from the doorway as I left.

'Bhabhi, even I wanted to speak to Maharaj...' she sulked, making a face.

Chhotu was bawling. Pointing in his direction, I said, 'The line just went dead suddenly. You know these Mumbai connections. Even I didn't say goodbye.'

Thirteen

'Mere sapno ki rani, kab ayegi tu?'

My hunch about Mohan was right. He was there before time, waiting for me in front of Churchgate station, his eyes eager, searching every face that poured out of the incoming Byculla local.

From a distance, Mohan looked fleetingly boyish, my heart skipping a beat at the first sight of his cleft, as he used his hands to wipe his face. His fitted brown trousers carefully cupping the round of his buttocks, its ends slightly flared. I tried recalling when he had worn the off-white, striped shirt before. His hair was neatly combed back. His moustache was trimmed to perfection. I felt a strange sense of ownership and pride. My Mohan was a handsome man.

I saw him stop a passer-by, asking him what the time was, pointing urgently to his wrist. Mohan's watch lying forgotten by our bedside table.

'Sure it's twenty past six?' he then repeated, raising his eyebrows, resembling an anxious parent. Like Bapuji, cycling furiously after dusk, manoeuvring between rows of paddy, his flimsy, cotton kurta aflutter, his hands placed near his eyes, as he squinted, bellowing Kartik's name, his voice echoing eerily. 'Kartik!' I too would scream hoarsely, chasing Bapuji's cycle, nursing a fleeting emptiness.

This was a temporary separation.

'Mohan,' I called out to him. Our glances met over the crowd.

'What will we tell Ba, in case she ever finds out? What if she asks me about this evening later? She always brings things up, when one is least expecting,' I spoke in a hushed voice, as soon as we had slipped into our cheap rexine seats; Mohan's hands having guided me down a shadowy aisle.

Giant images flickered up and down on a translucent screen up ahead; the sound was deafening. I kept my eyes fixed on the ground as we moved forward, lest I trip. My heart beat frantically; my throat was parched from the heat.

This was our first outing after marriage... alone. This was my first outing with a man. Ever. How would this evening end?

'What took you so long? Didn't you board the train I had instructed you to? It shouldn't have taken you this much time to reach Churchgate; we've missed the 6 p.m. show. We're lucky they had a later one,' Mohan remarked in an equally low tone, sounding slightly annoyed.

'Here, have some popcorn... you didn't eat anything earlier too, on our way out from the station. Now that we've only managed to catch the 8.45 show, we'll reach home really late. *Aradhana* is a long picture, maybe we should leave before it ends...' he resumed, passing me the bag. Back in Sinor, the popcorn was plain: no butter; usually something we indulged in at the village fair. I licked my lips savouring the taste.

'Umm... this is delicious!' I groaned.

Mohan smiled. 'Drink this when you're done; I've purchased a cola for us. You tend to get thirsty after too many of these, I always do...' Mohan added clasping a cola bottle firmly. He went on: 'I've asked Bansi to spend the night at the new shop, in case I'm not back by half past ten, which frankly looks like a distant possibility now. Actually I bribed him by saying I would fill in the whole of next week...' Mohan resumed, after I'd taken my first sip.

Our glances met once more before Mohan slipped his fingers into mine, his left knee brushing against my right thigh, our lips grease-lined.

'Isn't Sharmila Tagore really beautiful?' he mused dreamily, leaning in closer.

'Why couldn't we have sat there instead? Most of the seats are empty in the front rows... look? I can hardly see the heroine's face, so many tall people crowding our view. Couldn't we have got something other than this last row, and, and that too the corner most seats,' I sullenly retorted, my eyes travelling down the length of the auditorium.

'These seats are special. Trust me, they are the best in the house, we are lucky these were not taken,' Mohan chided, cupping my cheeks lightly.

I shivered, blushing at being touched in a public place, feeling like a newlywed for the first time.

For a while, we watched the movie in silence. Sharmila Tagore, the leading lady was indeed breathtaking. But, it was Rajesh Khanna who stole the show; his slanted smile making me deliciously giddy every time he'd saunter in, torn between serenading his lady love and flying a fighter jet.

'You know, this film does seem oddly familiar. I think I've seen a poster of it back home,' I murmured, my eyes riveted.

Mohan munched on popcorn. 'Could be... *Aradhana* broke all records when it released. No wonder it's has been re-released in Mumbai so many times, in various halls around town. Such films never really get old, Meera. So, now you know why this hall is so deserted! Thank God for that, though,' he added candidly, shrugging his shoulders.

A song had started by then, a train passing us by, taking me back in time.

I was miles away when all of a sudden I felt Mohan's hand climb up my right thigh, pausing expectantly at the entry to my sex. I pushed it back, a shudder running down my spine. Mohan grinned suggestively, inching closer, my denial turning him on, his eyes ablaze.

'*Mere sapno ki rani, kab ayegi tu?*' Rajesh Khanna crooned, his strawberry lips moving in slow motion. Like Mohan's fingers that probed insistently at my flesh, sifting impatiently through the folds of my expensive gharchola sari, a gift from Binal. *'Wear this on the day your husband first takes you out... when you both are alone... just the two of you. It slides off easily – look,'* I remembered her whispering in my ears; months before my wedding had been formalized.

'God! You women really know how to frustrate a man... this sari knot takes forever to undo. Did you have to fasten it so damn tightly? And... and this petticoat also...' he muttered, his movements restive.

Slowly, I turned to face Mohan, his moustache grazing my upper lip, before his left hand dug into my blouse, squeezing me through the soft fabric.

'What, what if someone sees us like this?' I whispered huskily, grabbing his collar.

Without a word, Mohan plunged lower on my breasts, sucking slowly at the top, his tongue ice-cold, his fingers pulling at the tips.

Just then someone coughed noisily in the row behind us. I jerked off his mouth in haste, pulling up my pallu at once, my insides aflame.

Mohan returned to watching the movie.

The song had ended.

❧

Before long, Mohan had started stroking me again, pushing my sari down clumsily, his hands probing, as did his tongue. I was dripping wet, the moistness starting to flow out of me, like the warm butter from the popcorn oozing down our fingers.

I clamped my thighs, desperate to keep my eyes focused on the screen somehow. Sharmila Tagore and Rajesh Khanna were about to make love in a log cabin, their hands everywhere, their faces equally tortured. Before the scene ended, Mohan had pushed his left thumb right up my sex, throbbing with tenderness.

I lolled my head backward, trying to remember the words of the song as Mohan dug deeper and deeper. Opening and closing my eyes, my sari hitched up; my petticoat now loosened from the sides, a couple of my blouse hooks unfastened. When his hips pulsated up and down, I rotated my waist, picking up speed... before slowing down again; convulsing the minute his palms had cupped my rawness.

'Meeraaa...' he shuddered kicking off his sandals, his right foot riding up my side, forcing my legs apart.

I pressed into his toes, biting my lips in desperation.

'Ahhhhh,' I moaned feverishly, pulling his chin up, our tongues on fire.

Mohan's fingers kneaded my hips.

'Go, go slow...' I whispered before nestling my mouth at the side of his neck, reaching out for his trouser front at the same time.

'Nahiiiiiiiiiin,' someone shrieked hysterically on screen, catching me off-guard.

I sat up with a start. Rajesh Khanna's body was lying lifeless.

'What, oh God, what happened to him? To Rajesh... I mean...' I fumbled, curbing my own temptations.

Just then the lights came back on.

Mohan glanced down sneakily, his face stricken, his fingers glistening with my raw juices, his zipper undone.

'We can still do it, the hall's practically empty, at least on our side,' I urged, pretending to keep my eyes ahead, suddenly emboldened, my body craving more.

Mohan squirmed uncomfortably.

I dragged my sari over my knees, touching his arms once before I slowly parted his thighs. Hoping it would act as a sign.

'It's going to get dark again, right? The movie isn't over yet? I mean what about the other Rajesh Khanna you told me about earlier?' I spoke fast, running my hands lower to stroke his navel, squeezing the top of his organ, hoping to be rewarded.

The lights dying gradually as I delved deeper inside his inners, using my pallu to cover his crotch.

Another song was on by then.

'Mohan, what... what? What happened?' I gasped, letting go of his shaft at once, as he closed his knees, his lips tightly pursed. 'It's, it's, the... your...' I stammered, extricating my hands clumsily, as Mohan's sticky discharge spread rapidly in the spaces between my fingers.

Mohan looked away, his eyes frozen.

'I'm sorry Mohan, I... I didn't realize you've, that you had, so, so fast... I mean...' I paused, tongue-tied.

It was the first time I had really known something was wrong. I had been right about Mohan all along.

❦

We were quiet on our way back, my insides still flushed with dampness. The compartment was quite deserted. It was nearly midnight.

From time to time, I'd look up at Mohan's face, hoping to meet his eye, but he was quiet and withdrawn.

I began to wonder if it was my fault again that we had failed in a sense. Was sustaining his virility a problem? Or a part of something more complex? Was that why he could never fully penetrate me? His organ falling lifeless within a matter of seconds... or not coming to life at all?

Was that the reason I wasn't getting pregnant?

Thoughts raced through my head as I grappled with broaching the topic with Mohan. I reached out to hold his hand but he pushed me away.

'In every man there exists a good and an evil side, contradictions that possibly make us all human,' I replayed parts of my earlier conversation with Guruji, his concern mocking me now; the way I had probably sounded, supremely overconfident about being right about my own husband; needing to be right this time. Not realizing that it was me who I was actually wrong about.

I still cared.

Fourteen

'There was a fire...'

We'll have to walk home. It seems, there has been a major accident on the parallel line, all the incoming trains are stalled. Can't say exactly when the services will be resumed,' Mohan reported, as I sat clasping my purse, my eyes searching all over the station for him. It had been more than half an hour since he had gone along with some other male passengers, jumping off from our compartment onto the platform.

'How far is it? Home, I mean? Where are we exactly?' I questioned softly, looking up in his direction.

Mohan's face was in the shadows, his shirt completely drenched in sweat. 'Depends on how fast we can walk – shouldn't take more than forty minutes, I suppose,' he replied, dabbing his forehead.

'What accident was it?' I asked as Mohan helped me out.

'Apparently, a major fire broke out in one of the compartments... we'll know the details only tomorrow, in the morning papers,' he replied, panting laboriously, as we scurried up a narrow flight of stairs.

The walk back was long. It was also completely dark by then, most of the streetlights blurred in the ashen afterglow of the evening showers that had retreated since.

Mohan kept to himself. Every now and then I would lag behind by a few steps, my sari feeling slippery, like the moist pavements we treaded on.

'Mohan,' I cried out his name, standing at the entrance of a murky by-lane.

He was almost halfway down the middle.

'Mohan!' I yelled louder, taking slow steps, my soles tiring.

'What's the matter? C'mon buck up,' he cried from afar, holding his hands over his eyes, his chest panting, like mine.

I looked around. A mangy street dog slept soundly a few feet away, stretched out on its stomach, its tail twitching from time to time. There was no one except us.

For a couple of seconds, I remained motionless.

'What's the matter? It is not safe here, besides as I said, we should be home soon. Hurry up now, Meera,' Mohan barked, grabbing my shoulders, appearing out of the shadows.

I stood unmoved, my back pressed against a wall plastered with faded film posters, some still wet, a faint line of moisture trickling down the side of my face.

Mohan grabbed the top of my right arm, roughly poking my breasts. 'Don't you realize what time it is, Meera? God knows whether Vrinda Ben will even open the door for us at this unearthly hour? The damn trains also...' he spoke in a high-pitched tone, agitatedly glancing downwards as I vexed my toes.

'I, I wanted to say something... before we actually got home,' I replied slowly, leaning closer.

'Go on... what's all this sudden fuss? As if time is running away?'

'What if it is, Mohan?' I whispered, adding as I ran up to him, panting steadily, 'What if now is all we have? Everything else just happening for a reason...'

The dog let out a fierce growl.

I cringed, clutching Mohan's collar, as we held each other real close, our bodies pressed tautly.

'Meera, must we dissect each thing between us, and that too, at all odd hours? You ought to get your head examined...' he grumbled, before releasing himself.

'I know, but what I meant is maybe things didn't go as planned... in the hall earlier... for you. But tonight, this moment, Mohan isn't about who climaxed first or how long it took for us to get there... it was the first time we were ever alone... no Ba, no Bansi, no Vrinda... not even Chhotu. So call me selfish or foolish, but I don't want this night to end... to reach home,' I pressed my lips down on his, quickly slipping in my tongue.

Mohan pushed my face away with both his hands.

'You're not to ever breathe a word about what happened to anyone, Meera, do you understand? No one should ever know that we were out for a movie, like this, okay?' he growled, pushing up my chin, as I pulled him back, grabbing his buttocks roughly.

'I know when to lie, okay? Besides, Vrinda and Chhotu are probably fast asleep now, so, so there is no point really in rushing back home and waking them up. Let's make the most of what we have... this night,' I teased, kissing Mohan passionately once again, this time deeper.

Mohan didn't react at first. So I ran my fingers along his chest, planting wet kisses all over his shirt, reaching down for his crotch, before cupping his balls, feeling his stare solidify.

'C'mon, Meera, it's very late, this is dangerous... what if...' the rest of his words drowned as my hands stroked his shaft vigorously, pushing down the zipper impatiently, my hips pressed into his.

What if this was our last night alone? What if there was really one Mohan? The one who always felt so detached, so indifferent to my desires?

My thoughts collided with each other.

Slowly, Mohan began moving his mouth, initially to protest perhaps, as we locked lips lustily, grinding my waist sensuously against his trouser front.

I shuddered, feeling his fingers climb up my body, pausing just under my breasts, as I licked the bristles on his moustache, feeling strangely possessed.

A car passed on the parallel road, its headlights piercing the dark.

'Mohan, oh...' I moaned feverishly, feeling an inexplicable trepidation as he covered my mouth with his in an instant.

'*Shiiiiish*, keep your voice down, woman,' he said cautiously, his left thumb rolling inside.

It was enough to push me off the edge.

'Meera, stop, this is a public place...' Mohan groaned.

But it was too late, as I had sunk to my knees, caressing below his navel.

'Ohhh... Meera... you... must stop at once,' he spoke with great difficulty as I closed my mouth over his swollenness, feeling ravenous.

The dog was up. It snarled at us from a distance, baring its fangs, its eyes glowing sinisterly in the half-light. With his left arm entwined around my waist, Mohan dragged me behind the car, his trousers dropping down all at once.

The risk turning us both on.

Or maybe... our fears were the same.

❦

'What's the matter? Why is there such a huge crowd here now, huh?' Mohan repeated frantically, as we jostled inside our narrow lane, overflowing with faces.

Some familiar.

Some strange.

Some sad.

Some surprised.

Some grave.

Some gaunt.

Some with their eyes closed, as if they had been sleepwalking, their lips bloodless.

'What's going on? Will someone speak?' Mohan questioned in a shrill voice, urgently patting an elderly gentleman's stooping shoulders.

'Where were you all this while, beta? You are Mohan Patel, aren't you?' the man spoke in a slow voice, his eyes lowered.

'Yes, I am Mohan. Is, is something wrong with Vrinda Ben, I mean, my sister-in-law? Why are the lights on in all the flats... in ours too, this time of the night? Is Chhotu okay? I think I just saw someone standing with him by our window,' Mohan retorted frenziedly, his lips trembling.

'Mohan Bhai, where have you been you all this while? We've been looking all over for you. Where did you disappear this way? Vrinda Bhabhi said you'd gone to Matunga, for dinner, some distant cousin from Badi Bhabhi's native town apparently... so, so we went there too, asking around for the address that Meera Bhabhi had mentioned before she left alone to join you,' a young man, whom I had often noticed accompanying Bansi home from the shop said, dashing forward, his face lined with sweat, his shirt tattered in places, his cheeks darkened with soot. He smelt strange.

Grabbing him by the collar, Mohan now hollered, 'Will someone tell me what's the problem? And Raju, what the hell are you doing here this late? Weren't you supposed to give Bansi company at the new shop tonight, in case I didn't turn show up at the stipulated time? Is, is Bansi at home too? Was that his shadow I just saw? Answer me, Raju... why are you crying?'

Mr Deshmukh, our next-door neighbour raced out just then, clad in a crumpled, cotton kurta pajama, his beard unshaven, his eyelids swollen. 'Beta, we've been searching high and low for you. The police are here. You better go inside immediately,' he stated grimly.

'What, why are the police here? Good lord! I know I got late coming home with Meera... but that's because of that accident that took place, near Marine Lines. There was a fire,' Mohan explained clumsily, the crowds growing in strength.

My eyes scoured the stairway that faced us, hoping to at least locate Chhotu. Was he asleep? I asked myself.

A man in a khaki uniform stepped aside just then, pushing back a retinue of people. 'Mohan Patel?' he hollered, pointing up ahead.

I shifted back, covering my head at once.

'Are you Mr Mohan Patel?' he repeated as Mohan pushed his way ahead of me.

'Yes, yes... I am Mohan, Mohan Patel. Sorry sahib, I had just gone out. I mean, with my wife. We're newly married, you see. I had no idea one simple outing would create such a major hullabaloo, disturbing all the residents of the colony. Actually, my wife Meera, she, she's just come from her native town to Mumbai, so I'd taken her to watch a film, in Colaba side, sahib. Then we thought of stopping over to have some bhel... first time... you know how it is, sahib. It was a Rajesh Khanna picture also... super hit sahib, a real classic. She, my wife just wouldn't take no for an answer. You know how these dickris are no, sahib?' Mohan babbled in a juvenile fashion, folding his hands.

'Which show?' the Sub-Inspector probed, sizing me up from the corner of his eye.

I fidgeted uncomfortably, running my hands over my stomach. Was my sari completely dishevelled?

'8.45 sahib, we, actually couldn't make it for the earlier show... you see, she, my wife Meera missed the train that she was supposed to have taken... she's new here, inexperienced in all this... it was all her fault...' he stuttered, looking flummoxed.

'What? What did you just say, Badi Bhabhi and you were out watching a film?'

In the distance I thought I heard Vrinda's voice.

'Mohan Bhaiyya, is, is it you... Mohan... Bhaiyya are you really back?' she ran into his arms, as everyone gasped, stepping aside to make space.

'Vrinda Ben, don't worry any more, I'm back now, as, as is Meera Bhabhi... all is well. I, I will never go away like this again... I swear on, on Chhotu,' he tried placating Vrinda as she clung to his shirt, mumbling incoherently as tears streamed down the sides of her face. Her lips pressed to Mohan's chest.

'There was really a fire Vrinda Ben, believe me. It's why we got unduly delayed. There was no way of informing you either, us stranded in the middle of nowhere, finally walking back home,' Mohan reiterated, pulling up her chin to wipe her eyes.

Vrinda remained inconsolable, whimpering like Chhotu, pulling Mohan into her.

'There, there was a fire, Mohan Bhaiyya,' she howled, burying her face into the side of his neck.

Mrs Deshmukh who had followed Vrinda out, along with some other ladies from our housing society, let out a deafening wail.

Vrinda collapsed to the ground. 'There was a fire, there... there was a fire Mohan Bhaiyya,' she kept wailing incoherently, saliva dribbling down her chin.

'Where's Chhotu? Someone tell me where is the little boy?' I interrupted, surging ahead impatiently, staring blankly at the faces in the assembled crowd, most of them bowing their heads low as soon as our glances confronted.

'Mr Mohan, we need you to come to the police station right away... do you understand? Hello...' the Sub-Inspector stated authoritatively, crouching beside Mohan as he too squatted on the ground.

He looked up slowly. 'But why, what have I done, sahib?' Mohan asked in bewilderment.

'There was a fire,' the inspector answered coldly.

'Mohan Bhaiyya,' Raju grimly interjected. 'A fire broke out at our shop, somewhere between 9.45 and 10 pm... spreading like wildfire within seconds... everything was gutted, gone in an instant. I was out to make a phone call. Someone snapped the electrical fuses it seems... nothing remains Bhaiyya... everything is charred, all, all the dress materials, the mannequins, the shelves, the cash... even the person inside... everything covered in soot.'

Mohan staggered behind a few steps, covering his mouth in horror.

'Praful!' he let out a violent cry.

'Bansi,' the inspector cut him short.

Mohan glanced up, tears starting to stream down his eyes this time.

'Your younger brother Bansi was at the shop when the fire broke out... only one dead body has been recovered until now, we need you to identify the corpse, so that post- mortem procedures can start. This is a police case,' he added matter-of-factly, beginning to drag Mohan away.

'What a night this has been... major fire at Marine Lines too it seems, have you people heard? God knows what's happening to this city... looks like we will burn in hell soon!' Mr Deshmukh mumbled, as the crowds began to disperse slowly.

Soon everyone had left. Except Vrinda.

She stood opposite me now, her lips trembling with an unspoken rage, before she pointed at me accusingly. It was a look I knew well.

Fifteen

Amavasya

Mohan only returned home the following evening, his eyes bloodshot, his face haggard, his lips chapped, his shirt soaking wet, his sandals covered with traces of ash, one of the straps torn. The house was filled with grieving relatives and family friends. Hushed whispers rose and fell, the air heavy with the scent of sandalwood agarbattis.

Ba had been informed. She was at the ashram. Raju diligently recounted how she had fainted on hearing the news. She had been apparently fasting since the night before.

It was the last Amavasya in the monthly lunar cycle. The curse of the dark moon is how Guruji would later describe the incident, on a long distance trunk call. He was away on a retreat to Rishikesh the night Bansi died, some of his disciples bitterly lamented, blaming his absence for the horrible tragedy that had befallen us.

It would take years for Mohan to recover the damages, one of our neighbours commented woefully, covering his mouth for a few seconds, fighting back his tears, his guilt-ridden eyes heavy with regret.

And what about the sky-high pile of staggering debts, the sahukars known to extract their pound of flesh? How on earth would they ever be repaid? By whom? From what? There was nothing left anyway. Everything we had managed to save from selling the old shop was stuck in investments for the second store that would now never see the light of day.

Only a trail of ashes remained... I overheard Vrinda sobbing hysterically, covering her face in her hands, every few seconds, as she squatted on the floor in Ba's room, surrounded by the colony women in their pale off-white saris. The bedsheet was crumpled. It's where she lay asleep with her son when the news first reached her, they whispered to one another, pulling their pallus closer.

I swallowed hard, my head reeling as I tried making sense of the events... Every now and then Bansi's ever-smiling face would flash before my eyes. He had been my only friend in this house... in this city... in my marriage. I took a deep breath thinking of the last time we had met. Here. In the same kitchen where I now stood.

'You look different, Bhabhi,' he had whispered, as I placed a hot toast on his steel plate.

I laughed.

'And you've been smoking again, Chhote?' I made a face, moving away.

It was a private joke.

Bansi followed me out as always and watched me hang out Mohan's underwear, which I had washed earlier. 'You look happy,' he had whispered under his breath.

I never asked him what he meant. I was too busy enjoying Mohan's attention as his eyes climbed my back from the hallway.

'Mere sapno ki rani...' the words drifted in from somewhere...

Like it was only yesterday...

My thoughts were suddenly disrupted when Chhotu let out a fierce wail, trying to locate his mother's plump breast, before she passed him on to someone else, again.

All day, I was in and out of the kitchen, making endless cups of tea and lime sherbet, refilling dozens of empty glasses, passing around stale biscuits on a rectangular steel tray.

I hadn't changed. The gharchola sari from Binal was now completely crumpled and in disarray... my eyes inflamed from crying...

There were people everywhere.

I barely registered when Mohan had actually walked in, or how long he had spent by Vrinda's side, constantly kissing Chhotu's forehead. He had left the house once again by the time most of our guests departed. This time for Bansi's cremation. Vrinda too was missing.

'She kept insisting that no one could stop her from seeing her husband's face one last time. With the post-mortem and all the formalities of investigation, it was pointless getting the body home, all the way to Byculla. Besides, his body was badly burnt. Mohan would have had to first seek permission from the Society Committee before bringing a hearse in through these gates. It's too much trouble and besides it's not as if Bansi will ever come back,' one of Ba's acquaintances rued, as I stood with my head lowered.

'Oh no... Badi Bahu, look!' one of the visiting women shrieked as soon as I'd left the entrance to Ba's room, my shoulders caving in with the weight of the tray, spilling over with heavy garlands and half-filled cups.

Most of the flowers had wilted.

'Badi Bahu... you are menstruating... just look at the blood on the floor. Didn't you know you were due?'

I tried saying something.

'This happens to be a sacred spot reserved for the performance of the puja for Bansi. Guruji has personally instructed us to conduct the formalities here, so that his soul can peacefully reach the next world. Just look at what you've done now, contaminating this entire area with your impure blood! We will have to cleanse the area with Gangajal, all over again...' she hollered frantically.

More blood streamed down my legs.

'I can clean it. Just give me a few minutes, please. I'll just change and be back within...' I muttered, lowering my eyes, embarrassed at the outrage, the collective ire of a bunch of women whom I bumped into, almost every day.

'No... no, please Badi Bahu, you'll ruin everything again. As it is, from the time you've stepped into this Patel parivaar, there has been one misfortune after another. God knows what more is in store for these poor folks?' someone else said, clicking her tongue in utter disdain.

'Means she's failed to conceive again... bechari...' another woman piped in.

I didn't look back.

'Arre, she must be suffering from some major gynaecological kharabi. No wonder the parents married off such a gorgeous looking girl to these Patels. Mohan is at least a decade older than her. I mean, who doesn't know the hardships this family has suffered, all their financial constraints... starting with the father's sudden death... forced to sell everything and relocate to Mumbai? To be honest, I was myself shocked when I saw Badi Bahu the first day. She looked like a queen, a high and mighty queen trapped in this modest colony. Peaches and cream complexion, ruby red lips, silky, wavy hair cascading down to her slim waist, long, black eyelashes... and what a perfect figure. She could easily have given these Mumbai actresses a run for their money...'

I grabbed a dining table chair, pressing my thighs together, desperate to stop myself from bleeding further, somehow.

The women continued to chatter idly amongst themselves.

'Maybe this will be Meera's agnipareeksha... if she does actually have an illicit affair. Bored with her own life, this marriage, no kids yet, trapped in this rotten hole, with a husband like Mohan who can never match her sex appeal... or...' the rest of the words trailed.

The word 'agnipareeksha' felt vaguely familiar. I swallowed hard, looking up as I did to confront a silent gaze. As a pair of doe-shaped eyes stared back from a printed portrait that hung on the opposite wall. A woman stood at its centre, bedecked in a rich Benarasi sari, dripping precious diamonds, her unruly tresses flowing like the night, her cherry lips parted. The man beside her balanced a heavy bow in his arms. His face was serene in comparison to hers. Ram and Sita.

'Agnipareeksha...' the word returned to my lips again and again, as I wondered what Sita's own life had meant?

Not the Goddess. The woman. The wife.

If she were trapped in a stale, lifeless marriage... or actually fell in love, after she had been kidnapped by Ravana? What if the man who destroyed her was the one who desired her the most? What if she was just paying the price? For the simple irony of her own fate. Condemned and tarnished because she was wanted by someone else. For a temptation that wasn't even hers.

'Sita's Curse,' I remembered Bapuji having once said.

The next few weeks were a blur. All I recall is the unending pujas and havans in our cramped apartment. Every corner of the house was smoke-infested, the chant of complex Sanskrit shlokas resounded everywhere, together with the aroma of desi ghee and heaps of white flowers. Men in saffron robes walked in and out of Ba's room, their lips pursed in sacred silence, their heads shaved, their eyes glowing starkly, even during the day, like Guruji's when he had asked me to kneel before him, commanding obedience.

I watched them from afar, nursing a fleeting attraction. Their torsos were bare; their privates covered by a scrap of unstitched clothing, their wooden clogs scraping the floor.

On Ba's orders, I had been confined to the other bedroom.

'Until she's completely well, Badi Bahu must remain inside... I don't want any further mishaps. We've already paid for one night of carelessness,' she instructed, before turning her face away obstinately.

I hardly saw Mohan in the weeks after Bansi's death.

Mrs Deshmukh would place my food before me on a daily basis, on the ground, outside the entrance. I had to wait till they departed, forbidden as I was from touching any of them. Most of the items were ice cold by the time I managed to finish my meal, in abject silence, staring out, secretly wishing for the rains, dreaming of waking up next to Kartik.

Wondering what he would have done if he were alive today. If he saw me this way, huddled in an airless corner, my tresses tangled, my eyelids heavy with exhaustion, my wrists bare. I shivered, running my hands over my thighs, one of my anklets slipping out just then, making a soft noise.

As if Kartik were listening. In hiding somewhere...

Like him, maybe Bansi too was better off being dead; I told myself, closing my eyes, envying him in a sense, especially, the fanfare about his life – the fastidiousness of all the rituals that were now being performed in his honour. As if the dead can ever be resurrected...

Could death be the safest way of staying alive then? Thoughts formed and melted...

❦

'May I come in?' someone asked in a hushed voice, pushing the door slightly ajar.

Guruji looked older, his face leaner, the muscles on his arms wired. His beard grizzled grey. Watching him walk towards me with a slight limp, I lowered my head.

'How are you, Meera? How have you been?' he cleared his throat, glancing in my direction, as I crouched by the bed.

I'd forgotten just how tall he was.

'I'm well. I, I don't know what else to say... I mean... you probably blame me for everything that's happened – like the rest of them,' my voice caved in as I shifted back a few inches, covering my toes with the coarse khadi cloth that I was made to don.

'You look beautiful, Meera... you always know how to take my breath away...' he responded serenely, bolting the door, before making his way up to me again.

I bit my lips, tasting my own blood.

'I don't know... everything seems to have changed overnight in this house... in my life, it's like I don't belong here anymore...' I grimaced, touching my own forehead, oozing dampness.

He bowed lower, staring at the movement of my mouth.

'Or maybe it is just the beginning, Meera; the real test of your faith...' he slanted his lips in a peculiar way.

Defensively, I placed my arms over my chest.

'Faith or fate? What kind of faith says you must lock up a woman this way?' I don't know why I screamed, my lower lip quivering in the oppressive afternoon heat.

Guruji flopped down beside me. Taking my hands in his, he whispered slowly, 'Fate and faith are the same, one always testing the other. You cannot escape it; it is nature's way. Suffering is universal... it is our karma.'

'Have you ever felt as if you don't have all the answers? I mean... that maybe this is all you will ever be? Searching, just like everyone else? A man of flesh and blood...' I cut him short, probably sounding embittered as his breath grazed the nape of my neck.

Guruji closed his eyes for a while, before slowly replying, 'As long as I don't forget... is that what you are trying to imply?'

'Forgetting is the hardest. It's all I want to do, these days... if only I could start afresh... if only we all got what we wanted... everything...' I sighed wistfully, my tresses falling limp over my eyes.

Guruji traced my lips with his fingers. Before wrapping his arms around me. 'If that were true... then where would we begin? Here, in this room... or... or where we left off?'

I shrugged my shoulders, trying to rise.

'I don't think about that night anymore. There is no point. Our worlds are different...' I couldn't complete the rest of the sentence.

Guruji pulled me roughly to his chest, muttering all the while, 'But, I can't ever forget you, Meera... no matter how hard I try. Your beauty is my sadhana... the sole object of my sanyas, my meditation, the reason I renounce this world... surrendering everything to live the life of an ascetic... I worship your Shakti... the power in those eyes... the way you destroy me...'

The rains commenced all of a sudden.

I made my way towards the open window, holding out my hands.

'Is my presence making you uncomfortable in some way, Meera? Or am I just asking too many difficult questions?' Guruji probed, the rudraksh beads around his neck rattling as he followed me to where I stood.

'Ba says I'm not to be in contact with anyone during this phase. What if I contaminate you too?' I professed vulnerably, shutting the window with a thud.

'I'm not the kind of man who is scared of consequences,' he asserted, tugging at my earlobes.

'You say that as if you are going away...' I raised my voice.

'That will depend on how you have viewed my absence... in all this while. All I can tell you, at this point, is that I wish to embark on an eternal maun vrat, travelling to a place much beyond the Himalayas this time. Further than the snow-capped mountains, to drown in the river of eternal truth, delving into the very sutra of human life, the way it has been described in our ancient texts. The Promised Land beckons, Meera... I depart tomorrow at the crack of dawn,' Guruji summarized, the ashen stripes on his forehead glowing forcefully.

I dropped my hands by my side.

'What if I followed you there?' I mused as he let out a loud laugh. 'Did I say something wrong? I was only trying to say goodbye...'

'Then say it again, Meera... say goodbye like you mean it... the way you and I had first... by the river... that flows from one birth to another... take me with you...' he chided, pulling my chin up tenderly, his beard caressing my cheeks.

Tears rolled down the side of my face. The evening havan had just started. Frenzied footsteps rose and fell outside the door.

'Why start something we can't end? Besides, it's time for you to conduct the prayers...' I held out, suddenly cautious.

'What's the worst that can happen, Meera? What is the maximum limit of your personal suffering? Before you realize it is all nothing but a trick being played by the universe, testing you again?' he probed philosophically, his swarthy hands resting on my breasts.

I eased away.

'I want to breathe... I want to taste the rains... drown in my own desires...' I exhaled after a lengthy pause.

'Desire has no language Meera... only signs,' Guruji whispered, undraping my sari slowly, before pushing my blouse over my head.

I wasn't wearing a brassiere.

'Maharaj...' I shuddered as he led me away; moving in swift strokes towards the clothes cupboard, yanking open one of its doors. We embraced, before I could speak, Guruji clasping me firmly as our bodies melted, like old times... like the first time.

By the time I opened my eyes, Guruji was standing stark naked facing me; his manhood oddly pressed between his brawny thighs. 'You look more serene in a way... it's what I wanted to say to you when you first walked in,' I confessed, staring deeply into his eyes.

'You should have then,' he took a deep breath, bringing his mouth down over mine.

I groaned as my insides came alive, the soreness of the past few days miraculously ebbing into nothingness. My breath quickened as Guruji's fingers reached for my navel, breathing in the scent of my own moistness. I thought of Mohan in the next room.

'Your hands feel the same... oh Meeraaaa...' Guruji murmured passionately, as I carefully arched my back, resting my hips on a pile of clothes stuffed haphazardly inside one of the many shelves, my nipples directly pointing at his face.

Guruji swirled his tongue around both, nibbling at them from beneath, while simultaneously shoving his knees between mine. All my memories rushed back as he pushed my shoulders down, thrusting my feet in the air. For a long time, we kissed like long lost lovers before he gently disentangled his mouth to run his tongue over my ankles instead, sucking on my soles with deliberate relish, his left thumb stroking my wetness all the while.

I locked my legs around Guruji's buttocks, wanting to be conquered by his suppleness.

'Meera...' was all he said, his eyes changing colour as he positioned my buttocks on the hard edge of the bed.

'Take me to the Promised Land... once,' I quivered, aflame on a slow fire, watching Guruji ease himself into me, while I stroked his swollenness.

I gripped his neck, moving up a few feet, as he shoved his manhood in me completely, plunging in and out with a crude force, squeezing my nipples, his left thumb rubbing on the opening of my sex.

'Take me with you...' I groaned, each time he pushed harder, his balls slapping against my skin, sending me into a sedated spell.

'I go where you go, it has been that way since the beginning...' he whispered at last, throwing my legs upwards.

I squealed, losing balance, before he expertly gripped my ankles, hauling the rest of me up, as I literally hung upside down on the mattress, balanced on my head, watching the world in reverse, a slow descent of sorts.

Guruji squatted over me, carefully inserting his thumb into my rear, grinding it in preparation of his final descent, his organ throbbing with ripeness.

I bit my lower lip, unable to fight back my own climax, moaning recklessly when he launched his full erection, my walls stretched to the hilt, his arms manoeuvring my limbs acrobatically, as we remained like that... like a sculpted mural on the walls of an ancient temple, somewhere.

My head falling backwards on the pillow as I writhed with pleasure, taking turns as we were... grinding my hips faster, to savour every ounce of Guruji's robustness... needing to be filled, and drunk... to be partaken... and punished.

'Turn over Meera... now...' someone commanded in a cold voice. It was torture to look up.

✦

'Badi Bahu, are you okay? Can you open your eyes...' was the first thing I heard.

'Think it's the heat... the havans over the past few weeks, the trauma of the last few days...' slowly I deciphered the second comment.

'Where is Mohan? Is he back?' someone else quizzed, yanking the cover off my face.

'You haven't been eating at all. Most of your food has remained untouched. You could've starved at this rate. Your blood pressure is dangerously low...' I recognized Mrs Mukherjee, one of our neighbours as she hovered above my face.

I tried saying something, but my throat felt completely parched. 'Where am I?' was all I could manage.

A tall man in a white coat forced me to lie still on my back. He had a stethoscope and was checking my vital signs.

'You are slightly better now Mrs Patel. Maybe it was the severe shock, coupled with the excessive bleeding... and the lack of food... the heat naturally adding to your fatigue... your ill health. You must take complete rest from now... your last cycle was very heavy. I will refer you to a good lady doctor, someone you can trust...' he said.

'Where is Guruji? Amarkant Maharaj? Has he left?' I frantically questioned, finding it tough to form a full sentence.

Ba pushed her way forward then.

'Guruji has not come at all, Badi Bahu. One of his disciples Swami Shivanand replaced him... Swamiji who has been one of Guruji's most trusted aides, ever since Amarkant Maharaj left his abode as a young man, in search of the Promised Land...' she paused prophetically, as I gulped for some air.

Someone pushed open the window. A warm breeze blew, caressing the corners of my mouth.

'Promised Land?' I questioned feebly, wiping my eyes.

Ba was speaking to the man who had examined me earlier. She glanced back in the direction of the bed, saying, 'Guruji does not like to talk about his life... mentioning only once during a satsang about how he had a dream as a teenager, of a young girl drowning in a mighty river, the water filling her lungs. Guruji had saved her it seems, diving into the rough waters... his eyes bleeding, as they clung on desperately, literally breathing life into one another.'

I sat up, my heart pounding.

'The vision was to alter the course of his own life, Guruji told us, before falling back into a meditative spell. "In her eyes, I saw Sita – the emblem of Shakti – the beginning of the path that I am to eventually take," his disciples often repeat his words. It was Guruji's mother who found him lying lifeless by the neighbouring river in their village, the next day, his body tinged blue, like he'd been bitten by a venomous cobra or something, rushing him at once to a renowned witch doctor, known to have brought back many children from the brink of death. Guruji recovered in time, though he claims he was never the same, the same dream recurring again after a few months, occuring almost every night till he finally disappeared, in search of that young girl who stared back at him ever so often. Her eyes haunting him every waking moment,' Ba let out a slow sigh, as I tried looking away.

'His followers at the ashram insist Guruji is only in the middle path of his sadhna... saying it's only a matter of time before he makes his final journey towards the Promised Land... beyond the veil of civilization...'

I gulped it down in silence.

'You are fortunate that on Guruji's request, Swami Shivanand came to Mumbai... just in time in a way, insisting on blessing you after the completion of Bansi's funeral, you must've done a lot of punya, Beti,' Mrs Deshmukh said, cupping my face.

'I don't remember anything... except I was alone in this room...' I think I raised my voice.

'You must have been unconscious by then, having collapsed by the side of the bed. It was Swamiji who discovered you unconscious. Insisting on being by your side for all the time you slipped in and out of your drowsiness, performing a yajna at dawn today to ward off the evil spirits from this house, before he finally departed,' she resumed.

'Where's, where is Mohan?' I questioned with difficulty, searching Ba's eyes.

'Mohan is out... he's found a job at one of the neighbouring shops in Crawford Market as a watchman. They've taken him in for now, more out of sympathy, till he finds something else, something better...' Ba informed stiffly.

'Watchman? How, how long has he been gone? How long have I been lying this way?' I shuddered, my thoughts confused.

'Your stars are all messed up, Badi Bahu. Shani is once again ascendant it seems in your birth chart, and so, this is the price my poor son has to pay... all of us having to suffer with him. Mohan, my darling boy, such an educated chap, such a good son... your parents cheated us and got you married...' Ba snapped, wailing loudly till she was led away.

I walked to the window. There was no moon that night, the Mumbai skyline a menacing mass of sameness. I took a deep breath, trying to segregate fact from fiction; a part of me still doubtful if I had dreamt it all up... Not knowing how long I actually stood there either. Not being sure of too much any longer, except that one half of my life had just concluded.

'Ghor amavasya... the dark cycle of the moon...' I recalled Mrs Mukherjee whisper while walking out of my room earlier, worry writ all over her face.

As I stared at the colony gates, I wondered how long I would have to wait before the next half of my journey commenced. And what would become of the years in between.

The ones in the middle... the ones no one talked about or wrote home about either. The difficult years, the diffident years, the years between the years... the ones often not counted... in the final tally.

The middle years...

Was this then the 'amavasya' of my marriage?

Part Two

Part Two

Sixteen

B-cup

Time is the best healer they say. But what if you had to heal from time itself? I asked myself many times as the months passed, some dragging more than others – as each of us tried in our own way to get over Bansi's untimely death... grappling with the aftermath of what it really meant.

Looking back, it was the financial woes that were probably the hardest, with Mohan most stressed of us all. A part of him died every day, as he worked tirelessly to pay back the moneylenders, the sari suppliers; keeping his problems bottled up inside and throwing away the key. Though we had managed to get back our bedroom – now that Vrinda and Chhotu had moved in with Ba – his sex drive had dwindled even further. Even the way he looked at me changed – as if he were miles away.

Our small house felt strangely empty; almost too large on occasion. I guess that's what the eternally jovial Bansi had meant to us all. He had always had a smile on his lips – as did the black and white portrait of him that now hung in our room. Mohan always made it a point to turn it around whenever he attempted to have half-hearted sex with me. Like he was suddenly scared; a part of him perhaps never forgiving himself for the tragedy that had befallen our family.

Only Chhotu grew up strangely unscathed by all this. Learning to talk, learning to run, to read, going to school every morning. His innocent laughter, in a way, the only memory left of Bansi...

Mohan's attitude to Chhotu changed drastically too, with him becoming more of the parent with each passing year. Scolding Chhotu if he erred or strewed his toys around; insisting that he studied diligently in the evenings; supervising his diet cautiously, always standing by as Chhotu played cricket with the other colony boys on Sunday afternoons, allowing him to go downstairs only after finishing a tall glass of milk, giving him the same lecture about the importance of his mental health every single weekend. Sometimes, I'd interrupt Mohan, trying to tell him to loosen up on the poor boy, but he would ignore me, pushing the glass closer to Chhotu's lips instead, protectively, as if scared of messing up a second time.

Vrinda would always be standing nearby, telling Chhotu to listen to Mohan, playing the role of a spouse almost; her back pressed to the wall, her once ample curves now sagging, her paunch shapeless, as she stared quietly, obediently, in Mohan's direction. I watched them talk to each other and felt a surge of sadness for all of us... at what we had become in the wake of Bansi's passing.

Mohan worked tirelessly and continued to change jobs over and over in the next couple of years, graduating on to more 'respectable professions,' until landing himself a full-time job as departmental manager in the lingerie section of a newly opened ladies' garment store in Crawford Market.

Brassiere

B-Cup

Lace

Lingerie

Panty

Bikini cut

Mohan repeated the following words every night, hoping to perfect their pronunciation, perennially tense about being pulled up by the store-owner for forgetting the finer details. All day Mohan sold imported underwear to the fairer sex. Like Vrinda, Mohan too had probably given up on himself in some way, thinning down considerably, his eyes weary, his face haggard. On most mornings, he forgot to drink the water, honey and lime concoction that I placed by his bedside. We spoke less and less about our needs, till they became like a forgotten language. Touching each other passionlessly on most occasions. Mohan mostly limp by the time I stepped out of my petticoat, his hands fatigued, as were mine from scraping the grease off the dishes.

'Mostly rich people visit our store – it's the only double-storeyed shop in the market that specializes purely in ladies' undergarments. There is free parking too, some of our customers' cars being as spacious as airplanes! I'll take you there sometime when I am a bit free. See to it that you are properly attired though, after all these ladies, my patrons, are not like you, Meera. They always make it a point to look tip-top. Always wearing lipstick; their face powder smooth as satin. They have no patience with petty salesmen like me. Which is why, the moment they stand at the counter, we're supposed to know what their cup size is. One guess only. Knowing we've got it right, when the ladies smile at us, before slowly removing their oversized sunglasses and asking us to show them what else we have in stock. Nowadays though, most of them come in wanting bikinis. It's so warm also, they all go swimming to these big clubs on Peddar Road side, their arms chiselled… their waists so delicate,' Mohan narrated one night, about a year or so later, chewing on his chapatti, occasionally glancing at Chhotu's face as we all ate our dinner.

Vrinda coughed a couple of times, probably a tad embarrassed by the discussion. Thankfully, Ba hadn't worn her new hearing aid. 'Bhaiyya,' she spoke after a while, clearing her throat. 'I'd like to say something if you don't mind. Make a request, actually. It's just that Chhotu too is in school almost all day. Then he goes for his tuitions… or is immersed in his homework, immediately heading downstairs to play with the other boys. Badi Bhabhi anyway manages the kitchen and does most of the cleaning… there's hardly anything for me to do in this house.'

Mohan frowned. Not saying anything.

'The thing is... I'm a graduate in mathematics. In fact Bansi always wanted me to work after marriage, if only I hadn't conceived so fast. Just before he passed away, he had promised me that once our new shop opened, he would talk to you and create a role just for me... something, anything... maybe in the accounts department, maybe taking care of the cash books, etc. So, so I was just thinking... maybe the time has come... the time to...'

Mohan glanced up after a few seconds, running his hands affectionately over Chhotu's curly mop. He had just turned ten.

'Actually, we do hire women sales personnel at the store, Vrinda Ben. Mostly ladies, coming from Bandra East side. They all speak with strange accents, coming for work in skirts and high heels. Minis as they call it amongst themselves, painting their faces to impress customers, who think them to be foreigners, just like our undergarments, mostly imported. But you might get a job in the accounts department. Your proficiency with numbers can be of an added advantage also, especially during stock taking and coordinating with our dealers. That way you could also travel back and forth with me daily... I mean... I can ensure that you're taken care of properly at the workplace even.'

'Don't you think you should consult Ba once before leading Vrinda on? I mean what if she turns you down?' I interrupted, touching his shoulder lightly, feeling a trifle jealous. But they both ignored me.

And just like that, a few months later, Vrinda had joined Mohan's store. Transforming completely within a matter of weeks as she traded in her simple saris for smart looking salwar kameezes and churidars and wore light coloured lipstick, always checking herself out in the bathroom mirror before she left every morning, accompanying Mohan, a spring in her step as they walked downstairs together. Her hair was cut shorter and she often left it open. Leaving the looking after of Ba and Chhotu to me. Like it was perfectly natural for her to do so.

✻

Diwali was now barely a week or so away. I had just fed Ba her lunch, and settled her down in her bed, knowing she would fall asleep within a matter of seconds.

'Badi Bahu, it's Mohan, he says it's urgent, hurry up and come down now,' Mrs Mukherjee hollered as I dried my hair one afternoon, facing the scathing sun. Our phone was dead again. I wondered if he had left something behind at home – his two-wheeler licence, his wallet or locker keys, perhaps – the one emblazoned with an emblem of the ashram.

I closed the window in haste, scampering down the stairs.

'Meera, where were you? The line's already got disconnected twice...' Mrs Mukherjee said again, as I entered her flat.

It was probably a routine call from Mohan, complaining about the lack of salt in his tiffin again, a ritual he repeated every few weeks or so, screaming at the top of his lungs. I mostly listened, knowing he'd forget by the time he made it back home, or simply prepared his favourite dish for dinner, instead. My marriage was based on convenient compensations and simple give and takes.

'Jai Sri Krishna,' Mohan said, before I could speak.

There was a moment of awkward silence.

'Why have you called?' I finally asked.

'Just like that...

'It's the first time you've rung from office to not discuss what was in your dabba. In, in all these years,' I spoke softly after the first few minutes, consumed by a passing tenderness, suppressing it at once, lest I be disappointed again. There was no point feeling dejected, I had taught myself again and again in the early years, when the rejections were harder, coming at regular intervals. Like the time Dr Anita the lady doctor had told me, sitting in her cramped chamber, somewhere in an up-market Bandra suburb, that I may never have children.

'You can always opt for other options... today India is also progressing in medical science and infertility is curable. But, it's very expensive Mrs Patel; the treatment costs could go up to lakhs. Besides, you would also have to convince your husband to come in for treatment...' she had paused to study my face. I had gone alone. 'I have one last suggestion. Please don't keep brooding about the same thing. There's no point. The truth is what it is and you can't possibly have everything in life, right? You'll see for yourself as time passes, that the sadness too will disappear after a while, like any other loss that is beyond your control,' I suddenly recollected her words as I stood facing a row of damp clothes fluttering in the afternoon breeze.

Mohan was saying something, when I cut him short asking, 'Are you coming home late? Should I inform Ba? Is that why you called? I have left the upstairs door open... and she is fast asleep...'

Mohan let out a wry laugh. 'Did you not hear anything I said?' he quizzed forcefully. 'Listen, I've managed to lay my hands on some free samples. I can bring them home tonight. I'm working late again, so Vrinda Ben will pick up Chhotu from his tuitions and come back on her own. You need to stand at the window around ten-ish, and send Chhotu downstairs as soon you see me entering the colony. I'll make him carry the packet up. No one will suspect a thing. Hello, are, are you there?'

'All well I hope?' Mrs Mukherjee suddenly dashed out from nowhere, casting suspicious glances all around as she pretended to dust her cabinet. Ba used the same tactic. I could always tell when someone was eavesdropping. As Binal had once written – it was an art most women developed post marriage; it was now my strongest survival strategy.

'Why will you be late again? Should I not prepare dinner for you then? And just what are you going to send up through Chhotu? Is it some food product, like that biryani masala you brought home last month, the one that Ba almost discovered tucked away in the topmost kitchen shelf? The one that I was then forced to throw away...' I spoke urgently bringing the receiver closer to my mouth.

'There are some silk panties and lace bras... C cup... I know you've put on a little bit of weight of late, especially on the sides of your breasts. Everyone wears foreign, branded items these days, even Vrinda Ben,' Mohan paused stiffly.

'And still her breasts are touching her ankles?' I scoffed, supressing a rising rage.

Mohan seemed to be flustered with my sudden bluntness. '*Shiiiish*, you really don't know what to say where. Besides, I didn't call you in the middle of a busy working day to discuss my sister-in-law's vital statistics. This is about you, Meera. You like orange, right? I've kept one aside already. With blue polka dots... soft, like a child's hands... and what can I say about the satin material, Meera, it melts your insides within seconds,' he panted, sounding very much the seasoned salesman. 'I can't wait to see you in it.'

It made me break out into a smile. 'Orange bra, you mean? And, what happens if Ba finds out, it's likely to show through my blouse, especially the cotton ones... they are always slightly transparent,' I said.

'No silly woman, I was actually talking about an orange panty... real skimpy, with just a tiny triangle covering your pee hole, leaving a major part of your buttocks bare, somewhat like a bikini, with string tie-ups on the side, like the rich ladies wear. Has a matching bra too. But you can't wear that, maybe too risky, as you earlier mentioned,' Mohan cut me short impatiently.

'Why would my buttocks stay uncovered like that? I mean, how would that help? I don't like it,' I remarked dismissively, making a sullen face.

'C'mon, don't you trust me at all? Who knows your body better than me, huh? Anyway, listen, don't waste any more of my time, and remember my plan,' he raced to finish as I let out a sigh.

Mrs Mukherjee had left by then to fetch her son Tamal from school, leaving her house keys in my safekeeping. She would be gone for at least an hour.

'Where are you now?' I questioned Mohan sharply, dragging the phone wire across the sofa.

'Why? Did Mrs Mukherjee say anything?' he sounded uptight.

'I am alone now... Ba won't wake up so soon either. So, I can talk some more, I mean, just in case, you're free for a while,' I replied settling back comfortably on the sofa.

Mohan remained silent for a while, before speaking up, 'I'm actually in Mr Mehta's cabin. He is travelling on a family holiday, abroad somewhere. I have locked it from inside. Maybe... maybe then you should do the same.'

Wordlessly, I got up and bolted the main door.

'So... go on... tell me about the rest of the panties, are there any more? Any other colours, more styles?' I questioned restlessly, arching my back, feeling a sudden rush of familiar pleasures.

I heard the sound of a packet being opened. 'You won't believe your luck... I have in fact got them in my hands as we speak. Just ripping apart the plastic packaging... wait, wait... let me tell you about the red first. The one that's especially popular with young girls, the unmarried types... typical South Mumbai customers, with long legs, those who go for swimming regularly,' he paused clumsily, as if he were inspecting it closely.

'And just what's so special about it?' I made a face.

'Actually, this one we also recommend to newlyweds; a lot of them preferring this style today. The panty just has a thin flap at the centre, the same fabric running around and covering the buttocks. It comes in a variety of colours and prints, including what we call "cheetah print" amongst ourselves at the store... The fabric too is the sheerest silk. All the to-be-weds and honeymooners are buying it. Hot favourite of the season.'

'Honeymoon...' the rest of my words trailed.

'What's the matter? Why are you so quiet?' he pryed, probably puzzled at my reticence.

'Nothing... I was thinking I wish I had worn something like this when we had gone to watch *Aradhana*. I mean imagine us in the dark... your hands brushing against that flap... anyway, tell me about the rest...' I resumed, closing my eyes.

'Yes, yes okay... umm... now this next one is my absolute personal favourite... it's a brassiere I am now talking about, the prettiest blue embellished with tiny, lace flowers... just at the nipples, more like rose buds,' he relayed, breathing heavily.

'How many? Rose buds I mean?' I interrupted, dabbing the corners of my face.

'Let me count. There are two on each side... the feel of the fabric is also heavenly. It's so soft; you can simply sink your teeth into the rose blooms. And again it comes with a matching panty, same colour, rose buds again,' he narrated with a certain bashfulness.

'Where are the flowers on the panty? Right in the centre?' I paused, running my hands over my breasts this time, gently rubbing at my nipples.

'Yes, right on your pee hole... just one big, blue satin rose, with... wait... let me see... yes, umm... four petals. I'm touching them now, the feeling akin to butter dripping down my fingers, like popcorn,' Mohan groaned, as I felt my insides tighten.

'What are you doing now? This minute?' I continued huskily, fiddling with my petticoat strings.

'Meera... I am stroking the orange panty, and thinking about you, and, and the fabric feels so nice you know... and the colour too. I can almost see it glow even with my eyes closed at this moment, like a fresh bloom in your Sinor garden,' he murmured, his breathing harsh. 'And you?' Mohan sounded equally nervous.

'I'm imagining what it would be to actually wear one of those, especially the orange one. It's my favourite from everything you have just mentioned... umm... can you manage to get me two of those?'

my lips trembled as I shuddered with eagerness. 'Umm, don't... don't stop talking, please,' I moaned into the mouthpiece, pretending it was his mouth, untying each panty string carefully, as his hands kneaded the folds of my buttocks at the same time. 'Are, are you holding it in your palms again? Tell me everything...' I begged as Mohan breathed into the speaker.

I convulsed, thinking of the bristles on his moustache brushing carelessly against my breasts. 'How does it smell?' I don't know why I blurted or when. Turning languidly on my side I clamped my thighs over my hands, the receiver landing on the floor with a thud.

Mohan was still on the line when I picked it up a couple of minutes later, relishing the pleasure of making him hear me groan, as I moved faster and faster, rubbing my navel against the rough upholstery, grinding my buttocks up and down, my nipples fully erect.

'It, it smells like you, Meera... your sex... after you've bathed... minutes after you stepped out from the toilet. You know, the times just after your cycle has ended, when you lather yourself with that special concoction... taking over an hour to finish your afternoon bath,' he stopped midway.

Mohan was grunting rigorously. It's all I heard for a while as I writhed on the sofa, using my thumb furiously... pulsating at the intense sensations. 'I'm so moist right now, Mohan...' I muttered, while sucking on my left thumb, the sore scent of my rawness almost sending me over the edge again.

'Are you, are you hard?' I whispered, gently lifting up my hips.

Mohan never answered.

Seventeen

Majnu

'Meera, a woman's body is everything. Learn to take better care of yourself. You've put on some weight, especially around your breasts. Look, what is all this?' Ma commented sternly as she doused my hair with hot jasmine oil mixed with amla, our backs to the July dampness.

I was back in Sinor after a long hiatus, or maybe it just felt that way. The passage of time was multiplied by the grief I felt seeing Bapuji's lifeless face, his lips bloodless, his cheeks shrunken... his bright eyes unseeing. Bapuji lay prostrate on a thin bamboo stretcher, his frail frame covered with a white sheet, his hands neatly folded at his chest, his toes parted, facing away from the darkness.

I was their only surviving child. Apparently, Ma had undergone three miscarriages before Kartik and I were born, nearly a decade or so after their marriage. Boys. Both times.

I had never asked my parents about either of them, I didn't care, to be honest. I had Kartik, and it had been enough... until, even he went away.

I had insisted on performing the final rites, arriving the night after Bapuji had succumbed to a sudden heart failure.

There was a huge showdown before I left Mumbai, Ba warning me severely not to light the funeral pyre, citing celestial consequences if I were to disobey. I lied to Mohan, assuring him I wouldn't dare go against her wishes. He said nothing as usual, silently helping me up on the train a couple of hours later.

'You're lucky you got a ticket so soon,' he panted, pushing my suitcase up, adding as an afterthought, 'You'll be back within a month, right?'

The station was overcrowded, as usual. I had simply nodded my head.

'Once Chhotu's school reopens, it'll be hard for Vrinda Ben to manage, there is always so much to do... you know how much Ba needs you, right?' he continued, looking around furtively.

I smiled wryly.

❀

'Are you even listening to me?' Ma resumed in a high-pitched voice.

I wiped the sides of my eyes.

'Meera, you are in your 30th year. It is not a joke, dickri. Listen carefully, you will have to exercise daily, remember the pranayam and kapalbhati that your Bapuji made you all do as children? Do it every morning, without fail, followed by at least fifty surya namaskars. Also, from now, as soon as you wake up, I'll make you drink hot water with a slice of lime and a dash of honey. And, start applying mustard oil on your ankles and elbows. Look how dry your skin has become, and... and what about the milk and haldi combination for your face? Every week...' she went on unabated.

I finally looked up, acknowledging Ma's concerned face. 'Just how do you know how old I am? We never really celebrated my birthday... here, at least. As if you can actually remember the exact day I was born,' I snapped, turning the tap on.

The cold water stung. As I reached out to touch my stomach, Ma laughed aloud saying, 'Silly girl, do you think a woman's age is ever calculated numerically? Then why do you suppose all women love reducing their age?'

Her words caught me by surprise.

'What do you mean? How is one's age supposed to be evaluated then?' I quizzed indolently.

Ma said, 'A woman's body is the real canvas of her age, dickri. Her hair, her skin, the roundness of her breasts, the tautness of her abdomen, the firmness of her sex, the way her fingertips feel at night, the moistness of her inner thighs at day break. You mustn't allow your body to age, Meera, no matter what the circumstances. Remember my words, keep yourself in shape, your face scrubbed clean and your hair conditioned with shikhakai and... and... always keep your sex perfumed... even when you're not well, taking extra care during your period days. Men are known to desire you the most when you are most inaccessible to them... never underestimate the thrill of a chase, for the opposite sex.'

I slipped my choli over my head and said, 'Sometimes it's hard to believe you never saw the city, Ma... just how do you know so much about men and women? You didn't even attend school. And, and as if you ever did all this for Bapuji, daily? It would be impossible, given all the daily chores there was, raising us... all the things that happened here, in, in this house?'

Ma was rinsing my panties. She lifted one of them saying softly, 'A woman can sense much more than a man, Meera... our instincts are everything... the way I was always scared of Kartik... the way he never left your side... treating you like his personal possession... that kind of attraction was not normal... it would never be understood... it worried me...'

I looked away distracted. Staring at a faint line in the sky above us... migratory birds I guessed.

'Did you know he was going to go away... then?' I spoke slowly, tears welling up in my eyes.

Ma reached out for my hands, trying to rise up, her face contorted with the difficulty of the movement.

'I wish I could know... then maybe these years wouldn't have felt the way they have... his face flashing before my eyes... the night I asked him to get out of your room... the time you started your periods... my dickra never forgave me... it was I who asked him to go away... first...' she swallowed hard.

'Maybe... maybe Kartik drowned, Ma. I mean... he always wanted to...' I couldn't complete the sentence.

'Come with me Meera,' she calmly ordered after a while and we walked down towards the river, hand in hand, rain clouds assimilating at a distance.

'You were right earlier. I didn't see the city, dickri... but I've seen enough of life,' she whispered.

'Did Bapuji ever take notice... all these things you did? Did he ever stop and check you out Ma, pay you a compliment even... were, were you really satisfied in your marriage... I mean in every sense?' I questioned, suddenly feeling closer to Ma.

For a while we walked on by, in silence. Then she said: 'How does it matter, my child? Others were attracted... you need that to keep going. To make sense of the years, all that time you end up being with the same man... sometimes without even realizing how the years between the both of you have lapsed. Watching yourselves as if from a great distance... the same man you once married, a stranger perhaps, at first, grow close... before drifting away slowly again... the intimacy ebbing... never intended to stay the same. Our bodies... they are our only source of power. You must always stay this way... supple, strong, sensuous,' she spoke assuredly, where we stopped, lightly touching my arms.

Behind us, the river flowed sanguinely.

'Can I ask you something else, Ma?' I paused, closing my eyes for a few seconds, my thoughts tranquil.

Not wanting this evening to end. The newfound intimacy between us, as women... someone played on a flute at a distance.

'Meera... every woman has many loves. Marriage is only a state; one state in a lifetime of myriad states and, and no state is ever complete on its own. People come and go... sometimes power lies in resisting them and sometimes in inviting them in. Now that you have turned older, you'll find yourself craving for more... more than what one state can ever offer... it's perfectly natural,' she said.

'I, I hardly step out; life in Mumbai is very different you see... there are a thousand errands. Besides I am not interested in all this, why complicate things?' I spoke defensively, lifting up my face.

Ma narrowed her eyes 'You don't have to, Meera... sometimes life surprises us in the most unexpected ways... on the inside. Just learn to keep your doors open, and don't be afraid of what it brings in. Never be scared of your own desires...'

My lips quivered.

Had Ma sensed the bitter truth about my life? Could she tell what lay ahead? As Guruji had once?

❦

I went back to Mumbai after nearly seven months. Bapuji had left behind some land. The sweet shop he had purchased a few years ago, after my marriage also had to be sold... everything took longer than usual in India's towns.

'Bhabhi, come inside, Meera Bhabhi...' I heard the words up close this time, as I finally located Vrinda on the main road just outside the main entrance to the station. I had just paid the coolie off and was searching for a cab to get home.

She looked different somehow. Or maybe it was the light. Dense rain clouds crowded the early evening sky.

I stepped back on the pavement at once, my heart skipping a beat as soon as I saw Mohan. Sitting behind the driving wheel of a small steel grey car! His eyes firmly focused on the road, as if he were studying the commuters waiting near the crossing in front.

'Bhabhi... surprise...' Vrinda yelled ecstatically, as she seated herself next to him, in front, the transparent pallu of her rose pink, synthetic sari flying out of the open window, her lips painted in the same colour, her tresses left open, tinged with streaks of henna.

'What are you doing here?' I spoke slowly, still standing outside.

It was then that Mohan finally looked into my eyes.

Vrinda burst out laughing. 'Listen to what Badi Bhabhi is saying! Did you not even inform her that you have purchased a car Bhaiyya, a brand, new Maruti that too? Pretty soon you too will also get addicted to the sheer speed...' she went on animatedly.

Mohan had stepped out in the meanwhile.

Storing my luggage away, he signalled to the back seat, saying, 'Better you sit there, Meera; a lot of people who've never sat in cars tend to throw up if sitting next to the driver.'

I shrugged my shoulders.

'Habit...' I whispered sitting crouched in the middle, my handbag to one side along with a tin of desi ghee that Ma insisted I carry back for my in-laws.

As the car sped along, I remembered coming to Mumbai for the first time. What it had meant then... the difference in its contours, the way I had felt about this city, at first.

We stopped at a traffic signal after a while. Vrinda insisted on buying an ice-cream for herself, saying she would like to pay for the same.

'Here, try some Bhabhi,' she moaned, smacking her lips.

I pushed back her hands slightly.

'No, thanks, I'm not fond of meetha. Besides, these things are plain unhealthy. The last thing I want is to look like a fat whale. After all, we're not getting any younger, any of us? And, who wants a fat, ugly wife, am I right, Mohan?' I retorted, turning my face away.

Mohan glared at me through the rear view mirror.

Vrinda too remained unusually silent for a while, her fingers sticky with the sugary red syrup, her face nearly the same shade. I closed my eyes, not feeling much, except the Mumbai rains that now came down slowly on my lips, tasting different, sweeter in many ways...

'Bhabhi... what are you doing?' Vrinda exclaimed, adding something about falling sick, as I rolled down the window just behind the driver's seat, gulping down the moist droplets.

Some people pointed in our direction. Children staring back in amusement. Men especially adjusted their rear view mirrors deftly. The ones I stopped counting a long while ago. My lips opening and closing, my kohl smudging at the edges, like the streetlights we passed.

'Looks like she has really missed the Mumbai rains,' Vrinda commented in a hushed voice, leaning closer to Mohan.

Our glances intersected again.

Lolling my head, back on the seat, I mused dreamily, 'This feels like flying...'

'Chhotu is waiting to go for a drive... he was asleep when we left... otherwise we would have brought him along too,' Vrinda resumed in a high-pitched tone, lightly touching Mohan's shoulders.

I was wiping my neck. Pushing my blouse lower. Before I began unravelling the tangles in my hair.

'Let's keep that outing for next Sunday... Meera needs help unpacking,' Mohan suddenly blurted, his earlobes reddened.

There was a confused silence.

'But you promised him,' Vrinda groaned, sounding desperate.

I lifted my arms over my head. Then tying my hair into a high bun, I said, 'I'm going to rub some hot oil all over my body... ... my, my hips feel so sore...'

Mohan was gaping at my breasts... the orange brassiere straps that peeked out precariously.

'Shall I come up with you and heat the oil?' he muttered under his breath, braking all of a sudden.

I lurched forward. My lips touching his neck.

I suppose I never answered his question.

Eighteen

'Bhukhi Atma'

Before long though, life had fallen back into the same dreary pattern. Mohan and Vrinda took Chhotu out on weekends, usually driving down to Chowpathy, gorging on fistfuls of piquant bhel, the saffron sea tumultuous, always at a distance. Or would stop by at Bandstand, passing by current heartthrob Salman's Khan breezy bachelor pad, hoping to catch him on his balcony, in case he stepped out.

Naturally, Sunday evenings were Chhotu's favourite time of the week. No tuitions, no homework... no pressure to perform.

Vrinda looked happy too. Becoming a working woman had lent her a whole new energy and self confidence. She had managed to shed some weight. Exchanging her cotton saris that Ba earlier insisted she wear at home for tight salwar kurtas fitted at the hips, paired with multi-coloured chiffon dupattas that trailed behind her girlishly when she'd run to unlock the main door, always the first to greet Mohan, her beady eyes sparkling. Mohan would say nothing. Sneaking surreptitious glances at Vrinda as she swayed her buxom behind, on her way towards the kitchen, her hands holding onto a greasy packet of aloo bondas or vada paos – Chhotu's favourite – that Mohan never forgot to carry home, since he had begun working half days on most Sundays, to earn more overtime, a greater chunk of commission as he frequently claimed.

Mohan wore a slight beard these days, and scratched it self-consciously when Vrinda dropped something near the kitchen entrance, her dupatta landing on the floor all of a sudden, her plump breasts popping out, unannounced. 'Oh no!' she would say, sounding exasperated, taking time to lift it up.

Mohan would continue to stare fixated, his hands folded neatly on his lap all the while, the nerve near his left eye twitching.

Was he erect? I thought to myself as I waved them goodbye, watching Vrinda's shoulders gently graze his, as their glances connected again, usually at the bottom of the stairway.

'Is that a new kameez you're wearing, Vrinda Ben? Looks really beautiful too... imported is it?' Mohan would bring his mouth closer to hers. Before Chhotu opened the back door, occupying his designated place and Vrinda sank into the front seat, her wet tresses billowing in the damp breeze, her smile mysterious.

Like mine each time I lied to Mohan, citing the same reason.

That Sunday, I made my usual excuse. Something about a splitting headache... or getting nauseous in his car: 'You guys go ahead. I don't want the seats to get soiled, besides Chhotu is eagerly waiting to tell you about his week... you must spend more time with him, it's the one day he gets you all to himself,' I said, as Mohan brusquely pushed my hands away, grabbing the keys from them. It had been more than three years since Mohan had brought the new car home, I calculated, listening to Vrinda ask Chhotu if he had finished all his tuition assignments, leading him out of the doorway.

'It's a pain growing up, isn't it? Study, study, study,' I interrupted, eager to see them off.

'I'll try and get you an autograph of Salman Khan, Kaki,' Chhotu shouted enthusiastically, ready to jump from the top stairs as I patted the top of his head.

'My hero is still Bachchan,' I smiled, lapsing back into the shadows, sensing Mohan's rushed breath, as Vrinda too scampered down the stairway.

'Jai Sri Krishna, Bhabhi, you sure you don't want to come along this time? The weather is just perfect and Ba too is away. We could all have dinner outside, somewhere fancy, you know. Why do you want to eat all by yourself? Every day?' Vrinda frowned, glancing back once, her maroon lip colour jarring.

'It's that bad acidity problem I've been having since the past week or so. You all enjoy your dinner and see that Chhotu doesn't have too much ice-cream. You don't want him to take after you now, do you, Vrinda? Better run along, your Mohan bhaiya, as you know, doesn't like to be kept waiting,' I slowly replied.

Suddenly feeling wicked, as I sucked in my stomach. I had lost six kilos since the time Bapuji died... since my last visit to Sinor.

I hadn't written home in a while either, I thought as I watched Mohan's car leave the colony gates, before disappearing onto a crowded thoroughfare.

Was aloneness an addiction?

❦

In the past, Binal had often referred to jealousy as the most fatal feminine trait.

'Men don't get jealous, Meera. They're not petty like us, fighting over a single piece of flesh. They can perhaps be termed possessive, like ferocious lions in a dense jungle, territorial about their mates. We women... we can be compared to cats, filthy, black, ill fed billis, perennially bhukhi, sneaking into someone else's kitchen, especially in the afternoons to lap up all their milk... covering the thali so immaculately so that no one even realizes all the milk has disappeared... bhukhi atmas,' she had declared, rolling her eyes.

I had always found the comparison rather lop-sided. After all, didn't the cat and the lion both belong to the feline family? Why then were we so different?

That day, within minutes of Mohan, Vrinda and Chhotu departing, I had bathed, lathering myself lovingly, pouring lukewarm water over my breasts, shampooing my tresses with generous amounts of shikakhai and amla, slowly forming a ball of foam, then parting my thighs, before pushing my index fingers into the folds of my sex to stroke my pubic hair tenderly. It felt blissful to have the house all to myself...

Like most Sundays, I had kept the television on in Ba's bedroom, turning the volume on high as I swayed seductively, as smooth as the soapsuds slithering down my navel.

'*Choli ke pecche kya hai?*' a woman in a husky voice crooned, making me shudder in anticipation.

I closed my eyes, dreamily recalling the first time I had heard the song on television while kneading the dough for the night's dinner. Mohan had been standing behind me in the kitchen, his trouser front pressed to my buttocks, his fingers rummaging through my hair.

'*Choli mein dil hai mera,*' the song gathered momentum, as I thrust my chest forward, my mouth slanted, my eyes languid. Trying to emulate Madhuri Dixit, the *dhak dhak* girl – in the way she gyrated her full hips, her movements desperate, a ghunghat pulled over her eyes, that glinted every time she bit her lower lip suggestively, trying to seduce the villain – a man who watched her, lustily.

'*Yeh dil mein dungi mere yaar ko...*' I sang, splashing about in the dark corner where we usually bathed, my toes pressed against a bucket of cold water, reserved for dry spells.

When the song concluded, I walked out, stark naked, leaving moist footprints all down the hallway. Ba's room was pitch dark by then. It's where I usually changed on Sundays, donning a bright red silk sari today, before stopping once to check myself out in the convex mirror. The choli I wore was completely backless... the one from my wedding night.

Some months ago one of the flats in our colony had been converted into a dance academy. I had always watched the rehearsals in secret, on my way up or down the stairway, sometimes leaving home early, just so that I could linger behind a mammoth, concrete pillar and gaze greedily at the group of young men and women toss their limbs in bold abandon, pouting their lips. The girls always wore stretch pants. The men were in jeans and ganjis.

One evening I had gone right up to the door, but didn't have the courage to knock. Just then the door opened. 'Arre Aunty, why are you hiding this way, all by yourself? Come in please,' Pratigya, our neighbour, Mrs Deshmukh's daughter, dragged me inside forcibly, not letting go of my hands till I set foot over the entrance.

'Hi, what's your name?' a young man had quizzed, his eyes the colour of rain.

'Arre, she lives upstairs only. Aunty is a fabulous dancer herself; she always corrects my steps whenever I visit them, especially before the Ganpati dance function that we organize every year in this colony. Please, Aunty, why don't you show me that step you were doing that day, standing before the mirror in your bedroom? You know, like this...' Pratigya said excitedly, breaking out into an impromptu jig.

'I, umm, was just passing by, I must leave, I have a lot of housework actually,' I said quickly. 'You all carry on.'

'Oh, c'mon Aunty, stay na please, we would all love to learn some desi, I mean, traditional Gujarati dance moves... we are really sick of the same steps day after day,' another girl in a short skirt yelled, pulling the bag from my hands. A few tomatoes spilled out.

Someone turned on the music just then.

'On one condition only... you people also have to teach me some steps of your dance form... it should be a fair deal... I have noticed that you all usually do Western kind of dance... with Hindi film songs... it's nice... like having the best of both worlds,' I broke into a smile, letting go of my inhibitions.

Everyone had laughed.

'A real barter then!' a tall, swarthy man, with salt and pepper hair and a beard bellowed, his eyes deep-set, fine lines around his mouth, his shirt buttons open up to his stomach. He had a thick, curly crop of hair on his chest.

'Aunty, this is our Sir,' Pratigya had whispered.

'Hey, stop calling her aunty for God's sake. You're insulting her classical Indian beauty. I mean, c'mon, she looks younger than many of you here and look at those, those hands – *mast*. She is a real Goddess; you guys should be ashamed, just see her figure, that slim waist, the curve of her ankles, as if she was born to dance. Please, will you please join us? It would be an honour to watch you dance, and, and maybe even learn something in return,' he interrupted Pratigya.

I glanced down, staring at my silver toe rings.

'No? You're turning me down then,' he sounded dejected, staring at me in silence for a while, his hands rubbing his chest. He wore a burnished silver bracelet on his left wrist. I had stared at the shape of his nails. My breath quickening at the sight of his long, muscular limbs, toned, perhaps from years of dance practice.

Pratigya was saying something to the others, their lithe frames swaying to the thumping beats. The track had just changed, this time playing louder than the last.

I don't think anyone heard when I had whispered, 'yes,' no one smiling back either in recognition, except the man with the sparkling eyes and the coarse chest hair.

⚓

'May I come in?' I asked that Sunday, clearing my throat nervously. My hair was still damp from my bath and I had left it loose, its wet edges dripping a little on my blouse. My sari was slippery in places. I had last worn it on my outing with Mohan. To watch *Aradhana*... a gift from Binal.

'Yes come on in, but, you're late... our classes commence at 6 p.m. sharp,' a voice replied from a distance.

There was no music.

Had I landed up on the wrong day?

'I, I remember you mentioning something about Indian dance class on Sunday evenings. Sorry if I got the timing wrong... I should have probably come in earlier, but the thing is... my husband...

Mohan, he only left home this Sunday. He was running a fever last week and before that, my mother-in-law was not keeping too well. Even now I almost wasn't making it... Mohan had some urgent work that kept him back in his workplace... and, and because it's a Sunday, I mean...' I paused breathlessly.

The shadows stirred.

Someone switched on a floor lamp, at a corner somewhere.

'You smell different,' I finally caught a glimpse of him, as a pair of sturdy hands reached out for me in the semi darkness.

'What, what do you mean?' I was suddenly scared to look up.

The man gave a wry laugh. 'I'm trying to tell you that you smell absolutely delicious, Meera... like fresh peaches or something. You know when they're sliced open right from the centre... so you can actually see their insides... pulpy, porous, passionate... pulsing with juice...' he spoke in a whisper, his arms holding down my shoulders.

I trembled. 'How do you know my name?' I questioned, feeling my mouth go dry as the man moved up ahead, blocking out the thin ray of light.

'Are you kidding? Every man in this colony knows your name... just that maybe they're too scared to say it out loud,' he answered, breathing in my face, before going on in a hushed tone, 'Look... I'm sorry if I've offended you in any way, perhaps I've said too much already. It's just that I've heard a lot of men here talk about you in the past, describing your beauty, your body, the shape of your hands... going on and on about the way you dry your hair. I'm sure you've noticed the retinue of guys who hang around under the stairs, gawking at you as you climb down to buy vegetables every morning?' he paused.

I glared back, my heart racing. 'And just what are you trying to get at?' I asked, suddenly feeling a pang of regret.

'Nothing, I'm only stating facts... being honest. Meera... you do happen to be the central object of male fantasy in this housing society. Men think of you when they are alone. Umm, okay let me put it this way, haven't you ever heard of married guys fantasizing in bed about famous starlets, for instance? Just yesterday, one of my friends told me that while having sex with his wife the previous night, he moaned uncontrollably.'

'Was he crying out my name? I mean your friend... while, while...' I tried forming a sentence.

The man burst out laughing. 'No, no, it's not what I meant at all. He, my friend was chanting Madhuri Dixit's name while doing it. "Madhuuuu" he'd groan every time his wife's hands moved faster on his privates,' he answered brazenly.

I don't know why I giggled, joining him. 'So, I am like some famous actress then?' I smiled to myself, walking away.

The man continued to watch me intently. I was nearly at the door when I felt him up close, his lips pressing into the back of my head. He was hard.

'Did you have something else to say? It's obvious there's not going to be any dance class here today,' I mused as the man pulled me in to his chest.

'Move for me, Meera, please, I want to watch you... move...' he said deliberately stressing the word 'move,' as his tongue touched the nape of my neck.

I turned around slowly. Staring at him in silence. My gaze fixated on his shirt buttons. At the dark passage of hair that plunged lower than his navel...

'Only... only if you teach me some of your dance steps... a real barter, remember?' I added teasingly, trying to maintain a safe distance, even as a part of me was enjoying this game... the thrill of a chase.

He nodded tamely, looking impressed by my frankness, and turned on the music... an instrumental track... slow. And so we danced, my body gliding effortlessly, as I swayed my hips, my limbs suddenly agile, graceful, as if freed from centuries of nothingness, my feet floating in the air.

His body glistened with sweat. My sari had unravelled, as I spun at a great speed, throwing back my shoulders... and then my arms... reaching out as if for the sky... the music adding to the slow surrender.

By the time I stopped, I was panting; my pallu lay limp on the tiled mosaic floor... my insides pulsating with moistness. 'I can't remember the last time I danced this way... I thought I had forgotten everything...' I cried ecstatically.

The man slipped out of his shirt. Not saying anything else before pressing himself into my side, 'Do it one more time, Meera.'

This time, I moved leisurely, on purpose, feeling myself casually graze his hardness... rubbing my hips over his crotch at each turn, wanting to push him to the very edge of his attraction. 'Oh, Meera,' he let out a stifled groan, lifting my left arm over my head, his fingers slipping into mine impatiently. I let him, before he placed both my hands on the sides of my waist, his fingers outlining the roundness of my breasts, as I tossed my head backwards; my nipples taut. I held my breath then, as he pushed me away roughly again, towards his right this time, lightly holding on to my wrists, as we circled in an anti-clockwise motion.

My sari was coming undone. He undraped me, wordlessly.

I didn't stop him. This time.

'Remove that too before it gets in the way,' he instructed decisively, his fingers pointed at my stomach as I quietly slipped out of my petticoat, my panties glistening in the half light.

'Run towards me, and, keep looking ahead... let your feet gather momentum,' he commanded.

I obeyed.

'I'm going to lift you up... teach you something new like you wanted,' he pronounced, stretching out his arms as I sprinted towards him. He lifted me powerfully in his arms.

I grabbed his back dizzily, digging my nails into his flesh, my legs entwined around his waist as we spun at a great speed.

'Hold on tight... I'm going to go faster...' he pushed back my tresses, to whisper.

I held his head, my breasts in his face, my heels digging into his taut buttocks, smiling giddily as if I were on a giant merry-go-round, a child once again whirling into oblivion with Kartik.

'Let go, spread your arms out. Don't be scared, Meera, I'm not going to drop you...' he promised. His legs were supple and deft, our lips touching each other's as we whirled round and round covering the entire length of the hall, our reflections dizzily passing through the mirrors plastered on all the four walls.

I don't know when he stopped and I collapsed to the ground, falling backwards as the room still whirled around me, spread out on all fours, the man lying beside me, our fingers delicately entwined. 'Did you like it?' he asked breathlessly, his voice from another world, his body leaning heavily over mine, its heat and sweat merging with my own.

His stomach was muscular, tight, unlike Mohan's. I felt my senses overwhelmed.

He licked my left arm, his tongue tracing the tattoo. 'When did you get this?'

'What else did the men say... in the colony, about me?' I interrupted, trembling as he pressed himself into my hips, his moves suddenly hurried, insistent, trying to pull down my panty. I braced my hips upwards, holding myself tense, my pubic hair moist, my breath heavy, my lips trembling.

'They, they said you had really good breasts, like foreigners'... bouncy and yet firm... they... some I mean said they wanted to suck on your nipples all night. You usually finish your bath by three-thirtyish or so in the late afternoons, right?' he paused awkwardly, flicking my nipples to and fro, securing his arms around my waist.

'What else?' I questioned my mind far away, my thoughts fuzzy. All I could focus on then was the way his hands felt... his nails... the rush of his afterbreath...

The man's erection was strong; I could feel it nudge my hips, as he clung tighter, hoisting his right thigh over my haunches, his zipper opened.

'They said... you were...' the rest of his words drowned.

Nineteen

Paris

I had been feeling sick all week, actually since the beginning of last month. My stomach felt bloated, I was nauseous after meals. I remember even throwing up a couple of times, usually within minutes of breakfast, my eyes red from sleeplessness, my feet swollen.

My arms throbbed all night, especially after Mohan tied my hands to the bedpost, his face frozen in a perverse slant, trying to sustain his erection at any cost. It was his latest experiment. Something he had once seen in a foreign film somewhere... set in Paris. A city of lights and love, as Chhotu had once mentioned, peering at a brightly lit screen displayed on a desktop Mohan had gifted him, after he passed his half yearly exams with distinction.

'This is a second-hand one, if you do better in your finals, I will buy you a laptop for your birthday,' he had promised Chhotu, as they went on to spend all of Sunday installing it, their eyes glinting with excitement when the device finally started working. There was also a new landline in our bedroom.

'By next week, we'll be connected to the Internet,' Vrinda declared proudly after dinner one night, as we scrubbed the utensils, standing in the dark, our hands often colliding.

'You should learn how to operate the computer. It's so simple, really. We all use it at the store nowadays; to process bills or while calculating stocks... no one does anything manually anymore. Information is at your fingertips. It's a brave, new world, Badi Bhabhi,' she had remarked somewhat sarcastically.

One night as Mohan tried to enter me again and again, I couldn't help but think of this brave, new world. Wondering if women were tied to their beds, sometimes, blindfolded? If they could actually speak their minds... share the things they loved... or hated?

'You're so damn tight, God knows what happens with you people on certain days,' Mohan grunted, sounding irked, fisting me furiously, his fingers probing my sex.

I glanced over his shoulder instead. There was always some light on, outside.

Like Paris, I imagined as Mohan slapped my breasts hard.

'Playing hard to get again, huh?' he gritted his teeth, hauling me up by my hair.

I chose silence.

Knowing it was easier to hate someone you love. My feelings for him trapped somewhere, between those two places. Our disappointments dull... after a point. The way his lips felt as I pulled them over mine at some point.

Not knowing who I might be... anymore.

🔽

'Do you think I am pregnant?' I questioned him one morning a few weeks later.

Mohan immediately covered his nose, pushing his chair back a couple of inches. 'Brush your teeth first, your mouth stinks,' he snapped, irritably, glancing up from the newspaper, a Gujarati daily.

'I vomited again this morning, it's happening way too regularly, you know,' I confessed in a soft voice, glancing down, the sight of the oily puris on his plate making me queasy instantly.

Mohan ate in silence.

'My cycle is yet to start... unduly late. Do you suppose we should go for a check-up, just... just in case? I have Dr Anita's new number jotted down somewhere, I can make an appointment... and you can join in, post work... I'm sure Vrinda can make it back on her own, one day?' I spoke in haste, covering my mouth this time.

Mohan looked stunned.

'I don't see any point in spending fifteen hundred rupees just because you think you may have conceived. I mean, going to that Anita woman invariably means her asking you to opt for a battery of tests. And then, like every time, she will make someone from her clinic call me also, blabbering some complicated medical jargon, forcing us to visit her once more... forgoing another crisp thousand rupee note, not to forget the to and fro travel. Naturally, we can't travel by train to such an upmarket place... remember last to last time, she even asked you how you came? Better we wait and watch. Besides, your cycle has always been wayward... like you!' he said sarcastically.

'But this time... my, my body feels different. My breasts heavier than before and... and, I feel my stomach is also growing. Look,' I interrupted, pressing his fingers into my navel.

Mohan brushed my hands off abruptly, his eyes scorching my face. 'Have you absolutely no shame, Meera? Chhotu is at home today. He's got such high fever from last night. Ba is doing her puja. What will they say seeing us in such a compromising state? There is a time for all this... are we animals?' he muttered, tearing into another puri on his plate.

'My grandmother always said a woman is the first to feel the changes in her own body, when she's with child. Perhaps it's just nature's way of preparing her for what lies ahead. Please let us get the tests done if she insists... please, Mohan,' I urged, picking up his empty plate.

'You actually feel you could get pregnant, huh? Now suddenly, after all these years of us being married? Meera you have crossed your 30s and me... well, I am going to be forty-two next to next month! What will people say?' he exclaimed, rising up from his chair.

I was walking back to the kitchen, trying to keep my eyes open. My head reeled, my mouth tasting strangely bitter again.

'A woman can conceive anytime, Mohan... and it isn't as though we haven't tried...' I snapped, glancing over my shoulders, adding bitterly under my breath, 'at least I have...'

'Who's damn kid is it?' Mohan yelped agitatedly, grabbing my shoulders, pulling me back unexpectedly, as I grimaced. 'I asked whose kid are you carrying? Taunting me this way, early in the morning... begging me so much to take you to Dr Anita. I remember it was you who mentioned the last time how the very sight of needles makes you nauseous... and now, just like that... you claim you've been feeling ill for a while. How come Ba is unaware of this or Vrinda Ben, for that matter? What's the big secret?' he quizzed eerily, staring at my face, shaking me up.

This time I burped in his face, emitting a stale stench.

'I was trying to save you... and you know that very well, Mohan... don't put words in my mouth,' I pushed him away brusquely.

'Really? You want to know what people say about you, huh? Sometime back, the men in the shops downstairs were gossiping about how there was something brewing between you and that dance master. Bloody, dick-less eunuch – teaching young boys and girls Western dance, as if he's ever gone abroad himself? Thank God, the society committee listened to my complaint and served him notice. Creating a bloody nuisance, encouraging youngsters to mix so freely, neglecting their studies, indulging in secret affairs, sans the consent of their parents'... good riddance,' Mohan continued unabated, sounding jealous.

'I didn't even know his name... we had only met one time. You can ask Pratigya, if you don't believe me,' I shrugged my shoulders.

Mohan's hands still held on to my wrists.

'And if you still doubt me, we can always opt for a test. I'm sure Dr Anita can recommend something, maybe to test *you* this time around, decide whether you are productive, in the first place. I think you are forgetting that earlier too she'd asked you to come and get yourself checked up. Remember?'

'Fine, *shiiish*, keep your voice down for heaven's sake now; let's see if we can go visit her on Sunday. Just don't tell anyone at home anything right away... I mean what's the point anyway? Let us first be sure ourselves, alright?' Mohan cut me short, getting fidgety all of a sudden.

I wiped my forehead, feeling drained by the heated exchange of words.

'And, and by the way, I didn't believe any of those men, okay,' Mohan added awkwardly after a few seconds, pressing himself into me.

My buttocks felt sore. I eased away at once. 'Even I was joking earlier about you undergoing any kind of test...' I smiled awkardly, staring back at his face.

Mohan tried to smile back. Running his fingers lightly over my mouth.

'I haven't brushed,' I abruptly said, pushing his hands away.

⚜

This wasn't the first time my womb had been invaded. In a hospital room, that is, by a stranger wearing thick rubber gloves and a green mask. And yet, this time around, things felt different. As the doctor investigating my insides, peered into a dimly-lit computer, my thoughts slowly drifted back to the last time I had seen the dance instructor. I had deliberately avoided him after our encounter. Not wanting to stroke any unneccesary complications. Scared in some sense. For the first time. Of my own heart, perhaps.

It was pitch dark when our paths crossed, after nine or so the following weekend. I was in the children's park, taking a short walk, in the lane behind our colony, desperate for some air, knowing it would be deserted by then.

'I knew I'd find you here,' I'd heard a muffled voice, before someone pulled me roughly into the surrounding unruly bushes.

'Leave me alone. What happened that day was a spur of the moment

thing really... I cannot see you again... this way. My family will be returning any moment... I have to get going,' I cried hurriedly, pushing back a few strands of hair from my face.

'Why have you been avoiding me? You seemed perfectly willing that evening, huh?' he retorted roughly grabbing my shoulders and pulling me into the thicket.

'I don't know. I don't have all the answers. Maybe I'm just not built that way. Maybe I grew up in a small town where we were taught to worship our husbands... kiss the ground they walked on. I don't know – maybe I'm still the little girl who believes in the eternal romance of Ram and Sita, the perfect marriage... saat janam and all that...' my lips quivered.

'And what about the agnipariksha Sita was made to undergo? You actually find that sort of humiliation romantic?' he questioned sharply, pulling my chin up.

I ran my hands over his cheeks. His jaws hardened. 'Marriages are not just about romance...' I stopped short. Had I said too much already?

'Then why the hell are you still trapped in one, Meera? Considering Mohan and you don't even have any children. I mean... let's be honest, I don't think he's ever satisfied you the way you would have wanted. Don't you see, Meera... there's absolutely nothing to hold you back to that family. And frankly, you should consider yourself lucky you never got knocked up by that loser. I mean imagine being a mother to his offspring... useless, piece of shit,' he sniggered, making a face.

We kissed clumsily, my body instantly warming to his touch.

'Meera, Meera please come away with me, say yes... please,' he cajoled persistently, his hands running up my back, squeezing my hips, before pulling out the clasp that held up my bun.

I touched his hardness, and he parted his thighs at once, to make more space, moaning aloud when I cupped his balls. 'Meera, can you not tell how much I want you? Come with me please... the dance hall is totally empty; I have the space for another night. We can make love there, on the floor, like last time... I want to be inside you so bad... watch

you wrap your legs around my waist, writhing in pleasure as we do it
again and again... this time, for real,' he pleaded passionately, slowly
rubbing my breasts.

I looked up, the lights from the street reflected in his eyes.

'Tell me about Paris,' I circled his lips.

He groaned, positioning his hips over mine.

'We can go there together, Meera; I'll arrange a passport, everything.
You know it's my dream to pursue ballet there. All we have to do is get
out of this city first, at the earliest, maybe right away, before they realize
you're gone for good. You can get a divorce eventually. We'll make love
under the lights of Champs-Élysées... just imagine going for boat rides
along the Seine river... and, and you can learn ballet with me too,
practicing daily. We can have kids of our own someday...' he went on
enthusiastically; sweat dripping down the sides of his brow.

'And what if I can't have children? If none of this is as simple as you
make it out to be?' I blurted, feeling his bulge dig into my upper thighs.

The man grabbed my waist, tugging at my silver waistband. I
shivered, slipping into his arms.

For a while, we locked lips, saying nothing.

'Anything is possible in Paris... it is the city of dreams after all,' he
replied impatiently, pushing my sari down, slipping his left thumb
inside my wetness.

'Paris,' he moaned as our tongues finally melted, our bodies merging
effortlessly.

I still hadn't asked him his name.

❦

'Meera, Meera,' I heard an insistent voice. Someone shook me
vigorously as I lay flat somewhere, my hair damp. Was I still wet? I
opened my eyelids with difficulty and stared at a blinding array of
lights.

'Open your eyes, Meera,' someone else ordered from the side.

'Paris...' I managed to say wearily, shivering of a sudden.

Was it the breeze from the River Seine? The one he had described so well.

'Meera, you need to look at me now,' someone said helping me sit up, propping up a few pillows behind me. My body felt limp, my hips immobile.

How long had he been inside me? Days? Weeks? Months? A whole year, perhaps? How many times did we do it? Standing? Squatting? Sideways? From the rear?

A hard, cold stethoscope was being pushed through the loose gown I wore, pressing over my left breast.

I grimaced, my eyes forced wide open.

'Meera, my name is Dr Batliwala. You were recommended to us by Dr Anita... I'm afraid you've suffered a miscarriage...' he paused. I listened in dazed silence, the smell of antiseptic overwhelming.

Ba stepped into view as soon as the doctor had walked away. 'Badi Bahu, you should have told us you were not feeling well that afternoon. It's only when you didn't come out of the bathroom for so long and I couldn't locate you anywhere else in the house, that I called for Mr Deshmukh. He had to break the door open with some other young boys he called in for assistance. You were discovered half naked. It was such a shameful sight... Mohan too was working late that day. Even Vrinda was not at home when all this happened. I tried getting you to look at me at first, say something... anything at all. But you just kept mumbling... saying some... some Pa something. Even now, it's what you were moaning in your sleep. Anyway, guess it's not your fate to give my son a child of his own... we must accept our lot...' she mourned, sounding bitter all over again.

'Where is he? Mohan?' I swallowed, wiping my face.

'At the store, where else? You've been in hospital for close to two weeks now. He can't possibly sit by your side all day, holding your hand. Someone has to pay these hefty bills. Anyway, visiting hours are nearly over, I better go down. Takes me forever to climb these stairs, and the lifts are way too crowded. Vrinda said she would come to fetch me. I have to wait at the entrance downstairs by a certain time,' she replied stiffly, getting up with difficulty.

When everyone left, I turned my head to the wall. A tear rolled down my cleavage.

'Shall I call for the nurse, sister?' a young woman lying in the next cubicle questioned in earnest, gazing at me, holding a green curtain away from her face.

'No,' I said, placing my feet on the floor.

'You shouldn't...' she stretched out her hands in panic, her lips colourless.

I smiled.

'I just want to pass urine,' I cut her short weakly, pointing in the direction of the toilet.

It was like learning to walk again.

As I walked out of one body and into the next... a week before I finally turned thirty-five. The age when you finally realize what it takes to dream again. Dream of love and loss, kisses and kites... dream of erotica and erections, of rivers and rescues... dream of silence and surrender, of marriage and masturbation, dream of butterflies and breasts, of pleasure and pain... dream of ballet and betrayal, in a place beyond Ward No. 3, Bed No. 22, JJ Hospital, Mumbai.

A streak of lightning flashed across the sky.

Twenty

Mumbai Lover

I returned home on a Sunday, a day after my 35th birthday. I remembered it because Ma never rang to enquire how I was, the phone lying lifeless by our bed.

'Meera, there is some news,' Mohan announced grimly, studying me from the corner of his eye, while surfing the Internet.

I was still a bit drowsy from the afternoon medication. I nodded my head.

'We heard a week or so back, actually... umm, your Mama's son Ramesh phoned us. Vrinda Ben... I mean it was actually Chhotu who received the call first. There was a lot of disturbance also. Umm, I was wondering whether or not to tell you about this at the hospital, but there was no point...' Mohan swallowed uncomfortably.

'Ramesh is my Fui's son,' I interrupted stiffly, gazing into the bright screen.

There was no other light in our bedroom that night. There was no need either. I had a splitting headache, my hips still bruised from the fall. My thoughts clouded. Every now and then, the pain of my last contraction would return, subconsciously, though I tried to fight it off... like a bad dream or something. Forcing myself to stop thinking of my child... the one I never saw...

'Do you want to go to Sinor? It's been ages since you last visited your native place? Vrinda Ben also feels it's where you will heal best. A change of place,' he paused again, eyeing me suspiciously.

I surveyed the streetlights. A couple of them were not on. There was no moon. The air was still, like it hadn't rained in weeks.

'She's right. You need a break, Meera. And, here you get hardly any rest. Guruji too is expected in Mumbai by the end of next month it seems; Vrinda Ben feels his arrival after all this time will naturally double up your exhaustion, what with hoards of visitors moving in and out of this place, havans to be organized, relatives from afar. You know how chaotic his darshans get. Besides, she insists on managing everything, this time...' Mohan resumed persuasively, bending to switch off the computer as I walked up to the window.

'Lie down; you are supposed to be on bed rest,' he screeched, trying to ease into a smile the very next instant.

'Had you thought of a name?' I spoke slowly, stretching my hand outside the rails.

'Name?' he was confused.

'Had our child been born, would you have wanted a girl or a boy?' I added under my breath, watching the stars appear, one by one.

'Honestly Meera, I didn't even think you would get pregnant in the first place. I mean, c'mon, we've been at this since the time we got married. Looked like we'd be trying all our damn lives!' he scoffed, unbuttoning his kurta.

I didn't look back this time.

'I wanted a boy... Kishen... Mohan and Meera's son... you know like Bhagwan Kishen,' I smiled wanly, resting my hips on the ledge.

Mohan let out a laugh. 'Like how? Meera and Mohan never really did it in real life... Meerabai spent her whole life singing bhajans. She was no Radha!' he retorted, loosening his pajama strings, his eyebrows raised.

An airplane passed just then, drowning the rest of his words.

'So, should I book your tickets then? I can do it from office tomorrow itself, it will not be a problem,' he repeated, getting to his side of the bed.

I returned to mine, untangling my hair. 'Don't bother. There is nothing left for me in Sinor,' I said taking my time.

'Meera...' Mohan stopped all of a sudden, his hands moving over my breasts, as our eyes met. 'Your, your Ma expired... it's what I wanted to tell you earlier. But, I didn't know how to broach the subject, I mean. I know you're probably still in mourning for the child, physically weak and all. She slipped on the riverbanks and apparently suffered a haemorrhage,' he couldn't complete the rest of the sentence.

I put my hand on his. 'I know everything...' I whispered.

Mohan was shell-shocked. 'How? Who the hell told you? The doctor told us not to breathe a word till you'd been discharged, since you had already suffered a major trauma... I don't understand...' he mumbled under his breath.

I let go of his hand. 'Vrinda told me yesterday...' I replied tonelessly, pushing my pallu away, suddenly feeling stifled by the weight of it.

'Vrinda Ben?' Mohan gasped, rolling his eyes. Then he scratched his chest nervously, 'I'm going to have a word with her right away... or, or maybe tomorrow, first thing, tomorrow, okay? How could she do this? I'll, I'll... get this sorted... umm, but, don't you think it's already so late... maybe Chhotu is asleep also, no?'

'Vrinda sleeps in the living room... alone. She says it's a lot cooler there. Besides, she's always awake till late... and it's not even eleven. On any other day, you'd all probably be just watching television,' I exhaled, continuing before he could reply, 'and really, don't worry, I'll be up and about soon. I already feel much stronger, seems the medicines are really working. Isn't it amazing what a long haul in hospital can do for you?'

Mohan stared intently at me.

'So are you saying you were not in shock about the child?' he reprised, resting on his elbow.

There was a power cut. I spoke into the stillness, feeling a lump form in my throat: 'I was in shock, I suppose, but I've been married long enough to know that babies aren't the result of miracles. I've made peace with what happened... besides, what's the point in grieving about something that can't be altered?'

Mohan pursed his lips tightly, probably wondering what to do next. His breath rushed as I removed my bra, placing it under the pillow. 'There's something I've been meaning to say to you too,' I spoke after a while.

Mohan remained motionless.

'You've put on too much weight again. Looks like no one has been making your food properly, with less oil, avoiding fried stuff and giving you the warm water concoction first thing in the morning. From tomorrow, I will personally monitor your meals again. Our bodies aren't the same, Mohan; they decay with time... like everything else,' I sighed, turning my back to him.

❀

Before we all knew it, it was time for Guruji's much-awaited visit to Mumbai. On Ba's insistence, Mohan had the living room white-washed just before his arrival, the off-white walls somehow resembling my ward in JJ Hospital. A strange shiver passed down my spine each time I went in, my attention arrested by Guruji's dark-rimmed eyes as he stared down from a life-size portrait that Ba had recently placed above the sofa-cum-bed... his chest bare. His lips parted... as if he was about to whisper into my ears. Was Guruji aware of my losses? Had he been informed? Had he guessed the future, as always? My fate? Was he concerned? Thoughts crowded my mind.

Only Chhotu seemed worried for me. Even teaching me how to use the computer to get my mind off things. He had crept up behind me one evening and wrapped his arms around my neck impulsively. His body drenched in sweat from playing downstairs. 'Kaki... come on, it's time,' he had whispered into my hair.

His touch always reminded me of Bansi... in a way. I had smiled. 'I was just coming to you... I know you promised to teach me how to use the Internet. I've been practising all afternoon also, while you were away taking your Sunday nap... the Word thing. I don't want to disappoint my teacher, after all,' I laughed, easing away, trying to make light of the moment.

Chhotu had pulled me back into his arms. 'You can never disappoint me, Kaki... you are my best friend...' he chided.

Now I switched on the computer.

'Learn something new, Meera. Don't take second chances lightly...' I recalled Dr Batliwala's parting lines in that instant.

Mohan

Mohan Patel

I slowly typed the user name and password, taking my time today, feeling my fingers tremble, as I tried desperately to concentrate, glancing periodically at the instruction sheet Chhotu had neatly pasted by the side of the study table, facing my bed. Holding my breath carefully as the screen came to life, infested with strange looking boxes of varied sizes and shapes. Wispy clouds floated in the background. I ran my fingers over them, slowly.

Wallpaper, I whispered, remembering the twinkle in Chhotu's eyes every time he taught me something.

Something new.

Press on the box (icon) that says Connect to Internet.

It's what I did next.

A jarring sound emanated from inside the monitor, like an old man clearing his throat in the mornings.

I quickly got up and bolted the door. The kirtans had already commenced. Guruji would be here any moment.

'Internet Connected,' a line flashed after a few seconds, next to it, a small visual of a telephone.

I tilted my neck sideways to decipher what was next on the instruction sheet.

Press on the box (icon) that says, 'Internet Explorer.'

I pressed hard, twice, my hands still unsteady.

Two identical looking, rectangular windows popped up. I suddenly panicked. Wondering what I was meant to do next. Reprimanding myself for forgetting the exact sequence...

Calling Chhotu or Mohan away from the havan was out of the question, I knew. Besides, Mohan would probably be livid seeing me operate the computer on my own. Having always told me to do so only under Chhotu's supervision...

I dabbed the sides of my face, instinctively pressing on the first window, on my right.

MSN something, it read. I stared blankly for a while, before crosschecking the sheet for something... anything.

This was beginning to feel complicated, so I quickly double clicked on the cross sign at the top right hand corner of the window like Chhotu had mentioned I should, if I wanted to shut down something. Referring to the window as a 'web page,' I murmured constantly.

The box immediately disappeared, emitting a funny sound again. I don't know why, but I got jittery this time around. What if I was doing something drastically wrong? What if the machine got damaged? I closed my eyes, imagining the extent of Mohan's ire.

Somehow, I had almost forgotten about the other window that was now minimized and flickered incessantly at the bottom. I pressed the middle key on the top, right hand corner, meant to amplify viewing. Still curious, I suppose...

'Mumbailover.com, thousands of horny Mumbai housewives online, 24 by 7 real, live action by young, hot bods, plus live sex chat, all this for free!' declared a crowded caption.

'Once a particular website/webpage opens, in the topmost search bar, type whatever it is you want to know, say a recipe for poha,' I quickly skimmed through Chhotu's instructions, almost having reached the end of the cue sheet by then.

I don't know what happened next.

A dozen tiny boxes appeared all over the original webpage, some interspersed with even smaller images. Wordlessly, I double-clicked on one of them, pushing hard on the mouse.

A middle-aged woman with plump breasts appeared out of the blue on the screen, darting her tongue out in my direction, pushing into the folds of her transparent sari, heaving uncontrollably, her tresses matted. She wasn't wearing a bra, I could tell from the way her breasts flopped sideways.

I stared in disbelief for some time, wondering how a simple Maharashtrian dish could be remotely related to all this.

Someone had begun chanting. Had Guruji already stepped inside our hallway? I tried deciphering from the apprehensive silence outside. It had been so long since we had last met. Had Guruji too changed? Like the rest of us, our pleasures perishable, like our pain?

Distractedly, I closed that particular box down, before proceeding hastily on to the next. There were literally hundreds now, crowding the page, each with a tiny picture – every person naked. This time, a young man's face cropped up, his trousers bunched near his ankles, his organ erect.

Impulsively, I enlarged the image, my heart racing. He was shaved, the red veins on his manhood pulsating.

'Fuck me Mumbai Lover,' a woman groaned, writhing on a wrought iron bed.

The man's back was to me. I moved closer, eyeing his well-sculpted buttocks... the way he ran his hands over his shaft once, occasionally grazing his fingers against his thighs.

I could tell he exercised daily.

'Ohhh, I'm so wet, fuck me now,' the woman moaned lustfully, parting her legs, her head dangling over the edge of the mattress.

She had a paunch, stretch marks on her breasts. She kneaded them repeatedly, as the man crouched on his haunches, stroking himself more rigorously.

I narrowed my eyes when he slowly removed a large, plastic object, phallic shaped, his hips braced upwards.

'Mumbai Lover, don't keep me waiting,' the woman groaned, rotating her waist, her hair descending in waves.

All of a sudden, the screen went blank.

I was sweating by then.

I redialled frantically, as Chhotu had said I should every time the line got disconnected.

At first, there was nothing, till the screen slowly started coming back to life, on its own, somehow, some of the images however, a tad pixillated.

With one push, the man inserted the object between the woman's legs... acrobatically placing her right knee over his shoulders. 'I'm going to come all over you Mumbai Lover,' she howled, rubbing him faster... and faster.

The man's face was partially hidden.

I couldn't stop myself from staring at the shape of his buttocks... tight, and yet tender.

'Mumbai Lover, fuck me Doggy style,' the woman now ranted in a raspy voice, sounding reckless, as he yanked the object out of her, deftly turning her over on her behind, standing with his hardness pressed under her thighs.

I turned down the volume to the bare minimum. Not able to take my eyes off the screen, even once. The man was plunging in and out of her buttock cheeks, his muscular hands gripping her thick waist to get a tighter grip. His chest was shaved too. I licked my lips, feeling slightly moist myself. Or maybe it was the humidity outside... I couldn't tell after a point... my fingers pressing over my sex as my hips braced against the chair to make more room for them.

Slowly, the man withdrew, licking the woman's rear this time, his organ still dangling between his legs, fully aroused. Sometimes, he would use his hands, stroking her lustfully.

The room too had fallen strangely silent. Till I heard Guruji's familiar baritone, instructing the women to bend down on their knees... close their eyes.

I pulled at my nipples, my eyes captivated by his hardness.

'Mumbai Lover...' I shivered deliciously, climaxing within seconds, my fingers overflowing with dampness.

'*Jai Ho... Jai Ho,*' the assembled chorus chanted.

I parted my lips.

As if I was there...

'Want to watch more horny housewives of Mumbai? Log on to www.mumbailover.com. Get the best fuck of your lives by the biggest and hardest online lovers. Get wet, fisted, sucked, licked, bondaged and pumped, 24/7,' a tiny message flickered over the same box.

'Meera, Meera open the door, Maharaj is in a real hurry, he has another satsang tonight... in Panvel,' I heard someone call out my name.

It wasn't Mohan.

❦

'I learnt about the miscarriage from Sarlaji, it must have caused a lot of anguish, coming at the same time as...'

I stared at Guruji's mouth, at the look of disquiet in his eyes. 'I really have no memory of that time. Or how long I had lain on my face, bleeding all the while, losing the child in those moments as Dr Batliwala, my doctor at JJ Hospital later explained...' I gulped, battling a familiar rawness, before adding weakly, 'it's as if that day didn't happen at all.'

I looked down at the tattoo on my left hand. The ink lighter...

'You look just as beautiful Meera, as if the years have not passed you by... beauty such as yours isn't marred by time,' he murmured, slowly walking towards the bed, my left hand in his, our fingers tightly entwined.

'Everything ages... everyone...' I said tersely, staring back into his intense, black eyes.

Guruji was rubbing the centre of my palms. His left thigh pressed into my right.

'Perhaps it's why I felt nothing seeing you... when you walked in through that door.' I glanced over my shoulder carelessly, before continuing in a low voice: 'You've always been here in a sense... after that night at the kutir... you always come back when I needed you the most... like that afternoon... the time I was locked here in this very room... the first time... when they blamed me for Bansi's death...'

Guruji was breathing roughly.

'I, I know it was you, it had to be your mouth over mine...' I mused, looking down, my kohl smudged.

'Are you happy, Meera?' Guruji interjected, pulling my knees closer.

I placed my head on his shoulder, the tiny follicles of hair at the back of his neck causing a sudden shiver.

'Happiness is not difficult,' I began slowly, adding as I ran my fingers over his chest, 'and neither does it require years of practice. All it really needs is some common sense. Like knowing when to look away... look away, first.'

Guruji walked away from me, bowing his head low, as if he were in deep contemplation. I settled my sari pleats. 'Maybe you have changed then, Meera,' he resumed after a while.

I smiled, slanting my head sideways. 'When you've been away from someone for so long, it's hard to tell the difference or, or maybe I have. I don't know. There's no point questioning the obvious. I think... it's better you leave now; there are a lot of people outside, anxious to be in your presence. It feels wrong to keep them all waiting... they've travelled here from such faraway places...' I exhaled, standing up and pointing towards the door.

'You think I didn't do enough for you to be blessed with a child, Meera... in, in all these years? Are you saying I failed you? We failed?' he raised his voice agitatedly, clumsily grabbing my hips, drawing me closer to him again.

I held on to Guruji for a while in silence, my buttocks pressed against his loins. 'Maybe I did, initially, in the early years, when I longed to talk to someone or just be touched in all the right places. I don't know for certain anymore... it's like they exchanged my body with another persons' at the hospital,' I replied, lolling my head backwards, feeling the succour in his arms.

'I have asked Sarlaji to send you to my ashram for a while,' he whispered, running his fingers through my damp tresses.

'Why?' I moaned, as his lips brushed past my forehead.

Guruji turned me around to face him, 'Don't you want to come back?' I placed my hands over his, as we stood with our backs pressed into the door. 'Sometimes, we must learn to physically separate our sadness Meera... the sense of loss that is known to diminish with distance... like, like the child...' Guruji drew me to him.

A tear formed and melted...

'Why? Why is everyone trying to get me to leave this house? This city? My, my child...' I cried, lifting my face up, overcome with pent-up anger.

Guruji secured his arms around me tightly, saying, 'What makes you think I am trying to do the same?'

I took a deep breath. Looking back into his eyes, I said, 'You once told me about fate and faith, standing at this exact spot, claiming they were inextricably connected... so all I am saying is that I'm ready to take on whatever lies ahead... the rest of my life is not in an ashram... Meera Patel is not dead. I, I just lost a child... I am still alive...'

Guruji shrugged his shoulders. 'And you are certain this is what you want?' he cupped my cheeks tenderly.

'I just... I...' I faltered, whimpering as he carried me in his arms back to bed, 'I just wanted to be loved... it's all I ever wanted, you know, to have someone look at me and see this Meera... this person... this person I am now...'

Guruji wordlessly undid my bun, watching my tresses cascade to my waist.

'Do... do you love me, Amarkant Maharaj? I mean can you say everything you said to me before a roomful of strangers?' my lips quivered as I tried stopping him.

Guruji plunged his head over my breasts. 'Meera... oh Meera, when will you understand this... this samsara... this is not the path I chose to walk on...' he paused, suddenly grabbing my shoulders.

There was an eerie stillness.

'I have never seen you in that way, Meera... what we share is different; above all this reciprocity and the bondage of human relationships... the suffering... the sins of our flesh. I am trying to unravel the mysteries of creation... and, and you, you Meera are my sadhana, my tapasya... not the samsara I have long ago surrendered... I can't go back now... even if I tried,' he added emphatically.

I watched him complete the rest of the sentence. Then holding up his face, I questioned, circling his lips with my fingers, 'And what gives you the right to decide that on my behalf? Samsara or sadhana? Who I must be?'

Guruji looked stunned. 'Meera... you have finally overcome the sins of your last birth... and the ones before. The night of your miscarriage was the moment your soul was recast... it's what made you lose so much blood too. The golden period of Vrihaspati has commenced, as per your birth chart. You are now free, to pursue whatever your heart desires. But beware naari, the samsara is alas, nothing but an illusion, everything wrapped in maya. Nothing will last, nothing can. It's the way the universe is designed. Never forget my last words... for it is these that will set you free in the end, again...' Guruji thundered fiercely nearly an hour later, as I lay prostrate before him, my head facing his genitals.

He was still erect.

'Amarkant Maharaj ki jai,' the rest of the women in the living room broke out into a belligerent chorus, their faces distorted.

Guruji's eyes were clamped shut by then, his face passive, the fractured-light haven now behind us.

Signalling the end in some way.

Or maybe I had finally come of age. I gazed at the rain clouds beginning to huddle closer together.

'Get an umbrella for him... now...' at a distance Ba hollered, waving her hands frantically in my direction.

I pretended I hadn't heard.

Knowing only this. Everyone wants things they can have. They just don't know it... yet.

Amarkant Maharaj was the first man I ever wholly rejected, sans regrets, sans anything... without caring about the consequences.

Twenty-one

Secrets

With Guruji gone, and most of his disciples from out of Mumbai leaving one by one by the end of the week, life gradually returned to normal. I resumed my daily chores slowly, relieving Vrinda of her additional responsibilities, taking care of the kitchen, preparing a list of things everyone needed, doing the groceries, cleaning the cupboards, rearranging the shelves, washing all the bed linen with my own hands... even agreeing to join an English coaching centre in Dadar.

It was Chhotu's idea, really. It was he who had convinced Mohan, telling him one night, almost six months after Guruji's departure that he would give up cricket on Sundays, to focus more on his impending exams, if his demand was met.

'Kaki is alone all day... and it must be so boring to be stuck at home all day... what's the use of her knowing the computer now, if she's not strong in English?' I can still recall his adolescent face, trying to win an argument with his uncle, while Mohan sat making a calculation of the month's expenses, grumbling constantly, fidgeting with his glasses.

'She is not interested in all that kind of stuff, beta... this is her life only. It's like going to office... or school... for us...' he tersely retorted after a while.

I was sweeping the kitchen floor. I looked up at the sound of Chhotu's voice. When had he shot up so much? His stature... the way he stood with his hands placed on his hips, an exact replica of Bansi... the manner in which he hoped to score a point with Mohan. Somehow.

'But I hate school, Kaka...' Chhotu answered, getting up abruptly from the dining table; some of his notebooks falling on the ground.

Mohan remained silent for a while. 'Then get all the information on the closest place she can go learn all this, from the Internet... this English thing you think will make your Kaki happy, but only after your homework, young man... and make sure it's a cheap option too... every damn thing in Mumbai is so costly nowadays... and as if Meera's knowing English will be of any great use to anyone? As if Kaki will start serving angrezi khana to us!' he added condescendingly.

Ba had just walked out of the toilet. 'What's the matter you both?' she wheezed, looking concerned, dabbing her face with her pallu.

'Your Badi Bahu has decided to resume her studies, she now wants to learn English...' Mohan sneered.

'Don't worry about him, okay? He'll forget everything once he sees my results... I promise, Kaki...' Chhotu whispered, walking up to me and squeezing my arm.

I smiled awkwardly.

'You look happy,' he smiled, touching my face for a fraction of a second.

Sounding like a man. At fourteen.

❦

'Guruji's auspicious footsteps have blessed this household again. Maharaj never leaves his devotees empty-handed, just one visit is enough for a miracle...' Ba declared victoriously, dabbing her eyes.

Chhotu's class eight results had just been declared. He had ranked third in class. But Vrinda and Mohan looked tense.

'What's the matter with you two, huh? Badi Bahu, prepare the puja thali, I must go to the neighbourhood temple this evening to offer my prayers. My grandson has scored a rank... that too, for the first time. And then, Mohan beta, all of us must plan a visit to Guruji's ashram for his two-week-long, annual satsang... we've been missing it for the last few years,' she continued.

Chhotu was out with his friends. I was about to go to the kitchen to make the evening tea, when from the corner of my eyes, I noticed Vrinda whisper something into Mohan's ears.

Change of plans, perhaps? I stopped in my tracks.

Not that it mattered. I wasn't planning on joining them in any case. Dr Batliwala had strictly prohibited travel after my latest check-up, telling Mohan the same on our last consult. 'Her insides are very weak and the hormonal treatment is ongoing, it may still take some time before she regains her strength... could even take a couple of months,' I recalled his parting words.

'Ba, there is something I wish to say... it is actually Chhotu's wish... the thing is, he's never been on a flight... so Mohan Bhaiyya promised to take him somewhere. I mean... now that he has his vacations, and anyway... I've been thinking of taking him along to Ahmedabad at some point. It's been so long since he met my side of the family... poor boy gets so bored here. All his friends go to all fancy holidays... those whose fathers are still living...' Vrinda stuttered eying Ba nervously.

'Nowadays, airfares are affordable, if you can bag a good deal, especially if you book online... there seems to be no dearth of travel websites. All his school friends have been on an airplane, Chhotu even tells me how he's the one being constantly teased about still using the train,' she spoke hurriedly, glancing at Mohan for approval.

I watched her go on and on. Trying to decipher what it was Vrinda really wanted. This time...

Mohan came to her rescue: 'Meera can come too, of course, and then we can all join you at the ashram, Ba. I will make all the necessary reservations required. Vrinda Ben is right... Chhotu needs a break... he has earned it. As we all have. So, why not make the most of these holidays. Besides, there's still some time left for

Guruji's Maha Satsang, so we can club both easily, travelling back to Mumbai together... one-way flight, one-way train... save some money too that way...'

Ba tried saying something, but I cut her short, 'No, Mohan, my evening classes are on. It's barely been a month and a half... and you've already spent so much money enrolling me into this course. It will all go waste.'

Vrinda looked at me wide-mouthed as I continued: 'And who knows how my body will react with all this airplane business? It sounds too risky. I'd rather stay back and look after the house. It's almost a year since I miscarried, how long will you people watch over me, this way? Really, go on, have a lovely, long holiday... and now, shall I bring out the dhoklas to celebrate?'

Chhotu had returned by then, his face flushed from the evening heat. 'Kaki why are you not coming? Aren't you happy with my results?' he said petulantly, rubbing his eyes.

'Of course I am... but there are some journeys we must make ourselves. You'll never have this time back, beta, trust me... make the most of it. And be sure to click lots of photos for me, like you do every Sunday when you all go out. I'm used to seeing the world through your eyes, it's nicer too... all the colours you capture, the stories you bring back for me... each time...' I laughed, gently patting his back.

His T-shirt was soaking wet. He stared blankly at my face. 'Bakwas!' he scoffed, moving away.

'What beta?' I called after Chhotu as he made his way into the bathroom, removing his vest.

'We can never see the world through anyone else's eyes, Kaki. How will you ever know what it's like to sit inside an airplane, flying over all these houses? I've even heard they serve delicious food on board. Or view the majestic Lal Quila in Delhi, or, or the road to Shimla... maybe even beyond... that is said to be lined with scented pine trees and snow-capped mountains. This time of the year they might probably be also laden with some left over snow. Have you ever seen snow, Kaki? Or, or mountains even?' Chhotu panted slightly, sticking his head out.

I gently removed the clothes from his hands, separating the coloured ones from the whites. 'It's why I have that thing, right?' I whispered, pointing at a shiny, new laptop that sat on our bed... a reward to Chhotu from Ba.

Mohan laughed loudly, almost sounding elated that I had declined his offer. 'So Meera, looks like you will have a lot of fun while we're all gone, huh? Chhotu be sure to teach your Kaki everything about the new laptop before we leave... he sure knows more than me... kids I tell you, these days!' he gesticulated wildly with his hands.

Ba had just removed her hearing aid.

'*Shiiish*, it's going to be our little secret,' I whispered meeting Chhotu's eager eyes, before vanishing back into the kitchen.

❧

It was the first day of my second month at Asha Centre for Spoken English, Dadar. Mohan dropped me to class that evening and I sat in the front seat of his car. Vrinda had accompanied Ba to the railway station, as she was leaving for Guruji's ashram.

'So you haven't said how are your classes are carrying on? I'm sure you are far ahead of the rest? I mean you've studied till the twelfth, after all... and you were always a bright student back in Sinor. At least it's what I told at the time our marriage was finalized. '*Temane ketalaka inglalisa jane,*' Mohan mimicked Baba telling him that I happened to know English, perhaps hoping to strike up a real conversation.

We had just stopped at a red light. I fumbled inside my bag.

'What time is your flight? You said it was around seven thirty or something...' I said instead.

'How does it matter, huh?' Mohan snapped, adding in an accusatory manner, 'as if you stayed back to see us off... anyway, yes, guess we'll be gone by the time you're back. Hope you've carried an extra set of keys and some cash? One just can't trust these trains at all nowadays.'

I smiled, pulling out my silver key ring.

'I could also take a taxi... I mean, just in case, it rains or something,' I mused, staring out of the window.

The cars restarted... the sun was about to slip into the horizon.

'Meera, I've been thinking; see the thing is... we're not going to have any kids of our own. After your miscarriage, it's now pretty plain; besides, neither are we getting any younger. I think of the future a lot these days you know... our future, this family's future... Everything I have been able to rebuild slowly... I mean, post Bansi's death, it's almost as if I am the only son... like Chhotu is perhaps also destined to be. So, what if I adopted him, legally, that is?' Mohan paused, sounding anxious.

A gust of breeze blew in; I closed my eyes for a few seconds.

'But he's already a Patel, the same bloodline. How will things change, apart from the legal nitty-gritty's? And it's not like we have a lot of property or anything...'

Mohan pondered this for a few seconds.

'Also, Meera, Vrinda Ben is getting on in years. How long do you suppose a single woman, a widow... can keep on at a job to support a family, huh? And, with me being promoted to store manager, probably in charge of another new departmental store, Mr Chopra claims he's planning to open, I will get a bigger salary... more perks hopefully. I want to leave something in Chhotu's name, bequeath something tangible... after I'm gone, that is. He never really saw his father... I mean if it wasn't for me asking Bansi to fill in that night at the shop, he would have still been alive today,' the rest of his words trailed.

I could see the entrance to the lane. Any moment now, we would reach. 'Seems you've already made up your mind then?' I said, removing my satchel from the back seat, my hips casually brushing Mohan's left arm.

'Have you lost even more weight or what? Your waist looks serpentine,' Mohan muttered, studying me in the mirror as I arched my back.

'Have I? I exercise a lot these days. I can do more than hundred surya namaskars,' I pursed my lips, returning to my seat.

'And, and just when do you do all this? How do you get the time? You've never told me any of this,' Mohan made a long face, applying the brakes suddenly, as I lunged forward. 'What else have you been hiding from me, huh, Mrs Meera Patel?' he hissed, roughly grabbing my arm, as I leaned sideways to open the door.

I shrugged my shoulders.

'You can't share all your secrets, Mohan...' I rued, staring back into his eyes.

❦

Tucked away in a dingy alley, minutes away from the bustling Dadar station, Asha Centre For Spoken English was located on the fourth floor of a dilapidated commercial building that belonged to no one, in a sense. Crawling with all sorts of tenants who operated non-descript, part-time offices, small Xerox and DTP typing units, each floor was teeming with occupants. The stairway was ill-lit. Stray dogs spread out idly on the steps, as I negotiated them carefully, never taking the lift... once.

The room we were designated had no windows. Not that I minded. I hardly had any time to look up from my textbooks. Besides, there were a lot of boys in the class, much younger than me. I couldn't really tell their ages though. All I knew was that from the moment I walked in till the time the class ended, every action of mine was being scrutinized closely by someone.

I could never be wrong about a stare. It's the only instinct in a woman that never really ages, no matter what the circumstances. This evening too, the same boy occupied the bench beside me. Unlike other days though, he sported a slight stubble. He was clad in white trousers, really tight at his crotch, teamed with a red, V-neck T-shirt. I smiled at him. 'You're Ramesh, right?'

His eyes lit up. 'Meera? Then he rephrased instantly, 'Mrs Meera Patel, it's nice to finally talk to you.'

'Hey Ramesh... yaar, looks like there will be no class today, want to take us to a film or something... you promised when you got your salary, remember?' the girl called Tarana, in her early twenties, sporting a fitted, orange salwar kurta and chunky wooden bangles tapped his shoulder impatiently. I had spoken to her a couple of times. She was from Delhi and wanted to work in a call centre. Of course, I never chatted much because I was always in a rush to go back home and get dinner ready.

'Hey Meera, want to come along with us?' Tarana asked spontaneously.

I arched my neck, hoping to catch a glimpse of the wall clock. Had Mohan already left? I wondered.

'Wow! I'm a lucky man – *bhai, acchi angrezi sikhne ka kuch toh faida hai*... a night out with so many lovely woman,' Ramesh grinned lewdly at me. ' Please, Meeraji, come with us.'

I stared him for a while, my eyes travelling down his flat stomach.

'Woman nahin... women... and Mr Romeo do not forgot about me, the married woman... *yaad hai na, bhaijaan*,' a girl in a burqa lifted up her veil, meeting my gaze fleetingly.

This time, I broke into a smile. 'Myself Meera Patel,' I cleared my throat, adding almost instantly, 'My husband Mohan Patel. We live in Byculla. With my Ba and... and today they have all gone on holiday...'

'Okay, so now officially welcome to our group, Meera.' The girl in the burqa said. '*Mera naam Tasneem Qureshi hai*... is it alright if I call you *appa jaan*...' she asked, wrapping her arms around me.

My pallu dropped slightly.

'*Ya Allah! Aaj toh toofan aane wala hai,*' Ramesh teased. '*Do do shaadi shuda aurat ek saath!*'

'*Lahaul vila kuwat...*' a chubby girl interjected dramatically, stepping forward.

'Meera meet Jayanti... the hot waitress... meet Meera... the hot housewife... meet Ramesh, the unemployed Mumbaiyya wannabe DJ... meet Tasneem, the Lucknowi begum... meet myself Tarana... the hottest *kudi* from Delhi...' Tarana threw up her arms in the air.

I grinned, suddenly feeling a lot happier than I had in a long, long time. It was 8 p.m.

'Meera, you're coming, right?' Jayanti whispered, handing over a fallen exercise book back into my palms.

'Of course... can't you see the look in her eyes, and before you ask, Meeraji, I, Ramesh Nene will drop you back in case it gets late... fine, sweetheart?' he offered gallantly.

Twenty-two

ASL

Mohan had left by the time I got back that night. We didn't end up going for a movie. Taking a taxi to Chowpathy instead to gorge on some spicy pao bhaji.

I don't remember the last time I'd had so much fun, as I splashed about in the waves, gazing at the murky horizon, laughing and joking with this carefree bunch, waving at children going up and down on a giant merry-go-round, their faces jubilant. Like Kartik and me during our village fairs, our tongues tinged orange and red.

My sari was still soaked when I returned home. At first I was a little thrown when I encountered the sudden darkness. For a while, I stood outside, in silence, my chappals sand-laden, my lips still burning from the tangy mint chutney. But the aloneness was also liberating.

With no one to ask me to fetch this, cook that... today... tomorrow... not for the next month and a half! No rules about when to wake up, what kind of paranthas to make, how much oil to pour, over the centre or on the sides? What flowers to arrange on Ba's puja thali? What vegetables to purchase for lunch? What clothes to hand out to the press wala downstairs? What the evening would bring? Before night fell... Which way Mohan would then want to have sex? Front? Back? Side? Upside down? Who would be on top, finally? Or would it just be myself, chewing on the last chapatti, slightly scorched at the edges, before lying alone in bed? Wondering if Mohan ever knew how I felt. Out of curiosity, if not anything else.

I decided to skip dinner, storing away the dough in the refrigerator, quickly changing into my night-time sari. There was no need to shut the bedroom lights as I undressed. So, I stood in front of the mirror for the longest time, my hands caressing below my navel.

Had I really lost that much weight?

I don't know for how long I stood gazing at my own reflection, smiling to myself every few seconds, pouting deliberately like I'd seen women do on billboards in front of the railway station, their lips always painted a robust red.

There were a few fine lines under my eyes... or, or was it just the lights? I ran my fingers over my cheekbones slowly and sat down at the computer.

Mohan

Mohan Patel

www.mumbailover. com I keyed in surreptitiously, hoping to get the spelling correct. Chhotu had taken extra care to explain the concept of upper and lower case to me.

Like the first time, there were more than a dozen video clips plastered all over the main webpage. Each accompanied with a brief description of what the footage probably contained. Bondage, Doggy, Blow Job, Pussy Fuck, Tit Cum... I scanned all the titles one by one... thinking all the while to myself what they actually denoted. Biting my lip, I peered into each individual box, for the next ten minutes or so, double clicking on most for barely a few seconds, impatient to locate the young man... the one with the intense stare. The one I just hadn't been able to get out of my head since the day Guruji had left...

From time to time I'd close my eyes, trying to imagine the curve of his buttocks, his perfectly chiselled chest... completely shaven, and the way his organ had slid effortlessly into the woman sprawled over the bed.

The connection was very slow.

I would've given up after a point, fanning myself furiously with my pallu, when all of a sudden, a tiny window popped up, emerging from a cluster of similar looking boxes on my left.

'Live Chat with Mumbai Lover' it read.

My heart raced, as I double clicked on the same.

A small screen lit up at once.

I took a deep breath, sensing the silhouette of a man sitting on a high chair. He was clad only in his underwear.

'ASL?' a thin line appeared simultaneously at the bottom of my page, in a rectangular box.

I blinked nervously, unsure what to do next.

'ASL?' the sentence reappeared.

I brought my face closer to the screen. The man was squatting in a manner that did not reveal his face. That his chest was shaved was the only thing I was sure of. The rest of his surroundings were dimly lit. For a few seconds, the empty box flickered.

'Hello...' I typed inside it at last, pausing anxiously after every letter.

'Hot?' the response followed immediately.

Was this graduating to a regular conversation? How long would it continue before I could see his face? Once? I ached to find out. The man on the stool was the one typing in the chat to me.

'Yes...' I typed, picking up speed, fiddling with my bra straps. I was perspiring heavily.

'Isn't there something about the darkness... just us? Here?' he responded after a second or two.

I pulled up my legs on the chair, leaning back to undo my bun. Somewhere a generator made a whirring sound.

'What are you wearing?' he asked as he shifted about on his stool.

'Why?' I retorted spontaneously, surprising myself with the sudden speed with which I was now operating the keys.

'Do you like my underwear?' he reverted.

I was about to ask him his name; instead I pressed the Delete button.

'First time on Live Chat?' he resumed, flopping down again, bringing his left hand over his organ.

'Yes,' I admitted, drinking a sip of water.

It was after 2 a.m.

'ASL?' he repeated again.

Then, before I could react, he added, 'Male, 30, Mumbai Lover.'

My face was flushed.

'What is ASL?' I questioned, nursing a gnawing nervousness.

'Age, sex, location... it's how we usually start a conversation here. How do you like to start things?' he countered, slowly stroking himself.

'Jai Sri Krishna,' I typed quickly, looking away from the screen once.

'Lol! That is funny; anyway, you are drop dead gorgeous. And thanks for turning on the camera, I like babes who are direct...' he stopped typing and reached for his organ.

It was partially erect.

'It's common to take God's name first... at, at the start things... anything,' I stopped abruptly, before resuming, 'I don't know about this camera thing, honestly... this is a new laptop actually, it must have come on just like that... actually this is not my laptop...'

The man waited for a while, his arms flopping to the side of his chair.

'Why aren't you naked?' he keyed in, scratching his chest.

'Can you see my face?' I panicked slightly, pushing back my chair in haste.

'Lol! I wish... nope... it's rather dark on your side... for now I can just about see you waist-downwards... and wait... hey now... now you're moving too far away from the screen. Though, to be frank, I like it this way. Who cares about faces, anyway?'

'I do not understand...' I pressed Enter, having decided to just go with the flow for a while.

'Okay, let's get straight to the point. Want me to cum for you? You have to pay after the first hour of free sex chatting... this is a porn site... so unless you are ready to swipe that card for me, baby, we are wasting precious time...'

I frowned, rapidly scrolling down the rest of his message.

'Porn?' I typed in a hurry.

'I mean... unless you wanna talk dirty or something... turn me on? How about showing me your hot pussy for a change. Build things up. It's what makes cyber sex all the more fun. Everything feels so real... all the lines, the fantasies, the foreplay... the orgasms... even the fears...'

'Fear... fears?' I phrased clumsily, thoughts racing through my head.

'Fears? Okay, so you like it kinky, huh? I should've known. One more horny Mumbai housewife!' he wrote.

'Yes I am a Mumbai housewife. And... and there's no one at home, you see... for sometime actually. And, I was just curious tonight I think, though I've been on this site before, one afternoon a long time back. Those days of course, I knew even less about these things,' I wrote, trying to suppress a childlike embarrassment.

'Lol! You've come to the right place then... curiosity is everything in sex!'

I gasped, narrowing my eyes. There was a minute or two of silence.

'Push down your sari, I want to look at your pussy NOW,' the man wrote, getting off the stool.

'Pussy?' I typed back, glancing down apprehensively.

I hadn't worn a panty after my bath. It was what Mohan usually liked.

There were shadows on the wall.

'Wet?' the man wrote next, gently cupping his balls.

'No,' I keyed in without reading his question really, feeling the blood rush to my head.

'Where do you want to do it?' came the next question.

I pushed the chair back slightly, tongue-tied.

'Is that a bed I see behind you?' he probed next.

'Yes,' I didn't know what else to say.

'Close your eyes and lie back on that... imagine me kissing you between your toes, first... sucking slowly on your big toe,' he resumed, before I could come up with my next line.

'Umm, love the way your skin smells... now I'm pushing your knees apart, to kiss you all the way inside that sari,' he suddenly stopped.

I shuddered, grabbing the edge of the study table... the laptop moving up a few inches by the sudden movement.

'Your chat ID just says Guest 127? What should I call you? In bed? Like to talk while fucking?' he questioned after a brief pause.

'My name is Meera... Mrs Meera Patel,' I almost wrote, my tresses falling limp over my navel, my nipples fully aroused. Before omitting the entire sentence.

❦

'*Besotted with her description by his younger sister and having sent his uncle disguised as a beautiful deer to the Dandaka forest, the demon king changed his own appearance, arriving as a helpless hermit, begging in front of the kutir's doorstep... before abducting her to his magnificent Kingdom... showering upon her the choicest gifts... the ten-headed Ravana is said to have been so obsessed with her... a woman who could never love him back... in the same way...*' I paused to look up slowly, beads of sweat clinging to my forehead.

Ramesh cleared his throat. The others staring at me wide-eyed.

'That's a damn strange book to choose for your reading practice...' Tasneem grinned, before asking in a low voice, 'any reason why you selected this in particular?'

'I don't know. I've always been curious about this tale... to read it in English, I suppose... Kartik used to have an English copy of the Ramayana...' I mused, slightly out of breath, adding slowly after a few seconds, 'I can change it though... I mean, in case you people feel it's not suitable.'

'No, it's cool really, the book we all have been asked to read before class next week should be one that we like, something we want to know more about. But what if Sir asks you questions about it? I mean it's not just any story we can easily dissect, right?' Tarana interjected.

'As in no one knows what *actually* transpired between Ravana and Sita while she was imprisoned in Lanka...' Tasneem continued, from behind her veil.

'Tasneem, I got married after my twelfth. I think I understand desire perfectly well. The Ramayana, maybe difficult for girls from the city... to some, to someone younger I suppose too. But, I, I grew up with it. Playing the part of Sita in our annual Dusshera play every single year... before... before my... Kartik,' I choked, my eyes filling.

Jayanti tried saying something, when I continued: 'Kartik was my twin brother. He expired just before Navratras ended...' I took a deep breath, before continuing in a soft voice: 'I'm not really worried that I selected the Ramayana for this assignment. Yes, it's not some new English book that everyone is talking about... in fact, to be absolutely frank, I can't even remember the last time I read something, anything. My English is still weak. But, this is a start... Sita is where I begin.'

There was a moment of stunned silence.

'*Paradaaraabhimarshaattu naanyat paapataram mahat...*' I recited in Sanskrit, closing my eyes, feeling the weight of their collective stare.

'There is no greater sin than coveting another man's wife...' Maaricha warned Ravana when the Demon King came to seek his help,' Tasneem said after a few seconds, looking me in the eye, lifting up her burqa.

Thanks to Sita though, I actually made new friends. I was usually the quietest, preferring to keep to myself, but reading Sita, brought back the Meera I used to be, all those years ago. In a strange way, maybe Sita gave me wings.

'M, it's okay right, if I called you that? Will you come for my birthday? It's my 25th and I'm having a party at a club in Yari Road to celebrate, please join in na,' Tarana said, settling her curly mop of hair.

It was pouring outside. The road outside the cafeteria flooded. 'Club? Expensive hoga?' was all I could ask, smiling awkwardly.

'Uff, M, what's all this "expensive" business? Stop sounding like my mother back home... always talking of debts and money problems... I mean c'mon, we are in Mumbai for God's sake. Now, now tell me first, are you coming or not?' she pouted, sounding slightly exasperated. 'You can meet my other friends too, M. Besides Gaurav, my boyfriend that is, and, and the drinks are on the house, he claims. Some company discount he's going to manage...'

'I'm not sure I can attend. Mohan usually rings on the landline at night. Besides, all this is for you... you, young people... what will I do there? I, I don't take drinks also,' I paused, finishing off my last sip of cold coffee.

'Hey chill... stop sounding like an old aunty and just say yes, this once!' she asserted, thumping the table.

That evening at the party Tarana introduced me to her friends as 'M'. We stood holding a fruit based concoction, and I glanced away, a tad embarrassed at my new name. I had worn a mustard, silk choli with elbow-length sleeves and tiny, polished mirrors sewn all over the chest and back, hand-stitched by Ma for my marriage, teaming it with a plain, peach sari with a thin woven border.

'M, I absolutely love your blouse. It's downright hot – backless and just so damn sexy... where's it from?' a girl who looked even younger than Tarana asked me cheerfully, extending her hand.

'It's what everyone wears back home actually... for anything fancy... like during Navratras, when we have these dandiya competitions. Tarana said there would be some dancing, so I thought of this...' I was flustered, my ears turning red.

'Well, in that case, may I have the first dance, M?' a well-built man clad in a light mauve shirt stepped forward and questioned. 'I've asked DJ Ramesh to get this party started,' he grinned mischievously, his hazel eyes lighting up as he looked admiringly into mine.

'Okay, I can see that you two have already met,' Tarana winked, slipping her fingers inside his, glancing up at his face to add, 'Can you believe it, Gaurav and I are from the same village even... of course that's something we hid from each other at first... somehow no one likes North Indians in this place, or, or maybe we were still new to Mumbai back then... about a year or so ago, right?'

I stepped aside. Touching Gaurav's arm lightly, I whispered, 'It's the first dance of the evening... don't let it go waste.'

'*Roop Tera Mastana...*' the song kicked off.

I closed my eyes. It was a song from *Aradhana*. I had practised the steps a million times in the bathroom.

❦

I reached home very late. It was past 1 p.m. The colony was absolutely deserted. I didn't change immediately. I tied my hair in a high bun, switching on the bedside lamp, taking my time to do everything... savouring the slowness. I studied my face in the mirror, pulling in my stomach slightly.

My breasts looked heavier than before. My face was flushed.

I wasn't wearing a bra, my choli completely backless. I ran my hands over my cleavage once, carefully unhooking the burnished copper choker from around my neck... feeling strangely exposed.

I shuddered, inhaling the sour scent of rum and cola that still lingered on my breath. 'C'mon M, how on earth will you know that

you don't like something, unless you try it, once at least...' I recalled
Tarana's face as she brought the glass nearer my mouth. I liked the
taste... bitter and yet sweet. Like the time Mohan and I had sipped
on our first cola together, in a movie hall.

'Where were you? You said you'd log on after 12 tonight. I've
been waiting for you all this while, declining so many other chat
requests. Thought you had left me high and dry, considering you
never even told me your name!' I read the first message as I loosened
my petticoat.

'M...' I typed, feeling my pulse quicken.

There was a minute or two of silence.

'You can call me M,' I took a deep breath, running my hands
over the screen.

'M... I like the sound of that... you look so sexy tonight M... I am
undoing that choli of yours... stooping to hungrily kiss your breasts...
I can't resist pushing my tongue into your mouth... my legs riding up
your sides, grabbing your waist...' he spoke as if he was right beside
me. I felt the immediacy of his desire.

'We're standing by this huge window, it's the only one... the river
breeze blows on our faces,' I paused to compose my next sentence,
lolling my head backwards, adding, 'I touch your chest...'

'I'm here... still...' his next message said.

'I, I kiss you... the taste... it's like swallowing the sky...' I was
breathing hard by then. 'I touch your face... your eyelashes... I, I want
to... taste... your...' my fingers trembled slightly.

It was the first time I had articulated what I wanted. In the way
I wanted.

'Say it... say "dick",' he cut me short. 'Say it, M...'

I scrolled down, opening and closing my eyelids, clamping down
my thighs.

'Dick... dick... dick...' I slowly typed, my nipples fully aroused.

'Sorry Bhabhi, Mohan had rung, he couldn't get through earlier it seems,' I hurriedly explained the next morning, as Mrs Deshmukh studied me from head to toe. 'Is anything the matter?' I stopped, biting my lip.

'Meera, have you done something to your face?' she spoke at last, easing into a smile, touching the milk packet I clasped in both my palms. 'Why, Bhabhi?' I answered, trying to force a smile.

'You've been glowing these days... yesterday too, when you went out, everyone in the colony was talking about how you have begun to look years younger. Mohan is in for trouble, he better head back home soon,' she chuckled, leading me down the balcony.

I glanced down. 'What's this?' I quizzed sharply, looking ahead after a few minutes.

'I wanted you to meet someone, Meera, it's why I was searching for you since morning today,' she paused, pointing ahead.

A bright, green parrot fluttered inside a tin cage.

'The cage... it's a bit small, no?' I spoke slowly, as the bird fluttered its wings incessantly, restricted in its new environment.

'Arre Meera, how many times we took this damn parrot outside since morning... hoping it would fly away, but it just wouldn't budge. Maybe it got scared seeing the torrential rains. Was actually there... sitting on my ledge. Honestly, I would've kept her inside my bedroom only, but you know how Uncle hates pets, anything new actually in the house,' Mrs Deshmukh made a sad face, her eyes drifting to the horizon.

'Does it talk?' I questioned, coming closer and gently patting the corners of the cage.

'Ram Ram, Ram Ram,' the parrot squawked in a harsh voice.

'That's all it says. Must have been someone's pet. But it refuses to leave because of the rains,' Mrs Deshmukh muttered under her breath.

The parrot had a piercing gaze; it was hard to look away.

'Have you come up with a name?' I asked as we strolled back.

'Madhubala,' she answered, glancing back at me once.

I stood motionless, overcome as if with a sudden bout of sadness.

'What's the matter?' Mrs Deshmukh patted my shoulders, walking back.

'Nothing. I was, was just thinking about the name... Madhubala dying so young, much before her time,' I shuddered.

It had started drizzling again.

Twenty-three

Early days

The first three weeks without Mohan passed quite uneventfully. The only constant being Mumbai Lover. Like the rains outside... imaginary, at times, no better than a fleeting pastime, something that helped me grapple with my own loneliness... a mere night-time pursuit, which invariably died a slow death the following morning, buried under the mundane... a boring habit that posed no threat, at least, not in any real sense.

'Hey Meera, ever had a fling with someone outside your marriage? I mean, don't get me wrong, but most married folks seem to be indulging in affairs these days,' Ramesh asked one day, removing the 'ji' from my name all of a sudden. We were coming back from a night show of an English film... my first in all these years. I was miles away, imagining all the characters in my head... all over again... the actors, the sets... the sunsets... the way the lovers kissed with their tongues, recklessly, without a care.

'How do you know she's also not hiding someone, huh? Hmm... what say, Meera? Frankly, if you ask me, this is the right time to have a steamy affair. Sometimes, it's just what men need to take more notice of us,' Jayanti responded playfully, winking at Ramesh.

Tasneem was pregnant again. She had just broken the news to us that very evening. 'Appa jaan, say something please, is it true what these people are insinuating?' she questioned naively.

I smiled, glancing down at my hands.

'Arre, Tasneem darling, ask me,' Ramesh hollered, fumbling for something in his backpack, before adding excitedly, 'You probably won't believe me guys... but I've nursed a huge crush on Meera's hands for the longest time. See, all the pictures I secretly clicked on my phone... sometimes it's all I can think about... even after I get home... and am in bed...'

'In bed?' I stuttered, somehow taken aback at Ramesh's confession.

'You mean when you are with Jasmine?' Tarana squealed, rolling her eyes at him.

'Sometimes...' Ramesh winked, throwing me a kiss, before jumping off the train.

I laughed. It was easy to feel carefree these days.

❦

'You're late again tonight,' he typed, as I undressed leisurely.

'What time is it?' I questioned, unhooking my bra.

'Late enough. Want to turn off that lamp?' he added after a few seconds.

'No, I want us to see everything.' His hair was damp. Like he had just bathed... the muscles on his chest gleamed. I ran my eyes down his collarbones. His ribs glowing in the semi-darkness...

'I want you to touch me,' he messaged, slowly parting his thighs, adding after a few seconds, 'I want you to do as you please tonight... I want to climax in your hands while you rub me... to savour my own nakedness... this nothingness. Okay?'

I inserted a finger inside my sex, and leaned back on a pile of pillows.

'Stop...' he instructed. 'It's not about you and me... not any more. Not after this... take me between those fingers, take me everywhere...' he resumed after a few seconds.

I ran my hands over the screen once. His jaw line was so firm...

'Describe what you're doing... each thing...'

'I turn... to face you... you're naked... all I can see is your eyes,' I shivered, as a chill ran down my spine.

The man was standing, his organ protruded.

I watched it for a while... its tiny lips opening and closing, as if to match the rhythm of my waist.

'I feel you... as you push it into the softness of my palms... I hold still, just to... to watch you grow,' I gulped hard, my throat aching as I moved closer to the laptop, adding, 'I push the skin back...'

The man stepped back a step or two... breathing heavily, the sound of his grunts more prominent with every passing second.

'Slowly, I unwrap your hands from my breasts; to push your organ inside them... making you jump almost, reacting as if to your own touch...' I keyed in, spreading my hips wider.

'I... I love the way your left nipple tends to slant slightly on one side. It makes me so hard as I flick it backwards with my nails, entangling my hands after a while to grip my dick, placing your fingers over mine... holding still... the safeness of skin over skin...' he responded.

I closed my eyes.

'I like it that you shaved...' I entered, lightly licking my right thumb.

'Together we move our hands on my dick... again and again... my balls grazing against your wrists, our chests pressed against each other's, our tongues in each others' mouth...' I scrolled down, bringing my mouth near the screen, swirling my tongue around his broadness, arching back at the same time, so that he could view my sex.

'Like my taste on your hands?' he asked after a while, his mouth parted.

I pushed my left hand deeper, shifting clumsily on the mattress, my breasts taut with tenderness.

'Or yours?' he typed.

'I like it when you watch me... I feel safe... somehow... like you've already been there... to all the places inside... you... I...' I bit my lower lip in heat, my chest still heaving.

'Yosuf,' was all he said in response.

'Yusuf...' I retyped, pulling the sheets slowly over my shoulders.

'Yosuf...' he corrected.

It was the closest I had ever felt to anyone.

Twenty-four

Convenience!

'Happy birthday to you, Meera,' Ramesh and Jayanti crooned as Tasneem clapped noisily, her eyes gleaming gleefully, like a child's.

Tarana stood beside me, helping me to cut a large cake placed on the dining table, decorated with fruits of different colours. Gaurav clicked photographs, facing us, part of his face camouflaged by his camera.

'Say cheese,' he'd shout every few seconds.

I covered my eyes.

'There you go again, Meera. You're supposed to be the birthday girl, soniye,' he made a face, shrugging his shoulders.

'Let her be, Gaurav... you should've been a professional photographer. God, you're obsessed with clicking people,' Tarana scoffed, neatly slicing the cake.

'These eggless things are pretty tasty, I'm impressed,' Ramesh cut her short, his lips smeared with toffee coloured cream.

Mohan had been away for a whole month. It was July. Tarana was lying on Gaurav's lap. Ramesh was busy texting his girlfriend Jasmine, away in Goa on a holiday.

'Hope your in-laws won't mind that we dropped by. I mean, eventually, when they're back, middle of this month, appa jaan, right?' Tasneem probed protectively.

I shook my head. 'No, this feels good actually. Having people over, the house gets so empty after a while, especially on Sundays,' I rued, walking up alone to the window.

'So, what do you do all by yourself, in the nights and stuff, especially?' Ramesh cut me short, his eyes searching my face.

'I like the way this friend of yours always comes straight to the point, each time!' Gaurav laughed, pointing at Ramesh. Everyone was sprawled out on my bed.

'Look who's talking, as if my boyfriend here is any different,' Tarana smirked, pulling his head closer as Gaurav gave her a slight peck.

'Get a room you two!' Jayanti groaned, turning over on her stomach. 'But on a serious note, Meera, don't you ever get lonely? I mean look around... this room for instance, what do you have here? Except for this laptop?'

'Hey, guess what, one of my married cousins is having an affair with this guy she met in some chat room or something,' Tasneem interrupted in a low voice, adding, 'And they've never met in person. Yet they've discussed everything, it seems. She looks so satisfied these days, radiant as a newlywed.'

Ramesh was walking to the window; he turned to ask, 'What exactly do you mean by satisfied? Hinting at cyber sex, kya?'

Tasneem propped up a few pillows, then resting her back against them, she replied, 'I think so. Tasfiya says that they chat for hours together... and you know what, she even went ahead and purchased this really fancy cell phone from some imported shop in town, just so that they could SMS each other all day. *Tauba tauba,* sounds so dirty, no?'

Gaurav too raised his right hand in agreement. 'Guys, how can two people do it online? I mean okay, assuming that they're on these live sex chat sites... like Mumbailover.com say... even then... all this connection business sounds way too farfetched to me. It would feel like being in a sex education class with naked models all around... umm, big tits, tight ass... the works and yet you can't do anything, like really anything. Fuck!' he groaned, winking at Tarana.

'Which woman would actually visit such impure sites in the first place, especially if you are married and all?' Tasneem muttered angrily to herself, gently clasping her stomach.

'Oye M, you've been awfully quiet all this while, guys maybe we should get going now,' Tarana said looking at me.

I had been watching Madhubala all this while. She had a new cage.

'Guess you're really tired of this silly discussion we've been having, thanks to our male companions, right M?' Tarana smiled, securing her arms around my shoulders.

'Bloody unfair, Meera knows it was Tasneem who first started all this sex chat business,' Gaurav scowled, jumping off the bed.

'I wasn't judging... I'm no one to,' I mused, clearing my throat.

'Good girl!' Ramesh exclaimed, throwing me a kiss.

'But Meera, c'mon what's your take on all this? You think cyber sex can ever really be as real as sex in bed with your partner?' Gaurav quizzed, touching my back lightly.

'Ram Ram, Ram Ram,' Madhubala croaked loudly.

'I don't know... maybe, it's a question of convenience. That's all it is, perhaps. Everything starts from there...'

❧

'Do you ever want me to see you... umm... see me?' I slowly typed, my lips still quivering.

I had just climaxed, lying on my stomach on the bed. My laptop was perched on two pillows.

'And suppose I said yes, would you agree to meeting me anywhere else... outside this chat room?' he messaged after a few seconds of silence.

'Maybe, I could probably call you home,' I keyed in.

'Okay, rule number one, I never come to anyone's place... so, it would have to be a hotel. Two, I charge by the hour, three thousand bucks, plus conveyance. Besides, the in-room expenses of course, mini bar, etc... and, and I never agree below three stars, almost always preferring the town side. No Powai, Thane types. Too much traffic just to reach there... I'd fall asleep the second I hit an AC bed.'

I scrolled down the list. 'Nothing's cheap anymore, inflammation,' I keyed in, biting my nails.

'Lol! Your English teacher needs to be told you're making progress... *inflation nahin toh inflammation hi sahi,'* he responded, adding a smiley after the sentence ended.

I stuck out my tongue. 'Oh! Sorry... actually I have so many new words swimming about in my head all the time. Gets tough to remember what to use when,' I admitted, playing with my tresses.

'Okay, tell me, what's the word you're thinking of right now, say, as we speak?' he questioned instantly.

I removed my fingers from the keyboard.

'Umm... may I be completely honest?' I paused, suddenly tongue-tied.

'Go on,' he replied.

'Pussy,' I typed, with my left index finger.

'Lol! You are funny, M!' he typed.

I smiled. 'I'm slow at times,' I responded after a while.

'Slow? No way... that's one thing you're so not. Do you realize you climax the hardest when we do it unconventionally? Like day before, when I wanted to do it in a train toilet and you insisted on sitting on the pot...'

'But, but that was more out of convenience,' I confessed, rubbing the corners of my eye.

'Maybe, but just slamming in and out of you... holding your hands up against that door, your breasts in my mouth, your ankles grinding forcibly into my hips... your hair all over the place... it was just...' I exhaled, reading out my words to myself.

'9820236675,' he promptly responded.

'I don't have a mobile actually and the landline is risky.' All sorts of thoughts raced through my head.

'Have you thought of what you'll tell your husband, in case he asks, like why your phone bill is so high for the past month, huh?'

I clutched my chest, reading the rest of his chat and bit my lower lip. 'He knows I use the laptop... the Internet I mean, so I can always say I was reading up things for my class. Besides, I don't think he reads too much into all this. I manage all the household finances, and every month I put away some money. That way, I don't have to keep asking him for things, small things...' I entered, before adding in the next line: 'Besides, what am I supposed to do all by myself?'

'Sorry, but I think you're underestimating your husband. After we chat tonight, I'm going to teach you a few new tricks to erase all traces of our conversations from your laptop. Always good to end things professionally, no loose ends... you should always be prepared. Okay?'

❧

'Hi, it's me, M... calling from a neighbourhood phone booth. My landline has been down, which is why I've been cut off for the last few days. I've been thinking about what you said before... about us meeting... the paid thing I mean. I'm okay with the arrangement. My husband, he... he's back the coming Monday. Do you think we can meet up this Saturday? It's only Thursday morning, so if you need time to make up your mind, you have all day today and tomorrow. I'll call again on Saturday morning, by 11 from, from the same number...' I whispered, hanging up in a hurry, leaving Yosuf a brief recorded message, before I stumbled out nervously of the phone booth.

Was I putting too much at stake? Too soon?

Twenty-five

Surprise!

It was Saturday afternoon. I was in Mrs Deshmukh's flat and dialled as soon as she stepped out of the room.

'My landline is still dead; this is my neighbour's number. I will wait for you in front of Café Mondegar, in Colaba. It's at the start of the Causeway... one place that's always crowded... it'll be easier that way. Being invisible, I mean. And it's also the only place I know well. Actually, I, I was hoping you'd pick up your cell today at least. Anyway, I'll log on to the site if I can, somehow... if the line is up by the time I leave home. Try and be online... how have you been?' I paused, then added, *'Oh, and I'll be in a salwar kameez tonight. I'll leave my place around seven-ish... take the back gate, so no one really notices, you know how people talk around here... anyways... I hope you can make it. It's a red salwar kameez, with gold sequins in the front and a matching chiffon dupatta... sleeveless. I'm leaving my hair open... the way you tell me it looks best.'*

'How long has Mohan gone for this time? Seems like forever,' Mrs Deshmukh muttered to herself distractedly. I wondered how much she had heard.

'Just a few more days,' I steadied my voice.

We both nodded.

I had skipped lunch that afternoon, taking my time to shower instead, scrubbing my underarms for over twenty minutes with a coarse paste made from turmeric, besan and milk boiled to the brim. I decided to let the amla and shikakai hair pack stay on for a while... using a scented face-wash to cleanse my face. It was a gift from Ramesh, imported or something he'd mentioned. 'I've got the same one for Jasmine... if only she was as fair as you, jaaneman, if I could see the veins on her face, like fish at the bottom of a translucent ocean, like this...' he had moaned, moving closer to me on our train ride home.

'You think Ramesh and Jasmine are having problems?' I had asked Yosuf later that night.

'Maybe, he was just hitting on you, M... he's a guy after all. Perhaps, he's always fantasized about a fair chick and this Jacintha or someone is dark, fat and ugly... could be tired of fucking her... variety is the spice of life, as we all know...' he keyed in.

My eyes glared in the dark. 'It's Jasmine,' I corrected him, sitting upright.

'Whatever! Just stop reading between the lines and enjoy the attention,' he wrote, his consolation sounding strangely intimate.

'What makes you think I need attention?' I asked, wiping the sides of my face.

'You really shouldn't be asking me this question. I mean, you just made me lick your pussy... begging for more all the while, making me shag for you this time. Wanting to drink me again and again,' he responded, trying to make light of the moment.

'So? Someone I know once told me that most Internet porn surfers happen to be women... he'd read it somewhere... in some famous, magazine...' I don't know why I suddenly blurted, unafraid of speaking my mind.

'Lol! You sound like me these days. Cynical, cold... calculating almost,' he observed.

'You can't become someone else just by sleeping with them,' I retorted, trying to suppress my rising irritation.

'Ouch! You can kill a man with that sarcasm! Now, listen you can say what you wish to me... it's fine. And, hey forget all the stuff

I said earlier to you okay... I hardly knew you back then, it was like Day One or something...' he paused.

'And? What's changed?' I interrupted, getting restless.

'Me,' he replied.

❧

The red salwar kameez wasn't new. Mohan had picked it up for me, from a store in Crawford Market. He hadn't realized it was sleeveless then, he later claimed, when I wore it for the first time, lying beside him on bed, his hands fidgeting with the dupatta.

'It's perfect, thank you...' I had said, turning to face him.

'It makes your breasts look juicier... the only thing is... I mean... you can't wear this outside,' he'd interrupted stiffly, smacking his lips.

'Why?' I had quizzed, sitting upright and adding, 'Vrinda is always wearing these kinds of outfits while going out, even at home on weekends these days. How can the rules be different for two women in the same house?'

Mohan had grabbed my breasts roughly, propped on his elbow, his stomach pressed into the edge of the bed. 'What if any other man casts a look on these, huh?' he narrowed his eyes, squeezing hard on them.

I locked the main door carefully, checking out the stairway. There was no one. A function was in progress downstairs, a wedding party, perhaps. The latest film music blared from the speakers.

I slipped out of the back gate, the one facing the children's park. It was exactly 7 p.m.

It had been overcast all day, the sun having set earlier than usual. I decided on a cab, not wanting to reach Colaba late. As I waited in the dark for a taxi, I tried figuring out what excuse would work best, just in case someone spotted me sneaking out. A walk in the park to get some air, or maybe a function back at my school, in Dadar? Anything that could easily explain the sudden change in my appearance as well...

My hair billowed in the evening breeze. A pair of bright headlights flickered faraway. There were hardly any people on this road. 'Taxi,' I screamed, waving my arm desperately.

The taxi approached closer, its passengers cloaked in complete darkness. It was difficult to see anyone's face.

'Taxi... Colaba?' I spoke impatiently, my heart pounding, as I scurried to keep pace with the moving car, worried it would zip off or be beckoned by someone else.

'*Chaliye*,' I yelled once more, banging hard on the left hand side door, bringing the vehicle to a screeching halt, this time.

'*Marne ka irada hai kya, Madam?*' the driver agitatedly hollered, getting off, his face glistening with sweat.

'*Haan ya na bolo pehle, Colaba?*' I repeated in Hindi, sounding anxious.

It was nearly 7.15 p.m. '*Haan ya na?* What are you thinking so much? *Haan ya na?*' I shouted exasperatedly, my words piercing the surrounding stillness.

'*Haan*,' someone countered in a loud voice.

'*Haan*...' I whispered, taken aback, by the familiar voice, 'Mohan?' I don't know how many times I said his name. Or for how long I just stared at him.

'Just where are you going dressed like that? What's going on, huh?' Mohan raised his pitch, pointing his fingers accusingly at my face.

My throat was completely parched as Mohan looked at me suspiciously, before he got to the point: 'I tried calling you this morning again. But, the phone just rang a couple of times before going dead,' Mohan paused to survey me.

I couldn't look him in the face.

'Let's go inside, Meera. This isn't a safe place, and it's gotten so dark. These power cuts are so damn annoying,' he added after paying off the cab.

I carried a small suitcase.

'What's the matter?' I finally managed to speak up, following Mohan inside, my head still lowered.

'Haven't you read the news at all? It must be all over the place by now,' he glared at me. I remained silent as Mohan leaned forward, before whispering into my ears, 'It's Guruji.'

I looked at him in surprise.

'Maharaj has been remanded to a three-day police custody on charges of trying to molest a 19-year-old girl. Her in-laws had brought her to the ashram on the pretext of freeing her from evil spirits... she started screaming and kicking when he tried to allegedly touch her. It's on all the TV channels. Everyone at the ashram is being interrogated. Some rumours doing the rounds even suggest Guruji was operating some sleazy sex racket all this while. Apparently, there were stashes of notes found in various regional shivirs, mostly Dollars and Dirhams. The CBI might be roped in... the police are slated to raid the homes of all his primary devotees, those who housed him over the years... in Mumbai, in Gujarat, in USA... everywhere. It's why I rushed home in advance, just, you know, in case someone landed at our doorstep as well,' Mohan grimaced, his face flushed, flinging the main door wide open.

My shoulders were trembling. Guruji's news was so overpowering that Mohan had forgotten to ask me where I was going. We climbed the stairs to our house in complete silence.

When the power returned we switched on the TV.

'*Amarkant Maharaj a sexual predator?*'

'*Havas ke pujari Gujarat ke Guruji.*'

'*Were all of Amarkant's victims, actually innocent?*'

'*Basudev (warden of the gurukul) and Sharad Chandra (caretaker of the gurukul) reported missing...*'

'*Baki khabron ke liye dekhte rahiye India 24/7...*'

Twenty-six

'Heroine!'

Mohan left early the next morning, not even having breakfast, saying he had to instruct Guruji's other disciples in and around the city, about how to answer any questions the CBI posed. Just so that everyone was on the same page. 'No one is guilty of anything till the Courts declare Maharaj a criminal... and, for all you know the woman in question was actually the one desperate to have sex, must be just some bored housewife... or you never know it could even be a paid sting operation... these channels are ruthless!' he had grumbled as he dressed.

'But what about the medical tests, you said there was a proper check by the authorities, how can a woman make up all of that too?' I pointed out. I was preparing anda bhurji – Mohan's favourite, something he delighted in eating secretly, especially in Ba's absence. It was one of the few secrets we still had, as a couple.

'What medical tests are you going on and on about, huh?' he suddenly quizzed, grabbing my waist angrily. 'What do you understand of all this, anyway? Are you a lawyer or a doctor now? Or are you pretending to be a judge? Just because you now know two more words of English, you've started imagining yourself to be some real heroine these days! Who are you to pass such scathing remarks on his character; especially after everything he's done for us...'

'I was just repeating what you yourself mentioned last night. I saw the same stuff in the morning on television. I couldn't sleep, so

I turned on the TV while you went downstairs. I, I saw the girl...
she was howling hysterically...' I stuttered, switching off the gas,
suddenly self-conscious.

'Hah! So what if you heard her version this time? Do you have any
idea just how much masala these salacious TV channels deliberately
add, just to stir up a sordid controversy? The same reason why they
keep repeating the same stuff all day long, wanting to hammer their
carefully constructed lies into our system. Bloody scamsters... how
dare they insinuate all this nonsense about a man revered world-
over... do you know how many girls' schools and charitable hospitals
his trust runs?' he went on self-righteously.

'I wasn't passing any judgment. But he's a man after all... and
all men have desires, it's natural, it makes him only human. Maybe
Guruji was just attracted to this woman... it's only normal when the
doors are locked, the waves crashing at a distance... anything can
happen. I mean who has ever peeked into Guruji's world; maybe
he did cross the line. It doesn't make him any less of a saint to me,
maybe, maybe it was that one time he forgot his vow of abstinence...
his journey towards the Promised Land...' my words trailed, as I
drained the excess oil carefully.

Mohan was near the door; he turned all of a sudden.

'Oh like that! Then going by your inference, even you had spent
an entire night with Guruji, Meera, and, as far as I can recall, you
weren't an old hag yourself. You too were quite young, I mean it
was sometime just after Bansi's marriage if I remember correctly...
your body must have been way more curvaceous... besides, look at
those boobs, still so juicy and firm... and your backside so perfectly
rounded... it could turn any man on,' he suddenly started shouting,
narrowing his eyes as I grabbed the corners of the sideboard. 'How
old were you then, Meera? Do you remember when we got married?'
he barked, pointing at my face.

Wordlessly, I brought out the ketchup bottle.

'Nineteen I think…' was all I whispered, pouring out some on the side, before holding out the plate in Mohan's direction.

'Exactly my point! So, did you guys also do it? I mean was there this, this thing… what did you just call it… attraction or something on similar lines? Did Guruji grab those yummy boobs of yours and lick them all night or did you make him suck your sex first… and, and then did you both end up doing it like dogs? Perfectly human by your own admission! How does this analogy sound, huh?' he continued hoarsely, banging the plate down on the dining table.

My eyes stung, as I stood still. Arguments with Mohan were mostly pointless… it felt safer to just agree at times. Or say nothing at all, like now.

Perhaps it was also how we had survived this marriage. Why I never told him what transpired between Guruji and me… never, not once in all these years of us being together. Not even this morning, this moment when there was actually so little of us… left to salvage or surrender.

The anda bhurji was burnt.

Mohan left it untouched, barging out after a while, not looking back once.

⚜

I didn't hear from Mohan all day. Ba rang later the same night, from a railway station to let me know Chhotu would be staying on at Vrinda's maternal place for a while longer. There was a lot of commotion in the background.

'It's better the lad remains there for a while… at least till this storm abates, Badi Bahu. Who knows who will cast their evil eye on this family again… Chhotu has suffered so much already. He shouldn't be exposed to all this… the police, etc. He's grown up under Guruji's shadow; he seems utterly confused about what's suddenly gone wrong, and why we had to vacate the ashram almost overnight... just after the satsang had commenced,' she stopped to clear her throat.

'You never know what can happen in such a big ashram,' I repeated the words to myself, slowly switching on the laptop, trying to balance the receiver with my left hand at the same time. Relieved that the landline had been restored.

'Oh and one more thing... Mohan is putting up with Prakash Bhai, Guruji's disciple who runs his ashram in Karjat. He called us from there a few hours ago, saying he's resuming work from Tuesday also. He will only return home tomorrow night, after picking us up from the station. He mentioned the landline being dead or something, so there was no way of letting you know... earlier I mean. So, don't wait for him, Bahu, there's no point,' she remarked pithily, before hanging up.

❀

'Online? Invisible?' I typed furiously, my eyes searching inside the chat box. 'Hello? You there?' I retyped.

The line got disconnected.

'It's me, M. You there?' I keyed in again, studying Mohan's wristwatch lying on the table.

It was past 1 a.m.

'Our phone line has been dead for a while... have you been getting any of my messages? I, I called you from...' I keyed in, feeling helpless all of a sudden, desperate for answers.

'You were right about Colaba...' came the first line.

I clutched my chest.

'You, you mean, you, you actually came? You got my phone messages that means? Why didn't you pick up your number... not even once?' I wrote, holding back my tears.

'Maybe, maybe I just like things one-sided; why break the mystery of being strangers?' he responded after a while.

My fingers stopped. 'I'm sorry... I did try stepping out. Mohan is back, he, he took me completely by surprise, literally catching me red-handed as I stood facing the back gate. I stopped his cab by mistake...' I shuddered.

'Lol!' he retorted.

'Please, don't remind me of how things didn't turn out... there's no point, as if we can ever actually undo the past! We're here now, and... it's all that matters...' I wrote slowly, opening my hair.

'What if your landline didn't get repaired tonight? What if your husband was home which I am naturally assuming he is not? The past is probably the only thing we would have had in common... you can never wish it away so fast,' he literally cut me short.

I buried my face in my hands.

'Kiss me... deep, I, I want to feel you inside,' I said instead, parting my mouth. 'I wanted to just look into your eyes, Yosuf... you mentioned the sea being close by... the sun was about to set, you whispered as I kissed your earlobes,' I typed, slowly drinking a sip of water.

'Have you ever wondered what it would be to be blind, M?' he questioned out of turn.

'Yes, and it was a beautiful darkness... a little scary in the beginning, melting as soon as you had entered me the second time, thrusting my legs sideways, your organ heavily swollen, as I placed you in, folding my knees...' I couldn't type any longer.

'I finally made my way up your wetness... the last time, with you on my lap... this strange peace descending on me, all at once. Who knew surrender could be so powerful?' he typed after a while.

I smiled.

'Or so powerless?' I sighed, glancing outside.

'Meet me tomorrow?' he asked unexpectedly.

'Monday,' I wrote, slipping on my petticoat. 'It's too soon Yosuf... I am scared I won't manage to pull it off again... no...'

'Day after?' he cut me short obtrusively.

'Day after?' I repeated, rubbing my eyes.

'Yes, unless you make it tomorrow, you decide?' he added.

'Come where this time? Getting out is going to be tough with my mother-in-law also returning home... given that my tests also start from tomorrow... I will be at my Centre from ten thirty in the morning...' I paused wearily.

'Go to Ambrosia, it's a guest-house run by a Parsi couple in Colaba, don't take a cab, reach Dadar first, take the local like you do on most days... say you have some work at the Centre or that your friends and you are doing group studies, in case he happens to ask. Tuesday is a weekday, so I doubt he will, considering you also mentioned him resuming work from that day. Next take a cab from there to reach Ambrosia... it's a relatively known place... at least most local cabs know where it is. Wait for me in room 222, second floor, taking the first right after you walk out of the elevator.'

'Don't, don't wait for me. In case, I can't come, for whatever reason... I mean, let it be the end of things between us then, please. Don't try searching for any answers... or waiting for them, here... like I was tonight...' I wrote at last.

'Heroine!' was all he said before I logged off.

'Heroine...' I whispered, the word sounding too close for comfort.

Twenty-seven

Ambrosia

Ambrosia...' I said to myself, staring out of the moving train.

'Hey Meera, how did your paper go? Looks like I'm screwed... think I need another term to perfect my grammar,' Ramesh said, sounding dejected, flopping on the seat next to mine.

I remained pre-occupied, my eyes fixated on the station... at the teeming millions who always swarmed at the sidelines... eternally waiting.

Jayanti and Tarana joined in just then, peering into their respective notebooks, their faces still flushed.

'Meera, sure you're not joining us? What if this is the last time we are all going to be together?' Ramesh lent me a hand, sulking as soon as I had turned my back.

'You should've been in films...' I smiled.

'Arre Meera, haven't you heard the breaking news on India 24/7? There's a major storm brewing over the Arabian Sea, apparently... *sabh khatam ho jayega*. We'll all drown,' he hollered, raising his voice.

Jayanti gave Ramesh a punch.

'Don't listen to this mad man, Meera. Carry on. See you on Wednesday; these are nothing but silly rumours being spread by some dumb TV channel. *Kuch sansani khabar nahin toh flood prediction hi sahi*, stuff they incidentally keep repeating every second year. Stay indoors and all that nonsense, trying to infuse panic amongst ordinary people. Arre, this is Mumbai, even the bloodiest bomb blast could not stop this city...' she stated matter-of-factly; as I watched the train slowly move out.

I don't know why I ran after the train that afternoon.

'Left something behind?' Tarana asked anxiously, adding: 'Shall I ask Ramesh to pull the chain?'

'No, no I just wanted to say bye... in case... in case,' I stammered, out of breath.

'Ambrosia,' Tarana yelled, as I stumbled on my knees, bending down to hold my stomach.

'You wanted to know the meaning, right? Earlier? Eternal nectar... anyway Meera, byeeee for now,' she screeched desperately.

❧

There was a lot of traffic on the way back. I had stopped to pick up the groceries for the month. There were serpentine queues everywhere... in almost all the shops in the neighbourhood market. As if the city was preparing for the worst.

It was past eight by the time I returned, the sound of the hourly news bulletin percolating down the stairs as I walked up, slowly. Wondering whom I would be pulled up by for being out for so long. Ba or Mohan? Guessing which of them would have a go first.

Vrinda was in the kitchen when I entered. Heating up the food I had cooked and stored in the refrigerator, before I left. She had put on more weight during the time she'd been away from Mumbai, misshapen bulges appearing all over her back as she bent down to wash her hands in the kitchen sink, before serving dinner. Her hair was fastened with a plastic clutch clip. She wore no dupatta.

Sitting at the dining table in a dishevelled cotton sari, Ba looked frailer, as she mouthed prayers in silence, small, black beads sliding across her bony fingers. She hadn't touched her tea.

I looked around for Mohan. Finally locating him, as I stepped out of the toilet, watching television, his kurta soiled from something. He hadn't shaved either.

We didn't speak for the rest of the evening. Ba constantly blabbering about how unfair the entire police probe had been, calling it 'unnecessary' on more than one occasion. 'All Maharaj was trying to do... was cure her,' she kept repeating as we gobbled down our meal in silence.

Mohan looking down on more than one occasion, when our glances met, refusing an extra chappati, pushing away my hand, deliberately distant.

I had blow-dried my hair at the same parlour as Tarana, having pulling it back now into a high bun, hoping the change would pass unnoticed.

Everything looked different somehow... everyone's eyes were hollow. I suppose the last few days had taken their toll on all of us.

'Do you want a cup of tea or something?' I asked Mohan as he changed into his night kurta.

'Turn off the lights,' he cut me short, slipping out of his leather sandals.

'How are things with Guruji? Any hope of bail?' I spoke after sometime, turning around to face Mohan as he sat upright on the bed, stretching his back.

'Stop pretending you care about any of this, Meera, about what happens to our Guruji... I mean, not once did you bother asking Ba this question, or Vrinda Ben for that matter,' he alleged, as I reached out for his hands.

'Mohan... have you heard what India 24/7 has been saying all day long? Tomorrow is doom's day for Mumbai,' I paused awkwardly.

Mohan laughed. 'Oh so now you're analyzing the weather? Geography after English, is it?' he smirked.

I walked up to the window. 'I need to leave home early tomorrow... though my paper is only after lunch... everyone has decided on doing some sort of group study together in the morning, I should be home after six sometime, I've informed both Ba and Vrinda,' I went on matter-of-factly, looking out.

It was past midnight. The colony was deserted.

Mohan laughed again. 'You know what Ba was saying? That everything happens late for you... school... kids...' Mohan scoffed as I slowly swerved. 'Anyway, when Vrinda Ben decides to take a break from her job – as she deserves to, after all these years of untiringly supporting this household – we'll hopefully have another earning member.'

'Come here... for a second, please, Mohan,' I interrupted, holding out both my hands. 'It's a full moon night... come here, please... just for a little while,' I continued, raising my voice slightly.

'Forget it, Meera, we've seen many of those before,' he groaned, his legs dangling from the edge of the bed.

I helped him climb down, placing his rubber slippers under his feet.

'What the hell is it with you all of a sudden?' Mohan yelled irately after a minute or two had passed, pushing me away roughly.

'The moon, it was just here... maybe it went under a cloud or something, stay on for a bit longer, will you? What if tonight is really the last, for us?' I paused, rubbing my hands over his bare chest.

Mohan was fatigued. 'Thank God! Haven't you had enough of this one life, woman... this manhoos city... this house... this filthy colony... this, this marriage... everything?' he blurted out bitterly.

'Who knew surrender could be so powerful?' I replayed Yosuf's words in my mind, closing my eyes.

'Imagine if you also drowned? If the damn prophecy came true, Meera?' Mohan sniggered, as he lay down in his bed.

I watched him from afar, not covering him with the sheet as I usually did as soon as he had turned to his side. My thoughts still lingering with Yosuf.

'You don't need to be loved, M... you need to be desired,' he had said. I parted my lips slowly.

'Aren't they the same thing?' I ran my hands over my breasts.

'*Being desired is like drowning... you have to let go... of the life you had...*' a tear rolled out of my eyes.

Mohan snored steadily.

'*And... and what about love?*' I remembered asking, as I stared at his shrunken silhouette from afar.

'*Love... love is scary shit... love means you want to be saved...*' Yosuf had typed back.

Twenty-eight

Lakshmanrekha

So, you haven't kicked the bucket, huh? I thought there was some major storm brewing,' Mohan smirked, as soon as I had stepped inside the bathroom.

There was no sign of any rain the following morning.

'No, doesn't quite look like it,' I responded as I combed out my hair, adding, 'But, I don't know why I suddenly feel so alive this morning... maybe it's just the sun or something. Isn't it wonderful to have so much daylight, especially in the month of July?'

Mohan grinned, getting back to reading the Gujarati daily. Ba was up too, pottering about the dining table. 'Badi Bahu, must you step out today? Haven't we already witnessed enough tension in this household? Shani is in transit at present, that too with Rahu, it's not a good day for anything, especially exams,' she scowled, her face descending into a dark frown as she fixed her hearing aid.

I cleared my throat, looking around the house.

'Lost something?' Vrinda quizzed, sneaking up on me, as usual, looking rather plump in her tight churidar kameez. She was resuming work too, with Mohan.

'It's nothing,' I said, shrugging my shoulders. 'I must leave quickly... I don't want to be late today.'

Mohan was still munching on his paranthas. 'Aloo again,' he muttered disapprovingly.

'Aren't Vrinda and you also getting late for the store?' I cut him short.

'Yes, we should leave too, just that we have to stop by that mobile shop first... in Dadar, actually very close to your centre,' he stalled all of a sudden, slipping on his brown leather sandals.

'Really? Then why don't you both drop me there, first? It will save me the headache of taking the train.' I handed him a neatly pressed handkerchief and then bent to touch his feet before the exam. 'Jai Sri Krishna,' I whispered.

'Do well,' Mohan said, patting the back of my head self-consciously.

'My, my, Badi Bahu, when was the last time you took my beta's blessings?' Ba taunted from a distance, chewing on her supari.

'It's Bhabhi's papers today, right? No wonder she's seeking her *pati ka ashirwad*, he's parmeshwar after all,' Vrinda squealed mockingly.

'Please don't start all this now... Meera will soon begin her lecture on women's emancipation, how there's no such thing as pati parmeshwar anymore and I'm in no mood right now for her tall talk,' Mohan grumbled, lowering his head before Guruji's portrait that hung in the living room. Then he said, 'I'll drop you. But make sure you haven't forgotten anything. Remember how you once travelled almost half the distance before suddenly remembering your assignment folder or something, making me then drive back through maddening traffic? We have to deposit Vrinda Ben's mobile phone at the repair shop... besides it's almost office time. There is no way I am going to turn back the car today, you understand?'

Vrinda giggled like a schoolgirl, following him down the stairs as we all left the house.

Watching them together I was tempted to turn around, at least once. What if I had actually left behind something? I asked myself, not moving.

'Meera where the hell are you, woman? Always delaying me unnecessarily... looks like she's died before the so called floods!' Mohan screeched.

I grabbed the banister, clenching my jaw. There was no point. 'Coming...' I screamed in return, my gold waistband glistening in the sunlight.

Stepping out of my Lakshmanrekha.

❦

There wasn't a single drop of rain till we reached Dadar. Mohan eyed me from time to time through his rear-view mirror... maybe there was something in my expression that was making him suspicious.

'So, what time will you be back?' he suddenly quizzed, raising his voice, looking back one last time.

I banged the car door shut.

'Same time as I mentioned last night...' I replied calmly, quickly slipping my bag over my shoulders.

An hour or so later, I was at Ambrosia. I had reached earlier than planned and ordered a cup of coffee in Room 222. I was in the bathroom when someone banged hard on the door. 'Yes... leave the tray there,' I instructed awkwardly, through the door. 'Just, just keep it and leave...

It was then that I heard the sound. He was turning the key in the lock.

'What... what are you doing?' I yelped, peering through the bathroom door.

The man waited near the door, his back still obstinately turned.

'Where's the light? Light?' I repeated, panicking, stepping outside carefully.

Just then the man lunged forward unexpectedly, tightening his arms around my neck, clamping his hands down over my mouth. He was breathing heavily, the smell of nicotine overpowering.

'Let go of me... turn on the light, or I'll shout, who are you?' I screamed hoarsely, biting his right palm hard, desperate to wriggle out of his clutches as he darted away from the door in pain, jerking his hands off me that very instant.

'Ouch!' he winced, turning on the light.

'Oh! You're here... it's you, right? I, I thought you were never going to show up! Yosuf... it's really you... right?' I said, my shoulders trembling.

'And why wouldn't it be?' he whispered tenderly, extending his arm to switch off the fluorescent tube light. Making it turn dark again.

'*Sab khallas*,' Yosuf laughed, slowly parting my tresses, speaking in a strange accent.

'Khallas...' I rued, burying my face into his chest, the actual feel of him making all our cyber unions seem incomplete somehow.

'You're tickling me...' I broke into a weary smile, relaxing in his arms, my eyes overflowing, like my insides.

The lights changed everything...

❦

'Say something...' I spoke first.

The rains were coming down harder.

'Guess we should eat first... we can just order room service...' Yosuf spoke matter-of-factly as I shifted back a few inches, settling my sari pleats. 'How about we try this dhansak thingy... and, and maybe even this patrani macchi... or... I don't know... maybe we could just go with a basic burger and French fries,' he stopped brusquely, glancing in my direction directly for the first time, the menu open in his hands.

I stared expressionless.

'Parsi food is totally *mast*...' he smacked his lips.

I rose from the bed. 'I'm sorry but, I'm actually vegetarian,' I interrupted, inaudibly almost, my back towards him.

Yosuf laughed again. 'I was just teasing you, M... trying to break the ice.' He stuck out his tongue, his fingers travelling up my bare back, pressing down lightly while I stood facing the mirror... obstinately.

'As if you knew that I didn't touch non veg!' I made a face as our eyes met again.

'Big deal! You don't know a lot of things about me too... it's only natural when two people meet for the first time on...' he stopped. I lolled my head backwards. 'Mumbailover.com,' we cried out in unison, giggling like children.

'What is your full name? It may be a good way to begin... break the whatever you mentioned before – ice – right?' I spoke up after a few seconds.

'Like ASL?' Yosuf winked.

I wiped my eyes. 'Must you always bring that up? The age thing?' I snapped, moving away to pull back the curtains.

'Ismail... Yosuf Ismail,' he cut me short, adding in the same breath, before I could pose any further questions: 'I'm a Mumbaikar abhi, but originally from Pune, and what else... umm... I turned 22 last to last week... I think we chatted on my birthday also... remember the night I made you lick cake off my mouth...?'

I grabbed the window railings, closing my eyes. Yosuf was years younger, something I hadn't quite detected in the past... when details like this had never mattered... somehow...

'One chicken steak, one veg burger, two Cokes, one with ice... and oh, ek Classic Milds bhi,' it was the sound of Yosuf's voice that dispelled my thoughts as he placed the lunch order over the phone.

'I, I don't...' was all I managed to say, feeling his intimate stare, while I stood watching the endless rains for a while, the glass panes mostly frosted.

Yosuf lay back on the bed, with his shoes still on. He wasn't wearing any socks. 'It doesn't matter what you remember, M, it's the order in which you forget things...' he mused, clearing his throat as I walked up to him.

'You're 22, so young... I mean... so...' I stopped as he leaned across and undid my hair.

'And you're a buddhi, huh?' he retorted, smiling tenderly.

'Listen, I never told you I was young... besides, let's face it, even you lied about being 30, remember?' I frowned, wiping my fingers on a rectangular paper napkin as Yosuf strolled up to the window to light a cigarette.

'*Age ko sex se kya matlab?* It's not a big deal,' he remarked callously, blowing a ring of smoke.

Wordlessly, I walked back to bed, balancing myself on a pile of pillows, crossing my ankles.

'But anyway, since we are on introductions, what is your name? I mean your real name? I am certain it can't be just M,' he reprised, staring back at me keenly, storing his sneakers away.

'What if it spoils everything?' I rued, strangely tongue-tied.

Yosuf laughed slowly.

'I mean... *kuch bhi chalta hai... Sita... Gita... umm...*' he coughed once.

'Meera... Mrs Meera Patel,' I cut him short, picking up a bottle of Cola.

Yosuf laughed even louder, on his way to the toilet.

'What now? What's so funny?' I winced, feeling embarrassed.

'I like the way you say "Mrs Meera Patel"... as if we are standing in a passport office or something,' he exclaimed, unzipping his pants.

I couldn't take my eyes off him.

'It's my name...' I murmured, pulling up the sheets to cover my legs.

'*Pata hai*, it's funny. I mean I'm sure you've wondered yourself... *saala har* sad story *ke andar* why must the heroine be called Meera? Like she's some tragedy queen,' he continued, dropping his pants outside the toilet entrance.

Jockey – the waistband on his underwear read. I swallowed with difficulty as I watched Yosuf clench in his buttocks, his back arched straight as he peed in full public view, without a care. As if he knew I was looking. Relishing the sensation.

I covered my eyes, glancing down as he strutted towards the sink, his organ pointing ahead.

He was completely shaved.

'What makes you call this is a tragedy? I mean, I'm just curious... as in, are you referring to what we are doing here, right now, in this hotel room?' I resumed uneasily, my lips faintly quivering.

'Boss, tragedy sells... like sex, full paisa wasool...' he smacked his lips, taking the bottle out of my hands, some of the Cola spilling onto my sari, wetting the area around my sex.

Yosuf had strong arms. They held me close as I remained still.

'I was being honest... the truth being I was shell-shocked when I saw you first... I've never felt so cheap in all my life, Yosuf... you're a kid I told myself when our eyes met. I'm way older. It all seemed so wrong at that one moment... everything... this bed... us... this, this... hotel... this day...'

The rains were coming down again, as if timed to fill up the spaces. Yosuf remained expressionless.

'I know I asked you to come here... it was me all the way, I wanted this, so, so bad. But... when I saw your face today, the full face... it suddenly felt too real... I mean, I'm sure you felt the same way about me, right?' I couldn't help but pry.

Yosuf smiled wryly, before gently cupping my cheeks. 'So, I am allowed the same degree of honesty?' he clarified.

I nodded my head tamely.

'Okay, so I never thought you were actually this hot in real life. I mean you can never know, right? It's all so damn virtual at one point, after one point...' he paused before dropping his hands by his waist saying, 'I was completely blown away seeing you emerge from the loo. The very sight of your bare back made me hard. You are like a Goddess... in that light... so dream-like... *jaise* I've died and gone to heaven...'

I shivered as Yosuf's left thumb pressed into my spine.

'I thought you just mentioned this being a tragedy? The story of my life?' I sulked, turning around to face him this time.

'Maybe it is, who knows these things?' he answered in a low voice, his fingers tugging at my choli strings.

'Meaning?' I succumbed to his fingers, my shoulders caving in.

Jeena toh sabhi ko aata hai... mujhe to sirf marna hai... har bar... issi samundar mein... I want to drown in you, Mrs Meera Patel,' he groaned, burying his head into my hair.

'You are too young to talk of death so lightly,' I smiled, trying to ease away as he parted my tresses, breathing hard.

'And you? How old are you, really? How old do you want to be? Tell me everything...' Yosuf roughly grabbed my waist, his nails digging into my nerve endings.

'I... I don't know. For a woman age becomes irrelevant after a while... everything feels the same, almost as if you are just being pushed ahead by this strong current...' I answered in a low voice, as he cupped my buttocks lightly.

'My whole life is a lie, Meera, that is the truth, it's the only truth...' Yosuf muttered under his breath, parting his thighs and pulling me closer.

'I haven't worn a bra...' I don't know why I confessed as soon as his mouth touched my earlobes.

Yosuf sucked on them, before nuzzling my neck. 'That's exactly why this story is a bloody tragedy... no bra, me fully turned on, and yet... *dekho humme?*' he stalled, turning me around sharply.

I stood on my toes, my hands clutching his chest.

'All talk and no action for the past hour... *sab khallas!*' Yosuf raised his voice, before dramatically flopping down on the bed, his face pressed into my navel.

The tiny bristles on his chin pierced my soft flesh.

'But, isn't it the way these things usually begin?' I held up his chin tenderly.

'Maybe... but this is... different,' he paused, drawing me over him. His hands circled my mouth, as he slipped in his right thumb.

'How?' I murmured, sucking slowly.

Yosuf looked up for a few seconds, then rolling over with me on top, he whispered, *Yeh kahaani sirf tumhari hai... Meera...* just yours, Meera...'

I kissed his lower lip hungrily, watching the colour of his eyes change.

The sky outside painted a strange slate.

As if it had read my mind.

Twenty-nine

'Shani and Rahu'

It must've been past 2 p.m., but we were in no hurry, leisurely changing out of our clothes, staring at each other in the large mirror, our lips quivering. Yosuf was well worked out, just the way I had always imagined him, his abs well developed, his buttocks taut, his balls perfectly rotund, his nails well manicured.

He looked darker in person, his eyes a moody black, his hair longer than it had appeared on the net. A dimple appeared carelessly on his left cheek... his lower lip was thicker than the upper, his eyelashes were long... almost like a woman's. It was almost surreal how much he resembled Kartik. 'You look different... just as everything feels different... somehow,' I murmured.

Yosuf turned around to face me, his eyes travelling down my stomach as I lay back on the bed, and silently pulled down my panty.

It was the first time I had laid naked beside a man – desired but untouched. As if we were both suddenly scared... like I was a girl again... back in time.

Yosuf slowly stroked my navel. A warm shiver passed between my inner thighs, as I closed my eyes, as if what we had was in danger of breaking into a million, tiny pieces...

'You look thinner than before,' he said, stretching his arms out over his head.

'Meaning, all this while, you thought I am fat?' I covered my breasts clumsily. 'Fat, horny, Mumbai housewife... isn't that what you had said to me once?' I rolled over on my stomach, my arms grazing his.

'What would we say to each other... which truth would we begin with? Which dream would we want to dream, first?' he spoke in a muted voice.

'I'm scared of my dreams coming true, Yosuf. Some part... of some dreams...' I spoke softly, lying on a mass of my open, unruly hair.

'*Sapne kabhi adhe sach nahin aate, Meera...*' he wiped my eyes.

'Then... then how did we get here?' I mumbled.

'You say that with a certain type of regret... having second thoughts? Sex with a stranger, that too in a sidey hotel?' he sharply questioned, as I pressed my face against his moist palms.

'And suppose I said yes?' I added listlessly, staring outside from time to time.

Yosuf sat up to light a cigarette.

'Umm... we could just discuss the refund bit. I mean... I usually don't change my rates for these sessions because I'm the one making most of the hotel reservations, etc. And these days, most married women prefer places of this standard. Good, safe neighbourhood, well connected to the nearest station or taxi-stand, centrally located... AC... Western style toilet... safer, I suppose,' he paused to exhale, resuming after a lengthy drag, 'But, maybe, in your case, I will make an exception. You could pay me for the hotel booking, and perhaps reimburse my taxi fare, if that's cool. I've come all the way from Wadala... no joke, right, in these rains, that too?'

I turned sideways. 'I'm carrying the cash in my purse,' I cut him short.

Yosuf laughed, stubbing out his cigarette. The sound of his voice giving me goose-bumps. 'Know what I love most about this place, huh? These bloody Bawas allow you to smoke in all the rooms. In fancier hotels, smoking rooms are way more expensive. At least you can breathe in here. I mean, who doesn't want a puff before and after sex? You should try it too sometime... it's the ultimate high, way better than an orgasm at times. It's what I do, when women sometimes ask me to say stuff to them, especially post a lengthy sack session... the mushy sorts, getting all lovey dovey, cozying up, wanting more... more conversation... more intimacy. I just light up at that precise moment, saying nothing...' Yosuf sounded cold all of a sudden, fluttering his eyelashes.

'Why give me a special rate?' I raised my voice, touching his chest.

'Shit! I just did the look on you too?' he winked.

'You said an "after-sex" look... is there one for before too?' I questioned bluntly, reaching between his thighs.

'Oh... Meera,' he moaned, bracing his hips forward, as I pulled myself towards him. 'How the hell do you always read my mind?' he murmured, watching me stroke him using both hands.

Yosuf's hand steadily climbed up my waist.

'At least you can breathe in here,' I exhaled, biting his right earlobe.

Wordlessly, Yosuf slipped off my choli.

❦

'What if, if you fall in love some day? One day?' I asked as we lay back against the pillows.

'You mean after having sex? As in, what happens if I happen to wake up next to the woman of my dreams or something?' he yawned, scratching his chest.

'I meant this job of yours, Yosuf. It's so risky... I mean for all you know, you could actually develop feelings for a particular person you are sleeping with... and, and then what? What happens then? Most of the women, your clients as you refer to them... I am sure are like me? Married, some probably even with kids... bigger responsibilities... doesn't it get tough walking out, knowing where to draw the line exactly?' I exhaled.

Yosuf switched off the air conditioning.

There was a stifled silence.

'So, love and sex are two different commodities?' he retorted after a while, slipping into his trousers.

I pulled the sheets over my breasts, my nipples still aroused. The rains were coming down again... this time heavier than the last.

'You didn't answer me, Meera...' he lit up.

I coughed once or twice, the smoke entering my lungs.

'Which one?' I wiped the corners of my eyes.

'Love... and...' Yosuf paused, pulling me into him as I buried my face in his stomach.

I was still moist.

'Sex is natural between a man and a woman... as is love, eventually, I think... you can't really have one sans the other,' I sighed.

Yosuf's breath caressed the corners of my face; his left thumb circled my breasts, squeezing gently. 'Looks like you've answered your own question then,' he smiled wryly, stroking my inner thighs, drawing fine lines with his fingers.

I parted them using my own hands.

'No, what I meant was, what if, you fell in love with the person you're having sex with... just sex... this kind of sex. The kind that ends with some cash or an afternoon in an unknown Colaba hotel... while it pours outside,' I explained, running my hands through his tousled hair.

Yosuf looked up, touching his lips lightly to mine. 'So what if there is money involved? Are you saying it justifies sex between two strangers, Meera? Making an afternoon like this in an unknown Colaba hotel, any different, while it pours outside... more respectable, I mean?' he retorted stiffly, his tongue slipping out of my mine.

'I, I didn't mean it in that way,' I added awkwardly.

Yosuf laughed, the sound of his voice echoing within the four walls. 'Then stop trying to fight it... constantly...' he cut me short tersely, pulling the covers over the both of us.

❦

Afterwards Yosuf began talking: 'I was about seventeen or so *jab* I first came to this sheher. I dreamt of being a film star. Like SRK, my idol – this nobody from nowhere, who virtually dominates Mumbai's film universe now... a man with absolutely no connections... no filmi background, not a rich producer's son, etc. I wasn't called Yosuf back then though. Neither am I Muslim. My forefathers are staunch upper caste Hindu Brahmins, in fact. Priests, actually. My father was the first one to hold a job as a clerk in a nationalized bank; my mother embroidered saris, sowing rich brocade borders and lace details on petticoats and blouses, making me hand deliver them to her clients, on my bicycle... *sab saale bade log.*'

I pulled Yosuf closer, kissing his wrists.

'It's how I first met Prasad Naik. He was this chhota mota model coordinator who'd graduated into fashion designing. Naik was a celebrity back home in Pune... I used to make deliveries for my mother to his house, usually post my tuitions, late evening types. Phir, one night, I spotted Naik on television, *interview de raha tha,* claiming how he was the only designer from our city to participate in the first-ever Men's Fashion Week to be held soon in Mumbai...'

I turned away from Yosuf, as he held me from behind, talking with his face buried in my hair.

'Naik promised me work, claiming chikna guys were much in demand in Mumbai. Telling me how I could make a fast buck by modelling for him; insisting it was also the easiest route to filmdom. "*Tere ko Amol Palekar toh nahin ban na,*" he snubbed me once, after I showed him my portfolio... after I'd told him how badly I wanted to make it to the film institute. My father... he never understood why it was so important for me to get out of bloody Pune, constantly screaming at me for my poor grades, grimly reminding me to prepare for my banking exams... My twelfth results were not even out yet... maybe that's why my old man still nursed hopes... maybe that's why we had that fight one night. Or... or looking back now, maybe he was nothing more than a middle-class man... someone whose only measure of success lay in having reared an equally mediocre, middle-class son...'

'Know something... I really think you'll make a fine actor someday...' I remarked tenderly, kissing his palm.

Yosuf laughed again. 'That's exactly what Naik said after fucking me in his hotel suite... somewhere in Nariman Point, pushing his bulge up my backside... going up and down inside my asshole... saying I had the tightest butt... talent... he kept repeating that word...' Yosuf stared straight into my eyes.

I covered my mouth.

'Chill! This isn't your typical, sad industry saga of sexual exploitation, stuff you read in filmi magazines. Besides, I got over it eventually. You can't keep holding on to sadness for too long, that too on an empty stomach. *Yeh sheher mein talent shabd gaali ke barabar hai...*' he shrugged his shoulders.

I kissed him slowly. 'I, I honestly meant it, just look at yourself... you have a great body. Besides you're so young still... it's never too late to live out the rest of your dreams, Yosuf, no matter how they may have turned out... at, at first,' I stuttered, lost for words.

Yosuf fumbled on the bedside table for his lighter. 'I don't know, Meera. Initially I kept trying to make it work as a small-time model, perhaps believing in Naik's version of imagined stardom. Also, honestly speaking, sleeping with him had opened up some doors... work was starting to pick up... low budget ad films, part-time modelling shoots... I'd even changed my name to Yosuf by then... sounded more macho, I figured. I mean; half this industry is either Muslim or Punjabi anyway... so between an Akshay Kumar and a Salman or Shahrukh kind of name, I decided on Yosuf Ismail... mysterious, masculine... Mohammedan. Honestly Meera, can you imagine an actor... umm... called... let's say Ananta Shirali... sounds more like a freaking schoolteacher in a government college.'

'Ananta... I like that name... it's different,' I said after a few seconds of silence.

'But you can't fuck an Ananta! Think about it, Meera... imagine telling an Ananta, "c'mon suck my breasts, lick me please, I want you so bad Ananta,"' he laughed wryly, rubbing my sex.

I shivered, 'Ananta... I want you so bad, Ananta...' I whispered deliciously. 'Ananta...' I repeated again blowing gently on his eyelashes.

This time it didn't stop raining.

⚜

'What if I couldn't make it today?' I restarted, taking my first drag.

'Easy... easy now... you might choke, it's your first time...' Yosuf promptly pulled the cigarette out of my fingers.

'Who would have paid for the damages?' I asked, grabbing it back.

Yosuf was crouching on the carpet by then, trying to switch on the television. I wasn't sure if he heard me at all.

'What're you doing now?' I questioned softly, adjusting my choli over my shoulders.

'Trying to get this dabba started... you know on my way here, most of the radio channels were talking about how today may be the last day for this city... some Shani and Rahu transition, happens once in a lifetime or something,' he relayed, frowning over something.

'You're limp again. It's amazing how fast men seem to lose their erection, like someone getting up and switching off the main terminal,' I giggled, my eyes travelling down his buttocks, pausing in between.

Yosuf turned back, smiling. 'Looks like there's some major wiring problem in this room! I somehow managed to get the TV started and look... there's no picture at all, no sound even... just nothing...' he panted, flopping down on the bed, his organ wilted, slipping out from between my fingers.

'Shani and Rahu,' I murmured, sitting behind Yosuf, our arms entwined.

'*Setting sahi hai, boss,*' he spoke after a while.

I laughed, pressing my lips lightly into his back.

❧

'Guess what now... no power too, looks like there is some major electrical locha?' Yosuf exclaimed exasperatedly.

I had lost track of time.

'I called up the reception guy asking for another pack of ciggies... he said there was a helluva lot of water-logging and no electrician could come presently to inspect the damages... in fact, some of the phone lines also seem to have gone down,' he reported, knocking urgently on the toilet door.

'Just a minute,' I cried, before staring back at myself in the tiny mirror, its left side slightly cracked.

'Wow... that was fast, I always thought women were notorious for taking all the time in the world to dress,' he observed, as soon as I stepped out.

'I'm used to changing fast; we only have one loo at home. Besides, Mohan, my husband... he, he takes longer and, and Chhotu can't afford to miss his school bus, also... there is... Vrinda Ben...' I stalled all of a sudden.

This was the first time I had brought up Mohan. In all this while...

Yosuf was pouring me a cup of tea.

'*Meera ka Mohan*... or should it be the other way round?' he paused, juggling a couple of sugar cubes in his hands.

'I should probably get going Yosuf. It's nearly 4. I may not get a taxi back to Dadar,' I responded hurriedly, searching inside Tarana's clutch.

'Dadar?' he raised an eyebrow.

'I have to change back, right?' I shrugged my shoulders, straightening my choli.

'Meera... listen... I mean what time do you have to be back... home? We still have a couple of hours...' Yosuf interjected, rubbing my shoulders, pressing himself into me from behind.

My kohl was smudged.

'I know your rates are for eight hours... here, keep the cash... I could even pay your return cab fare... you headed back to Wadala?' I spoke fast, clenching my jaws, trying to keep the rest of my feelings at bay.

Yosuf caressed my neck, his hands softly kneading my buttocks.

'Nope... actually there's this bachelorette party coming up... some rich industrialist's only daughter getting hitched at the end of the month in Bali... big, fat desi wedding... real glitzy... designer clothes and all that jazz. They may even have SRK dancing at the sangeet. The wedding planner needed some male strippers for the hen party...' he laughed slowly, stepping aside.

'Really?' I raised my voice, meeting his eyes.

'Well, in Mumbai, sex is like any another day job... any job to be honest. All you need is the right attitude and a good body... works like a personalized CV really. It's something I realized pretty soon after Naik and I had split, after about a year when I took up a full-time job as a gym instructor, in some place on Carter Road. It's where I had my first paid sexual encounter eventually, doing it in the backseat of this really, massive car... in a hotel parking lot. It was almost dawn... the place was totally khali. I got paid five grand at one shot! I was pretty stunned, at first... I could've sworn I had felt there was a genuine attraction between us all this while. Maybe I wasn't all that wrong also. Two weeks or so later, my cell beeped. "*Akele ho*?" a husky voice probed. I was zapped. "*Kyon*?" I quizzed, startled. There was a lengthy pause. "Shazan Mallick's friend... she said you were very good," someone replied. I smiled. I knew it was time,' he recollected, wiping the corners of his mouth.

'When is this party you are talking about? As in what day is it?' I probed while tying my plait.

Yosuf was walking away towards the window.

'Pune... this Saturday night, at the Savoy Mansion, it's a newly opened property, real swanky, great views, huge rooftop pool, you know the usual...' he answered straightforwardly, pushing back the curtains.

'So, you're going to visit your home too? Pune right?' I asked, coming up by his side.

The streets were completely choked with water, cars floated at a distance... a couple of school-children waded home, their hands clasped tightly, forming a human chain of sorts, the water upto their chests. Yosuf stared at them; pretending not to have heard a single word.

'Here, here keep the money,' I spoke at last, dispelling the silence building up between us.

A police van passed just then, making some sort of frenzied announcement. There were hardly any private cars in sight.

'Maybe, you should wait a while, Meera,' Yosuf said, pressing the envelope back into my hands.

I stared wordlessly into his eyes.

'Leave at 5.30, in an hour or so from now, hopefully by then the water too would have subsided... rather than getting out immediately. You're unlikely to get a train also, most of the lines would be choked... and... cabs...' he bit his lips, sounding serious all of a sudden, more grown up.

'You mean what if I really drowned?' I smiled, smoothening out the creases on his shirt.

'Shani and Rahu,' Yosuf placed his lips over mine.

I closed my eyes.

Yosuf's fingers traced curious circles on my bare back, untying the choli strings once again...

'Wait, I just got dressed to leave,' I reminded him.

'Big deal!' he cut me short.

The power came back on

❦

'You think you'll get bored of the sex... eventually?' I pondered, stretching out on his stomach.

Yosuf was playing with my tresses, still panting slightly. I could feel his abdomen muscles contract and flex.

'Because... in a way nothing lasts... I mean, even this thing between us, the attraction was probably more viable because of the anonymity involved, working like a drug almost... forcing me to take so many risks, tell a bunch of lies, pretending that I had group study today, before checking in here alone... all because... because I feared time... what if time was really running out?' I took a deep breath, slowly rubbing his chest.

'And what if... say you want to meet me again? What if the first thing you do tomorrow night, I mean if your husband isn't around, is to log on to the site again and, and wait till I come online, Meera? What if it's never really that simple?' Yosuf interrupted roughly, pulling up my chin.

'Time always falls short... it has to... eventually... trust me. I've seen more of life, Yosuf... I know when something is nearing its end,' I mulled, caressing his eyelids.

'Bakwas... does every film have the same climax? Things would be so damn predictable, Meera. Think about it... maybe... maybe this is different, just one half... the, the first half,' he winked, lighting up.

'So, you're saying, what if we actually fell in love or something? Say I never went back home... if we just continued lying next to each other, here on this bed, in Room 222? If this day were to never end... like the rains, going on and on and on,' I gasped, pointing outside.

Yosuf placed his hands over my mouth.

'I never said anything about love, Mrs Meera Patel,' he said abruptly, taking a long puff.

I gave a dry laugh. 'Me too... was only trying to get my point across,' I forced a smile, sitting up.

'You know, I think you were wearing the same sari on the second night we chatted, I wanted to say that to you before,' Yosuf remarked in a low voice, studying me in the bathroom mirror.

The taxi would take another hour or so. We'd just been informed by the manager downstairs. It was already 5.45 p.m. It made more sense to change here and head home directly, rather than stop by at Dadar. Besides, the Centre would have also shut down, thanks to the incessant downpour.

'I remember this choli of yours... this particular fabric, the way your sari kept slithering off your shoulders... you were back from some party...' he whispered, coming up from behind.

I turned around.

'Listen... isn't there any way you can sneak out and come online again? Maybe tomorrow night... I mean if this hen party deal actually materializes, I will be heading for Pune only by Friday night? I'm certain you can cook up something, right? Or, what say we chat in the afternoon, huh? I know a good cyber café, where all this is allowed. They even have covered cubicles... close to Dadar station. Can you sneak out of the house like this again?' Yosuf's words were soaked in urgency.

I removed the kohl from my eyes using a piece of folded toilet paper; its dry corners stinging me.

'And hey... why the hell don't you carry a cell phone? We could even text, all day and night...' he grabbed my hands all of a sudden.

'It's too costly; besides what need do I have of one? I mostly stay at home; the only time I go out is for groceries or to the temple with Ba. And after this course is over, I will have no reason to travel all the way to Dadar... unless I pursue another course or something... it's far-fetched,' I exhaled, brushing out past him.

Yosuf leaned against the bathroom door. 'I could buy you one you know, the latest one...' he shouted behind my back.

'For what?' I threw up my hands.

'Don't be so stubborn, Meera... it's another world... believe me, the possibilities are endless, you can be so free...' Yosuf added emphatically, turning me around, as our hips aligned.

I traced his lips lightly.

'Just for the record, I'm happy being in my own world,' I paused, adding as I pressed into his dimple, 'and, honestly, I think I'll be lost anywhere else... in some other world, that is... beyond Byculla. Why try something that you are not sure of?'

'You're right. I mean at first, maybe... but nothing is meant to be permanent, anyway. Nothing lasts, c'mon you said so yourself. Maybe it's time, Mrs Meera Patel... time to fly away, to a faraway place, somewhere beyond your own cage... there is a world out there you know... beyond the boundaries of your narrow Byculla lane,' Yosuf pulled me possessively back into his arms.

I stayed there for a while, quietly watching the monotony of the rains, feeling his heart race against mine. 'So, why don't you go home then? Meet your parents in Pune, this weekend?' I resumed softly, planting tiny kisses on his nipples.

Yosuf glanced down after a while.

'Think about it, Saturday isn't so far away either, the hen party in Pune... I meant since you are anyway going to be in the same city,' I cajoled, gently squeezing his buttocks.

Yosuf let out a wry laugh.

'Go home for what? Can you imagine telling my old man the whole truth about my life, Meera? I can guarantee the bugger will be mortified... and my mother, she *toh* will faint. She was always the staider one... always wearing these really long sleeved blouses, covering her head demurely whenever my father entered a room, fasting every alternate day... for his wellbeing, and mine,' he sneered, holding me back.

'Don't... you shouldn't talk about your parents like that, ever,' I cut Yosuf short, covering his mouth, adding, 'it's not easy to know what goes on between a man and a woman in a marriage... maybe your mother was just trying hard to make her husband take notice of her, to fit into the system, the drudgery of a long-term relationship. Who can tell what happens behind closed doors? I'm sure, every single family has some issues... secrets and lies they keep locked away... covering them at times with years of silence. But that... that doesn't mean the gates to the house are shut forever? You, Yosuf... you can always find your way back in.'

Yosuf shook his head, slowly.

'Please, please just go home Yosuf, this once. Your parents must be worried sick ever since you left home... the years you have already spent estranged from them, here in this strange city, so distant from the life they imagined for you, their dreams... all their hopes. So many things could have also happened at their end... it's not fair to do this to them... please...' I raised my voice.

Yosuf was walking away towards the window, his head hung low.

'Holy shit!' he shrieked all of a sudden.

My heart sank.

'Meera... look, look Meera everything is floating... when, just when did the waters rise this high? I thought the rains were abating a little while back. This is no ordinary storm... and, and what time is it?' he sounded concerned.

'It's nothing; this sort of flooding happens every July. Maybe you are still new to the city. One day at least, Mumbai goes under... these media people also, these news channels have no other work than to hype up what is regular for most Mumbaikars,' I pushed back a strand of hair from my eyes.

'Meera,' Yosuf called out my name, suddenly holding out his arms in my direction, his lips slightly parted.

'If I promise I will come online again, will you give me your word to go home and meet your family, this time?' I said, as we hugged desperately.

'Promises are what you make when you're not sure of meeting the person again... the same person... the same way...' he rued, kissing my forehead. 'I have another condition,' Yosuf whispered, tracing my lips with his left thumb.

I kissed his fingertips, my hips rocking back and forth to a familiar rhythm.

Just then the phone rang.

'It's your cab, Meera. It should be here any minute the reception dude claims. The taxi stand is sending it over, however they have just one taxi at the moment,' Yosuf reported absent-mindedly, banging the receiver down.

He was still shirtless.

'What time is your meeting... about the hen party?' I spoke, while walking towards the bed.

Yosuf laughed. 'Well! Looks like I've missed that one... just one cab it is... and you better carry on first. You don't even have a cell on you; your family must be worried sick by now. The water-logging too seems to be getting worse by the minute. Why risk spending the night stranded in the middle of nowhere?' he met my eyes; as I bent down to pull out the envelope containing the cash.

My pallu dropped.

'Oh Meera,' Yosuf shuddered.

I closed my eyes... feeling nothing, except the dampness of his palms as they shoved my sari down clumsily.

'Same time, tomorrow?' he sunk his lips into my saltiness, peeling off my panty, squatting expertly on his haunches.

The wind raged through my tresses.

'Tomorrow...' I murmured, pulling his head closer.

We had left the window open...

❦

I don't know when Yosuf actually left... the exact time, I mean, or what were his last words to me. It was difficult to hear anything after a point. The rains were insistent, coming down faster, drenching everything, including us.

'Have you ever fallen in love, Meera?' he tenderly asked, leading me towards the bed.

'I... I don't know when I've been in love... I've now been married for...' I secured my arms around his neck, when he gently lifted me off the ground.

'No... not been... falling,' he panted slowly, as we kissed passionately, whispering while sucking between my toes, 'falling in love is different...'

It was the first time I had broken down. 'I, I can't breathe Yosuf...' I cried, at some point, the sequence of which was blurred, I suppose.

Mounting Yosuf, as I threw back his arms, our lips returning to one another... a strange stillness in our eyes.

'Meera...' his hoarse cries filled the room whenever Yosuf thrust his hips forward, as if invading my wetness... for the first time... all the places I hid.

I forced my eyes shut, biting forcefully on my lower lip, wanting to experience each shudder, as he gyrated back and forth, gripping my shoulders as we clung to each other.

Had the phone also rung once or twice, in the meanwhile?

I was past caring. Minutes away from reaching my own climax, when Yosuf scooped me off the bed again, as we stood near the window, our limbs tangled.

'Open your eyes, Meera...' he pleaded, pushing the panes open, his touch scorching.

'I can't... Yosuf...' I responded breathlessly, convulsing as soon as his hands gripped the soft cheeks of my buttocks.

Yosuf eased back slightly. 'I could just cancel that cab, Meera...' he cupped my face, tracing the shape of my mouth.

'What if...' I swallowed, drawing Yosuf into me, wanting to melt against the warmth of his skin... the lights off forever.

We kissed achingly, like long lost lovers reuniting after a season of separation. Scared to let go... unsure of the way back... in the end.

'Look at me once, Meera... before...' he softly chided, placing my head back on the soft pillow, his voice unsteady.

It was then that I looked up, staring over Yosuf's shoulders.

At the carnations that had been alive once... in the vase by the bedside.

Thirty

'No Ordinary Storm'

Yosuf was right. This was no ordinary storm. As I made my way home in a shared taxi, clutching my satchel over my chest, constantly shivering, my lips nearly colourless, my hair matted... it was easy to see just why.

Everywhere my gaze travelled, there were signs of water... sometimes in tiny pools, gurgling at the centre, sometimes gushing out like a mighty torrent, swallowing everything that came in its way... torn chappals, deflated plastic water bottles, discoloured ladies' handbags, bloated out of shape by now, a Mohameddan's white skull cap, someone's expensive wrist watch... fallen flowers, limp petals, tiny pebbles, wilted leaves... the sweat and grime of a city that was once in reckless motion.

'Deva! Is that your colony?' our taxi driver suddenly yelped, glancing back fretfully.

I was still thinking of Yosuf... the shape of his buttocks, as he slipped on his white corduroy pants, not glancing back even once... perhaps imagining me to be asleep.

I never stopped him... pretending it was easy.

'Excuse me Behenji, too much water on that side of the street, looks like you may have to actually walk home,' a middle-aged gentleman sitting beside me, interrupted in a peculiar whining tone, nudging me hard.

I wiped my face. The skies were still ominously grey.

'Yes Madam, my taxi's already conked out twice, if water enters the engine once more, *bilkul bandh ho jayega apan ki gadi.* I can't take another chance. This lane looks severely flooded... better you join the human chain. Look, there, all those people at a distance, walking hand in hand, slowly trying to make it back home. Suggest you too join in, you may even know someone... am sure they all live in the same lane...' the driver continued impatiently, rolling down his window at once, as if to prove the same point.

I adjusted my pallu, handing him a crisp five-hundred rupee note.

'Beti...' another co-passenger whispered, before holding my hands to caringly add, 'be careful, samjhi... the city looks totally submerged. I wonder why no one took those flood warnings seriously all this while? All the phone lines are also down. *Pata nahin* what time we will get home... if at all, we can make it back today, that is. The highways are the worst affected...'

I stared back at her eyes.

I tried to smile.

'Don't worry so much, Maji...' I reassured, patting her weathered hands.

'Alright then,' the gentleman shouted impatiently, waving at me from the backseat.

Slowly, I dismounted, feeling the current steadily climb inside my petticoat, drenching me waist downwards. Another cab passed us by, spitting up a pool of slush, wetting the back of my blouse also. My lips had already begun to taste like salt, from the muggy water that had probably seeped into my mouth. I tried spitting a couple of times, but my throat was completely parched. My eyes burnt. I looked at my wristwatch.

The second hand was frozen.

'Meera... Meera, it's me, Meeraaaaa,' I heard someone desperately holler as I arched my neck sideways.

'Meera, it's me, Mrs Deshmukh! God... what a manhoos day! You know I've roamed the entire city searching for Uncle... he left home to buy some books, mentioning some obscure book store yesterday afternoon, on the other side of town... the one where he says he always manages to get a heavy discount, second-hand *wale kitab*...' she paused apprehensively, water streaming out of her mouth.

I grabbed her wrists roughly.

'Thank, thanks Meera... would have slipped and fallen, my slippers are also already lost somewhere... and I've left my spectacles at home... can't see properly,' she muttered anxiously, as I manoeuvred forward, pushing back the current with each step, my clothes soaking wet.

'Don't leave my hand at any cost,' I shrieked, when we waded in deeper, one of my own sandals drifting ahead.

'Careful everyone, open manholes on this stretch,' a young man hollered, throwing his arms about.

I stopped in my tracks. My pallu weighed me down, making it difficult to even breathe normally. Mrs Deshmukh also panted sonorously, sweat furiously streaming down the sides of her rotund face.

'How far do we have?' someone asked aloud, sounding as if he were in some kind of physical pain, tugging clumsily at my left arm.

I finally looked up... the colony gates looming before us, as we now stood just a few metres away from the first block... my bedroom window flung open.

Ba held on to the railings... her eyes vaguely distant.

'Looks like Mohan still hasn't made it back,' Mrs Deshmukh cringed, shaking her head.

I grabbed my chest, my fingers slipping out of hers.

'Isn't that your mother-in-law there, by the window, up ahead? Ba was standing in the same place when I left home! Thank God, Vrinda at least returned early yesterday, luckily having taken a half day she told me, when I caught her getting off an auto, saying she had developed a bad stomach all of a sudden. Must be the train food she had said frantically, dashing up the stairway,' she narrated, carefully wiping her bag.

'*Yesterday?*' I slowly repeated the word to myself, tasting the rains once again.

'What, what are you saying, Meera? Come on and walk fast. Make haste,' Mrs Deshmukh implored impatiently, dragging me on.

'*Yesterday,*' the word continued to reel in my head.

How long had it been since I left these gates? Lying to Ba and Vrinda... and...

❦

July 26, 2005.

A day many Mumbaikars like me, will never forget. Not only because the city had braved its worst flooding since 1974, but because of the sum total of our losses. The counting of which had only just started.

'Are you sure you don't want to eat anything, Badi Bhabhi?' Vrinda implored again, as I stood behind Ba's bed, massaging her temples.

It was after lunch. Ba was running a high fever, worry writ large all over her bony face, her eyes puffy from lack of sleep, the prayers beads tightly clasped in her hands.

'At least have some amrut... you don't look too well yourself,' Vrinda continued, pouring her a glass of warm milk.

I propped up the cushions, helping Ba sit up, my hands shrivelled from being in the water for so long, reddish insect bites in some places.

I shook my head vehemently.

'Thank God, you made it back home safe and sound, Bahu; we were so tense all this while. Just Chhoti Bahu and me at home, all of yesterday, no other male member also who I could've sent out to look for Mohan and you, like some other families have been doing in the colony, hoping to locate those misplaced. There are thousands missing apparently... still...' she muttered incoherently, turning on the television higher.

The same visuals of water beamed everywhere... a city in turmoil, on almost every channel.

'Has Mr Deshmukh been traced, yet?' I interrupted, turning my face away from the screen, my eyes itching.

'Not yet... Aunty was saying one of her relatives thinks he spotted him in a taxi near Mulund, but you can never tell...' Vrinda pensively replied, clutching her chest, before dramatically flopping down on the bed, tears streaming out of her eyes.

Slowly, I wiped her face.

'Switch off this thing Ba, there's nothing but bad news as of now. What's the point of watching the same depressing telecast? Can these people come back? The ones...' my words trailed as I grabbed the remote out of her hands.

'Actually, the electricity just got restored, Bhabhi... there was no power since late last afternoon... two people were even charred to death in front of our colony gates. That Mrs Dixit's younger son Arun... all of 20...' Vrinda sobbed harder, her shoulders trembling violently.

'I know, I heard... now Ba get some rest, please. I'm going to the society meeting downstairs... some local boys were talking earlier about forming a search squad, splitting themselves into groups and spreading themselves out all over the city... searching everywhere... in hospitals, police stations, hotels, bus depots for those still missing from amongst us. They depart at dawn. I told them I would hand in some photographs of Mohan, just... just in case,' I felt a knot tighten at the base of my stomach.

'Badi Bahu,' Ba suddenly shrieked, before adding wearily, 'do you... do you also think my Mohan is dead? Like, like the others...'

I grabbed the back of the armchair. 'No,' I bit my lower lip hard.

'How, just how are you so strong, Bhabhi, to not be affected by all this? This flood...' Vrinda looked visibly stunned, her face flushed.

I smiled weakly.

'I'm used to waiting, perhaps... I... I have been waiting for Mohan all my life...' I rushed to finish, unbolting the door, and running down the stairs.

❀

By midnight, the rains had somewhat retreated. Now, only its ruins remained... like a pile of molten ashes, after the dead are burnt. Lying scattered in places. Ba had switched the television back on again. Vrinda too remained awake. We had just finished dinner, still hopeful of Mohan's return.

If only he had come back then...

'What happened to the verdict on Guruji?' I asked Vrinda, hoping to get my mind off his absence. Thoughts of Yosuf filtering in... whenever I was by myself... the sound of his voice... his hands... the taste of nicotine on his tongue.

'There's another hearing day after. Who knows what the Court will decree then. There are all sorts of versions being speculated on television. Thank goodness, Chhotu isn't here yet...' she looked up from scrubbing the utensils.

I continued wiping the gas.

'Ba switched the TV back on as soon as you'd gone downstairs... they were showing this news about a couple of children belonging to some school in the suburbs then. Think it was Kalina... on their way for a picnic in a tempo traveller. The driver lost control in the torrential downpour, leading to the Matador skidding off a flyover. All 26 of them, gone... all of them died... some of the bodies washed away within seconds, the tides merciless,' she grimaced, holding her stomach.

My hands stopped rinsing for a few seconds.

'What time is it?' I cleared my throat.

'Almost one,' Vrinda said, slowly picking up the clean plates.

'Let's go to bed. I am exhausted; guess the day is finally taking a toll on me. Besides, I want to meet the society people once more in the morning before they finally disperse. We should sleep... I mean what's the point of crying over spilt milk, anyway? A tragedy like this affects us all in the same way... right?' I said cryptically, hanging out the towel to dry.

✤

The chat box was empty.

I bit my lower lip hard. 'You there?' I keyed in, turning down the volume at once.

'It's me M... Meera,' I added, untangling my plait in haste. 'I made it back home safe... and, and you? How did the meeting in Andheri go? I'm so glad you took that cab out first, instead of me. I guess the flooding was bound to get worse with time, as you'd correctly estimated. Vrinda, my, my sister-in-law was in fact just telling me about the casualties... the schoolchildren in Kalina,' I stopped, hoping he had joined in by then.

It was the exact time we had decided upon yesterday at the hotel.

I closed my eyes... Just then, I noticed a tiny envelope pop up on the right side of the chat window. I double-clicked on it frantically, my heart pounding.

'See, knew it... you had to turn up, who says promises are meant to be broken, Mrs Meera Patel? Oops this is a bad habit! From now onwards, I'm going to call you Meera... just Meera... my Meera... Meera...' I read the lines out to myself.

'What are you wearing Meera, just this minute? Did I tell you that choli of yours is a real tease... I couldn't stop dreaming of your bare back... the way your breasts felt when I touched them for the first time. Listen, will you wear it once more for me, someday? Please... say yes...' I scrolled down impatiently, using my left index finger, my lips opening and closing.

A streak of lightning lashed across the night sky just then. 'Hold me Yosuf... I need you tonight,' I keyed in, grabbing the edges of the table.

'*Pata hai,* Meera... we both are just the same... you and I. We have the same fears too, I suppose. I've been thinking of it all this while... trying to come up with an answer... figure out the real reason you suddenly changed your mind about leaving first, forcing me to leave Ambrosia in such a hurry. I mean was it just because you wanted me to reach my Andheri meeting on time or, or because... you hated the thought of saying goodbye yourself... saying it first? I mean this could be it! The grand finale... where the movie ends... the climax... or should I say, anti-climax!'

I narrowed my eyes, tears welling up instantly. Wiping them, I slowly entered, 'Maybe both... I don't know. Anyway, where are you now?' I swallowed hard.

The air smelt different. Could it be raining again?

'I'll meet you on the other side... wait for me, Meera... and... and listen, promise me you'll never wear a bra again. Lol!' I smiled, going through the remaining part of his message, again and again.

Unhooking my blouse, rubbing my nipples up and down. Trying to imagine the last time Yosuf had touched them... minutes after we had climaxed together... for the first time.

'*The taxi is waiting... you should go,*' I had whispered, touching his shoulders.

Yosuf had looked up startled.

'*There's just one cab and it's for you, Ma'am,*' he bit my chin playfully.

'*No, it's not what we discussed earlier, remember? You leave first... I can always get another one. The reception mentioned there are more cabs coming along in a while... and I could probably pool in with some others living in and around my area. I'm only going back home, Yosuf... You're the one who has to go further... faraway... I meant. Don't waste any more time... I'll settle any dues that may remain,*' I'd cut him short, kissing him lightly over his eyelashes.

'*So, kahani mein naya twist?*' Yosuf had grinned as I lowered my eyes.

'And, what happens if your family comes looking or something? They must be waiting for you to show up...' he urgently retorted, gazing outside in silence.

'And, and yours?' I stopped, sensing his cold, hard stare.

'Don't start that chapter all over again, Meera... not now... please,' Yosuf placed his hands over my mouth.

The phone rang noisily just then. The cab driver was getting impatient.

'Sure?' he had questioned again.

'Hmm...' I let go of his hands, turning over on my stomach.

'And what do I get for this noble sacrifice?' he raised his eyebrows, reaching across to touch my stomach.

'What sacrifice? You're just leaving a little before me... you really do have the makings of a fine actor! SRK better watch out,' I laughed, caressing his chest, feigning a yawn.

'You never know... today is doomsday and what not. Looks like this city could be really drowning... and here you are, sending me headlong into the raging floods?' he had panted, as I sat up slightly, pressing my breasts down on him.

'You are not alone...' I had whispered, my lips grazing Yosuf's neck, as I repeated tenderly: 'You just have to go home this time...'

Yosuf had pulled me into his arms at that moment.

'I want you inside me... where are you now?' I let out a muffled moan. My fingers stopping at the entrance of my sex, my nipples pointing at the screen.

There was a sharp breeze.

'Yosuf...' I breathed into the stillness.

'Chat messages will be delivered when Mumbai Lover29 is online,' a thin line reappeared at the bottom.

I wiped my eyes.

Had my earlier messages too remained Not Delivered?

'Last message from Mumbai Lover29 sent at 9.25 p.m., Tuesday, July 26,' it stated above that.

I pulled my petticoat down urgently.

July 26th?

Had Yosuf lied to me about his so-called meeting in Andheri yesterday? If not, then what was he doing online sending me all these messages? Was the hen party in Pune then nothing but a carefully constructed lie?

Like everything else...

'Are you online?' I entered one last time, battling severe exhaustion.

There was still no reply, even as I tried calculating the exact sequence of events. Why Yosuf was suddenly missing tonight after all that he had made me promise?

Absconding... like Mohan?

Thirty-one

Purush ya Mahapurush

I couldn't sleep much that night, waking up exactly at quarter past five, and rushing downstairs, clutching a few of Mohan's old photographs in my right hand.

'You will ring me right, if you hear anything...?' I was out of breath.

'He's not at the JJ Hospital Morgue or the Bombay Hospital one either... we've already checked, Bhabhi,' a young man in his early twenties, wearing a pink, striped T-shirt uttered passively, taking the pictures out of my hand.

'I didn't mean it that way,' I cut him mid-way, swallowing awkwardly, before adding, 'I'm certain my husband is still stuck somewhere. Do you know how many people continue to be stranded all over Mumbai? Haven't you all been following the news? It's too early to assume the worst...'

In all our years together, Mohan and I had never discussed death; perhaps knowing it was inevitable... brushing it off like everyone else. And yet over time, it was death that kept us together, in a way, strangely numbing us to the smaller failures, inevitable in any marriage, parts of us that kept getting chipped away. Irrevocably.

✦

'Are you sure you have the right number?' the owner of the STD booth questioned stiffly, removing his thick spectacles.

I placed the cloth bag of groceries on the ground, spilling some potatoes. It was almost lunchtime on the 28th of July. There was still no news of Mohan.

'Just how many times will I repeat myself?' I snarled, picking them up slowly, my pallu descending.

The man coughed once or twice, forcing himself to look away.

'*Arre Madam, khamokha gussa karte ho? Apan ka fault thodich hai,*' he frowned, handing me back the loose change.

'Then stop asking me the same question a thousand times,' I snapped brusquely, glancing back over my shoulder. Someone else had occupied the cramped booth by then, anxiously punching in the digits, stealing glances from time to time in my direction.

'Madam, how many times have you visited my shop since morning, *batao*? Every time you dial the same number only,' he retaliated, add after a few seconds while scratching his chest, '9820236675, right? *Bees baar se zyaada kiya hoga try subeh se.* Tell me, what wrong thing have I said to you, huh? The particular cell is still switched off, it's been that way ever since you started calling...'

I banged the cloth bag down on the counter, wiping my face. 'It is the right number... it is the only number,' I gritted my teeth.

The woman in the booth stepped out just then, her hands shivering uncontrollably. 'Unavailable...' she sighed, meeting the shopkeeper's intrepid gaze, as he thumped the counter hard. '*Lo kar lo baat... dekha,* Madam, you're not the only one,' he made a face, pointing at me.

I was walking towards the booth again.

'My husband... he hasn't come home since Tuesday, used to work in Lower Parel... at the mall, in an Indian restaurant... *ghar nahin aaye abhi tak*... the eatery is still closed, I guess. Even the manager's cell phone is switched off. I, I've checked everywhere...' the woman flopped down on a plastic stool, pressing her forehead.

'Have you tried calling his cell phone?' I paused, taking an umbrella out of her hands.

She shook her head, her eyes vacant.

'My daughter is getting married next month... we were saving up. We thought of gifting our son-in-law an expensive handset. Everyone carries one these days,' she gulped for air.

The shopkeeper seemed to be getting restless, eyeing me suspiciously from time to time.

'*Arre* Madam, trying the same number, again? *Kitni baar bolu aap ko, switched off hai.*'

The woman stared at his face nervously, biting her nails.

'Listen to me,' I brought my mouth closer to his, and said fiercely, 'my landline is down since dawn... I haven't slept in three days... I will call again... I will be back. This isn't about dead people, all right? It's about finding those still alive... knowing where they disappeared, this way... how someone can just leave, without a trace? Without saying goodbye, even? Once?'

The man looked down, embarrassed.

'I hope you find him, Behen...' the woman muttered awkwardly, as I climbed down a slim flight of wrought iron steps, my eyes brimming with helpless tears.

❦

In an hour, Guruji would be on television, in his first-ever, televised interview on a national news channel. The country waiting with baited breath, eager for answers. The way I ached for Yosuf to answer my questions. Hoping as I was, to reach him... somehow... somewhere.

I could barely focus on the impending interview.

'*Hawas ya havan?*'

'*Sex ya sadhana?*'

'*Purush ya mahapurush?*'

Numerous versions of the same truth were being flashed on screen since the time Ba had switched back on the television. Or was it all just one big lie, in the end? The one that now confronted me, as I made it back home, taking small steps, my arms throbbing with the weight of the groceries.

Could a man ever rise above his flesh? To fall in love with a woman he just has sex with?

Once? Twice? Thrice?

Inside a kutir? On a hotel bed? In a chat room?

In the darkness?

Anywhere...

❧

'Welcome to India 24/7, Metro News, on this special episode, we feature an exclusive interview with one of the country's most revered godmen, Amarkant Maharaj, worshipped by millions of Gujaratis the world-over. Here in his first ever televised chat, recorded a few days ago at his kutir, where he is presently under house arrest, till the Court hands a final decision,' a thin man in a dark business suit spoke solemnly, looking ahead with conviction, adjusting his neck-tie every once in a while.

I watched Ba and Vrinda as they listened rapt to the news.

'Amarkant Maharaj, are the charges framed against you by Mrs Mandavi Seth true? Did you touch the 19-year-old woman in an inappropriate manner, on the night of July 20?' was the first question.

'Is it true that you asked Mrs Seth for unwarranted sexual favours that night, saying she should allow you, and I quote from her statement recorded by the local police, 'to help inspect her womb,' the reporter continued, glaring at Guruji's looming silhouette.

I leaned forward slightly, hoping to catch a glimpse of his face, curious to see Guruji again. Had he aged this time? My mind raced, even as I desperately tried to concentrate.

There was pin drop silence.

' "Maharaj told me to undress... saying I needed to lie down in front of him, so that he could inspect my womb," Mandavi Seth has gone

on record to allege,' the journalist repeated in an accusatory tone, pointing ahead, his eyes narrowed.

'Yes,' it was then that I first heard Guruji's voice, composed as always. I swallowed hard, grabbing my stomach.

'So, you are admitting to the charges framed against you then? Are you going on record now... here, on this special bulletin of Metro News, on the country's number one news channel India 24/7...' the reporter raged, his chest palpitating, as Guruji simply nodded his head.

Ba let out a loud wail at this exact point.

'Meaning... you are saying you actually had sexual relations with Mrs Mandavi Seth, on the night of July 20? I repeat July 20, 2005?' the reporter recapped persuasively, perhaps, a tad perplexed himself.

Guruji stayed silent this time, like the rest of the people who had assembled to watch his dramatized court martial. 'It all depends on what your definition of sex is,' he spoke up finally, his face averted.

The reporter tried interrupting, but Guruji raised his right hand, and continued to speak: 'Are you talking about love-making... the kinds that goes on between lovers, between man and wife, for instance? Or lust? The sudden attraction between an older man and say his daughter's friend or between a sister-in-law and her husband's younger brother, also labelled as infidelity or adultery, at times? Or are you implying homosexuality? Love between the same sex?'

'Amarkant Maharaj, how would you define what transpired between the victim and you, on the night of July 20, 2005? I repeat July 20, 2005,' the reporter snarled, smarting from being provoked on national television.

Guruji brought his hand down after a few seconds. I studied the familiar gaps between his slender fingers. 'I would label it as being part of a treatment... purely transactional, nothing else; there was no exchange of emotions, if that is what you are implying like the rest of the investigators have been attempting. What happened between us was clinical, to say the least, not like I was having an affair with her... or attempting to seduce her, especially in the manner that is now being widely reported,' he answered nonchalantly, before sinking back into the chair.

'*And just who are you, Amarkant Maharaj? Some kind of a medical practitioner, huh? I mean… we all know that your followers swear by your miracles, claiming that just chanting your name resurrects people from the grasp of death… your bhibhuti making the crippled take their first steps… helping infertile women bear healthy sons, your herbal jaribootis legendary for curing impotency in men,*' the reporter paused to take a deep breath.

Guruji gave a wry laugh. 'There have been daughters as well, in the past. Of course, the ratio of boys to girls is much higher, I agree. But that as science will probably explain is nothing but a chromosomal coincidence,' he rejoindered light-heartedly, practically dismissing the accusations.

The reporter grimaced. Then, wiping his mouth he hurled his next question. '*Are you trying to suggest it was consensual in that case? Also, is it just a mere coincidence, Amarkant Maharaj, that most of your followers also happen to be women? I mean, is that too purely a matter of chance?*'

Guruji shook his head once more. 'What's wrong if my disciples are mainly women? I am proud of the fact that I have been able to communicate with the fairer sex… the prototype of Shakti… Kali… Durga, Sita. I mean… isn't half of your so-called TV viewing audience also these same women? Isn't that how reality television is surviving, not to mention the soap operas that are gaining so much momentum nowadays…' Guruji cut him short abruptly, sounding irritated for the first time.

The reporter chuckled. '*Amarkant Maharaj… let's get back to what we were talking about. I asked you a straightforward question, which I will again repeat, in case we have our viewers joining in at this point. Was the exchange between 19-year-old Mrs Mandavi Seth and you sexual? And if so, was it also consensual? And kindly stick to the topic, this time,*' he grit his teeth, looking mean all of a sudden.

'Sex... as you constantly label it... between a woman and the man, she is perhaps meeting for the first time, can never be fully consensual... at least not so soon, not so easily either. Not until there is a certain melting of one's own defences... a basic level of attraction, even if its very nature maybe transient and fleeting, slightly primordial. It was no different with Mandavi. I knew she'd resist my techniques, put up a fight, perhaps. But, I had made a vow to her mother-in-law who has been coming to me for several years now. Their family business happened to be in the doldrums... an heir was needed at all costs... there was no other way... and her in-laws seemed to be somehow convinced that Mandavi was possessed by evil spirits,' Guruji exhaled, running his fingers through his dreadlocks.

This time round it was the reporter who laughed. *'So, are you claiming to be this modern day, reincarnate of someone, like the ancient Surya Devta who had once blessed the queen Kunti with Karna, the famed warrior in the Mahabharata? Is that what you are implying here on the nation's number one channel?'* he shouted, clearing his throat.

'I'm afraid, it seems you've got your facts all wrong. I suggest you revisit the Mahabharata when you find time. In any case, here are some details for your immediate consumption. Kunti was given a mantra by Rishi Durvasa whereby she could summon any devta and conceive a child by him. When a young Kunti questioned why he had taught her this particular mantra, Durvasa answered saying it would prove beneficial in her later life. However, Kunti mistrusted the great sage, deciding to try it once, on her own. Surya devta duly appeared. When Kunti begged him to return, he insisted he had no choice but to fulfil the mantra. It's why Karna was later also abandoned by Kunti, as you must remember,' Guruji cited confidently, neatly folding his arms across his chest.

A few people clapped.

The reporter was scribbling some notes. He glanced up after a while to ask, *'So, Amarkant Maharaj, what exactly was Mrs Mandavi Seth's particular ailment? What exactly were you trying to heal, that too in the intimacy of your kutir tucked away on a remote hilltop, far away from the rest of your ashram?'*

'Her husband Devesh suffered from a medical problem, they have had a long standing history running in the Seth family, it is very unfortunate, though... especially since Mandavi was clearly unaware of this... it's what caused her such extreme mental anguish,' Guruji blurted out, unexpectedly, his voice booming in the stillness.

Vrinda gasped loudly, sticking out her tongue, clutching the floor mat at once.

'But, surely the Seth family could have just consulted a fertility expert to treat their son or taken their daughter-in-law to a hospital for proper treatment, in case she was displaying signs of mental instability, as you claim? What qualifies you for the job?' the reporter retorted agitatedly, appearing to be losing his calm.

'Well, maybe it's because I've never failed a woman who has sought my help or a family that has faith in my healing methods. I have never let anyone down... I mean... apart from once maybe... just that one time...' Guruji suddenly lowered his voice, his shoulders drooping.

I closed my eyes, stopping myself from staring at his chest.

'I'm sorry... but this is what I infer Amarkant Maharaj... what you are saying on this channel, the country's number one news network, is that you actually have sex with women whose husbands are... umm... probably sterile... with the blessings of their family elders, of course!'

Guruji shifted in his chair. He was bare-bodied. His thick rudraksh necklace flashed occasionally.

'Now I am sure you very well understand that such an act is a serious offence, even punishable under the Indian law? And, that brings me to my next question... something that I am sure is intriguing to our audience... exactly what do you get in return Amarkant Maharaj? Dollars? Pounds? Dirhams? Are these nefarious activities all actually a part of a larger sex racket you are allegedly running? Under the guise of being this revered miracle-maker of course?' the reporter sharply alleged, pointing directly at Guruji's face.

'*Answer me, Amarkant Maharaj... we are running out of time here...*' he howled after a minute or two of pent-up suspense.

Ba looked shell-shocked by the sudden turn of events, Guruji's unabashed admission... the inferences of this telecast.

'Do you know how the great Pandava Arjuna was conceived, since you seem to be keenly interested in Hindu mythology?' Guruji restarted the conversation, sounding completely unfazed.

The reporter glared back.

'Once a Brahmin rishi, Kindama and his wife were making love in the forest when Arjuna's father Pandu accidentally shot at them, mistaking them for deer. Pandu was cursed by Kindama, before the latter breathed his last, saying that the mighty king too would merit the same fate, if he ever had intercourse with his wife. Pandu could therefore never father children. Also, he was so shattered with the gruesome murder he had unwittingly committed, he went on to abdicate the throne of Hastinapura to his blind brother Dhritarashtra,' Guruji stopped short.

'*Amarkant Maharaj, we're running out of time...*' the reporter yelled brashly, waving his ballpoint pen in his face this time.

'Pandu's disability forced his wife Kunti to invoke Indra, King of the Heavens, using the same boon bestowed to her in the past by Rishi Durvasa, consequently giving birth to Arjuna. In fact, it was also how the other Pandavas were conceived, in time...' he continued, taking short breaths.

I wiped my face. Feeling mouth over mine...

'*And, and exactly how does this justify your own actions with reference to the present context? Amarkant Maharaj you here are being charged with alleged molestation, and not some divine sexual prowess! Besides, we happen to be in the 21st century; not the Dark Ages... this is about a woman's dignity... not some mythical reality,*' the reporter had grown relentless, glancing at his watch irritably, his lips twisted.

Guruji laughed again.

'Mandavi is a child... she doesn't realize what she has to fight against, in case she cannot bear a child in the long run. The wrath of her in-laws, the incessant medical probes, the witch doctors who will be eventually summoned in her native village, the painful assumption that she's been the frigid one all along, the snide remarks that will hound her for the rest of her life. Coupled with the sky high costs of treatment that will inevitably push the Seths towards further bankruptcy. It is what awaits Mandavi, after all this media speculation and police chakkar eventually dies its natural death. The world is very cruel, you see. And, and women... their bodies... have merely one purpose, that which has been decreed since time immemorial, made all the more stringent since our Vedic ages, propelled by staunch Brahminical customs and timeless traditions. A *nari's sharir* exists purely to give pleasure to a man... to hold his seed in her womb... suffer the pain of his penance... the agonizing trauma of childbirth. And yes, to answer your earlier question, I am no doctor with a fancy medical degree, you are correct in all your previous insinuations. But I am a man of faith. And if I, Amarkant Maharaj, can help women assuage their mortal sufferings, with the family's implicit understanding and their own consent... I don't think I am being wrong or unlawful in any matter, to any of the parties involved. My own salvation is in the absolution of their fate... my body; the strength I harness through my rigorous meditation is nothing but a medium. I have never considered myself anything other than a mere instrument... powerless when confronted by Sree Shakti...' he declared decisively, wiping his mouth with both his hands.

'*But, Mrs Mandavi Seth is reported to have resisted your advances... the police report clearly mentions that there was some sort of scuffle. More than once?*' the reporter interjected abrasively, glancing down at his notes.

Guruji was lost in thoughts. 'Perhaps it was Mandavi's fate then. I know what it feels like, I've been there... my own heart divided with love for someone else, to not surrender, come what may, holding out in every possible way to temptation. I know she was married against her wishes. Mandavi told me she was in love with someone else... her own first cousin. She lost her purity to him,' he took a deep breath.

A tear slowly rolled out my eyes.

'But, despite the present circumstances, I bear no grudges about her FIR, the fact that she publicly tainted my name, saying I harmed her physically, supposedly molesting her in my kutir. How come the scratches on Mandavi's thighs, are now suddenly being related as the result of a childhood fall? And... and just why is the state police hell bent on politicizing, calling me a resurrected Hindu saint who conned women? I have nothing to hide... I have said it before and I say it again here on the country's number one news channel... I am ready to face trial,' Guruji stated resolutely, sounding triumphant.

'*Amarkant Maharaj... we thank you for your bold submission. Let me assure you that not just us, at India 24/7, the country's number top news channel, but the whole nation is eager to hear the Court's verdict. However, before we wrap up this special segment of Metro News, is there anything you'd like to say, to anyone in particular? To any of your disciples maybe, some of whom are on an indefinite fast, praying that you're speedily acquitted,*' the reporter paused to scratch his forehead.

Guruji remained absolutely motionless before, lifting up his face up to reply, 'I've heard about the grave situation in Mumbai... the floods... the loss of lives...'

'*We are completely out of time,*' the reporter cut him short.

'I hope you are well? I know we will meet again... in some other birth, maybe... once the cycle of this life culminates... when I am free... to drown... in the river of light...'

'*Who are you talking to? I mean...*' he quizzed coarsely, his fingers just about to detach the tiny microphone attached to his shirt collar.

'Someone I fear I may have lost to the rains, someone who wasn't scared to drown... my moksha... my...' he shuddered, solemnly bowing his head.

'What's wrong, Badi Bahu?' Ba pryed a couple of hours later, pushing open my bedroom door slightly, adding pithily, 'Vrinda said you didn't touch your dinner.' Ba blew her nose into her pallu, glancing at me from time to time.

'Do you believe in the charges yourself? Do you think Guruji was actually helping that Mandavi woman?' I raised my voice, walking back towards the bed.

Ba shuddered at the very mention of the victim's name, her lips trembling as she framed her next sentence, 'Badi Bahu, do you think anyone would have dared posed this question had she just borne a child?'

The candle melted. There was a powercut again.

'What do you mean?' I whispered, staring down at her frail frame.

'I... I mean had this Mandavi girl just given in... once... surrendered to Guruji's luminescence, placing her trust in his powers of magnificence? Listening to her mother-in-law... her family...' her lips quivered violently.

I grabbed Ba's bony shoulders, my feet unsteady.

'I know the Seths for a long time, they have a long family history of infertility... the son, especially... he supposedly can't even...' she paused uncomfortably, pushing back my hands.

I fought back my own tears, feeling cheated... vindicated as if today, for the years of silence. *Had Ba known about Mohan too, all along?* Thoughts formed and melted...

'Their entire bloodline will be wiped out. How dare a chit of a woman like Mandavi go against the order, betraying the divinity of Guruji's own flesh?' she hissed, her dentures making a hollow sound.

Her words stung. My eyes blazed in the dark... all the secrets I had borne without grudge... the hurt coming back in short sharp waves. The first night at Guruji's ashram... the memory of Ba turning her back to me, walking away, her shoulders stooped... Mohan's eyes as he ripped open my sari... forcing me to bend over... till... the evening I passed out in the toilet...

*Guruji always being summoned when I was at my weakest...
Confined to this very room... here by this bed...*

'Bahu... are, are you there?' Ba groped clumsily.

Her fingers groped for mine...

Was Guruji my punishment? Or her penance?

The phone rang.

'Hello?' I shouted into the mouthpiece, my heart racing. Hoping it was Yosuf... this time.

'Hello,' I repeated louder as the line was disconnected.

'Hello,' I screamed harder, as she slowly turned around.

'Who's this? Hello, can you hear me?' I was beginning to sound desperate.

Someone coughed once.

I grabbed the edge of the computer table, panic stricken.

Standing a few feet away, Ba stared at me.

'Yosuf?' I breathed into the mouthpiece, hoping to avoid her piercing gaze.

Someone coughed again.

A tear rolled down the side of my face. '*Yosuf, please, please tell me it's you? Please...*' I shouted urgently, dropping the receiver down in the heat of the moment.

Ba was at my side by then. She crouched to pick it up, shoving me aside roughly.

'It's no one... wrong number I think. I, I was... I was just hanging up...' I stammered out of breath, trying to snatch back the cordless from her hands.

Ba raised her eyebrows, straining her ears, placing the receiver close to her right ear.

'Who is it?' I quizzed in a shrill tone, not moving, blinking nervously.

Vrinda was in the room by then, bearing Ba's medicine box... balancing the stainless steel kit in her hands.

'Who is it, Bhabhi?' she enquired sneakily, scrutinizing both our faces.

'It's my son,' Ba cut her short authoritatively. She bowed her head low, folding her hands in prayer. 'Chhoti Bahu, light all the candles in the house. My Mohan is headed back. My beta was stuck in Panvel all this while... having gone there for some vendor meeting or something... took shelter in a stranger's home. He couldn't get through to our landline he complained,' she paused pensively, sighing as she completed the rest of her sentence: 'It's all Guruji's benevolence... how could he leave his most devout disciple empty-handed, again?'

Thirty-two

Chai

The next day, the State Government issued a storm warning. There was some cyclonic development over the Coast of Gujarat again. The roads wore a deserted look, most schools shutting down, wives frantically dialling their husbands, forcing them to apply for a half day... in case, just in case, something bad happened... again.

It wasn't raining though. Not yet, that is.

Translucent clouds played hide and seek pitted against a jealous July sun. From time to time, a cluster of vultures would circle the afternoon haze, hovering hungrily above the gilded island of Mumbai... probably hoping to spot more carcasses. More than a thousand people had already lost their lives... many more were still missing.

'Going in to work late today? Or have you applied for a holiday?' I asked Mohan; he was lying on his stomach.

'Is the landline working? How strange, the way it just went dead again, minutes after you rang us last night? To inform us that you were getting back...' I drank a sip of water.

Mohan grabbed my left wrist all of a sudden, forcing me down beside him.

'Heard you were crying a lot... Vrinda Ben mentioned you didn't eat anything last night again. What did you think, Meera, that I was dead... like the rest?' his words stung as he buried his face in my cleavage.

I squirmed, covering his mouth. 'No,' I exhaled, adding slowly, 'I knew you would make it back... somehow.'

'So Vrinda Ben was lying?' Mohan rudely interrupted, running his hands over my waist.

'What difference does it make? You're home now, sleeping soundly beside me. Where were you since the day of the flood? What you were doing in Panvel, all of a sudden? I mean, who cares, as long as you are safe... as long as you came back to this house, to us?' I exclaimed, hoping to ward him off.

Mohan stared back in silence, not knowing how to react next, watching me as I slowly got off the bed. 'I'm going to have a bath. It's dreadfully muggy outside; heard some of the women downstairs mention something about a water shortage problem, again. Was out buying Ba's medicines... couldn't get everything in one shop, as usual,' I spoke fast, unlocking the cupboard.

Mohan banged one of the doors shut, taking me by surprise.

'What were you doing in Colaba, huh?' he snarled, narrowing his eyes menacingly, his breath falling on my face.

I glanced up. 'Colaba?' I repeated, quickly pulling out an off-white kota sari from one of the shelves.

Mohan snatched it out of my hands.

'Vrinda Ben told me about you spending the night at some hotel there... some Ambrosia or something you had apparently said after you returned home, the next afternoon. But, I thought I dropped you off at Dadar that same morning? In fact, when the rains started, I even managed to get through to your Centre; someone called Prakash picked up the phone after a long time. Think he didn't follow Hindi too well... all he could convey was that there was no one there,' he frowned, studying my expressions.

I brushed his hands off me.

'How the hell did you land up in that Ambrosia, place? Do you know what kind of people go to such joints even? Answer me, woman...' he added agitatedly, shaking me by the shoulders.

'People like us!' I shouted back, before walking away, tucking the silver key ring back into my waist.

'What do you mean by that?' he was relentless, his voice echoing creepily.

I was at the door by then. Slowly, I turned around.

'People like you and me, Mohan. Everyday people... ones who are just trying to survive... to make it through... a bad day, a bad week... a bad year, at the most... a bad flood in the end. Not knowing what lies outside... preferring to remain tucked away in an air-conditioned, hotel room... locking the door cautiously, pretending it's just another day in their lives. Normal people, Mohan, people without too many choices, trying to hold on to the little they have... just wanting to breathe,' I gasped, hoping to avoid his cold gaze.

Mohan tried saying something else, when Vrinda knocked sharply on our door.

'You're back early too, just in time for lunch,' I cleared my throat before she stomped in briskly, balancing a large packet in her hands. 'Brownies,' she giggled, panting slightly, handing them over to Mohan, lowering her voice adding, 'Special brownies... eggless... I got them specially for you.'

Mohan shoved them aside, appearing flabbergasted.

'Here, Bhabhi, why don't you try one also?' Vrinda wiped her mouth, looking searchingly in my direction.

I tied my tresses into a high bun.

'Come on, I travelled all the way to get these and now no one seems to be interested only,' she scowled childishly at Mohan.

'Do you want me to keep them in the kitchen then? Seems no one's going to taste a single brownie... all my effort has gone to waste,' she continued in her trademark nasal whine, as soon as I set foot outside the room.

'No,' I retorted, swerving unexpectedly.

Vrinda looked up from counting the brownies, her lips parted.

'He will have one. They've come all the way from Colaba, Theo Broma, right? Don't waste them, Mohan. They're eggless too, like Vrinda mentioned...' I spoke wryly.

✦

I don't know why I decided to watch television that afternoon after lunch with everyone else. Mohan's face remained scowling as he flipped channels every few seconds, his eyes lighting up whenever any new headline flashed.

The Court was still in session. Thousands of Guruji's disciples thronged the main thoroughfare outside... mostly women, their heads covered, some carrying their children in their arms, some waiting in silence, their eyes vacant, mouthing solemn prayers, hands folded in reverence.

'I should've been there too,' Mohan said, adding, 'If Guruji is acquitted, I'm taking the first night train out to pay my respects. We owe him so much, all of us...'

I was serving tea. I stopped, looking up to study Mohan's face, the way it suddenly looking bonier. The light falling behind his shoulders... the cleft camouflaged in dense facial foliage.

Ba was grumbling about something and ordered Vrinda to draw the curtains. The room was plunged into a thick cover of darkness except for a small patch of light, emanating from a lone diya that flickered near her bedside, falling directly on a framed photograph of Guruji with Bansi by his side. Fresh marigold garlands adorned both their necks; their lips were slanted, their eyes sleepy, their thick hair cascaded down to their shoulders – both strangely identical. I looked at Ba, a new realization dawning on me.

'I had forgotten just how handsome he looked... Bansi I meant, of course,' I paused awkwardly, feeling the weight of Ba's scrutinizing glare.

'Oh, I thought you were talking about Maharaj that way...' Vrinda gave a sarcastic laugh, spreading out on the mat below.

'Good lord! Look... look everyone... *shiiish*... Vrinda Ben shut up...' Mohan hollered, taking us all by complete surprise, as our attention immediately veered back towards the screen.

'What is this? Oh no...' Vrinda exclaimed panic-stricken, literally jumping up from her place, her dupatta slipping off.

'Is this Mumbai? I mean... I thought,' even Ba stuttered nervously, covering her mouth in shock.

I grabbed the edge of the armchair, transfixed at the steady stream of images being flashed on the news channel at present.

'Turn it louder Mohan, now...' I yelped, urgently pointing towards the remote, lying beside Ba.

'Sixteen new dead bodies have just been recovered from the Western Express Highway. All victims of the flood; eight women, five men and three infants – choked when their vehicles submerged in the steadily rising levels of the floods on Tuesday, the night of July 26th, claims DCP Mrinal Damle,' a female news-reader reported staring mechanically at a teleprompter, her own eyes slightly moist.

'Why... I mean... couldn't they just get off from their cars or something? What sense does it make to keep sitting inside as the waters rose this high? Couldn't they tell they were going to die?' Vrinda remarked noisily.

A passport-sized photograph of a woman and her child was being flashed, a hydraulic device pulling up the sedan they had both been trapped in... at the time of their death.

'We still have to carry out the post mortem, to examine the exact moment they breathed their last but, it's obviously a case of suffocation. All the cars had central locking, so as the water limits rose, the system must have got jammed,' a man with unruly greyish hair was saying. Someone held an umbrella over his head.

I had seen him before. DCP Mrinal Damle, a caption running below reaffirming the same.

'Looks like it's started raining again,' Mohan muttered

distractedly, as Ba shoved her left hand in his face, telling him to remain quiet, quickly stuffing in her hearing aid.

'*Of the cars retrieved... three were personal vehicles bearing a Mumbai registration,*' the newsreader paused, as aerial shots of the Western Expressway came back up.

The highway still appeared to be severely flooded in parts, inflatable rubber boats carrying the Indian navy insignia floating around in the murky waters, as part of the ongoing relief operations.

'*Sir, have all the victims been identified, yet?*' the reporter in the studio resumed in a jarring tone.

I covered my ears.

'Yes, all but one... male, aged around 30 years or so, well built, approximately 5 feet 11 inches tall... his body was severely damaged, unrecognizable almost at the beginning, remaining for nearly 72 hours in all this water. It took us more than four hours to break the top of the car. We'll be announcing all the names of the deceased shortly to the media,' DCP Damle answered grimly, peering from time to time at a wad of papers he clutched in his hands.

I shuddered, closing my eyes. The television blared, as we watched the dead being air-lifted one by one, out of their mangled cars, in silence, their limp bodies suspended upside down, like a bunch of lifeless puppets manipulated by flimsy strings.

'Actually, the forensic team involved in our rescue operations has just in fact handed me an identity card of some sort, supposedly recovered from our last male victim's trouser pocket. The ink marks have mostly faded though, along with most of the other papers in his wallet... currency notes, etc... the rexine completely disintegrated. It says here... umm...' He frowned stiffly.

'Why the hell don't they just flash the man's photograph for a change and finish off? I mean, what if his family is also sitting in front of the TV, like us?' Mohan sounded irked, fanning his face with a newspaper.

'Meera... open your eyes once... before... before I go...' I kept hearing Yosuf's voice. Somewhere.

I should have looked up... tried stopping him... cancelled the taxi... stayed back in Room 222... lying beside him, naked... watching the rains... for the rest of the day... for more, maybe... even told him how I felt... everything...

My thoughts raced.

'Kahani mein naya twist,' I thought I heard him laugh softly, parting my tresses...

I yanked the remote from Mohan's hands. My eyes burning.

'The car with the registration number MH 6679 was a licensed tourist vehicle. Our sources have just confirmed that it was being self-driven, having been rented from Lucky Tour & Travels, located in Mahim East. The owner of the transport company has given his statement claiming that the white, Maruti Zen, was, in fact hired on the night of July 26, sometime after 9 pm,' the news reader had also changed in the interim.

'We categorically told him there were no taxis available, the ones that we normally used for outstation tours, I mean. Also, most of our good vehicles were stuck at various junctures in the city, thanks to the flooding situation all over Mumbai on that day. But he was so damn insistent... even doling out extra cash right then. He mentioned if there were no drivers willing to venture out in these torrential rains, he was game with even driving himself. "Been a while since I've been on the road alone, Chacha,"' Mr Sulaman Aziz, proprietor of Lucky Tour & Travels in Mahim revealed to the special correspondent, Neelima Ray.

'I told him several times it wasn't safe at all. But he assured me, saying, "Allah saath hai iss baar". He laughed. "Ghar ja raha hun, Chacha, saalon baad mauka mila hai... iss baar toh koi bhi khuda mujhe rok nahin sakta,"' a pot-bellied man in his late 50s, sporting a shiny polyester shirt narrated.

The reporter, Neelima Ray, grabbed the mike from his trembling hands, continuing softly, *'Shankar, this really is the saddest part... if only the victim had waited a little while longer, he may have actually been able to make it home, as Mr Aziz was mentioning earlier. If only he wasn't so desperate to head out in the middle of the raging rains and...'*

'Neelima, Neelima can you hear me now? Did, did Mr Aziz mention where the victim was actually headed? I mean, are there any further details emerging on where his home may have actually been?' the man seated at the news desk interrupted urgently, scratching his goatee, as the monitor zoomed in on Mr Aziz and Neelima's faces again.

'Why aren't they showing his face?' I quizzed in a shrill overtone, my lips suddenly dry.

'This here is the image of the one unidentified male victim, aged approximately 30 years, amongst the 16 corpses found dead in their cars at various points along the Western Express Highway. The latest recoveries of the July 25th flood – one of the darkest days in Mumbai's personal history, so far,' the news reporter announced after a brief, commercial break, her face forbidding.

I began to tremble as my hands dropped by my side. 'Yosuf... Ismail...' I muttered inaudibly, slowly moving my face away, as tears began to course down my cheeks.

'We would like to inform our viewers that according to the latest reports filtering in, the last male victim amongst the 16 found dead this afternoon on the Western Expressway has finally been identified as one Mr Yosuf Ismail... aged 30, a resident of Wadala, Mumbai. Ismail's body is now being dispatched for post mortem...'

Mohan was tightening his pajama strings. He lunged forward all of a sudden. Gritting his teeth, he muttered, 'So much dard? C'mon Meera, he was probably just an ordinary Mussalman... bloody infidels all of them. One less of them! Who cares?'

I thrust Mohan back forcibly. *'Leave me, leave me now!'* I shrieked, falling on the TV screen as a slightly blurred image came to life in the background. *'Yosuf... no... it just can't... my Yosuf...'* I rambled breathlessly.

'Meera turn this damn TV off right away... I told you before also, the visual is bound to make you sick to the pit of your stomach,' Mohan hollered, tightening his grip on my shoulders.

'No... no, don't. Don't you dare touch Yosuf!' I snarled, adding sharply: 'Is that, is that... is it blood? Near his eyes?'

Mohan stood unmoved, the remote dropping from my hands, landing on the ground with a thud.

'His lips are swollen so much... and, his, his face... he looks... Yosuf... he looks so old suddenly...' I clasped my mouth.

'His capillaries must have burst. It's pretty normal when you die like that... most of his body also would have melted by now. Didn't you hear what the news reader reported before?' Mohan interjected, shrugging his shoulders dismissively.

'If you happen to know this man by the name of Mr Yosuf Ismail, please contact DCP Damle's office on 022-346479, or 022-346480.'

'Yosuf... it can't be you... you, you said your meeting was in Andheri somewhere that night. Yosuf, answer me. Yosuf talk to me, please... say something Yosuf...' I repeated frantically, clawing the TV like a woman possessed.

Mohan tried dragging me away, picking me up from the ground where I had collapsed.

'Just what's gotten into you, Meera?' he hollered, violently shaking my forearms, his nails piercing my skin.

'It was I,' I took a took deep breath, adding under my breath as my voice cracked: 'I sent him out first... it was me... I, I killed Yosuf Ismail...'

Mohan was frowning fiercely, his hands resting squarely on his hips.

'For all you know, it's some stupid girlfriend chakkar... these youngsters also, nowadays, trying hard to impress, taking unnecessary risks, being so damn impulsive,' he barked, adding under his breath: 'Serves him right! Bloody idiot!'

'Yosuf... Yosuf...' I stammered.

Mohan shook off my arm, and let me fall in a heap. 'Looks like your Badi Bhabhi is in mourning for that road-side Mussalman Romeo, let her say goodbye. Go on and prepare the chai this evening, Vrinda Ben,' I heard Mohan snort in disgust, brushing past me, kicking my hips, with his right foot.

Between my sobs I looked outside. Wondering why life always hurt us back in the same places? Training us to forget and then punishing us... treating our stolen moments of joy like it was our biggest crime.

'Allah Ho Akbar!' The evening prayers had just commenced in our neighbourhood mosque. As if Yosuf had timed his own death... the way he had perhaps led most of his life... in a rush to reach someplace. Someplace else...

My whole life is a lie, Meera... that is the truth. That is the only truth,' I remembered him saying as dusk began to fall, the light slowly slipping away from between my fingers.

Leaving behind nothing, except a labyrinth of lost time.

Thirty-three

Byculla

I had a strange dream. At least I think I was dreaming.

Details of which I can still recall, including the way the rains smelt, as I slowly opened my eyes. My mouth still rancid from the number of times I had thrown up last night, before Mohan dragged me out of the toilet at some point, before walking out of our bedroom himself. There was no water bottle by our bed either.

Ba and Vrinda were probably in their room now.

Sluggishly, I pushed my hand below my navel, shuddering at the coarseness of my pubis. I wasn't wearing a panty.

'Mohan,' I tried speaking, forcing my eyes wider, adding, as I gulped my own spit down, 'is anyone, is someone here? Can someone pass me a drink of water... please?'

There was no reply.

Had Mohan already left by the late night train?

There were bruises all over my left arm. I could barely move it beyond a point. '*Meera ka Mohan*,' I writhed, biting my lower lip in desperation.

It was 4.11 a.m. or something.

I cringed at the way things repeated themselves, the rezai gently slipping off me, while I stared at myself in a cracked mirror attached to the built-in cupboard. My thighs parted, partially revealing the shape of my sex. I looked down at once, feeling exposed in some way... a slight shiver that comes only while touching yourself... abhorred from shame or stain... intimately alone, and, and yet...

'Meera!' someone shouted angrily.

I gasped.

Was Mohan watching me all this while?

'Open the damn door just now...' the voice grew more threatening as I lolled my head backwards, studying my fingers in the fleeting shadows, my hips braced upwards.

'What are you doing inside?' would be the next question.

I sighed, parts of the dream coming back... in waves. Like the tiny chills each time I stroked my breasts, my nipples pointed straight, its ends hardened.

'*Mar gayi manhoos*, better break open the door, what if she's hung herself or something...' It was Vrinda.

With the knuckles on my left hand, I lightly rubbed my knees.

'Meera, this is my last warning, you understand... I'm not lying okay? I will kick open this door...' the rest of the words trailed, replaced by an almost deathly silence.

I parted my lips, tears rolling out of my eyes... everything coming back... almost as if it were part of a slow moving sequence, beginning with the following sentences...

'I am not lying,' I had confessed at some point, I recalled, my eyes travelling to the door once again. The lock was broken.

'Just what do you mean? Were you screwing him or something? That, that son of a bitch Mussalman... the one you can't stop howling about right now! Answer me, Meera. I want a straightforward reply at once... I'll smash your face like I broke the bedroom door open... you understand? You are not going to get away so easily...' the words dissipated as another tear formed, my hands grasping my stomach.

'Depends on what your definition of screwing is...' I had retaliated at that point, my eyes smouldering.

'Good God! Ba, Badi Bhabhi has gone crazy. How will we show our faces in this colony, ever again? And... and, what if, Chhotu is told about all this?' Vrinda screamed in the hallway.

Mohan was livid. He grabbed me by the arm. 'Screwing, screwing my foot! Shall I show you what the word really means? Haven't you understood in all these years of being with a man, huh? Mrs Meera Patel,' he had belted hoarsely, pushing me flat on the ground, my right arm hitting the corner of the computer table, bruising within seconds. 'And just how the hell are you so calm, after all that's happened in this house? You think it's all a bloody joke? You think I am going to stand by and watch you... you, you,' Mohan ranted at the top of his lungs; kicking me in the side.

'Answer me, Meera... what is your exact relationship with that Mussalman? What, what was that bastard's name... that *maderchod*...' Mohan flew into a fit of rage, his eyes glaring precariously.

'I, I don't know... I don't know anything for sure, anymore, Mohan... everything was a lie... everything else,' I responded weakly, painfully lifting myself up and limping towards the bed.

'See... I told you Mohan Bhaiyya; there must have been some misunderstanding. I knew it from the word go, in fact. From where will Bhabhi know some Muslim fellow? I mean she hardly ever leaves this house... maximum she goes is to buy subzi downstairs or purchase Ba's medicines, sometimes accompanying Chhotu to his tutions, maybe. And listen, Bhaiyya, if there was something cooking between Bhabhi and someone, wouldn't Chhotu have come back and reported everything to me verbatim? You know how my son tells me everything... he's always been like that... honest like his father,' Vrinda had interjected all of a sudden; inching back towards our entrance, taking calculated steps.

'You are absolutely correct, Chhotu is very honest... I'm assuming then that he's already told you about someone surfing adult chat sites on his new laptop? I mean, I'm assuming it's not our son on these sex websites?' I cut Vrinda short brusquely, as she stood frozen in her tracks, shell-shocked.

'Badi Bhabhi, what, what are you saying! Have you no shame, at all!' she pretended to cringe, dramatically clutching her chest.

It was at that moment that Mohan had slapped me across my face, his fingers stinging, like his afterbreath.

'No, no of course, it wasn't Chhotu, Vrinda Ben... it couldn't be. And Meera, don't you dare talk back to her like that, you understand? How dare you disrespect my family? Especially Chhotu, knowing full well he, he is... he is my son... now...' Mohan fought back embittered, banging the door shut on Vrinda's face, as I slowly turned my back.

'So are you saying I don't have to feel guilty that I was the only one seeking an ounce of external pleasure, Mohan? I mean, now that it's open secret that it was most likely none other than you frequenting porn sites, on Chhotu's new laptop, huh? Tell me, you tell me something now; did you ever indulge in a live, sex chat yourself? I mean have you... have you ever made love to someone sans a face? Or been touched in the gloom of your own bedroom? Every single night... have you ever pleasured yourself, imagining it to be someone? Someone just like you, desperate to drown... to, to give in... be completely naked... be sucked and savoured... to be fondled and found... be drunk again and again. Answer me, Mohan!' I breathed roughly, gripping the bedpost to steady my steps.

Mohan had shaken shook his head in utter disbelief several times, all the while muttering incoherently.

'*Answer me Mr Mohan Patel, do you not know what goes in this bedroom? In this house? In this colony? In this lane? In Byculla?*' I screamed like a woman possessed.

✦

Parts of the dream were diminishing in strength... shrinking as if. Perhaps it was only natural too, considering most of my body was now numb. After Mohan had ripped open my sari, slapping the buckle down over my navel, watching me howl in agony, each time the leather strap eased out of me... everywhere.

I didn't cry much.

Maybe there were no more tears left either. Or perhaps the pill had really worked... the one Mohan forced me to swallow, dragging me up on the mattress.

'Don't you ever repeat this mistake again, you understand? At your age you should be ashamed, Meera... going to meet some random guy you chatted with on an adult site, lying blatantly to your husband and his family, before travelling all the way to some seedy Colaba hotel? For what? Just to have sex with a stranger, right?' he breathed down my face.

'Did you not *once* think how I will I ever show my face to this family, especially after all this has now come to light so publicly? What if they were to discover the whole truth, Meera? Why, why did you do this to me? Cross the line?' his voice quivered, as he tightened the belt around my neck.

'Wipe... just... wipe the blood on the floor... Mohan...' I trembled, biting my lips painfully to add, 'bloodstains are the hardest to remove, once they solidify. You don't want the Patel parivaar to know you hit your wife, do you? Or that you practically raped her one night, tearing into her privates with the same belt... or just how much you love tying her to a bedpost, blindfolding her, forcing her to watch all this so-called dirty stuff, in silence?' I could barely breathe.

Mohan raised his left hand, narrowing his eyes.

'Before she's then made to touch herself... as, as you lie back, watching in silence? All in the name of some marital variety, right? Unless of course you can justify it saying it was nothing but a simple means... to, to help you get a stiffer erection... sustain it enough to penetrate me... everything you subjected me to... anything... just to get that male heir for this, this great family? Just like... Ba... parading me to Guruji's ashram after we were married... knowing I would be too ashamed to open my mouth... after...' I pushed back his hand forcefully.

Mohan clenched his jaws, suddenly looking tortured.

'You... you've hated me all these years, haven't you? Be honest Meera... you could never really love me completely... right from the start... I knew it...' his voice quivered, as he grabbed my cheeks, digging into my cheekbones.

My lips were swollen partially, making conversation difficult.

'I... I have tried Mohan... but, but maybe I did fail in the end. And before you ask me how...' I took a deep breath, resuming weakly, 'because, because this afternoon... earlier on... when they were showing Yosuf's face. From, from the very first time that image came up on the television screen, I, I swear... with every particle in my body, with every living cell I possess, I wished to God it was you... you, Mohan, instead of Yosuf. I wished you were dead!' I spoke fast, holding his face closer to mine.

'What!' Mohan convulsed, the belt dropping out of his hands as I glanced down at the bolster. 'I, 'I thought it was over by now. I mean... isn't the bastard dead? And, and hasn't this been a big enough lesson for you already? How can you dare say all this to me after what transpired earlier... the way you kept shouting out that boy's name, shaming me in front of my whole family, stroking unnecessary suspicions about your so-called relationship... your character... this marriage, me?' he stood over me.

'I mean... did you hear yourself once? "Yosuf, Yosuf, Yosuf..." you wouldn't stop, Meera. Not even after I had clamped my hands over your mouth, literally begging you to shut up... from creating this huge scene,' he wheezed, letting go of my shoulders to add, 'I mean, fine he's dead... killed in some freak road accident. A guy you had sex with a couple of times, perhaps. We could have just let it pass, Meera... bury it as a secret... within these four walls, and, and... maybe with time, I would've even forgiven you for this grave sin, this betrayal. Who knows? I mean for all practical purposes, maybe you were really desperate or something, considering you've always been the needy kinds anyway, not easily satisfied during sex. So... perhaps your philandering was just that... you were just another horny Mumbai housewife that afternoon... the afternoon of July 26th.'

I stared at the laptop stored at a safe distance.

'But, but no Meera, you had to bring the whole house down with your public meltdown. Why, why, huh? Why the hell couldn't you simply let it pass? Like any other person would normally do in such a case... accepting it was a mistake on your part, just, just this once? Or, or make up something... I mean, what purpose did your confession serve anyway? As if your lover will now come back from the dead to rescue you... Yosuf Ismail...' Mohan snarled, perspiring profusely.

I was finding it difficult to breathe normally; my jaws smarted and yet somehow I managed.

'Mohan... have you ever... have you ever killed someone? Have you ever known what it would be to push someone over the brink, blindfolded towards their own death? Do you know the guilt that comes from taking someone's life? Someone who had no clue they may never see another day? Someone so young... with so much to live for... dreams and desires, hopes and happiness? Do you know how that feels? When you... when you are the only reason they are not breathing today... when it is all *your* fault, when you never even said goodbye... once... like Bansi...' my voice broke, my shoulders caving in.

'I don't understand this melodrama, Meera... even when I'm willing to forgive you... eventually,' Mohan cut me short.

'You won't understand... you can't Mohan... actually it's not even meant to be that way. So simple, so easy... unless you really loved the person... how what you offer now is not enough... it never was...' I sobbed into my palms.

Mohan glanced back over his shoulders one last time, his eyes bloodshot, like mine.

'So, why the hell did you come back? You should have stayed back in that... what was that C-grade hotel you had fun in, Ambrosia or whatever, right? Who told you to wade back through the floodwaters, risking your own life, just to reach back home, Meera?' he shot back one last time.

'You came back to this house because you had nowhere else to go. This Byculla lane, this squalid colony, this damp bedroom, that lone window up ahead... this is the extent of your world, Mrs Meera Patel. Admit it... you can't think beyond this life for yourself. Which is why you scampered back, like a terrified little bakri, lying to everyone through your teeth about your whereabouts on the night of the flood, petrified as you must have been yourself, of the consequences... the after effects of your sins... your bhukh... your vasna... this, this constant need to want more... from your own life...' Mohan had pointed accusingly at my face, spitting up venom.

I nodded.

'You're right Mohan,' I'd slowly whispered, looking up.

'About what, Meera? Being a horny housewife from Byculla, Mumbai? Are you admitting that you, Mrs Meera Patel are nothing but a cheap whore?' he repeated agitatedly, shoving the door open with both hands.

'What is the difference between a wife, a whore, and a woman, Mohan? What... what if being a woman is enough? Just, just once?' I pursed my lips tightly.

Mohan never answered.

'Your hot water and... and lime...' I remembered murmuring dully as soon as Mohan's back was turned. Watching wordlessly as his silhouette faded into the surrounding shadows, his shoulders stooped low.

It was then that I passed out...

Knowing it was to be my last image of my husband. Perhaps Mohan was hurt too... in the course of everything that had transpired, I told myself, as his face slowly melted... drifting as if to a secret hiding place... beyond our four-poster bed... and...

Helping me make the most important decisions of my own life.

Teaching me that leaving home wasn't hard. It's choosing which part to leave behind that was.

It's a lesson I could have only learnt from Mohan... and our marriage.

❧

Ever since I was a little girl, I had heard the phrase, 'weaker sex', being applied to women. Occasionally, even Kartik teased me about it, charging ahead in our daily race to reach home on time. 'You girls are always so dheela in everything... walk fast now, at this rate, we'll never make it back before sunset,' he would holler, his arms placed over his head, as we trudged through fields of golden paddy.

Our favourite short-cut.

As I walked slowly down the steps of our house now, with nothing, except a small bag that contained the money I had been saving over the last few months, and my wedding sari, I don't know why but I suddenly recalled Kartik's comment.

Mohan had left earlier the same morning. He was probably already on his way to the ashram, hoping to hold Guruji in his arms or sit with his eyes closed during a night long satsang... maybe it's all he had left in a way... after last night's violent argument, after... after Yosuf's death... after the television was turned off... after the rains of July 26th...

Vrinda slept next to Ba, both of them snoring mildly. I had chosen not to bathe, quickly changing into a crumpled salwar suit. It was the same one I'd worn on the night Yosuf and I were to first meet.

I sighed, slipping it over my head, not knowing why I chose that particular outfit again... perhaps something about the way it still smelt... all the memories it evoked subconsciously... bringing Yosuf back, in a manner only I recognized.

As if he had never really left... like Kartik.

'C'mon Meeru... you can do better,' I imagined Kartik yelling, as I quickened my steps towards the back gate.

There was no one in sight this morning. No cabs either, not even a stray auto rickshaw. No sign of any movement. 'Sorry Madam, I already have a sawari waiting, *aap utro*,' the cab driver cried tensely, as soon I had scrambled onto the back seat.

'But, but I spotted you here, from a distance. You have been khali for a while... ...it's why I came running all this way, there was no one in your taxi,' I explained clumsily, feeling slightly out of breath by then.

'*Arre, kya bolun apan*, this lady I picked up... guess she's sanki or something. Been asking me to take her all around town since last night, Madam... and now, all of a sudden, she tells me she thinks she has found what she was looking for. Phir... before I could even protest, she literally dived out of the backseat. *Lagta hai* she's in this children's park only. I would've ditched her a long time back and taken you instead, but it's just that she owes me a helluva lot of cab fare. If she doesn't come back in the next few minutes, I'm going to haul her back personally. *Mazak hai kya!*' he thundered angrily.

'Is that her over there? I think I can see a woman...' I interjected awkwardly, craning my neck.

'*Haan*, yes, that is her... please Madam; do me a favour now... go fetch her back, please. Say that I want to be paid off once and for all. I'll then take you anywhere you ask, all right? This is a no-parking zone this time of the morning, so I can't leave my cab unmanned. *Police ka locha ho jayega*,' he spoke hurriedly, pointing outside his window.

I wiped my eyes. 'Hello, hello you there...' I shouted, waving my arms desperately as I walked towards the park entrance. Our eyes finally met after a few seconds, as an elderly lady clad in a crushed brown silk sari, broke into a weary smile. A thin gold chain glinted in the fuzzy light. Her eyelashes grey.

It was dawn.

❧

'So, you reached home finally, I see?' she questioned softly, as soon as our paths had crossed.

The grass felt damp. I had left my slippers back in the cab. I narrowed my eyes, asking, 'Have, have we met before? Somewhere else, I mean?'

The woman passively nodded. Green glass bangles clinked softly.

'I'm sorry... but I can't seem to place you somehow, a lot's happened in the last few days too... I maybe a bit disoriented myself... my, my head feels...' I mumbled incoherently, my gaze restless.

'What happened to your elbow, Beti? And, and your lips, they look bruised... are you okay?' she touched my left hand, as I flopped down on a wrought iron bench.

'Actually... I'm in a real rush... I have to be somewhere urgently... somewhere else, that is. I can't answer all these questions. The thing is, I needed that cab... the one there, parked next to the main gate from where I just entered. Will, will you be getting off here? Paying him off?' I cut her short, adding as she caressed my upper arms, 'This, this is nothing, really. I happened to fall. It's nothing... trust me.'

The lady seemed distracted.

'Hello, Maji, did you hear anything I just said? I really must get going now. You need this cab or what?' I shoved her hands off me in haste.

'Everyone's in some sort of hurry, it seems... in this city... is Mumbai always like this? Always in a rush?' she grabbed my wrists lightly as I tried getting up.

'First time to Mumbai?' I spoke fast.

The cab driver was waving frantically in my direction, hoping to catch my attention.

She nodded tamely.

'Actually it's a bad time to visit... we've just survived a major tragedy, everyone's probably looking for an escape route at the moment, perhaps fearing death coming again,' my lips quivered.

'Death...' she repeated the word wryly a couple of times, before looking at my face searchingly to add, 'can death ever come twice, Beti?'

I had begun to walk away from the bench.

'Do you need the cab or what, Maji? The driver is getting very restless; saying you owe him a lot of fare too... so, if you want to stay on in this park for longer, you can. Just pay him off, please, okay?' I retorted tersely, glancing over my shoulders once.

The lady looked up after a couple of seconds, tugging clumsily at her blouse sleeves. Some of the stitches missing near her right elbow... 'I, I don't know where I have kept my purse, Beti. I've been to so many places since the time I landed in Mumbai, you see... after my son rang me two-three days ago, telling me he was headed home to us.'

'So? Why did you follow him to Mumbai? Didn't you hear of the flood warnings? It was all over the television... radio...' I intruded impatiently, hovering over her.

'It's precisely why I came to this city... to save his life. Something told me he was in some sort of danger... the TV channels also were full of warnings as you rightly mentioned; I thought I should show up at his door first... take him in my arms. We had fallen out a few years back, actually. Some family trouble... I hadn't seen my boy in a long, long time. Maybe it was my way of making amends for all the seasons we had been estranged,' she grimaced, wiping her eyes.

'Madam, what's going on? You both seem to be having a *mast* chat, *mujhe paisa do aur choddo aap, bahut meherbani hogi,*' the cab driver glared menacingly at the lady now, his fingers pointed firmly at her face.

'Beta... trust me... I have really misplaced my purse,' she gulped anxiously, managing to stand up.

'*Matlab?*' he snarled, adding threateningly, '*Sun budiya zyaada shana na ban... saala akkha raat ghumeli, aur fhir park mein aake aapan ko topi pehnati hain.* Shall I call the *hawaldar sahib? Do char danda pada toh sab kuch yaad aa jayega tereko, samjhi?*'

'How dare you shout this way... listen, just listen, come with me now, okay? I will pay you off; just tell me how much this woman here owes you, fine? C'mon fast now, or should I look for another taxi? Or maybe I too should search for the hawaldar sahib?' I yelled at the driver.

He shoved me aside, asking curtly, '*Kyun? Door ki rishtedaar hain kya, yeh saali budiya?*'

'Yes, yes, she is... a friend of my mother-in-law's, now, now will you stand here and keep yelling this way... or, or can we proceed?' I spoke agitatedly, putting my arm around the elderly lady.

Thirty-four

Ananta

'Meera,' Yosuf shuddered as I slipped my lips over his organ, swallowing his swollen head gently, parting his thighs with my hands.

We were lying inside an old bathtub, placed diagonally, facing the window.

It was Yosuf's idea.

'This kind of rains happen only once in a lifetime, I just... want to take a picture,' he'd said while pulling the antique tub out from the toilet, the veins on his neck stretched, his shoulders vexed outwards, his eyes drunken, as if.

Yosuf dragged the tub towards his right, gritting his teeth, a thick line of sweat trailing down his chest, the bluish veins near his navel, pronounced.

'Aren't you supposed to fill these things with water, first?' I mused, turning over on my stomach.

Yosuf pointed in my direction, his breathing roguish. Wordlessly, I slipped out of bed, my pallu trailing on the ground, my waistband making a soft murmur, as I slowly walked ahead, our eyes fixated on each other. Like a lifeguard guarding the shore... his gaze permanent, not floundering, once.

The carpet was completely soaked by then, as was the armchair, its faded, green upholstery rendered softer, somehow. Or maybe it was just the change of light. Things always looked different when it was darker. Feeling older in some way. More familiar. Like being tucked in the arms of an old lover.

It's what we did, in any case. Yosuf's tongue seeking mine, each time I tried saying something. Anything. His right thumb rolling inside my mouth, forcing it open, dizzyingly defiant, like his thighs that pushed mine apart insistently.

Our toes wrapped around each other's.

'What are we doing? Here?' I finally dissipated the quiet, shuddering as Yosuf's hardness rubbed against my palm.

My elbows smarted from being slouched inside a waterless bathtub for the last fifteen minutes, or so.

'We're surviving this storm... hiding for as long as we can... Meera,' he murmured.

I slowly stretched his organ to its full length, watching in silence as its girth expanded, reacting to my fingers that had begun to collect momentum, in the meanwhile.

Before I let go, nestling my head on Yosuf's nipples, licking around the reddened corners.

'You know this is the first time I've wanted things to go on...' I circled my fingers around his navel.

Yosuf swallowed hard, sucking in his stomach.

'What else do you want, Meera?' he gently pulled my chin up.

'Nothing,' I trembled, my insides turning to dust.

Yosuf inserted his right palm inside my sex, probing gently.

'That's dangerous... not knowing stuff. It's what I've always feared... it's the only thing I am sure of, in fact... despite everything that's happened in my own life so far... I always know what I want... and...' he exhaled.

We kissed deeply, as Yosuf whispered, 'I always know how to get there... to where I want to be in life...'

I climbed over Yosuf. Most of the hooks on my blouse now open.

'And what if I said I always wanted to drown... to know how it feels... to lose myself completely... to not fear... anything... losing things, losing people... losing who I am... being free...' I convulsed.

Yosuf clasped my shoulders, positioning me over his member, standing upright.

'So... what's stopping you, here?' he rued, his tone suddenly warmer, his mouth seeking mine.

It thundered vociferously.

'I don't understand...'

Yosuf was outlining my breasts, his fingers moistened with my juices, its tips tepid. 'Why are you so scared to be alone, Meera? With me? This way?' he stared back into my eyes.

I shoved my left breast inside his mouth.

'We are alone, remember Mumbai Lover... it's why we connected with each other. We were always alone... just the two of us...' I answered in a hushed voice, spreading my hips wider.

Yosuf wiped the corners of my eyes.

'Have you ever wondered Meera... what if my name wasn't Yosuf Ismail... what if we hadn't met in a dark chat room... or agreed to have paid sex?' he paused all of a sudden, the rest of his words trailing as I swirled my tongue in his... squatting faster on his swollenness, as he massaged my buttocks, his left thumb disappearing into my dampness, our bodies buoyant.

He glided under me just then, like a fish swimming in deep waters, bringing up his face by parting my knees, his tongue drenched in my moistness, some of it dripping down his chin.

I struggled to breathe, as Yosuf expertly manoeuvred us both, sinking in his teeth deeper, as I lay stretched over him, our stomachs pressed tightly together, our tongues on fire.

The room damp, emitting a musty odour. Like the scent of clothes hung out to dry on a flimsy clothesline, its borders shapeless, stretching out its sleeves towards an open sky... as we did, each time either of us happened to slip out of one another... somehow.

'So... so tell me your real name then...' I murmured, minutes after Yosuf had exploded inside my mouth, before I gulped him down greedily, *my eyes watering from the potency of his discharge, the way it tasted.*

'You... you promise you won't laugh... I mean... I, I usually don't like talking about all this...' he paused awkwardly, burying his head in my breasts, the area between them rife with dampness.

I caressed the top of Yosuf's head, planting tiny kisses as I rummaged through his thick crop.

'Let it be for now then... let's leave that for another time... another place, maybe...' I murmured, looking up.

❧

'Madam, Madam... hello...' the cab driver bellowed, waving his hands frantically from his window, while backing the car.

I had just paid him off.

'What is it?' I sounded impatient, ducking my head lower.

'Actually *woich*, that *park wali buddhi*, Madam,' he pursed his lips, fidgeting inside his tattered shirt pocket, his eyes strangely fixated on my face.

It had started to drizzle again, the skies menacingly morose.

'I gave you the exact amount you said she owed you... add to that my morning fare... umm... apart from the surcharge of course. Have I paid you less by any chance?' I raised my voice.

We stood face to face, the waves crashing at a distance.

'Keep this, please, Madam... consider it a personal favour... *apko Khuda ki kasam...*' he pressed a few crumpled notes back inside my palm.

'Listen... I, I don't understand... Were the notes I gave you damaged or something?' I cut him short.

'Madam, I shouldn't have misbehaved with that budiya. The, the, the thing is... I hadn't slept in all this time. Ever since the damn flood; all I've been doing is ferrying passengers, nonstop... daily, sans a single night's rest. I'd actually fallen into a deep sleep, when she suddenly scrambled onto the backseat of my taxi, not asking once, if I was in any position to drive. I hadn't eaten anything either. She kept begging me to take her to Saki Naka,' the driver glanced upwards.

I wiped a few drops of rain from my lips.

'I tried protesting initially, Madam, before agreeing in the last moment. I don't know why I relented, to be honest... maybe I felt bad for her at some point. Anyway, to cut a long story short, I waited nearly for half an hour, in a darkened alley; before she got back in, begging me to proceed towards Bandra, this time around. I kept glaring at her rudely from the mirror, hoping she'd tell me exactly what she wanted, once and for all. But she constantly changed her mind about her destination. *Phir bhi... Bandra pahunche apan log...* then... then from there again she insisted on going somewhere else... *phir* Wadala Wadala *bolne lagi... achanak...*'

'Wadala? Why, why Wadala all of a sudden?' I ran my hands over my cleavage, shuddering at the memories it resurrected.

'I asked her the same thing, I swear on my children, Madam,' the driver recalled persuasively, urgently lighting a bidi to add, 'she was looking for her son, she confessed at long last... saying they hadn't met in years, or something. She seemed totally distraught, constantly blabbering to herself in the backseat. Staring blankly in my direction, from time to time, her eyes blood shot. Her anxiety drove me crazy at some level... coupled with her confusing instructions. *Saala kabhi idhar, toh kabhi udhar... akkha raat bhar!*'

I lifted up my face.

'She had apparently landed in Mumbai, at the crack of dawn, after the floods on July 27th, waiting alone in VT station for sometime... outside it was badly waterlogged... she sounded *lachar* at that point,' the driver restarted, as if on cue.

A BST bus passed us by just then, billowing hot fumes in our faces. I coughed awkwardly, my lower lip swollen, smarting under the surface.

'Oh God! Could it... I mean was it, what if it was the same woman from the cab on the afternoon of July 27th, when I returned home to

Byculla... to my colony, from Colaba? Could it be the same person? Who had got up with me... together from Ambrosia... she'd been loitering in the Reception area, begging for a ride back... having taken shelter, like many others...' I gasped, covering my mouth with both my hands.

We crossed the road in silence, the driver running after me.

'You knew her *kya, sach mein*, Madam?' he appeared stunned, eyeing me suspiciously.

'*Phir*? What... what else did she say? I mean... did she tell you anything else about her son?' I mumbled, myriad thoughts racing through my head, all at once.

'*Kuch khaas nahin...* she'd just tell me where to go before staring out of her window again, her eyes frozen... It was me who finally took the call to drive up to the nearest police station. I mean how long could we have driven around aimlessly? Missing Persons lists had been hung in each local thana... on the notice boards, bahar, I told her heatedly, refusing to pay heed to any of her pleas or theories of where her boy maybe. I knew about these lists, Madam... from actually having ferried some dead people on the day just after the flood. There were bodies floating everywhere... it was a mess, the intolerable stench... bloated, disfigured corpses strewn about carelessly everywhere... *bacche log bhi...*' he gulped agonizingly, as our glances intersected.

My shoulders trembled... as Yosuf's face flashed before my eyes... his lips lifeless.

'*Udhar seich*, they sent her to the Bombay Hospital morgue, saying some dead bodies were still lying there, unclaimed ones, it seems. She insisted on going inside the *haspatal* alone, though at that point, I genuinely felt sorry and requested she take me along. It was also quite late by then. But she didn't bother replying, walking inside by herself, not looking back once. I had no choice... *apan wait kiya dubara*,' he chucked his bidi on the wayside.

My throat was completely parched.

'Returning almost after an hour or so, she then requested me to drive her to the nearest STD booth... repeating that it was an emergency. Most of the booths were however closed. It's why I actually brought her to Byculla side, earlier this morning, suddenly having remembered seeing this one, solitary STD booth that usually opens very early, mostly by the crack of dawn. I often come that side to drink tea in a small stall opposite the same booth... facing the children's park, from where you spotted me also, I think. I slowed down, hoping to locate the booth owner, when she suddenly scurried off. Before I could tell her where to go and make the call... *kuch bhi nahin kaha*... it exasperated the hell out me...' he wiped his eyes, visibly strained by the lengthy exchange of words.

A knot was tightening at the base of my stomach.

'It's okay... you were just doing your job. Thank you... I mean thanks for bringing me here too. I, I, I must really leave now, *namaste*,' I spoke hastily, on purpose, folding my hands, wanting to cut short the dialogue.

'Madam, *ek minute... suniye...*' the driver screeched desperately behind my back.

'*Uss budiya ka beta mar gaya*, Madam,' he clenched his jaws, as I swerved, taking my time.

'Allah forgive me for my insensitivity, for trying to make money, at a time like this...' he sounded repentant.

I forced a laugh, stealing a glance.

'Just how can you infer that, Bhai Sahib?' I took a deep breath, before resuming, 'you yourself said that the lady hadn't located her son, all of last night. I mean, even after the morgue visit... after she re-entered your taxi, post her Bombay Hospital stopover, she didn't utter a word about his death, right?' I placed my hands across his chest, in an attempt to get him to back off.

'Here, Madam, *isse dekho pehle aap*... the budiya happened to leave this behind... it had fallen on the ground, perhaps. *Aap ne bhi shayad dekha nahin theek se*... it was lying on the back seat, all this while...' the driver intruded hoarsely.

I glanced at the photograph. The skies were darkening. There was a robust gust of wind. Most people had opened their umbrellas, scurrying faster, their arms entwined, their eyes blinking nervously.

I closed mine, drinking in the first drops, shuddering as I had the first time.

'It's not what you remember, Meera... it's the order in which you forget things...' I heard the words again and again...

❦

'Close the window, the sheets are soaking,' I said, lying naked, my head hanging over the edge of the mattress, covering my chest clumsily.

Yosuf's back faced me. My eyes travelling down the firmness of his curves, pausing to gaze at his penis slouching between his brawny thighs.

'What's wrong?' he questioned softly, nibbling behind my ears.

'I don't know... just that sometimes I wish... that I wasn't this person...' I answered feebly, touching his chest.

Yosuf laughed loudly, holding my hands up over my head, his fingers outlining the area under my breasts.

'What?' I mused, grabbing him closer, as we sat ensconced in each other's arms, listening to the monotony of the rains.

'And what if there is no before Meera... if this were where it all begins... and...' he stubbed out his cigarette, tracing my collarbone with his left index finger.

I shivered, biting the edge of the sheets.

'Is that all? Everything you wanted to say?' I don't know why I had blurted then, feeling Yosuf play with my tresses.

'It's never enough Meera... words... they take away so much... the meaning of things...' he reprised slowly, as I ran my fingers over his hardness.

'You know... sometimes I wonder who I really am? Who this woman is? The one I see daily? The one I stopped talking to a long time ago... making eye contact with, when... as I watched them all leave... one by

one... till... until I became this person. Mrs Meera Patel of Byculla, Mumbai who logs onto Mumbailover.com, practically every single night. Mrs Meera Patel who lied to her husband Mohan of so many years... escaping the life she had all this while... Mrs Meera Patel who never bore any children... or saw a different city... another life... like the lights of Paris, maybe... Mrs, Meera Patel... who... who had nothing, really... except...' I gazed at my own hands.

Yosuf lowered his gaze, his breath balmy.

'Mrs Meera Patel who pays to have sex with a 22-year-old boy, in a hotel in Colaba one afternoon... someone called Yosuf Ismail...' I exhaled, reaching out for his arms.

Yosuf rose up from the bed...

'You can get as far away from the noise...' he cut me short abruptly, staring outside.

'What if I don't know how to...' I swallowed desperately.

'All you have to do is keep your eyes open. Listen to all the things you see... the sound of this falling rain... the laughter of a child... the birds making a curious semi-circle... the waves crashing on ochre sands... the way your skin feels... safe... the pattern of things,' Yosuf took a deep breath.

I buried my face.

'Not shapes... patterns... Meera...' his words trailed.

❧

'Is this, is he your son?' a woman clad in Western formals asked me, breaking my reverie, shaking my right arm, forcibly.

I placed my hands over my eyes.

We stood facing a string of muted fairy lights that glowed precariously, at some distance, my toes nearly sinking in the moist sand... Chowpathy strangely deserted this morning. The balloon sellers missing... the carefree laughter... the lovers... the food stalls mostly vacant.

'I guess this just dropped out of your hands...' she resumed handing me the photograph. 'He... has the most angelic features...

as if nothing can ever destroy him... what is his name?' she called out from behind my back, in a shrill tone.

I didn't look back, my tresses blowing in the breeze, my eyes smouldering. The light was smudged. Dim rain clouds grazing the South Mumbai skyline. Making it difficult to see much...

Except... his smile... the way his one dimple melted deep into the folds of his left cheek...

Everything the same, mocking time, as if.

It was a picture of Yosuf as a young boy, tall for his age, sitting behind the steering wheel of a car, most probably imported. His face was camouflaged by all the mechanical paraphernalia... except, the look in his eyes, glazed with an adolescent bravado... desperate to turn the ignition on... anytime... never stopping.

I ran my fingers... smoothening out the creased edges... the paper mostly bluish green... imagining them to be the veins under his skin... turning the picture over, slowly.

'Ananta Shirali, *chowda varsha,* Pune,...' the ink marks had also begun to fade.

I waded into the water

'*Imagine Ananta Shirali – sounds like a schoolteacher in a Government college, wearing soda glasses...*'

'Anantaaaaa,' I moaned, the rest of the pieces slipping back into place...

'*You can't fuck an Ananta, think about it... imagine telling an Ananta, "c'mon suck my breasts, lick me... please, I want you so bad Ananta..."*'

I covered my face in my hands, the water rushing up my salwar, tiny ripples that insistently rocked my hips back and forth, as if I was still in bed with him.

'*I like your name... it's different... Ananta...*' I sank to my knees.

The tide arose steadily against my spine, some of the saline water coming into my mouth.

'Imagine a world where you'd never have to wake up?'

I lolled my head backwards, seeing Kartik now, as he touched my waist lightly, his lips parting... beckoning me deeper into the water.

I pushed back a strand of hair from my eyes... wanting to stare back equally... knowing it was the last time we were meeting.

It had to be.

A host of other faces flashed by dizzily. Some I recognized instantly... others turned away...

'Meera ka Mohan,' I outlined the letters, tracing them in the water, one by one, listening to the roar of the waves... the way they retreated... leaving behind nothing...

'The samsara is alas, nothing but an illusion, everything wrapped in maya. Nothing will last, nothing can. Our body is just a medium, the marg is something else... mine, yours, ours. Unlike the atma... the soul that is ananta... limitless.'

I glanced upwards at the sky. Its darkened contours resembling Guruji's black eyelashes.

The picture fell out of my hands, gently. Carried forward on its own... making its own way inside...

I followed it for as long as I could.

'Na hanyate hanyamane sarire...' I shouted into the wind.

The rains were coming down heavily...

I drank the first drop. Drowning out the noise.

Acknowledgements

Sita's Curse wasn't supposed to be my second novel. Or at least it wasn't the book I wrote after completing *Faraway Music*, published last year. Maybe looking back, *Sita's Curse* wasn't meant to be a book at all, to begin with at least. As I stood facing her – Our lips slightly parted. Our hair damp. The rain clouds huddling closer together. Our chests heaving up and down; slowly. Our gaze distracted. Distant. Like the rest of the city around us. The metropolis of Mumbai – always crowded, always cacophonic, always in a rush to reach someplace else. Surrounded by a vast mass of nothingness. The sea – the infinite, the only constant. Strangely.

I was a relative newcomer back then. A young journalist. It's all I had. The few rushed seconds with her. An aloneness so familiar, it almost made me wonder. Each night. Waiting to see her the day after. At exactly where I left her. Each afternoon as my worn down Mumbai taxi stopped at a busy red-light, standing a few feet below a dingy Byculla chawl. Faded undergarments flitted on a nylon clothesline, a green *tota* screamed hoarsely, young boys whispered into cell phones, their scrawny legs dangling from the banister. Nothing to really catch one's eyes – except the sight of her. A middle-class Gujarati housewife who stood with her hands stretched outwards, her pallu slipping surreptitiously. Her hips protruded. Her breasts perfectly rounded... her cheap cotton blouse damp... her tresses uncombed... a silver key chain tucked into her waist... sinking in deeper. Like my glance. As I followed her, daily. Into a place of hushed whispers and slow stares. An imagined paradise, for a woman I called Meera.

Sita's Curse is my tribute to her. To the memory of what things were. To the way she tasted the rains, licking her lower lip lusciously, her tongue darting in and out... her greedy glance, the times I caught her caressing her own cleavage, lost in stray thoughts. Asking myself on many such occasions, if she had a lover. Someone who desired Meera back. Wanting her to be wanted and loved. To be relished and pleasured. Knowing if she was in a stale marriage. Drawing mental caricatures of the man whose wife she may have actually been. The suffocating bedroom that was theirs. The bed on which she made love. Or masturbated. Or secretly smuggled in lovers. Being selfish and sensuous, at the same time. Being a woman. Being every woman. Wanting better for Meera. Than this. This rut. This ruin. This ravaged reality that contrasted so starkly with her physicality, her sexual prowess, the way she always looked back at me. As if she always knew I was watching her. A safety to which we both surrendered.

For almost a year, Meera remained my weakness, till the tragedy of the July 26, 2005 floods that ravaged the city of Mumbai. I still remember the previous afternoon... clearly... her eyes... searching as she bit the corner of her pallu. Was she crying? Was she ever sad? Was happiness not hers? Did Meera have kids? Was she barren? Was her life celebrated? Was she tortured? Thoughts formed and melted...

I suppose I will never know now, having never seen her after I resumed work, three weeks later, battling a severe viral infection, having walked back home, two days later, making way through the waves... water everywhere... the sound of death and decay... up close.

This is her story.

And mine.

In bringing this closer to a larger audience, I thank my editor Nandita Aggarwal who challenged me to see Meera the way you will. I hope. As a creature of fact and fiction. Of fantasy and foreplay. Of love and lust. Of pain and pleasure.

Because in the end. Nothing lasts.

'Na Hanyate Hanyamane Sarire...'

Go on, Meera... fly away. Fly now... forever...